Estella's Fury

Barbara Havelocke is an international bestselling author, whose psychological thrillers have topped Amazon and Kobo.

Her writing career started in journalism, interviewing the real victims of crime - and the perpetrators. The realistic, complex characters who populate her fiction reflect this deep understanding. When not writing, Barbara is found walking her two dogs, Scamp and Buddy, or taking photos of wildlife.

Also by Barbara Havelocke

Estella's Revenge
Estella's Fury

BARBARA HAVELOCKE

Estella's Fury

hera

 Penguin
Random
House

First published in the United Kingdom in 2025 by

Hera Books, an imprint of
Canelo Digital Publishing Limited,
20 Vauxhall Bridge Road,
London SW1V 2SA
United Kingdom

A Penguin Random House Company
The authorised representative in the EEA is Dorling Kindersley Verlag GmbH. Arnulfstr. 124, 80636
Munich, Germany

A CIP catalogue record for this book is available from the British Library.

Print ISBN 978 1 83598 157 3
Ebook ISBN 978 1 80436 706 3

Zallman-Caps used for drop caps by D. Rakowski

Cover design by Mark Swan

Cover images © The Metropolitan Museum of Art: Dale T. Johnson Fund, 2009 (eye)

Printed and bound in Great Britain by Clays Ltd, Elcograf S.p.A.

Look for more great books at
www.herabooks.com | www.dk.com

For Rory

I'll see you later x

'A woman, a dog and a walnut tree, the more they are beaten, the better they'll be.'

PROLOGUE

There is something about walking around a house that is empty except for oneself which is relaxing and thrilling at the same time. The only sound to be heard is that of your own feet moving softly across thick-pile wool rugs, your own breath gentle yet amplified by the lack of all else. Then you hear something – the coal shifting as it burns in the fireplace, perhaps, or even a shout from outside – that makes your heart leap as you still, frozen with conviction that there is someone else in the residence with you.

This is how he feels as he pads through Estella Drummle's London townhouse. He is enjoying the solace as he gets to know her: an oxymoron, he knows, but it's true nevertheless. Sometimes it is easier to become acquainted with someone's true self when they are not around to present their day-to-day façade.

So far, he has investigated all the reception rooms on the ground floor before moving up the house. Now he is in her bedroom, and he stands on the silk rug beside her bed, and imagines her waking, stretching, throwing back the blankets and lifting her head from the pillow. For a moment, he closes his eyes and breathes in the aromas of Estella's perfume, beeswax polish, and the white roses and lilies in a vase on the cabinet…

There is no discernible scent of a man anywhere. Which is curious, given that Estella is married. But she does keep an exceptionally clean and tidy home, so perhaps that is the reason. Even the drawers he has gently rifled through have been neatly ordered.

He throws open the doors of her wardrobe, and runs his hands over the velvet, silk, devoré, fur, muslins, finest cottons, every material possible, assaulting them with squeezes.

They hold no secrets in their pockets.

The dressing table is the same. It's a curious piece that does not match the square mahogany furniture of the rest of the house at all.

This is slight in comparison, with the elegantly curved legs that were favoured several decades earlier. He picks up a jewel or two, holds them aloft so they twinkle in the soft gaslit lamps, then sets them back exactly where they were.

There is nowhere left to explore now but the attic.

Up the stairs he treads, careful as a hunter stalking a deer. Halfway up… a step creaks.

He freezes, holding his breath, then slowly releasing it. No one is coming.

At the top of the staircase is a single door, painted dark green, with a brass knob shining brightly. A thrill of illicit excitement shivers through him as he reaches out and twists the knob, but nothing happens. The door is locked. The key is right there, though, already in place. It turns easily, with a neat click, and then the door swings inwards.

Someone is on a bed. Lying curled up on their side. Blissfully ignorant in their slumber.

He takes a step towards the bed. Then another.

They don't wake. They don't even stir.

He pulls a long knife free from the sheath of his inside jacket pocket. It makes the softest rasp. Even that doesn't get eyelids fluttering open.

A few more steps and he is by the bedside. Gazing down at the peaceful face, his lips twitch into something that is half smile and half snarl. They are so sound asleep that a trail of drool has pooled on the pillow. There's barely any weight to the knife as he leans over the reposed body…

Bentley Drummle sleeps on. His liberator sighs. Impatience, resignation, it's hard to identify exactly what is going through his head at that moment. But then, so few people can read him at the best of times, though many think they know him.

He holds the point of the blade against Bentley's throat until a scarlet bead forms then trickles across his skin like a slash.

The eyes fly open, red as the drop of blood. They roam around the room as Bentley roars like a bull in search of someone to charge at.

The knife brings him to a halt.

'Bentley Drummle, I presume?' asks the man. 'Cease your slumbers. It's time for scores to be settled.'

CHAPTER ONE

Away from grief at the passing of my mother, away from fears of my secret being discovered, away from my terrifying husband… Each roll of the wheels of my carriage took me further from my life, and towards rest, peace, and the good company of my friend, Elizabeth. London – that great, heaving city – disappeared into the distance.

Yet my troubles did not.

What was I going to do about Bentley? My solution for dealing with my violent husband would not hold for much longer. His friend, Startop, kept paying calls in the hope of seeing him. For how much longer would he accept that he had 'just missed' his friend, and start asking questions of his true whereabouts? What if he brought the constabulary with him next time? And – my breath caught at the thought – they searched the house?

If that happened they would discover him, drugged and chained in the attic.

There were other secrets, too. Far darker even than that.

Hours passed, but no solution came. Determined to escape my mental turmoil, I stuck my chin out stubbornly and stared through the window at the undulating fog that had gathered.

London fog was almost solid. It felt as if one could cut a slice from it as one would cake – though this cake was filled with sinister ingredients: the choking smoke from countless chimneys; the heady scent of humanity crammed together in the world's largest city; the noxious vapours of a million industries rising ceaselessly into the air. It could linger for a week, and be so dense that even by daylight one might struggle to read, despite being seated beside a window.

Country mist was different, and the journey to Wynterton Manor was shrouded in the stuff. It filled the hollows of undulating fields, piled gently against hedges, and seemed to capture and increase the golden light of sunset as it faded into indigo. It softened the crunch of the wheels over the road. It blotted out the world until it seemed as if the carriage remained still, while trees appeared suddenly, leered over me, then lurched away.

Through the mist I glared, searching for a sign of how much farther Wynterton Manor was. I grew weary of the journey, and longed to see Elizabeth in her new home.

Though we corresponded regularly, it had been ten months since we last saw each other. In fact, it had been at my wedding reception: a time filled with hope and future plans. Since then, my husband had shown who he truly was by locking me in a room at his family home in Paris, and attacking me repeatedly until he sent me to the edge of death. It had changed me forever. Violence had always lived in my heart, curled like a half-asleep cat that watched the world through slitted eyes, but after what Bentley did to me it fully awoke.

My daring escape from my honeymoon and all its horrors was followed up just two months later by Mother's death.

Mother, mother, mother, how I miss you.

To others she was mad Miss Havisham, who had been jilted on her wedding day, and ever after shut herself away in a dark house, stopped the clocks, and wore always her wedding gown. To me she was Mother, adopting me at the age of three, and raising me to be her tool of vengeance against all men – for she believed they were all cruel and abused their power over women.

'Never love. Never trust. Break their hearts,' she whispered to me every day. Every. Single. Day. 'Make them love you, that you might destroy them.'

Raise a child to shut off emotions and eventually something inside them breaks permanently. I did not feel the way other people seemed to, did not react to situations in the same manner. I was a thing apart from the rest of humanity.

Without Mother's indoctrination, and Bentley's brutality, I might not have killed that man.

Don't think about that!

I straightened slightly and forced my mind back towards Elizabeth. It would be good to see her.

The coach lurched over a great bump in the road, sending me into disarray. My *Frankenstein* novel slid to the floor. With a sigh, I picked it up, righted myself, and gazed outside again. Before I could gather my thoughts, there came the sounds of shouting and laughter. Laughter with a cutting edge.

The shape of another carriage – a public coach, in fact – emerged from the fog as we gained on it. And something else, far smaller.

A tiny figure, running.

'Come on, catch us up and we'll toss you some pennies.'

'Just a bit farther. Here's a shiny shilling. Come and get it!'

The jeers were aimed at a boy of about eight, who raced to catch up. Shoeless. Clothes filthy and ragged. As we flashed past, I saw more. His pallor was as white as the mist surrounding him, his eyes red-rimmed, with black shadows beneath. His thin limbs pumped desperately, trying in vain to reach the coach and the promised money that would buy him a long-overdue meal.

'Gah, he's not trying hard enough. Doesn't deserve it,' came a shout, followed by mob-like laughter.

Those riding atop the stagecoach leaned forward, eager to bait the beggar boy. They held shiny coins aloft, but their grip was firm. They had no intention of giving anything away, no matter how needy the child; their offer was for entertainment only.

They soon fell away into the distance. Their vile taunts rode with me, though. How I hated bullies!

When we passed an inn soon after, I knocked with the metal-worked handle of my parasol on the blue pin-tucked satin-covered ceiling of my carriage, to signify that I wished to stop.

'I require some refreshments,' I called.

That was not all I had in mind as we pulled into the courtyard and one of the footmen went inside to organise my repast. I alighted and stretched my weary limbs… and waited.

Moments later, the stagecoach arrived, just as I had hoped. Time for a lesson to be learned, and I was the governess to teach it.

CHAPTER TWO

I espied almost immediately the two men who had been the chief ringleaders in torturing that poor beggar boy. They were seated on a bench outside the inn's main entrance, showing the bottom of their tankards to the sky as they downed their pints. My rage at their merciless teasing of someone in dire need hid beneath my composed exterior as I stood beside them, the perfect gentlewoman, feigning reluctance to enter the building unchaperoned.

I would neither kill nor maim them. The inn was far too public for such tomfoolery. Besides, I was keen never to again take a life, and had instead spent the summer trying to make friends, of all things... No, my plan was simple poetic justice: I would steal from them and give the proceeds to the pauper child.

Pickpocketing was not a usual skill among the gentry, but my – shall we say, unusual? – upbringing meant I had secret skills. My old friend, Yvette, had taught me the art of slipping money onto my shoe, then sliding it in place beside an unsuspecting mark. A simple comment would draw their attention to it on the ground, and when they checked if the money was theirs they revealed where their wallet was – thus allowing me to know which pocket to lighten.

With a bend as if dusting myself off, and a little twist as if trying to discreetly stretch, I straightened suddenly and pointed.

'Pardon my intruding, but have either of you gentlemen' – they both visibly preened in surprise at the compliment – 'lost some money?'

They were mirrors of confusion until they followed my gaze. There was a five-pound note on the ground beside their feet.

'Yes!' they replied in unison.

I smiled. 'Which of you is it? For it cannot be both.'

The nod that passed between them was almost imperceptible. They both got their wallets out and checked, and the man on the right said:

'Twas I who lost it. What a good job you noticed it. I thank you for your kindness.'

'I wish you good day.' I watched him stuff the note into his wallet, noting its return to his front inside pocket. The other man had his own drawstring purse attached to his belt by leather strings.

I swept away, peered around the inn's door, and beckoned my footman to bring the food to the carriage so that I might eat in privacy (for the inn was too down-at-heel for a lady such as myself to dine without causing notice). As I departed, he hurried ahead to set up my makeshift repast in my carriage. I made to follow, but turned one last time towards the two men, who were red-faced with cheer.

They enthusiastically raised their refilled tankards to me, and wished me a good day. What I needed was to create some misdirection. All it took was a clumsy little nudge and…

'Oh, good sirs, I have spilled your beer all over you. How silly of me!'

I fussed with my handkerchief, dabbing at them both with one hand, while in my other was a knife that snicked through the leather ties of the man's purse. Unseen. Unfelt.

The man with my five-pound note slumbering peacefully in his wallet did not notice my hand slide into his inside pocket, as I wiped at him.

'My apologies, good sirs. Let my man replace your drinks at my expense.'

Thus, they would not need to check for their money for a while yet. When they did, though… Ah, if only I could stay to see their faces as they realised what I had done.

I was taking my seat in my coach when the beggar boy arrived with stumbling steps, so weary his feet dragged. He eyed the two men warily, but there was hope, too. Poor, naive fool, I could almost hear him thinking that if he was lucky, someone might feel pity and throw some leftover food his way.

If he was *unlucky*, he would be arrested for vagrancy and jailed. Possibly even transported to Australia. He was not yet into double figures in age, but would be tried as an adult, and punished harshly all for trying to stay alive.

'Boy!' I called. 'Come here. Do not fear.'

Once inside, I offered him food and asked him where he was heading.

'I ran away from my employer. He beat me badly.' He ate like a starved dog.

'You have no family to whom you might turn?'

He shook his head. The only sound was of chewing and gulping as he devoured half of a pie. The other half disappeared into his pocket.

'You are most welcome to travel a way down the road with me.'

How happy he looked! He nodded his head so hard it was in danger of dropping off.

We set off; the horses' hooves on the dusty road and the boy's cheerful chewing were the only sounds. What would become of him, I wondered. Yes, I had fed him and would give him some money, but modern life was cruel to children who had no one to protect them.

Since Mother's death I had often thought of my extraordinary luck at being adopted by her, despite her strange foibles. For I had been an orphan, like the boy; no one else would have wanted me. Often in those early days of grief for Mother, I also found myself sentimentally grieving the loss of my birth parents. I wondered what fate had befallen them; who they were; what they were like; if they loved one another. I pondered which traces of them I saw in the mirror. When seeing the threadbare street urchins that littered almost every street of London, I contemplated what my fate would have been had I not been adopted by the richest woman in Kent.

The boy and I continued along the road companionably for several miles – me taking care of some correspondence that might just help this lad in the future; him eating – before he leaned back, finally sated, his stomach a visible bump of fullness. He gave a sigh of contentment – then started.

'You have realised at last the potential danger of riding in the carriage of a stranger, heading who knows where,' I observed.

'Please, don't hurt me. I'm a good boy—'

'You've nothing to fear from me. Remember this lesson, however. You saw how those men pretended to want to help you, only to snatch it from you for their entertainment. Yet you climbed into my carriage, all because I promised food.' I sighed. 'Most people are good, but those who are bad will end you as quickly as you gobbled up that pie. Faster.'

He had a skeletal frame; his huge eyes stared from pale but grubby skin. Cuts, bruises and open sores bloomed all over him.

'You have run away, you say? I do not blame you. They clearly mistreated you.'

'You won't take me back? Please, don't—!'

'I swear to you on everything I hold dear.' Which was precious little, but he was not to know.

'I-I've come from the mines.'

That explained everything. No wonder the boy wished to escape the back-breaking work, the danger of shaft collapse or explosion from coming across pockets of gas. Why should he not instead long to see the sun and feel the wind? Someone had to descend the depths of the earth, though, and gouge out the riches, and who better than the poor, uneducated children? To the well-fed, well-born owners of the mines, it was a simple practicality. They argued that without employment, such children would become lazy or turn criminal. Thus they felt no guilt at putting poor children to work in the mines, where they toiled from six a.m. to ten p.m. All of it perfectly legal.

To treat anyone this way, let alone children, seemed an abomination to *me*. It was yet another sign that my thinking strayed from the norm.

'There is a village up ahead.' I gestured to the cluster of houses growing closer. 'You can alight here, or go a little further with me, for I travel to Wynterton; do you know it?'

He did not speak, but his eyes grew wider as he listened.

'Here is a letter of recommendation, saying that you are a hard-working boy. I hope it will encourage someone to employ you. The food can go into this bag of mine, which you may take, along with this.'

When he saw what I was proffering, he shrank back. It was quite a sum of money. There was a five-pound note from me, plus the combined contents of the two men's wallets. The men would surely be furious when they realised they had been robbed, but the finger of blame was unlikely to point my way because I was a gentlewoman of means. No one would believe them. I did rather wish I could see the

9

expressions on their greedy faces. Let it be hoped they learned their lesson and, in future, would not be so cruel to those in need.

Though the boy's gaze was glued to the monies, he did not take it.

'I expect nothing from you for this. Think of it as proof of kindness in a harsh world.'

A line appeared between his eyes, but his hesitant fingers took it.

At my knock, the carriage stopped. The moment the door opened, the boy flew from it, a bird freed from a cage. He paused a few steps away, though, staring, waving, mouthing 'thank you'.

'Do not forget, child: trust no one,' I called.

'Wait!' His shout surprised me. 'Make sure you don't trust no one, neither, me lady. Even down the mines we've heard tell of Wynterton.'

Then he bolted. What on earth could he mean? Though I pondered, I found no answer.

Onward the coach swept, gobbling up the miles to the Suffolk–Essex border, and Elizabeth's home on its far side. We had initially become friendly because I thought she would be useful in advancing the plans my husband and I had shared. Like a plant that is easy to tend, our friendship had grown. At the time, Bentley had been fixated on the fact he was 'almost a baronet', despite several people – including his godfather, Sir John Taykall – having to die for that to happen. It had taken time to hammer into his thick skull that he was wasting his time waiting for the almost impossible to happen; instead I offered an alternative plan.

Sir John had been determined to find himself a wife – a young woman with whom he would try to have more sons. If we found him someone suitable, we would have his eternal gratitude. What's more, by choosing someone of the correct gentle, malleable demeanour, we could exert influence through her. She could constantly recommend us to her husband, above even Sir John's son, Winston. He would back Bentley's ambitions to become an MP. Elizabeth was that woman, recruited by me.

As I thought, a most ferocious aroma of manure assaulted me from outside. I held my nosegay up, and breathed deeply. How apt that such an odour should appear just as I thought of Sir John, for his breath had to be encountered to be believed.

'Imagine kissing him,' I muttered aloud.

Hopefully, he would be dead soon, for he was much older than my friend, and then she would find herself a rich widow as payment for putting up with him.

Was that a terrible thing to think?

I caught myself and studied it. Yes, that was exactly the kind of comment that others would not think, let alone say aloud. Since Mother's death – ah, see how all thoughts returned to her! – since then, I had felt adrift, for she had always been my anchor even when I had longed to be cut free. The ache of missing her did not lessen, only deepened. I had never felt so alone. And so, this summer, I had tried to befriend other women, not because they might be useful but simply to spend time in their company. It was unfamiliar territory; my childhood friends had been the mice and spiders that nested in the rotting remnants of Mother's wedding feast. Them and Pip, a boy my age, forced to visit purely for me to sharpen my cruelty on. Yet my summer of studying 'normal' people and trying to be like them was clearly having a beneficial impact on me, for I was starting to amend my thinking. It could be exhausting trying to break the threads of myself, attempting to weave a new personality, but progress was being made.

A spectre-like glow appeared in the mist. It was Wynterton Manor, all lit up to welcome visitors. Windows like mean little eyes squinted from medieval walls, their timbers on show, listed and bowed. Other styles of architecture throughout the ages had been jammed on without thought, including the Georgian front. The mishmash made me think of a strange beast squatting in the mist.

'Waiting to pounce,' I whispered aloud. I thought again of the boy's warning.

A shiver ran through me, almost as if it were a premonition.

CHAPTER THREE

ootmen appeared swiftly to take care of my things. Elizabeth swept forth to welcome me with an enthusiastic embrace before taking my hand to lead me inside.

'It was a wonderful surprise to hear you were coming, Estella. You look well – married life must be suiting you.'

'Far more than ever I anticipated.' The thought of Bentley back at home, locked up in my attic, lent fervour to my voice. 'How are you?'

'Let me show you to your room, and then we will catch up properly.' She smiled and squeezed my hand, then looked behind me and her face dropped a little. 'No lady's maid?'

'We have a small household at the moment,' I reminded her. She led me across the wide entrance hall, panelled from floor to ceiling with wood so dark it seemed to almost absorb the light, and stopped at the foot of the staircase. 'I wrote mentioning it, remember? How I found it necessary to start afresh with the staff – you understand what it is like, coming in and trying to enforce new ideas when people are stuck in the old ways. I thought you might be able to spare someone while I'm here – I hope it isn't too much of an imposition?'

Elizabeth made a noise of understanding, but it wasn't enough to cover the slightest hesitation.

'Silly of me, I do remember now. We shall find someone for you.'

Without realising it, I had imposed. Embarrassed, I dropped her hand. The assumption that there would be more than enough staff to absorb my request had seemed reasonable given the size of Wynterton Manor. 'Bentley's needs come first, obviously, and so I left my staff behind for him,' I added.

Getting rid of all Bentley's staff and bringing in those who had spent their lives being loyal to the Havisham family had given me the freedom to make Bentley my prisoner. Lydia, who was my housekeeper, lady's

12

maid, and confidante, was taking over my role of jailer for a few days. She knew how to maintain Bentley's regular doses of laudanum in order to keep him a docile prisoner. For if the opiate wore off and he regained his strength it would surely be impossible to entrap him again. That was a fear that lived with me constantly, akin to the dull ache of a bad tooth.

'We're in a little disarray ourselves,' Elizabeth said. 'The staff turnover here is unbelievable – it was bad enough at home to keep hold of the good ones, but here it seems impossible. One of the girls did a flit the other day, just upped and left without so much as a by your leave, and we have not yet replaced her. One simply cannot get reliable staff these days.'

Shadows under her eyes seemed to deepen as she spoke. It was my turn to reach out to her and give a comforting squeeze. 'It must be quite a shock having to manage such a large household. I'm sure you're doing admirably.'

'I must confess it is far beyond anything my family and I ever envisaged for me. There is always so much to think about, things that I never even considered. Not in my most wild dreams. And there is something odd—' Her head jerked as if waking from a dream, and she smiled widely, falsely, embarrassed. 'No matter. Let us get you settled in. Excuse me for just one moment.'

She stepped away, leaving me at the bottom of the stairs, while she spoke with a woman, who was presumably the housekeeper. The sensible black dress, high-necked and stiff as a brick wall, gave her the look of an impenetrable fortress. Starched white collar and cuffs lent a puritanical air. She must have been attractive once; the vestiges could still be seen, if one looked closely enough.

She glanced in my direction. Lemon-sucking lips drawing even tighter together, but nodding as she strode away, a chatelaine of heavy keys which hung about her waist swinging as if the house were a jail and she its chief warden. At her approach, a maid scuttled out of her way as if in fear of her life.

Was she the reason why Elizabeth was pale and seemed to be struggling a little under the pressure of running this house? Were the servants fleeing the house to escape the clutches of a tyrannical housekeeper? It wouldn't be the first time.

It wasn't uncommon for some staff to cling to the old ways of having things done, rather than embrace the changes of a new mistress. If that was their attitude, then it was best for all concerned to part ways.

As Elizabeth walked towards me again, she threw a nervous glance to her left down a dark corridor. What was there? I pretended to be looking around in interest, studying the columns that swept up into the ceiling, splitting and forming arches, twining so that they looked like tree roots. Like I had been buried alive.

By the time Elizabeth reached my side, she had smoothed the line of worry between her eyebrows, but there was a pinch to her mouth that looked like fear.

CHAPTER FOUR

My room was beautiful, with a four-poster bed, a full-length cheval mirror and a huge bay window.

'It is a shame you have arrived to darkness. I chose this room particularly for you because it has the best view of the garden of any guest room. Tomorrow I shall show you all of Wynterton's best assets. Sir John is famously proud of his gardens, both formal and informal.' Elizabeth beamed, but fidgeted as she spoke.

As well as escaping the complications of my own life, I had wanted to check on how my friend was coping with life married to Sir John. I felt responsible for her, because I had known he was not the best of men when I proposed their union. A greedy, gassy old windbag he was, whose breath was so bad it was possible to smell him before he entered the room; a man for whom women existed purely to provide heirs. Even though I had warned her, and she had gone into the marriage willingly, still concern nibbled at me. I had thought myself so all-knowing and cynical back then, so prepared for everything men could throw at me. My own marriage had quickly proved what a naive fool I had been – and I feared that same foolishness had led Elizabeth into a dark life.

'Although you cannot see it from the house, there is a lake at the back,' she said. 'This room does give a lovely view of the fountain, however. The gardens truly are a wonder; Sir John employs countless gardeners and staff for its maintenance.'

'I shall look forward to seeing, if not everything, at least a taste of Wynterton's splendour,' I replied.

There were several dots of burgundy splashed on the white window ledge. I have never been able to abide mess, so as we spoke I rubbed at them.

'Oh, yes!' she enthused. 'Over there you can, perhaps, make out the beginning of the orchard. That wall there – you see it? – encloses Sir

John's pride and joy, his rose garden. He is very particular about his roses, and takes care of them himself.'

It was too dark outside to see anything but our own reflections in the glass, but I nodded anyway. I surreptitiously licked my finger and rubbed again at the stains. The dots smeared like blood. Even here, in the safety of my friend's home, I could not escape my black imagination.

Elizabeth twittered on enthusiastically about her life. I watched her carefully. She had lost a little of her youthful roundness since marriage, and looked more like a grown woman. Yet as she spoke about her husband she did not seem afraid – and that was a relief. I admired the way she was making the most of her situation, for she had always struck me as sensible, level-headed and determined to carve out a place for herself despite fate dealing her the unfortunate cards of being born into a family with a title but not a single son, only daughters. As a result, she and her sisters were doomed to struggle, for their family did not have enough money for good dowries for seven daughters.

The first time I met her had been at an afternoon roust where I had been surrounded by suitors and utterly bored by them, and I believe I muttered something aloud expressing my frustration at never being left alone. Elizabeth had the spark of spirit to reply that some would have given everything to have that, to have even one man interested in her.

'My fate is sealed by whether or not a man desires me. But I was born plain and pragmatic rather than sparkling, and I am not an heiress. Do not complain about having everything, Miss Estella, when you stand beside others who have nothing.'

There had been no trace of rancour in her words, or even anger. Those emotions would, I confess, have made me slice back at her with a cutting remark. Instead, I recognised that she spoke truth as she saw it.

We had conversed for some time after that, and she had told me of her situation, which was exacerbated by her being the middle sibling in birth, and bottom in beauty. Her prospects of making a good marriage were slim, and as the years on the marriage mart increased, her chances of any suitor decreased. When I had voiced certain views about how society was in the wrong for giving women only marriage as a way of securing their futures, instead of giving them the freedom to earn their own living, she had looked both scandalised and delighted, whispering that she agreed with me.

After that, we had seen one another, inevitably, at almost every ball and social gathering. Her acceptance of her situation for what it was, coupled with determination to change her future, impressed me. That she could do all of that in genuine good humour intrigued me, too, for the same could not be said for me at that time, filled as I was with a cold frustration and smothering boredom with every aspect of my life.

Thus, when I'd heard that Sir John had been widowed and realised that he would quickly be on the hunt for a replacement wife, I had asked Elizabeth if she might be interested.

Now she stood before me, raised up to the status of lady. So why was I still worrying about her? Her delight was genuine as she told me about her new home.

'You are in one of the newer rooms, built by Sir John himself, when he expanded the manor after first inheriting it. He was keen to add some luxury for himself and guests.'

'It's lovely. You mentioned a few moments ago that something was odd, though, and I wondered what you were referring to—'

A gentle knock on the bedroom door ended the discussion before it could begin. Elizabeth jumped and checked her pocket watch before giving permission for the person to enter. It was Mrs Switchley, the stern housekeeper, and behind her was a twig-thin servant girl.

'This is Nora.' Switchley's voice was that of a guard introducing a prisoner. 'Nora, you will act with the decorum required of a lady's maid. Remember your place. And don't dawdle – if you are not in this room, you are down in the kitchen, or you will have me to deal with. Do you understand?'

All this was said without acknowledging Elizabeth. My friend turned around as if lost. Frowned. Then shook herself.

'Estella, I had not realised the time. I shall leave you in young Nora's capable hands while I change for dinner.' She rose, checking the time again, as if she could not believe her own eyes.

'Sir John has permitted you to forgo dinner this evening, Lady Taykall, that you and your friend might enjoy a more informal supper in the Cedar Room,' Mrs Switchley intoned.

Elizabeth gave her assent. 'If it is agreeable with you, of course, Estella.'

'I had rather a generous repast during my journey, but something light such as tea and sandwiches would be wonderful,' I replied.

Mrs Switchley then did the most remarkable thing. She took hold of Elizabeth's elbow and actually led her from the room, as if she were in charge. The impertinence! I waited for the mistress of the house to reprimand her, but instead Elizabeth went, meek as a lamb going to slaughter.

CHAPTER FIVE

ith Elizabeth gone, I had a little time to settle into the room I would be staying in for the next few days, while Nora unpacked my things.

There was something winning about her. Nora was clearly nervous as she bustled about the room, but determined to shine, carrying my clothing as if it were the most precious of treasures.

'Where would madam like her... these?' She looked at the undergarments in her hands, the like of which she had clearly never encountered before. She spoke very slowly and carefully, as if each word was a weighty thing which must be manhandled into place. Below it could be heard a strong Kent accent, fighting all attempts to suffocate it.

I indicated my answer, then returned to gazing out of the window while watching her from the corner of my eye.

She had a mob cap on, which only housemaids or lower wore. She seemed to realise, whipping it off when I turned my back, which made me smile to myself, but I pretended not to notice so as not to embarrass her. Her hair was the soft brown of a field mouse, and her movements reminded me of such creatures, too. She was neat as a pin.

'How old are you?' I asked.

'Fifteen.' She was tiny, only reaching to my armpit. Her hands, which were so cleanly scrubbed the skin was the bright pink of a bullfinch's breast, gave a little twitch. I raised my eyebrows. 'Twelve, miss, missus, ma'am. But being young just means I can learn quick.' Her accent was winning its fight to be heard, and her speech was speeding up.

My reply was warm. 'I shall change into the lavender gown now, please find it. You can unpack everything else while I dine.'

'Yes, miss. I mean, missus, you're a missus, ma'am. Sorry.' Her blush started simultaneously on her nose, cheeks and ear tips, and spread until the pink patches met. 'Nerves.' The word blurted out before she could stop herself, it seemed. She realised too late she wasn't supposed to admit to such a thing, and the pink deepened. Then she pulled herself so upright that she almost toppled backward.

'Nora, is this by any chance your first time serving as a lady's maid? Because if it is, do not worry. I don't bite.' Although I had been known to threaten…

She threw her head back and laughed. 'Me? No, I'm very experienced, miss, ma'am, missus.' Then her head dropped to her chest. 'I'm sorry. Would you like me to get you someone else?'

Her moods were as swift as her movements. I put my finger beneath her chin and lifted it so she could see my smile. 'We shall get along famously, I'm sure. Everyone must start somewhere. Now then, fetch me the lavender gown, and tell me about yourself while I dress.'

It would be the first gown I had worn since Mother died that was not black, and it felt momentous. I had observed the mourning period rigorously, but felt this visit marked a time to end it.

As Nora started to relax, she chattered happily, with me interrupting only to ask questions or give her directions on her work. She wasn't a mouse, I decided. When she smiled she reminded me of a starling on a branch, the way it can look dull brown and sharp and ordinary, and then a slight shift transforms its feathers into an iridescent rainbow of colours.

'How long have you worked here at Wynterton Manor? Oh, and if I might suggest that in future the water be warm rather than cold for me to wash in. No need to worry about it now, this will suffice.'

Thank goodness my childhood had left me hardy, thanks to winters growing up in Satis House, where fires were lit only in a handful of rooms while the remainder were so cold I could see my breath and my fingers went blue if I was still for too long. The water Nora was using reminded me strongly of those old days.

'Only been here a few weeks, miss, missus, ma'am.'

'Ma'am. Or Mrs Drummle, if absolutely necessary.' I took a breath. 'Actually, call me miss, as it's only the two of us.' My marriage was an utter sham. Acknowledging that in some small way felt so beautifully rebellious that I barely flinched as Nora cleansed the back of my neck with the icy cloth. She continued talking.

'I come straight from an orphanage. Well, sort of. Coming here is my chance to get a better life, improve meself, like. Now here I am'

– she met my eye in the mirror and her shy smile grew – 'talking with the likes of you. I can't hardly believe it.'

'Hard work always prospers.'

'It must do! Never could I have imagined half a year ago that I'd be out of the orphanage, let alone working in a big house like this! I've never been allowed upstairs before, not unless it's to lay the fires.'

'You're a scullery maid?' My surprise was barely concealed. In the hierarchy of servants, lady's maid was one of the best, for they were above all other female servants beside housekeeper. Lowest of all servants was the scullery maid. How curious that a housemaid not be given the opportunity to serve me instead, for they would be the obvious choice, working as they did upstairs.

'That's right, miss, missus, ma'am. All the housemaids were busy because one of them upped sticks and left without notice. There's always a to-do when that happens,' said Nora. 'So I put myself forward. But, if I can make so bold, if I can learn the skills of a lady's maid, well, who knows what my future could hold. Perhaps I could become the lady's maid to the mistress of this fine place.'

'A fine ambition, and one to be encouraged,' I agreed. 'I shall do my utmost to help you in that endeavour.'

There was a brittleness to my smile, though, because what Nora said made little sense. I would have imagined the housemaids would have been fighting between themselves for the opportunity to gain this preferment, for a lady's maid not only dressed their gentlewomen mistresses, but often also acted as companions, accompanying them wherever they went.

Were there rumours about me? Was that why no one wished to serve me? Did people suspect the awful truth about me, despite all my hard work to hide it?

CHAPTER SIX

hatever the reason for Nora becoming my makeshift lady's maid, I was impressed by her determination to better herself – although clearly she was going to have to work hard as she knew absolutely nothing about the task. I knew what it was like to have dreams stymied, and so I decided to do what little I could to aid her by teaching her all it was possible to in my short visit to Wynterton Manor. Certainly I didn't want to give any ammunition that might lead to her being told off by the housekeeper, who I had a feeling would be looking for any excuse to tell anyone off over anything.

'Your greatest hurdle in becoming a lady's maid is to learn about style, for not everyone has it. The ability to know what will suit your mistress, and to pick out what will be best for her day ahead is what makes the difference between an invaluable lady's maid and a mediocre one. That and the capacity to be always discreet, for you will be a companion and often a confidante.'

Nora's face was the picture of concentration, her eyes wide to take in the information all the better.

'Now, because of the gauze sleeves in this day dress, the obvious choice of jewellery is this pair of bracelets with the cameos,' I explained. 'And these drop earrings...'

'Have I done this up right? It don't look right.' Nora stood back, viewing my laces with a screwed-up expression.

I looked in a mirror to see what she had done. 'Ah, no, you need to tuck that bit in there, see?'

She did a twirl, looking for somewhere to place my silver-backed hairbrush, which she had inexplicably picked up, and finally opened up a small hatch in the wall, at about waist height, and popped it there rather than back on the dressing table where she had found it. A small bell inside the compartment tinkled, for she must have brushed against it. And with that, the cupboard interior suddenly began to move, disappearing downwards.

'Oh! Oh, no! That'll put the cat amongst the pigeons,' she tittered. Then her face paled. 'Mrs Switchley'll have my guts for garters for making such a silly mistake.'

'What on earth has happened to my brush?'

'It's a platform what goes down to the kitchen. It's only in the new rooms. It's so as the kitchen can send up food and drink direct to your room. It's useful at night, see. You just ring for a servant or send a footman downstairs with a message saying what you want, then they send it up in this.'

'How clever.' I peered down into the dark shaft – just as the ropes started moving again.

'Watch out! They must be sending the brush back up.'

We both pulled our heads back with a laugh.

Nora showed me to the parlour, known as the Cedar Room, where I was to meet Elizabeth. My new lady's maid kept up a steady stream of chatter.

'That was Betsy all over. Once she made up her mind, lor', but there was no changing it. I dint think she…'

As we walked, I was struck by the gloom of the house. The corridor's mean windows allowed little light even in daytime, I imagined, and the candles lining the walls (for there was no gas) seemed only to soften the darkness rather than expel it. This corridor, I realised, was the one down which Elizabeth had looked with apprehension when I first arrived. That made me study it with more interest.

'She said she was going to leave,' twittered Nora, words as fast as her feet, 'just as soon as ever she could and go to London – wanted me to go with her, but I says to her…'

There was a strange sense of time having stood still, which also reminded me of Satis House, and of a rot setting in.

'She didn't even wait out the couple of months, though. Left without me, she did. Without even a farewell. I've no regrets, though, because look at me now! Raised up, I've been!' Nora pattered ahead of me down an even darker corridor. 'It's just this way, miss. I-I think…'

The corridor grew dimmer, colder. A musky smell grew with each step. Dark wood panels were replaced with limed walls pockmarked with blooms of damp. A large, slate-grey stain crept up from the floor.

'We're going in the correct direction?' I asked.

'P'rhaps it's just around the corner?'

There was nothing there but deepening gloom. The smell was stronger; almost animal. A gentle draught came and went, came and went, as if the house were breathing.

We stood there, servant and gentlewoman. Waiting. Holding our breath. Edging closer together.

Goosebumps blossomed across my skin. I rubbed my arms, pulled myself taller.

'Let us turn back and correct course,' I said. 'Come.'

A movement in the corner of my eye…

'Mrs Drummle.' The housekeeper seemed to appear from the deepest shadows like an apparition. 'No one comes to this section of the house. It is dangerous.'

'Dangerous?' I repeated, disbelieving.

'Parts of the ceiling in some rooms have fallen. You were going to the Cedar Room to see Lady Taykall, correct?'

She took charge with a 'follow me' that showed how used she was to being obeyed. Bumping against her skirt with every step she took was the chatelaine of huge, heavy keys, along with the usual array of useful items such as scissors, a comb, and a knife in a plain leather sheath.

My goosebumps faded as we walked back towards the light. But what was it about this place that made my flesh creep as if someone were walking over my grave?

Having finally located the parlour, Elizabeth and I caught up a little more over a light supper.

'This is my very own room, given to me by Sir John with the express purpose of being a place in which to relax and repose when he is working hard in his office. Many of the rooms are named after trees or animals, for they are a passion of Sir John's; this is the Cedar Room, because of a large cedar that rather dominates the view outside.'

As she spoke, she poured tea from a large Staffordshire Wedgwood creamware teapot, decorated with a depiction in black of a man and woman sitting beneath an oak tree, in the style of clothing popular around the time Sir John was born, judging by the lady's wide gown and towering wig.

'Sir John works many hours, despite his age. I have suggested that his son, Winston – have you ever met him? No? Why, we must rectify that, for he is a good man – I have suggested that he take over some of the more time-consuming jobs now that Sir John is getting older. For surely it would be a good idea for Winston to get used to running the estate before he inherits.'

My laugh was sharp, and out before I could stop it. 'Apologies, Elizabeth, but I can imagine that did not sit well with Sir John.'

'Indeed.' She bowed her head like a penitent at church. 'He felt it was a judgement on his vigour. As a result he seems to spend more time than ever locked away in his study.'

What a relief, I wanted to quip, but held my thoughts inside and instead helped myself to the proffered sugar, before looking around the room. It had dark wood panels, dark paintings on the walls, dark corners where the candlelight did not reach. There were touches of femininity here and there. A cloth over the table, embroidered with drakes in flight across a lake. A large frame which held a tapestry that Elizabeth must have been working on. Flowers on every surface; their perfume failing to overcome the strange, musty smell that hung in the air. All were little sparks of life the new mistress of Wynterton had ignited. Yet even in that room, there was a stagnancy akin to Satis House – worse, even; for while our rooms had been alive with creatures, from mice to spiders, this place was filled with dead things brought back from Sir John's various hunts. There was even a stuffed lioness at bay in the corner of the parlour, forever protecting the moth-eaten cubs gambolling at her feet in oblivious innocence.

Elizabeth saw where my gaze fell.

'They are not quite what I envisaged for my parlour, but Sir John is so fond of them. He went on safari to Africa and India years ago, when he was still a young man. There he shot big game.' She gave a brave attempt at a proud smile.

That explained why the house was so filled with dead creatures posed to mimic life. Of course! I had learned all about his past and taste in women when looking for a suitable bride for him. Both his first and second wives died in childbirth, along with the children – a tragic but all too common tale. By all accounts, he was left particularly bereft after the death of his second wife; it seemed so cruel for history to repeat itself. After she, too, was buried alongside her infant daughter in the family cemetery, Sir John went away on safari.

Eventually, after about four years away, Sir John returned to his family seat, but he had still clearly been grieving, for the very mention of his deceased second wife's name, Ffion, was, by all accounts, banned from the house. Sir John found it too upsetting to hear.

It wasn't until another six years had passed that Sir John married his third wife, Jemima, the identical twin of his younger brother's wife. It was she who bore him two sons, thus securing an heir and a spare for him at long last. Further heartbreak was ahead, however, for the eldest son, Benjamin, died aged fifteen, from a sweating fever.

That lioness kept staring at me. Something about a mother frozen forever in a moment, unable to escape it, brought to mind my own mother, recently deceased. My hand went to her ring, which hung about my neck on a fine chain of gold and tiny seed pearls, and I shifted slightly so my back was to the poor lioness.

'Do you have plans to redecorate?' I asked.

'I prefer to keep things the way Sir John likes. As an older gentleman, he is more set in his ways than a younger husband might be,' she confessed. Then put her hand over her mouth, eyes widening. 'Not that I would want him to change!'

The lady doth protest too much, methinks. 'Of course not. The flowers in every room look wonderful – do I detect your touch there?'

Brightening the gloom in the parlour were huge displays of salmon pink geraniums that seemed to strain to break free of their pots so they might escape to sunnier locations.

She blushed in pleasure. 'They are all from Sir John's gardens and hothouses.'

'Yours now, too.' A necessary reminder, it felt. Nowhere else in the house apart from this room bore her mark, from what I had seen thus far.

'And how are you and Bentley? Sir John is so fond of him.'

'I, that is to say, we…' My usual quick wits abandoned me. My mind was a blank. She stared at me.

'Estella? Is all well?'

She was going to realise. The truth would be out, Bentley released from his bonds, and I would be pilloried at best. Hanged at worst.

CHAPTER SEVEN

I feigned a coughing fit. It was all I could think of as panic enveloped me. Damnation, I should have realised that coming to see Elizabeth would not be the escape I desired. Sir John was close to my husband, of course he was going to ask after him. The fear of discovery that constantly threatened to smother me back in London appeared once more, as if someone were pushing a pillow down over my face, stopping me from taking a breath.

Elizabeth patted me on the back with such vigour I truly did start coughing. She poured a glass of refreshing cordial for me to drink, and watched intently as I sipped and caught my breath. Thanks to the *petit-drame*, she forgot her question.

'I must ask, and hope you do not take offence at my bluntness, but… are you truly happy here… with Sir John?' I asked, to start the conversation in a different place.

She blinked rapidly. Picked up a tiered stand of sandwiches, the crusts all removed, and proffered them. Finally, she spoke.

'Happiness is what we make of a situation. I have found contentment here.'

'What is the secret to your contentment?' My curiosity was genuine. Was it truly possible to be married to a man such as Sir John and enjoy it?

'My situation is secure at last, Estella. Hours are no longer spent worrying what will become of me as I age. Sir John has his foibles, don't we all, but on the whole I have my diversions and he his. The running of the house keeps me busy.' She paused and gave me a smile that spoke of confidences shared. 'Besides, this house has rooms enough for me to hide in, if Sir John is feeling particularly amorous and I am not.'

My nose wrinkled. I tried to disguise it by giving a discreet cough behind my handkerchief.

Ever since my disastrous honeymoon in Paris, I could not imagine even kissing anyone again. The terrible dreams, and moments when I would be walking along a street and something would happen that flung me back to that horrific time, were only a part of it. There was not only fear of what a man might do to me – I was scared what I might do to a man.

For I was a murderess. The word conjured the image of pools of blood and cackling laughter, of evil so perverse there could be no hiding it or justifying it.

Was there any justification for my actions after stumbling across that man attacking his former beau? The sound of the woman's cries – thin, yet raw with pain and terror – had dragged me back to the moments when Bentley had held me trembling on the edge of death. At that moment I had not simply been remembering but *reliving*, and had been fighting as much for my life as for hers; and as much to punish Bentley, as the stranger. Fighting back had felt good. Strangling the man had almost been easy. The energy filling me had been a lightning strike: raw and powerful and deadly, yet exhilarating. My blood had pounded and every part of my body tingled, making me feel more alive than ever before. At that moment, I had felt that I was finally whole. I had wanted more. I had wanted to punish *every man in the world* for their violence against women, and Mother had seemed to be there with me, whispering encouragement, as she always had.

Afterwards, however, an exhaustion had overwhelmed me and for days it was impossible to drag myself from my bed. My reaction had been unnatural. Shame and disgust mingled with a terrified determination that this could not be the person I had become, no matter how natural it felt.

And so the battle against my two natures had begun in true earnest. In the ensuing summer months, I had turned my back on the violent beast inside me, and instead socialised with normal women. Studied them, aped their actions, desperate to become like them because the alternative was too hideous to contemplate. Somehow I smiled, made polite conversation, listened to chatter about rose gardens and worried about friends as if I was exactly like other women…

I finished my roast beef sandwich and swallowed down any fears that dared rise within me.

'You've gone rather red, Estella. You aren't going to start coughing again, are you? Is the mustard too strong for your liking?'

'It is perfection.' I beamed. 'Now, tell me: is managing the house suiting you?' Something was troubling Elizabeth, and if it was not her husband, it might be the housekeeper. I leaned in. 'I am filled with admiration for you, managing such a large house. I don't know how you do it – I am certain it would be beyond me.'

The lie was to give her confidence. Given the opportunity I would have relished running not only the Wynterton estate but all the Taykall businesses. There was still a longing inside me to find a purpose to my life and perhaps become a woman of business.

Elizabeth sighed, deep and heavy, as she contemplated my question. Then offered the stand of sandwiches again. Before I could take one, she spoke, moving it just out of reach as she did so.

'The housekeeper, Mrs Switchley, has been here forever, and is very particular about how things are done. She runs a tight ship, though, so… it is unforgivable of me to criticise.'

'Are you? Criticising, I mean?' I leaned forward, attempting to reach the sandwiches.

'A little… in my heart. Change can be difficult for someone in her position, however, and so I forbear. There are some alterations I have proposed, but although she nods and appears to listen, they never seem to happen. I don't like to remind her in case of seeming… well, nagging.' She set the stand down, on the far side of the table from me.

'Elizabeth, you are mistress here, not she. Perhaps it is time to remind her of that.'

'Why, Estella, you've barely eaten a thing. Wouldn't you like a sandwich?' She picked up the tiers of neat triangles once again. 'It does rather feel sometimes as if it is the servants in charge of the house rather than Sir John and myself.' It was set down again as she spoke. My stomach gave an unladylike grumble. 'Sir John does not seem to notice, much less mind. Mrs Switchley and the butler – did you notice him? Tall. Face like a bloodhound. Name of Worthybrook – hold absolute dominion over everyone. Even when I ask a maid to do something, fetch the simplest item even, I swear I see them glance over at Switchley or Worthybrook first, as if to ask silent permission. It is most vexing. I believe the pair of them scare the young girls so much that they look for alternative employ as soon as they start here, for we cannot hold on to any girl for long.'

'Why is the butler interested in the maids?' I asked. 'That is house-keeper work.'

Elizabeth nibbled on the edge of her sandwich. It looked like it was cucumber. I was rather fond of them.

'Sometimes it is permissible to not ask but tell people how things are going to be. If that makes you uncomfortable, perhaps you could couch it as though it were a question, while making it an order. For example' – I folded my hands on my lap – 'those sandwiches do look delicious. Would you be so kind as to pass me one?' The snap in my voice was that of a whip over an unruly horse.

'Oh! My! That was impressive, Estella.' She scrambled to pass them. I took two, to show I meant business. With my help, my friend would take charge of her household and anyone who argued would rue it. 'I shall try to be more like you,' Elizabeth announced.

'Only in some ways, dear; I would not recommend it in all...'

'Returning to the subject of the butler, for a moment...' Elizabeth sounded reluctant even as she spoke. 'I don't wish to seem uncharitable, or say anything untoward, but he does seem overly concerned with the maids. He is always watching them.'

I froze. 'Is he now?' I said, my voice careful.

If I had but known what was ahead of us, perhaps I would have shown her how to defend herself. Certainly I would have taken action myself, rather than allow the conversation to move on to the delights of decorative tea caddies... But those were innocent days bathed in sunlight, compared to the storm that was to come.

CHAPTER EIGHT

After eating, my journey from London to the countryside started to rather take its toll. 'It is amazing how tiring sitting in a carriage is,' I observed.

'Let me walk you back to your room.' Elizabeth offered me her arm companionably as we left her parlour, and generously pretended not to notice when I could not contain a yawn. When we arrived at my door, she said her good nights. 'Incidentally, we shall be joined for dinner tomorrow by two guests; they will not be overnighting. Mr Coutts and his man of business, Mr Blincoe, are great friends of Sir John's. Sleep well, Estella.'

'Coutts?' Elizabeth had started to walk away but my query made her stop. 'Where have I heard that name?'

She turned. 'He is a viscount. His father was an inveterate gambler and lost everything – even the family home.'

'How scandalous!'

'Indeed. But I admire the way he is now making quite the name for himself thanks to his bold fabrics. Why, you are probably wearing cloth woven in one of his manufactories.'

'Goodness.' I looked down at the lavender silk damask and found myself very much doubting her statement. Still, I had remembered where I knew the name from – the *eligible bachelor* Mr Coutts, who had got all the ladies' fans fluttering at Mrs Brandley's afternoon tea.

The tea had been staged just a few days earlier. Mrs Brandley had been kind enough to extend an invitation to me and a number of other newly married ladies for us to join her and her daughter Lucy – of whom I was extremely fond. As we nibbled on cucumber sandwiches, Lady Cecilia Forfar gave a sigh and announced: 'Ladies, I need your advice. I simply can't decide what to do about my country ball.'

This constituted a terrible calamity, judging from the reaction of the others. I was learning more about navigating these afternoon gatherings, trying to fit in with people who did not think like me. Pretending to be like them was hard and tiring, but I was determined to be normal after having taken the life of that man. And so, noting how seriously all the others took Cecilia's pronouncement, and the way Cecilia herself pouted and flounced, I arranged my face into an expression of sympathy as the terrible trials and tribulations of organising a ball were expounded.

'There's such an expectation that one must always outdo oneself. The last ball was such a marvellous success that I fear having made a rod for my own back to be beaten with.'

Cue noises of sympathy. I patted her shoulder, because I had noticed that people liked being petted like a dog when they required comfort. The other ladies were also making suggestions for themes the ball could have and I wracked my brains to find something useful to offer.

'There doesn't have to be a theme,' offered Daphne Fitzwilliams. 'The opportunity to gather with friends and dance and enjoy music is surely enough. It will be grand to get out of the city and gather at your country seat.'

'A straightforward affair in Essex will not get a write-up in the society paper, Daphne.' Mrs Avis Crocombe wagged her finger as she spoke.

'A masked ball, then. They can be fun.'

'I'm bored of those.' Cecilia yawned. 'Letitia Fitz-Simmonds held one only last month and it was so tired, and a little tawdry.'

'Fancy dress could be fun?'

'Yes! Italian-style fancy dress—'

'Oh, you don't want to do that. They were all well and good two years ago but they are a little passé these days.' Avis again.

'Estella, you're very quiet. Do you have any suggestions?' Cecilia asked.

'Yes, Estella, what are they doing in Paris? You were there recently, weren't you?'

The mention of my honeymoon was a bucket of iced water thrown over me, but I hid my shivers. I thought back to happier times in the French capital, in my younger days, while attending a Parisian finishing school for gentlewomen, to prepare me for snaring a husband. The fashions then would be old hat now, though.

'Who will you invite?' asked Daphne. Her dark blonde ringlets trembled with excitement. She was a woman with a lively mind and a generous nature, who had fallen with child swiftly and was desperate for company other than her husband and baby.

'Mr Coutts would be a delightful addition. Perhaps he might be a good fit for my sister; she has come out this season and is being very picky,' said Avis. She picked a crumb from her red bombazine dress and, when she thought no one was looking, popped it into her mouth.

'I hear he is determined to find himself a wife this season,' added Daphne.

There was much fluttering of fans at this comment. Presumably Mr Coutts was rich or handsome – or both.

'New money.' The wrinkle of Mrs Matthew Pocket's nose spoke eloquently. 'Or is he? He is a viscount, but does not allow anyone to call him Lord Coutts, simply because he has no *family* money left after his father ruined them. How ridiculous! And the money he now has comes from… *working*. Surely he cannot be trusted if he hides his illustrious heritage.'

'Perhaps it is pride,' said I. 'Or that he would rather be known for his achievements, than his title. The way he has changed his fortunes sounds admirable.'

'It is vulgar to speak of money.' Emily Harkness leaned forward as she spoke. Her eyes were dark as chocolate, her skin pale as a lily, but two bright spots of red on her cheeks betrayed excitement. 'But my goodness, what money he has! I hear—'

'What is the point of talking of guests if there is no ball to speak of?' Cecilia exclaimed. She gave a vexatious tap of her fan into her palm.

Daphne tilted her head in thought. 'A black and white ball is always elegant.'

'Always. That is precisely why I cannot do it, for it is not at all original. I need to create something unexpected, that no one else has done, something that will have all the ton talking, not fall to the *obvious*. Oh, forgive me, Daphne, desperation is making me mean.'

'Perhaps at this ball the men should wear the corsets and the ladies go free, so that they may realise the purgatory we live in. That has not been done before,' said Lucy, baring her teeth before biting into a bonbon. Cries of shock broke out.

'Really, you must apologise.' Her mother sighed.

The shock was turning into giggles.

'A man would never wear such a thing,' said Cecilia. She covered her mouth to hide her daring at such a statement.

'My point exactly,' replied Lucy. 'Corsets are becoming tighter and tighter. Only a few years ago women had far more freedom of movement; now our clothes are once again beginning to constrict our movement, and even our breath. This is more than fashion. It is control.'

'It does create a most attractive silhouette,' I countered. I was far fonder of my corset since it had stopped me from being stabbed to death by an attacker wielding my own knitting needle.

For a moment I was back in that alley, barely able to see, moving on instinct as I fought to save a stranger from having her virtue violently stolen by a beau she did not want.

'Look deeper than the surface. Come, you are more than capable.' Lucy replied to me but looked around in appeal at everyone gathered. 'It seems to me that society is so scared of women that we must be physically restrained from reaching our full potential. How long before the latest mode is for us to be locked in a box? Think what we could achieve if only we could dress and act the way men do – if we had their freedom.'

It reminded me of something.

'You know, in Paris such balls are all the rage.' All eyes turned to me. 'It's true. The rich and fashionable think it amusing to stage balls where they dress like beggars. There are even some ladies who dress as men, and men who dress as ladies.'

Stunned silence was followed by hesitant titters that grew to outright laughter.

'My word, what will they think of next?'

'It's outrageous—'

'Yes… everyone would be talking about it.'

'It would certainly get a write-up in the society papers.'

'The scandal sheets, more like!'

'Dare you?'

35

'I don't think you need go quite that far.'

'If it's good enough for Parisians then why should we not do it? Are we not as chic as they?'

'Well, I don't care what the theme of the ball is, provided Mr Coutts is invited,' declared Avis. 'He is simply perfect for my sister – she really must meet her match before the end of the season, or what will people think?'

'Father says he has amassed an absolute fortune in under two years. He started from nothing,' said Emily.

'Oooh, he must be quite cut-throat. I do love a man who knows what he wants and lets nothing get in his way.'

'The look in your eyes is positively lascivious, Daphne!'

And thus the conversation circled back to Mr Coutts, and again the fans fluttered for the eligible gentleman. As did mine, for an idea was forming. For Mr Coutts to have gained such wealth in such a short time he must be a sharp operator, tough in business, and also a truly modern man. Perhaps as such he would be open to a revolutionary idea – partnering with a woman filled with ideas and determination. An independent income separate from the fortune Mother had left me (which was now technically Bentley's since I had wed him) might prove useful indeed if my husband were ever to gain the upper hand again. It might provide a secret nest egg for me to raid, if I ever again needed to flee my husband.

My eyes flew open to darkness just as deep as if they had stayed tight shut. The bed, the sheets, the very air felt unfamiliar; where was I? A few heartbeats passed before my disorientation cleared and I remembered. Of course, I was not at my house but at the home of my good friend, who had walked me to this room after a lovely evening of conversation and the occasional passing sandwich.

What had woken me, though? I couldn't say, for strain though I did, there seemed no sound amiss. Yet my skin prickled and my heart beat faster, as if aware of danger. The air filled with blinding white light and the smell of sulphur as I struck a lucifer and lit a candle, which I raised around the room, peering into shadows. There was no one there.

A creak outside my bedroom door sounded, as if someone was shifting their weight. A gentle susurration. Shading the candle with my hand to limit the light it threw, I crept towards the door. The sound on the other side became clearer. Someone was whispering. A man and a woman. I pressed my ear against the door.

Only an occasional word could be deciphered. Their voices rose a little as they grew more animated. Only a little, but enough.

'…watch her… must stop…' The man.

'…leave her for now…' The woman. '…doing everything we can…'

'Same time tomorrow.'

'As usual.'

'Don't be seen.'

Soft footfalls receding.

Licking thumb and forefinger, I snuffed my candle and pinched the wick to reduce the smoke, the smell of which might otherwise give me away. Then I eased open the door, holding my breath as if that might prevent any telltale creak from the hinges. There was none. I looked to my right. The neat, poker-straight back of the housekeeper disappeared. To my left was the butler's tall but slightly stooped figure.

Why had they held a clandestine meeting outside my door? And if I was the 'she' they referred to, what did they wish to prevent me from doing?

Or were they talking of Elizabeth, their mistress? She had said they acted as if they were in charge of the house, rather than she. Could she be in danger somehow?

I thought of the beggar boy's words. I remembered those drops of red on my windowsill – blood? Recalled also Mrs Switchley's knife on her chatelaine. And the butler's interest in the maids. Not to mention Elizabeth's almost servile demeanour around her housekeeper. There was something very wrong in Wynterton.

No, it was too ridiculous a thought; the kind that only seemed likely in the middle of the night but did not survive scrutiny in daylight.

Yet, for all my scoffing, sleep did not return.

CHAPTER NINE

The day dawned bright and mild. One of those wonderfully mellow autumn days that can fool one into imagining winter will slumber forever, and summer will stretch her long fingers through all the 'ber' months.

The sunshine burned through my sluggish haze. I had tossed and turned most of the night, listening to the sounds of this unfamiliar house. Once again I had been reminded of Satis House but, unlike my childhood home, I was not familiar with every scent, every noise, and even the way the air moved. There were no comforting moans from Mother as she paced, endlessly mourning the life she could have had. Instead, every creak of the house as its timbers settled had me burrowing deeper beneath my tangled bed sheets, until I fetched my favourite fan: the one with the small knife hidden inside the decorative boning of the handle. I held it to me, and at last sleep found me.

I had slept until Nora woke me with my breakfast. The speed at which she was learning was impressive, and dressing went smoothly. Still, as I walked along the corridor to find Elizabeth, I surreptitiously removed several hairpins from my top bun that Nora had speared my skull with.

Sir John rounded the corner and almost bumped into me, putting his hands out. They were filthy with soil, and I shrank away for fear he would dirty my beautiful cornflower-blue gown which, despite being only a simple day dress, had such fashionably wide sleeves that I had pillows tied to my arms.

'Ah, Mrs Drummle, good to see you. And how is Bentley, eh? Eh?' Sir John leered towards me, wiggling two furry caterpillar eyebrows in a way that would have had me baulking had I not been raised to be a gentlewoman, and therefore always kept emotion in check. There was no escaping his breath, however, so I flicked my fan open with aplomb and fluttered it between us demurely. 'Ha, yes! We newly-weds, eh?' Then he held his hands up and waggled them. 'Love to get my hands dirty. One must never be above getting one's hands dirty, eh, girl?' he boomed, jaundiced eyes dancing beneath those bushy eyebrows, stained yellow-brown from cigar smoke.

Goosebumps crept over my skin. Was he going to enquire more about Bentley? He was fond of my husband, and saw him of something of a protégé, particularly since we had been asking Sir John to sponsor Bentley's political career – which would now, hopefully, never be launched.

'Have you seen the gardens yet?' he asked instead. 'For the most part they are managed by my gardeners, of course, but there is a section I like to call my own. Was inspired by the old king, don' cher know.'

Ah, old King George III – or Farmer George, as he had been affectionately known before his death fifteen years earlier. Sir John was considerably younger, having been born in 1774, but because he had sometimes frequented court he still liked to dress in the old-fashioned style of silk knee breeches, and a peruke so severely powdered that he sometimes was followed by a small cloud about his head. Sir John was an old man fighting progress, at bay against the changing times.

Elizabeth appeared from around the corner, almost colliding with him in much the same way I had.

'Goodness, this is quite the party.' She laughed.

'Show Estella the grounds, my dear.' It was an order, not a suggestion. 'It is a bright enough day. Or perhaps go to the meadows to hunt for butterflies. I shall be busy attending to my own visitors, so accept my apologies for my absence.'

He gave a bow, surprisingly low and courtly for a man of his age, then trotted off, one finger exploring the recesses of his ear.

My friend was in the first flushes of trying to find common ground with her new husband, and so she had seized on Sir John's suggestion of 'butterflying', as she put it.

'It is a most pleasing hobby Sir John and I can share. It is useful, don't you find, to create interests together?' She spoke as we walked side by side through the grounds, followed by two footmen, whose presence foiled my hopes of being able to tackle Elizabeth about the whispered conversation between Mrs Switchley and Mr Worthybrook last night. One had a large bag over his shoulder, which tinkled musically as he followed us. The other carried two large but incredibly fine nets on the end of sticks.

'Oh, yes, Bentley and I share a surprising number of hobbies and interests. Redecorating our new home.' *Preparing the attic bedroom that is now his prison.* 'Medicinal preparations.' *I administer the laudanum, and he receives it with trembling gratitude.* 'Prison reform.' *Certainly he is being taught a lesson he will not forget in a hurry.*

'Goodness.' Her eyes were wide but she nodded, thoughtfully. 'You seem to share many serious outlooks – that is surely the sign of a perfect match.'

'We are certainly finding our way through these first months of marriage most agreeably.'

As we walked there was something strange about the grounds that nagged at me. Then I realised: it was uncannily quiet. There were no sounds of servants calling to one another, no whistling or singing. It was disconcerting.

The garden was split into formal and semi-formal, and many of the trees and bushes had been trimmed into all manner of fantastical shapes, from simple spheres to a pair of elephants with their trunks held high to trumpet to the world. It was an impressive show of humanity's ability to subjugate nature, but the sight made me long instead for the gardens of my childhood home. My heart ached to see again the overgrown tangles of Satis House's grounds, and walk along paths that could barely be seen, or hide among the foliage as I had as a youth.

The fountains, the walled orchard, the walled rose garden, an impressive herb patch, which smelled divine: all was pointed out to me with shy pride. At one point we saw Sir John beside a stand of short-trunked, wide-crowned walnut trees, talking with one of his staff: a gardener, from his garb. His voice carried on the soft air.

'…increase harvest. What's that saying I'm thinking of?'

'A woman, a dog and a walnut tree, the more they are beaten, the better they be.'

'That's the one!' Sir John gave a chortle.

Perhaps I should beat him and see how much it improves him.

Whether in London or the country there was no escaping how little men thought of women. How trapped I was in a world where I could never gain power.

Finally we walked through a grove of beech trees, where speckled wood butterflies danced in patches of sunlight. Elizabeth pressed on until we reached the other side.

'Here we are,' she declared.

Meadowland opened up all around us. Beyond its gentle undulations lay fields, tucking into one another, and cut up into a patchwork by mile upon mile of criss-crossed hedges. The sun warmed my skin and for the first time in many months a sense of ease rolled through me, lowering my shoulders.

'It is very late in the season, but here we may see some butterflies,' said Elizabeth, taking the net handed to her by the silent footman. I did the same.

'Oh! Look!' I pointed, for there among the long grasses a butterfly flew in gentle skipping motion over the tops.

Elizabeth leapt forward, swung her great net and... missed.

'There is another,' I said. This time it was I who wielded the net. The butterfly skipped away, wily for all its delicacy.

We two raced around, giggling and spinning. Calling breathlessly to one another, pointing this way and then that. Memories filled me of rare moments of innocent childhood joy, when I had played with my friends, the mice and spiders in Satis House, their little feet tickling as they clambered onto my shoulder for a titbit of food before the game began again.

'Well done, Estella! You got one.'

Inside the fine netting was a small butterfly with fiery orange wings, bordered with chocolate brown. Pride swelled through me at being the first to capture an insect, even if it had been all luck and no judgement.

'A small copper – common, but a fine specimen. Wait there a moment.' Elizabeth walked to the discarded bag and pulled out a jar.

'So that was what was clinking,' I exclaimed.

'And this is where the magic happens. Watch...'

With gentle precision, she emptied the net into the jar and quickly put the lid on. The butterfly fluttered against the glass, and although I felt sorry for it, I peered closer, for this was a fascinating opportunity to study it. Its antennae were striped brown and white, the buds on the ends of them were either deepest brown or black: which, I could not decide.

'There's the thinnest border of cream around the wings,' I gasped. 'And… are their wings made of scales? I would never have noticed this. Thank you.' I looked up and met Elizabeth's eyes. She beamed.

'Just as Sir John has opened up this world to me, I am pleased to do the same for you. It truly is a wonder, is it not? Now, then.'

She took some wadding and opened another bottle from the bag, this one filled with liquid. Then she opened the butterfly's jar – but instead of letting the small copper go, she popped the wad of damp cloth inside.

'What—?' I began, but stopped. For it was already obvious. There was some kind of poisonous chemical in action.

The butterfly battered its frail body against the glass, a futile battle to reach the freedom it could plainly see. Each fluttering was already weaker. Each beat more desperate. The wings flickered. It fell to the bottom of the jar.

Another sad tremble and it fell to its side. A twitch. No more.

I bit my lip to stop the tears that threatened to brim over. Set my face so Elizabeth would have no clue that inside I was screaming.

Murderess!

Knowing that I had saved a woman's life by killing her attacker did not make me feel better. Surely only monsters snuffed out lives as easily as others did candles?

Somehow, watching the butterfly captured in the killing jar, I felt monstrous all over again. That poor insect. Trapped. Scrutinised. Killed. Simply for being itself. And dead because of me.

Everywhere I went, death seemed to follow, as naturally as night followed day.

CHAPTER TEN

My mood of overwhelming sadness cast a pall over the remainder of the butterfly hunt, try as I might to hide it. Finally, Elizabeth sent the footman back to the house with the equipment, and instead suggested we take in some more of the grounds. The weather was starting to cool, and although it was warm in the sunshine, it was cold in the shade. The resultant combination of flushes and shivers reminded me of having a fever.

Elizabeth drew her arm through mine as we strolled once more through the formal gardens, pointing out areas of interest to me. To reach the meadows we had veered to the left of the house, whereas now we explored the back and traversed mainly downhill. Eventually the formal layout that Sir John's ancestors had created many moons ago thinned until a view opened up to a lake so still it was a huge mirror to the sky. We stopped beside it and as I looked down at the darkening clouds above me I had the oddest sensation of both falling and floating, and my stomach clenched as if sensing danger.

Elizabeth pulled her arm from mine and stepped ahead of me, standing apart. The spot where her arm had been grew cold before she spoke.

'You would not guess to look at it, to see how tranquil it is, but this lake hides great dangers. Sir John's wife drowned here last year.'

'It was here? I had not realised it was in the grounds.' It had happened around the same time as Bentley had begun courting me in earnest. The details that he had shared with me at the time were scant but sufficient.

'He blames himself for her death, you know. I'm not sure he'll ever get over the loss – they were together for thirty years, more or less; can you imagine? All that shared history, the hopes and dreams, raising a family, grieving for the lost children…' Elizabeth herself seemed lost. Her eyes were huge as she stared at the still black waters, and she could not seem to tear her eyes away. She leaned towards the surface imperceptibly. I had an urge to grab her and shake her from her watery reverie.

Sir John had certainly been keen to fill his dead wife's shoes after her death. At my wedding, just three months after she had passed away, he had been champing at the bit – hence my arranging for he and Elizabeth to meet.

But then I remembered the ten-year wait between his second and third marriage. My summer of trying to think like 'normal' people had changed me a little, and so I paused to wonder if perhaps Sir John was capable of finer feelings after all. Perhaps I had misjudged him. Burying one's emotions was not the same as not feeling them.

'He loved her?' I asked hesitantly.

At last Elizabeth looked away from the water. 'Surely it isn't possible to be together for so long and not have love for one another?'

No matter how many years passed, I would never hold Bentley in affection – not unless suffering from a severe blow to the head that left me a fool, perhaps. Our circumstances were probably unique, however…

Curiosity tugged at my skirts, wanting attention. 'Why does he blame himself?'

'He… Perhaps I am breaking a confidence between man and wife. However, it is common knowledge here, so I do not think that can be true. It was a hot September day and Sir John's wife, Jemima, loved to go on the water. She was out of sorts that day; however, Sir John was rather insistent that she accompany him – he thought it would cheer her once she was on the boat. One of the men offered to row for him, but again, he wouldn't hear of it. You know men and their pride.'

Indeed I did. All women did.

'When they got to the middle of the lake, Sir John was overcome. His heart was gripped in a vice and he could not catch his breath; he felt quite weak. Jemima panicked. As Sir John passed out, he heard a splash. When he came around again several hours later, he had drifted to the edge of the lake and the boat had come to rest amongst some reeds – just over there, in fact. There was no sign of Jemima. He called for her, his voice weak. She didn't reply. He began to crawl slowly, painfully, back to the house but was spotted by the chief gardener, who carried him to the house and then raised the alarm amongst the other men. A search party was raised, but Jemima was not found. The lake has still not given her up, not even the ring she always wore, bearing her initial.'

How awful. Even the hardest of hearts can be softened by the suffering of tragedy, and this loss put Sir John in a whole new light for me. I vowed to be more charitable towards him – although that would involve a lot of fan use...

Gathering clouds were darkening, bruising the light, and I noticed Elizabeth shiver. We turned back towards the house, which crouched low over the top of the hill, a mishmash of disparate parts that suggested a creature waiting. Brooding. Patient. This was not a happy house. It was a place where tragedy seemed to seep from its walls and run from it in rivulets right down to the forbidding stillness of the lake.

I put my arm through Elizabeth's.

'Come, let's walk back, for you look like you are growing chilly,' I said, unable or unwilling to show my own sudden vulnerability.

We set off, and she leaned against me, her steps leaden.

'What on earth is wrong? You should not upset yourself over the past this way,' I said.

'No, no, it is not that.' Instead of speaking further, she concentrated her energy on putting one foot in front of the other.

'Something is amiss, Elizabeth.'

More silence. Her lips drew a stubborn line. At last, we reached the garden proper. As we approached the walled rose garden, I spied a bench and veered towards it.

'You can't go in there.' The voice was deep and authoritative.

I turned, my arm still through Elizabeth's, and gave one of my best haughty stares to the man in front of me who dared tell me where I might or might not go. He wore thick work boots, coarse trousers and shirt, and an apron of sacking. His hands were filthy with soil, a smear of which was across his forehead, where he must have been pushing his bushy black hair back off his face. He would have been handsome had it not been for the scowl on his face and the anger that tightened his eyes into a glare.

'Have a care who you address in that manner, boy,' I ordered. He flinched at the 'boy,' as I had guessed he would. He was clearly a man – strong, at that, judging from his forearms, which showed because his shirtsleeves were rolled up – but men tend to be so satisfyingly sensitive about not being perceived as 'manly', whatever that might be. 'Do you not recognise the lady of the house when you see her? Show some respect.'

'Estella…' Elizabeth looked positively blue as she swayed.

The man darted forward. 'Are you unwell, m'lady?'

'She's feeling faint,' I replied for her. 'I was trying to get her to that bench so she could sit down.'

'Better to get her to the house. With your permission, m'lady?' Without waiting for a reply, he scooped her up and marched up the incline towards the house.

'The bench is over there. What on earth are you—?'

'The roses have had a feed. Sir John did it himself. The smell won't do anyone any good, let alone a lady in swoon.' He still sounded more like someone used to giving orders than receiving them. Despite carrying my friend, he walked so quickly up the hill that I was forced to scurry after him, which annoyed me intensely.

Still, if horse muck had been spread to feed the roses, he was right that the aroma would not have aided Elizabeth in her weakened state. The admission that he was right irritated me even more.

'Who are you, anyway?' I demanded.

'Robin Bellis, miss. Head gardener. Could you—'

Pre-empting the request, I opened the door before us, which led into the library. Bellis put Elizabeth down on a high-backed Queen Anne chair. With a silent nod at us both, the muscles in his jaw clenched as if we had insulted him, he left the room as quickly as he had come.

'Well!' It took me a moment before I remembered myself enough to kneel beside my friend and take her hand. 'Are you feeling any better? I'm starting to see exactly what you mean about the servants acting as if they are in charge – the head gardener was most put out that I wanted to take you into the rose garden. The way he just marched you here!'

There was a little more pink to her cheeks as she nodded.

'I haven't ever spoken with him before,' she said. Her voice seemed slightly stronger. 'I have heard about him, however. He is said to have a fearful temper; and although his given name is Robin, no one calls him by anything but Brock, because he is as stubborn as a badger, they say. Still, I was glad he came along, even if he was...'

'Inappropriate.' I said what she was too polite to. 'Do you know what caused you to feel so faint?'

Her face was a picture of hesitation, but her hand gave away her secret. It fell across her stomach, protective and nurturing all at once.

'Elizabeth,' I gasped. 'Are you...? Could it be...?'

A slow, shy smile spread across her face as she nodded. 'It is too early to be sure, but yes, I believe I might be with child.'

This would secure Elizabeth once and for all within the Taykall family and Wynterton. She no longer needed my protection.

Yet goosebumps bloomed when I thought about the gardener's anger, the butler's proprietary air, the way the housekeeper acted, lording it over the household and her mistress.

Something was happening in that house. Something beyond servants getting above their station. My instincts had been honed through years of surviving numerous attempts on my life, from the cunning to the blatant, and now they were vibrating like the silk of a spider's web being plucked by the blunderings of a hapless fly that did not realise death was about to pounce...

CHAPTER ELEVEN

t had been an unexpectedly emotional day, worsened by lack of sleep the night before. Elizabeth and I spent the remainder of the afternoon in the house, reading aloud.

I took the opportunity to keep an eye on Mrs Switchley and Mr Worthybrook whenever possible. Their whispered conversation had fired my curiosity and, ever fascinated by a puzzle, I was determined to discover their secret.

Mrs Switchley ran a tight ship. If she caught housemaids lingering above stairs as they cleared a table, or a scullery maid taking her time tending the fires, the housekeeper swept all before her with swift reprimands.

There was nothing untoward in what I witnessed, however.

In between reading to one another, Elizabeth told me more about the expected visitors for dinner: Mr Coutts and Mr Blincoe. Coutts and Sir John had started doing business together at about the time the cloth factory went from profitable to a virtual gold mine. Sir John might look like a fool, yet he was as sharp as a scalpel regarding business. If he thought something was worth investing in, then it was a good thing.

Elizabeth confessed that she would be dressing with care for dinner. Never one to be outdone, I decided to do the same. A man of fashion and taste was coming, who was also bold, successful, and able to begin rebuilding his family's lost fortune. This was a rare man indeed, and one who might have the vision to see past the rules of society that stopped a woman from owning an industry. As such, I was keen to impress this fascinating lord who chose business over title, and I told Nora as much once I was in my room.

'Apparently, he thinks of himself as an *arbiter elegantiarum*: someone who could even replace Beau Brummell now that he has moved to France,' I said.

'What's a arboretum eagle ta-ra-rum?' Her face was a picture of fascinated horror, and I could only assume she was imagining some kind of fantastical bird man.

I repeated the phrase and made her say it again until she had the correct pronunciation. Such knowledge could be useful to her. 'It's nothing rude,' I added with a smile. 'It means that he considers himself an authority on social behaviour and dress that can be summed up in a single word: taste.'

Nora and I chose a gown of daffodil yellow, with slashes about the neck and hemline, through which showed blonde lace. It felt good helping her in these first steps towards achieving her dream life. I thought of the beggar boy. How I hoped he would find employment, or at least a roof over his head until such time as he could. Perhaps it was foolish to settle such a large sum on him, but he deserved the opportunity to make something of himself. I felt a strange sort of kinship with both of them, for I was an orphan, too.

As for Nora, it was no trouble to aid her. She was most entertaining company and a satisfyingly fast learner. Upon explaining that the evening required a more elaborate hairstyle, she attempted to conquer her fear of the curling tongs, heated by the fire's glowing coals.

'Fold the curl paper about the section of hair – that's it – and that will protect the hair,' I explained.

'I'm more afeared of catching you than the hair.' She shuddered.

'The more you fear something, Nora, the more likely you are to make a mistake. Confidence is key.'

By the time she was finished, perfectly cylindrical curls framed my face, my centre parting was straight as a ruler, and the bun at the top of my head was decorated with ribbons and damask roses.

The finishing touch was a pearl necklace, with matching pearl drop earrings. Tucked into my bodice was the end of a long chain, on the end of which hung a ring of Mother's. I had some trouble deciding on which fan to use, but eventually, for reasons that escaped me, I opted for my favourite, the Parisian one, with its hidden weapon.

The drawing room was cold. I was grateful for my many petticoats beneath my dress, while simultaneously cursing my bare shoulders, because a great draught slipped through the huge, closed windows. It was all I could think of as I tried to attend to the men I was being introduced to.

'Lord Coutts.' I greeted him with a low curtsy suitable for one of his rank.

'Oh, no – "mister", please. I can no longer answer to the title I was born to, for I am not worthy of it. It should have been lost when all else was.'

He took hold of my hand and bowed so low that I could see little of him but his sandy-blond hair.

'It's a pleasure to meet you, Mrs Drummle,' he said, finally looking up. He had a long, elegant, perfectly straight nose, and keen, bright blue eyes. Between the shade of his hair and his eyes, his colouring reminded me of looking at the sea on a summer's day.

Mr Francis Coutts was a conundrum. A viscount who refused to be recognised as such. A gentleman, but not – for he worked for his income. He had earned enough money to be forgiven for that, however, and was causing quite a stir among those of the ton looking for business to invest in. His rise had been meteoric, for no one had heard of him two years ago, yet now he was the talk of the town – helped no doubt by the fact he was not only successful but of marriageable age and single. All of which had been gleaned from gossip, but now the man himself stood before me I was determined to get my own measure.

Perhaps, with a little persuasion and the offer of a large investment sum, I could become a partner, I thought.

'I do hope you can forgive my intrusion upon your visit to Wynterton Manor.'

'Not at all, Mr Coutts. Your arrival makes me feel less as if I have intruded on the newly-weds.'

As I spoke, I tried to shuffle closer to the fire which roared in the huge fireplace. Into the stone surround were carved two monstrous dog-like creatures, rearing on their hind legs, mouths gaping in mid-roar. Perhaps they had gobbled up all the heat, for despite the flames crackling from the huge logs, nothing seemed to warm the room. The dark wood panelling on every wall absorbed the light in the same manner.

Coutts' replying smile was gallant, and perfectly symmetrical. He took a step closer to the fire, too. 'No one could find fault with your company, I am certain, Mrs Drummle. Is Mr Drummle with you?'

My reply in the negative had him pulling an expression of sadness that was flirtatiously fake.

'A tragedy. This is my man, Mr John Blincoe, by the by.'

Mr Blincoe stood a little behind his master, and met my eye only to say his greeting then bow his head in subservience. The rest of the time his gaze was on the floor, as far as it was possible to tell given that his eyes were permanently hidden by light reflecting on the wire-framed glasses he wore. A thick, pale scar was discernible on one side of his face, running from the cheekbone down into his greying, neatly trimmed beard.

Both men were dressed in fine clothes, though of course the master was dressed more ostentatiously than his clerk of business. Coutts' peacock-blue coat, with velvet collar, was contrasted against a buff waistcoat, across which was a massive gold link watch chain. On his bottom half were black trousers and boots, which ensured his top half remained the focus. On the ring finger of his right hand was a plain gold band.

'You run a cloth mill, is that correct, Mr Coutts?' I asked. The warmth from the fire played over my shoulders.

'Cloth is my business and passion. Why, I can look at any person from across the room and tell the type and quality they are clothed in. From observing the way a person moves I know what style of clothing will suit them best: what to accentuate and what to disguise.'

'You judge the cut of a person by the cut of their cloth,' I quipped.

'There is much can be told from people's clothing. Their social position, an idea of their income, even their priorities in life. Clothes are more than merely practical, they are a declaration to the world of the way we want to be perceived by others.' His reply did not reflect my own light tone.

'Clothes maketh the man, rather than manners?' The fire was rather ferocious. One half of me was burning, while the half furthest from the flames was resolutely freezing. I shifted position surreptitiously.

'Clothes show the intention, the façade; manners show the truth,' Coutts replied.

'In my experience, both can be easily faked. I have known people who pull manners about them and throw them off as easily as a cloak.'

He frowned, then quickly cleared his face along with his throat. 'You, for example, are showing impeccable taste with this silk crepe over satin – gorgeous.' He leaned forward and lowered his voice. 'You are a light in this dark, gloomy house.'

Coutts was clearly charming and handsome, but there was no hint of the businessman rumoured to be as sharp as a cut-throat razor – and by all accounts he was ruthless. According to Daphne, who had heard it from her father, Coutts had been quietly building a name for himself and then around two years ago had begun aggressively taking over competitors. A year ago this became even more marked. I admired how he had taken control of his life. He was old money, and could have sunk without a trace in a vain struggle to cling on to status. Instead, he had launched himself into the new industrialised world, in much the same way as I would like to.

His mild-mannered appearance must be a costume he wears to lull opponents into a false sense of security, I thought.

Long had I desired to use my brain in this world, but Mother had always prevented it, saying that the business of revenge was all I needed. Bentley had won me with false promises of partnership and a marriage of equals, with him determined to become prime minister and me the charm and acumen behind the decision-making. How quickly after the wedding he had smashed that illusion – I still bore the scars, luckily hidden beneath my clothing.

The remembrance made me pull myself taller, as if to disprove my weakness. It also made me decide to be bold.

'Are all the fabrics you wear from your own manufactories?' I asked. He nodded. 'And Mr Blincoe's?'

The salt-and-pepper-haired clerk wore deepest black, broken only by a stark white shirt and necktie, but the quality of the cloth was obvious – velvet, silk, the finest wool. He wore a black cameo oval mourning ring; a watch chain of silver stood out against his black waistcoat, while a jet bead dangled from it, glimmering in the light.

'It is possible to tell much from a person by the way they treat those over whom they have power—'

I stopped because Mr Blincoe had pulled his watch from his waist-coat pocket, glanced at it, and with the lightest of touches on the elbow attracted the attention of his master. Coutts halted our conversation by raising a finger, and listened instead to whatever his clerk was whispering into his ear.

Annoyed, I took the opportunity to turn the burned half of my body away from the fire, to heat the cold half of my body again, like a pig on a spit.

Coutts gave a curt nod that sent Blincoe hurrying away. 'Do excuse him, he has several letters that must be written before dinner. Now, where were we?'

'It is unusual to travel with one's clerk, is it not?' I asked.

He opened his hands in a gesture of apologetic surrender. 'In order to find success I have had to do things differently from others. If that means embracing less than usual practices, such as having my trusted clerk always by my side, so be it. He not only takes care of the dull day-to-day details of things, freeing me to oversee everything unfettered, but is also there to enact my ideas as and when they come. For when inspiration strikes it must be acted upon quickly in this brave new world we have created, where everything changes far swifter than in bygone days.'

'How interesting that you should speak of doing things differently. For I believe that women could offer much to business, if only given the chance.'

The noise he made was a careful midpoint between agreement and disbelief. I pressed on, despite my sinking feeling.

'If you are looking for investors then I – that is, my husband and I – would be interested in investigating—'

His nostrils flared. 'Speaking of interesting,' he replied, 'I couldn't help noticing the ring you wear about your neck. It is an unusual design. I would love to hear more about it.'

Without realising, at some point I had pulled the ring free from my bodice, and begun playing with it. It was a habit that gave me comfort but of which I did not approve. Ladies did not fidget. I tried to keep the conversation going.

'I have ideas to offer as well as money. Have you considered—'

He reared back, eyes rolling like a horse about to bolt, and seemed to look around as if searching for someone to rescue him. There was no one near enough.

'Forgive me, but that ring really is lovely. May I?' He peered in determined fashion, desperate to stop me embarrassing myself with men's talk. 'Yes, most elegant. The way—'

My hand moved to protect it from his gaze. Ladies, however, must also not act in such a rude fashion. At the silent reminder, I forced my fingers to uncurl and instead hold the ring out.

'A most elegant design,' Coutts muttered, taking in the large red stone, surrounded by smaller diamonds. Only, they were not diamonds at all.

'It has no monetary value but the sentimental value is great.'

For a moment I was no longer in the cold drawing room of Wynterton and was instead in another icy house: Satis. There was Mother, sitting before me in her wedding weeds; the finest lace, once white, turned the yellow of old bone from being worn every day for years on end. She leaned forward, holding the ring between forefinger and thumb as she told me how it had been her engagement ring from the man who destroyed her life. How the jewels were nothing but cheap paste, as worthless as Everard Compeyson's heart. Once again I saw her curl her fist about it, so tight with anger that blood dripped from her hand and onto her gown.

'Are you feeling unwell, Mrs Drummle?'

His voice seemed as distant as if he were shouting at me from the other end of a tunnel. All I could see was Mother. Calling me. Screaming a warning I could not hear…

'Mrs Drummle?'

What is it, Mother? What are you trying to tell me?

CHAPTER TWELVE

I dragged my mind's eye away from the imagined phantom before me and forced my gaze back on to the living. 'I am quite fine, thank you. Forgive me, my mother passed away recently.'

'And the ring was hers? I am sorry for your loss.'

'I found it while sorting through Mother's things. Wearing it makes me feel closer to her again.' My only comfort at her death was that she would be enjoying herself in the afterlife as self-appointed torturer of her former fiancé: the two of them joined together at last in hell.

Why had my imagination conjured her before me, though? Did part of me fear that if she were still alive she would berate me for abandoning her quest to destroy all men? She herself had begged me to turn from that path, though, in those final weeks before her death. For those precious two months we had been closer than ever before.

Perhaps she had come back to judge me for murdering that man...

The half of my mind that was on Mr Coutts noticed that he had become thoughtful. When he spoke again, he was gentle.

'It is the firsts that are the hardest, and give the sharpest pain. Through the first year one is constantly looking back to "this time last year" when they still lived. Yearning for their presence, or at least for the foresight to have treasured each moment keenly.' He played with the stem of his wine goblet as he spoke. 'To have known it would be the last time their touch was felt, the last good night spoken, even the last bickering words exchanged, would have altered them from the commonplace to moments to be cherished. Yet their very ordinariness renders them indistinct.'

'I would have branded every detail on to my memory for all time had I known.' I nodded.

We were both still. Silent.

'Who was it you lost, Mr Coutts?' I asked, velvet soft.

At last, I felt I was seeing the man behind the façade. His eyes were distant, lost in some remembered pain, so I repeated my question.

'Who was it you lost, sir?'

Coutts threw his wine back and swallowed hard. 'Gosh, no one. One only has to have a heart to guess at your pain.' He gave a laugh that rang loud after our shared sorrow. 'Damnation, woman, why won't you stop your questioning?'

Liar. His strange reaction made it clear he had lost someone, but whom? And why would he not admit as much?

He is a dissembler, like all men, Mother seemed to whisper to me. It was good to hear her again. *Only being sympathetic in order to create a false bond with you so that you will lower your guard.*

Who had he lost? Perhaps it was too upsetting for him to talk of it in company; I could understand that, for I had felt moved almost to tears as I spoke. His rudeness was unnecessary, however, and somewhat shocking.

'Ah, Mrs Taykall!' Coutts exclaimed, holding his hands out to Elizabeth as she approached us. 'My, the cut of that jacquard is exquisite! May I?'

His smile was as bright as a gas lamp's light. And as unnatural.

Dinner was a frustrating comedy of errors, where each of us seemed to want something at odds with what the others desired, while simultaneously trying to stop everyone else from getting what they wanted.

I wanted to speak business; to seize the rare opportunity of being in the company of someone who had made a success of themselves. The men – Coutts, Sir John, and even Mr Blincoe, in his own quiet, understated way – wanted to stop me. Always, they steered the conversation away, stymieing me. Sometimes they simply changed the subject; other times Sir John would remark on how I should speak with Bentley about it later and that I needn't 'worry my pretty little head about such manly things'. It was intensely irritating, and the only thing that made me smooth my ruffled feathers was the fear that he might start questioning me about Bentley's whereabouts lately.

Luckily, Sir John had been all too eager to accept that his protégé was too busy working to accompany his wife on this visit. How much longer that excuse would hold could only be guessed at. And then what? The thought made me feel breathless, as if my corset were too tight. Like it or not, the control I had over my life was illusory only, and once people began to question in earnest I would be in the most terrible trouble.

That is a worry for the future, I reminded myself, and returned to looking about the table.

Mr Coutts, ever the jester now his flash of temper was over, diverted the conversation to vacuous topics. 'Did you see what Sir Tewks wore the other day to the races? The tails on his jacket were scandalously short. It looked appalling.'

Mr Blincoe barely spoke, but when he did, his voice was most charming, well spoken, with enough honey to have kept an entire hive busy for a year. He was the only one who attempted to engage me.

'You are interested in investments?' he asked.

'Most certainly. Why, I long—'

'Here's a jolly jape!' Sir John guffawed, blasting his breath across the table.

Simultaneously, Coutts interjected: 'What a wonder your cravat is, sir! You must teach me how to tie it that way!'

A footman poured gravy onto my plate until it swam.

Coutts clearly wanted something from Sir John, for no sane person would compliment his dress. Sir John was incredibly formal for dinner, in an old-fashioned way – whether out of a special effort for his guests or because this was how he always dressed, I could not tell. His collar was so starched he couldn't look down to see his feet. I could have waved a five-pound note beneath his nose, and he would hardly have noticed. Also, although my friends and I had laughed at the idea of a modern man wearing corsetry, dandies and fops of the last generation had been known to, and Sir John clearly still did, from the way he creaked like a ship at sail.

Elizabeth, meanwhile, was clearly scheming for an opportunity to tell her husband about her pregnancy. Sir John, blissfully unaware, simply wanted to eat his meal in peace and crack his terrible puns, his booming voice trying hard to create an air of festivity that was entirely lacking. Not least because of the long-faced servants who stood around, serving us while their expressions yearned for the end of the day.

And then there were the animals.

Behind Sir John, a stuffed bear stood on its hind legs, rearing over his shoulder, teeth on show as if it was ready to lunge forward and take a bite from him. Its two forepaws raised to swipe. As Sir John spoke, I wondered: would it devour him or me first?

Behind Mr Blincoe, several doe-eyed rabbits stood poised to bolt for safety. It seemed rather appropriate for a man who appeared so innocuous.

Mr Blincoe's eyes were hard to read, always hidden behind the reflection on his glasses, but there were moments – a gesture or a muttered aside to Mr Coutts – that told me much. Though he seemed to fade into the background, always deferring to his master, I suspected his efficiency was the key to Mr Coutts' success. Coutts himself all but confirmed this with strange joking comments peppered into their conversation.

'You know, we two are tied, there's no escaping,' Coutts teased at one point. Blincoe only looked rather embarrassed, running a finger between his collar and neck as though it were suddenly constricting him.

The butler, Worthybrook, could do with a lesson in manners from Blincoe. Between Elizabeth's comments about his attitude towards the maids, and then the whispered conversation outside my room, I kept a close eye on him. Who was the 'she' he and the housekeeper were so concerned about? During the meal, Worthybrook didn't seem interested in either Elizabeth or me. Instead, his bloodhound face vanished around the door as he whispered fiercely to someone unseen, his sibilants hissing like an angry snake.

'...do not shilly-shally... Pick up your feet, girl, or I'll dock your wages.'

I glanced at the lord and lady of the house. Neither seemed to notice the butler's outburst. Elizabeth was intensely focused on her plate, cutting her bloody beef with such vigour I thought she might saw the plate in two. Sir John's mastication didn't miss a beat. He tended to act as if the staff were invisible and inaudible, unless he required something that needed direct interaction. As soon as his needs were met, the servants once again stopped existing, as far as he was concerned.

Under the table, I nudged Elizabeth's foot. She started, met my eye, and raised her brows in a silent appeal: *don't make a fuss.*

It was someone else's home, and so I did as I was asked. But I sliced my beef with uncharacteristic aggression.

Elizabeth was right: the servants did run the place with little respect for their employers. How ridiculous! How—

No. That wasn't entirely correct. Glancing around, I noticed something different. The footmen were unnervingly jumpy. The one who had flooded my plate with gravy had done so because his hands were shaking. None of them met our eyes. This wasn't unheard of in some old-fashioned households, but what was unusual was that even when addressed directly, their gazes slid away uncomfortably.

Why? Elizabeth was the picture of graciousness. Sir John was too oblivious to even notice them. He would no more become angry with a member of staff than with the sideboard, it seemed. Like most people who considered themselves to be of impeccable breeding, he felt that his servants were property, not people, and so they did not warrant consideration. All apart from Bellis, who advised him on his beloved roses.

It had to be Worthybrook they feared in the same way the girls reacted to Switchley. Those two ran the house. And perhaps, I posited, Bellis ran the estate? What emboldened the three of them so?

CHAPTER THIRTEEN

s dinner concluded, Sir John wiped his mouth so vigorously that his chin reddened beneath the tender, saffron-hued smile he shared with his wife.

'Time for we men to talk business,' he said, pushing his wonky peruke wig straight. 'Worthybrook, cigars and brandy.'

The butler moved to fulfil his orders, and the men stood. This was the signal for we ladies to withdraw. Typical that I would not get to hear the most interesting part of the evening.

'Elizabeth!' Sir John called after his wife. 'You ladies like pretty things, don't you? Show Mrs Drummle my Cabinet of Curiosities – she'll like that.'

As the door began to close behind us, I heard Sir John speak suddenly, urgently now that the women were out of the way.

'The supply needs to kick up a notch, old chap. There's not only me to consider but the others waiting – special friends of mine, old chap, who don't like to be kept waiting.'

Mr Coutts cut in. 'I-I do not think we have… the capacity to accommodate such a request.'

'On the contrary,' came Mr Blincoe's soothing voice, drifting through the closing door, 'we can sort out logistics so that—'

The door clicked shut.

I longed to be part of the conversation. Instead, I was banished from the room.

Elizabeth bustled across the hall, past the stuffed wolf and several closed doors, until she reached the one she desired. I paused to catch the attention of a footman. My bare shoulders were icy cold, so I asked him to send Nora to me with my lace pelerine cape.

'The Cabinet of Curiosities, as Sir John calls it, really is spectacular,' said Elizabeth, fiddling with the doorknob, which was proving difficult to turn. 'It must be seen to be believed – oh, Mrs Switchley, could you come here a moment, please? I can't seem to...' She gestured in frustration.

'Sir John wishes you to enter?' asked Mrs Switchley.

'He suggested I show our guest his collection.'

I caught Elizabeth's eye and frowned, trying to convey that she need not explain herself to her staff. She was too busy smiling in gratitude at her housekeeper, who took a large key from her chatelaine and unlocked the door.

The room was dark and silent as we stepped inside. A gust of air both musty and chemical enveloped me. Light from the hallway behind us spilled in through the open door, making hidden objects glimmer as if jewels were scattered within. When Elizabeth lit a candle, I gasped at what was revealed before me. From floor to ceiling, wall to wall, were glass-fronted display cases filled with countless tiny insects, skewered into the velvet. Butterflies of all hues, shapes, and sizes – some as large as I had never imagined – spread their delicate wings in death.

'Some of these have wings the size of my hand,' I whispered in awe.

'Sir John is particularly proud of those,' Elizabeth said, her voice warm with enthusiasm. 'Aren't they magnificent! They're from all over the world. Some collectors use cyanide, because it kills quickly, but Sir John realised it leaves the specimens brittle and changed.'

She spoke as if showing me treasures, but all I could see were the remnants of beauty killed to fulfil a passing whim. Spiders in brilliant shades of blue, red, pink, and orange lined the cases. My heart clenched at the sight. As a child, spiders and mice had been my only playmates; for me, this room felt like a graveyard of friends.

Elizabeth lit more candles, and the renewed light caught on the wings of beetles, their jewel-like shells twinkling back every colour of the rainbow.

They're only insects, I reminded myself. I had killed a man, after all, and that was inarguably far worse.

But I had done it to save that woman. He would have killed her.

And yet... and yet...

The truth was more complicated. Together, she and I had fought him, strangled him with his own scarf until he lost consciousness. A desperate move in our struggle to survive.

But after she fled, leaving him there, alive but incapacitated, something shifted inside me. I could have left, too. He wasn't in any state to pursue us. Instead, I returned to him, stood over his senseless form, and made the cold, deliberate choice to strangle him until his life force drained away.

Beside me, Elizabeth pointed out various creatures, telling me stories of their exotic origins or explaining the ingenious methods used to preserve them. I smiled, nodded, and made polite noises of interest, but I could barely hear her over the pounding of blood in my ears. The strange aroma of the room smothered me.

Its neatly arranged carcasses took me back to that alley with my victim. The godlike power I had felt over life and death when I made the conscious decision to take his. How much I had enjoyed it. Too much. So much that I knew it must never be repeated.

Or I would become addicted. Addicted like Sir John was to killing insects and displaying them.

When I emerged from the Cabinet of Curiosities, I was shivering, though whether from cold or something deeper within, I could not say. Perhaps I was falling ill, but it felt as if something about that house had seeped into my bones, like a dampness creating an ague of the spirit. As much as I had looked forward to visiting Elizabeth, I was now glad that I would be leaving the day after tomorrow. I could not wait to leave that strange, dark house, but as tempted as I was to make an excuse and leave early, it would have seemed impolite.

But that night was not yet over, as much as I longed to retreat to bed. The men would soon be finishing their conversation, and we ladies had been asked to say our farewells to Mr Coutts and Mr Blincoe.

Elizabeth was still inside, blowing out candles and checking that nothing had been disturbed before locking the Cabinet of Curiosities. As I waited in the hall for her to join me, another chill ran through me.

Where was Nora? She was not waiting for me with my pelerine cape, as I had requested. Irritated, I looked around and spotted her near the staircase, shrinking away from Worthybrook, the butler.

'What are you doing up there? You're not allowed above stairs.' He wasn't shouting – his words came as a low hiss, mere inches from her face, as he backed her into a corner.

Nora held the blonde lace pelerine in her hands as if it were a newborn babe, her chin trembling. Then she thrust it out defiantly.

'I ain't – haven't – done nothing… anything wrong. I'm a lady's maid now, ain't I, Mrs Switchley?'

'Aren't I.' The housekeeper corrected with a withering look. 'That you are. However, that does not give you leave to be in this part of the house, you stupid girl. You belong either below stairs or in Mrs Drummle's room – and you use the back stairs to travel between the two worlds.'

Worthybrook nodded, his jowls shaking with the motion. 'There is never any excuse for you to be here. Do you understand?'

His cheeks were mottled with rising anger. My little starling looked terrified, and I could not stand the bullying and berating a moment longer.

'Ah, I see you have my pelerine, Nora,' I called out, stepping from the shadows. 'Thank you for bringing it down exactly as I told you.'

Nora scurried over, relief written across her face. 'I brought this, too,' she added quickly, handing me a cashmere shawl. 'In case you were feeling chilly.'

'That is perfect,' I replied, softening my tone. 'You really are proving invaluable. Now, off you go.'

I spoke with the confident authority of someone who expected every word to be heeded. Mrs Switchley and Worthybrook could only bow their heads in grudging acknowledgement as their prey escaped.

I vowed to inform Elizabeth before I left that the butler and house-keeper were working together to terrorise the staff. They were the reason she could not retain her servants. They were the ones exerting control over the entire household. The oppressive atmosphere of that house emanated from them – they were at its epicentre – and once they were removed, Elizabeth would finally be able to run her household as she should. Though I had not found the rest and relaxation I had sought in my visit to Wynterton, by passing on that information to my friend at least something good would come from it.

Mr Coutts appeared from the dining room, puffing on a cigar, still deep in conversation with Sir John.

'Ah, ladies,' he called. 'Thank you for a delightful evening. Now, I must bid you a reluctant farewell.'

He bowed low over my hand and kissed it in the same manner he had when greeting me, giving me a view of the top of his thick sandy-blond hair. In turn, I dropped a barely-there curtsy. The faithful

Blincoe, a black crow trailing silently behind him, had his head bowed in subservience.

'It has been a pleasure,' Mr Coutts said.

I hesitated, wondering whether to try once more to speak of business. Blincoe had already disappeared through the huge double entrance doors, and Coutts was turning to follow before I made up my mind.

'Do not forget, I desire to invest in a business, and—'

'Not mine.' Coutts' handsome face contorted, lips puckered in anger. His stare was so hard I stepped back, expecting him to strike me. 'I won't hear of it—'

'Sir?' Blincoe appeared again. 'Is all well?'

The viscount's face smoothed. He bowed, and walked through the front door looking the picture of elegance.

Behind him, darkness had fallen, and the sky was a deep blue, scattered with stars. Coutts had been all charm as he took his leave, his mercurial changes reminding me of Bentley when he had been courting me. There was no sense of a dance of death, however; no out-of-control manipulation or desire in me to win his approval at any cost. Coutts was a different animal from Bentley, and the reason for his changes were obvious, occurring when I spoke about his business. He thought that, as a woman, my thoughts were unimportant. How annoyingly short-sighted of him. If only I could get him to see past his prejudices and fears of how society might judge him for doing business with me…

A word spoken outside caught my attention. A name. Had I just heard *Jaggers* being spoken of? It made my ears prick with interest, but there was no context, nothing else to be heard, and I could not go outside to listen better, for it would have appeared unseemly.

Jaggers was a criminal barrister with a fierce reputation, and he had also looked after my mother's business interests. He was someone I had known for as long as I could remember – literally, for my first memories involved him carrying me away from my parents, to the woman who would adopt me.

If Jaggers was involved with Coutts, then perhaps he might be able to speak on my behalf. All hope was not yet lost. Yet did I want to get involved with someone who might be brilliant, but was also so changeable? I was unsure, but still buoyed, and so I joined with

Elizabeth in the drawing room, rather than following my original plan of going to bed. We both took a seat beside the window and sighed.

'Although it is lovely to have visitors, it is sometimes a relief when they leave,' my friend said. 'I prefer the company of friends to acquaintances.'

'Always.' As I smiled in agreement, behind her through the window I saw Coutts climbing into his coach, a footman of unusually heavy build holding a lantern aloft so that Coutts might see where the step up was. Another lantern hung on the coach itself which, although not a landau, was a sleek thing, clearly built with speed in mind. Only the best for Mr Coutts, it seemed. Mr Blincoe was just setting his foot on the step to follow his master when a movement to one side, past the coach, drew my attention. Someone was there, standing in the dark of the bushes, trying not to be seen.

I recognised that silhouette.

It was Nora.

She shifted position, and her face was illuminated for the slightest sliver of time. Her whole being was concentrated on Mr Coutts. Eyebrows knitted, nostrils flared, mouth parted.

Then she disappeared completely into the shadow. What had she been doing out there? Did she know Mr Coutts? How on earth could that be?

I thought about her expression. There could only be one interpretation: she was fearful.

CHAPTER FOURTEEN

On my way to bed, I went via the southern conservatory, which had a fountain that made a sound most soothing to my fractious nerves. Keen for fresh air, I first turned out the light and then opened the door to the outside. It felt good standing on the threshold and breathing in the cold air. Turning out the light had been a whim, but it instantly made me feel calmer, as it always did. Darkness was my home, no matter where I happened to be, and it held no fear for me, for I had grown up in it in Satis House, where sunlight had been barred from its interior. Staring up at the pinpricks of light I had been named after, for Mother had named me to be her guiding light from the darkness of her life, I saw that the stars gave me nothing but cold bright winks, as if they held the answers to all questions but were too mischievous to share such knowledge with mere mortals.

I heard rustling. Ah, it was as I had hoped – Nora was coming this way.

No. The noise was too heavy. On instinct, I drew back slightly into deeper shadows. Two people. One pursuing the other. Almost in front of me, they stopped, when the hunter took hold of the arm of its prey.

'You want to watch yourself, Nora. I mean it. Do what I say, or there'll be trouble.' The growl of Brock Bellis, the head gardener.

'I am doing! Leave me be.' She sounded angry.

Bellis' arms fell from her and hung loose by his sides, judging from the faint outline I could see courtesy of the stars. 'Take heed, girl. Or you'll pay a terrible price.'

Nora squeaked then, like a frightened mouse. I was about to step from the shadows, but Bellis ran his hands through his hair and then stalked away. This time he walked over gravel, for all to hear, his feet crunching in the direction of the servants' entrance.

Nora slid through the open door of the conservatory with no idea that I crouched mere inches away.

Shame stopped me from revealing myself. I was still that nasty little spy of my childhood, creeping around and listening to the plans dreamed up by my grown-up cousins Camilla and Sarah Pocket, so that they might be rid of me permanently and thus inherit my mother's fortune when she passed away.

The taunts heard as a child are the ones that scar the most, for that is when we are at our softest and most malleable. I heard in my mind my cousins' taunts and ridicule, saw their hateful glances; I would not open myself to anything like that again.

I waited until all was quiet and still once more. Finally, I moved, heading towards the staircase and bed at last.

In the alcove created by the sweep of the stairs stood Bellis and Worthybrook, talking together and casting narrow-eyed glances at the housemaids tidying up now that the guests had left. I pulled my shawl closer around me to ward off the goosebumps stealing across the back of my neck. The men seemed so intent on those young women that they reminded me of wolves around sheep, choosing which to gobble up next.

Nora appeared in my bedroom almost the instant I rang for her. Bright, eager, no sign of all the trouble that had befallen her that night – and what a busy night it had been for her: bullied and berated by the butler and housekeeper for simply doing her job; spying on Coutts; threatened by the gardener.

As she helped me disrobe I tried to think of a subtle way of asking her about it all – especially Bellis. My blood was up every time I thought about the way he had spoken to her, which made it harder to think strategically. So I started to talk about what to wear the following day, in order to at least get a conversation going.

'I thought perhaps the chequered day dress because it's in a heavier cotton. The weather is getting colder,' she replied. 'With this bonnet?'

'Excellent suggestions,' I said with a smile that ignited her own. 'This bonnet will be better, though, for the wider brim balances the wideness of the skirt, see?'

'I'm awful sorry, miss, missus, ma'am. I'll try harder—'

'It wasn't a criticism. You could not have known this detail without having seen the outfit modelled.'

Her eyes seemed suspiciously sparkly. I had only mentioned it so that she might learn, but should have realised that she would be sensitive after the night she had endured.

She blinked her eyes rapidly until they glittered a little less, and soon she seemed as happy as that most sociable of birds, the starling.

The thought of hurting this young girl's feelings was something that gave me pain. For in my youth I had been a most terrible bully to my only true friend, Pip. Slapping him for no reason, and hurling hurtful barbs. Yet we had grown fond of each other, until my engagement to Bentley broke our friendship. How I missed him!

'I myself am an orphan,' I said, sitting down before the dressing table and handing her the hairbrush. 'Did you know?'

'So… how was you raised up so, miss? If you don't mind my asking?'

'I was fortunate, Nora. I was adopted by a very special woman. Though I won't deny there were challenges, still, I was lucky. We are two orphans together, Nora, and I admire your determination to improve your lot after your difficult beginnings.'

'It was a 'ard place to be raised,' she said. For a moment her eyes dimmed in remembrance.

'An orphanage, yes?'

'Sort of. Near as no matter. Who my parents were I've no idea.'

'Nor I mine. Do you ever wonder about them? I did not at your age, but since my adoptive mother died, they have leapt to the forefront of my mind often, for some reason.'

'I don't need no parents. I have a big sister, Nancy: eighteen months my elder. Close we was, but she left – the man what run the, well, orphanage, Koblin, his name is, he found a place for her in the Smoke.'

'London? Do you see her often?'

The brushstrokes on my hair slowed for a moment, then resumed at normal pace. 'Nah, not much. She ran away and ended up falling in with the wrong type for a while. Some real Blackguard types if you get my meaning.'

Everyone was aware of the Blackguards of London. While many condemned the gangs of orphan children who banded together, I took a different view. What did it say about society if it was happy to abandon the innocent before they had even hit double digits in age – for not all were taken in by authorities to live in orphanages. If we left them to their own devices, with no support, no one to look out for them, it was hypocritical to then act with shock and condemnation when they were forced to make a choice between dying of starvation and exposure, or banding together and turning to crime in order to survive.

'It's enough to know she's happy and sorted in life these days,' continued Nora. 'Last I heard through friends of friends was that she's got herself a nice young man, name of Bill Sikes, who looks after her well apparently.'

'Do you miss her terribly?'

'That I do.' She looked down, but only momentarily. 'It'd be a treat to set eyes on her again, but I'm happy here. I've got me a future and security in this manor – something I dint ever think I'd have.'

'Do you have a sweetheart?'

'Lor', miss, missus, ma'am, there's plenty of time for that. I'm too young an' busy for such nonsense.'

Of course she was. My desperation to get her to open up had made me stupid. I pushed on, though, as I could think of no other way.

'You're a wise girl. Mr Coutts, for example, he's a handsome man – would someone such as he attract your attention?'

'Mr Coutts?'

'The gentleman who came to dinner tonight. I thought I saw you outside, looking at him.'

She met my eye in the mirror. 'I've never heard of Mr Coutts. I was outside, miss, missus, ma'am, but I never noticed no handsome gentleman. Was it he who was getting into the carriage? Along with an older man?'

'That's right.'

She nodded slowly, as if thinking. 'No, I couldn't see either man properly in that light.' Then she gave me a cheeky wink. 'Trust me to miss the chance to see a handsome man, Mrs Drummle.'

She turned down the bedcovers for me. As I slipped inside, I tried again.

'Did I see you talking to the gardener? Is he more your sort of fellow?'

Did I imagine the stutter in her movements as she smoothed my counterpane?

CHAPTER FIFTEEN

I lay in bed wondering what had woken me. It was my restless mind, tugging in all directions at the knots of Wynterton's secrets. The staff were hiding something, that was certain. How much did it impact my friend, Elizabeth?

'...*watch her... must stop...*' That was all I had heard from the butler's whispered conversation in the dead of the previous night, but it had been enough. There was a sinister ring to it, which seemed to amplify each time I thought about the way Worthybrook and Switchley acted as if they were in charge more than Sir John and Elizabeth.

Then there was Nora and Coutts.

And Nora and the ever-angry Bellis...

Secrets always made me restless. I did not like them, did not enjoy the way they made me feel. Being on the outside while others were on the inside of the knowledge, knowing and talking and exchanging looks in a way I was unable to decipher, was hateful. Perhaps it was because from childhood I had felt like someone on the outside, looking in, pressing my nose up against the glass pane through which I could view the rest of the world, but it was always muffled and distorted. Or perhaps—

My head tilted to one side quickly, trying to capture the sound. Was it real or imagined?

Imagined. With a sigh, I turned on my side. Whatever was going on was nothing important and certainly nothing to do with me. What were a servant's troubles to do with a lady? Especially one who wasn't even their mistress—

The sound again.

What was it?

Throwing my sheets back, I stepped into the middle of the room. Waiting. Nothing. I tiptoed carefully to the bedroom door, to the window, and back again, but heard no sounds. Perhaps the butler and housekeeper had once more met outside my room and whispered to one another. Was that what had woken me?

There! A fox was giving its shrieking call. Such a chilling sound, though one I was used to, having grown up in the countryside.

A shiver that was purely corporeal ran through me. I climbed back into bed and tried to leech the vestiges of heat I had left on the mattress and sheets. But I could not get back to sleep. Finally, I signalled defeat by ringing for a servant.

It was Nora who came to my door.

'Might you fetch me a glass of warm milk, please? I'm sorry to disturb you.'

'I was up anyway.' She crossed her arms about herself and glanced over her shoulder as if looking for something. No doubt an escape route, after my having broken her sleep.

'I would fetch it myself, but as I'm a guest here...' I trailed off and bit my lip. Yes, I knew I had a certain reputation for cold imperiousness, so this might have surprised some, but when I lived in Paris, at the ladies' finishing school Mother had sent me to, I had been great friends with Yvette, a servant in the household and my lady's maid. I knew how hard they had to work and my gratitude – and guilt – was genuine. 'I've had an idea,' I said. 'You could save yourself returning up here by sending my drink up in that strange platform thing. What do you call it?'

Nora looked at it, her mouth skew-whiff. Shook her head. 'Oooh, miss, I hate that thing. It gives me the shivers.' She leaned closer. 'I keep thinking there's something hiding in it, in the darkness, that will jump out at me when I open it.'

'There's an image that will help me sleep.' I laughed.

Nora's smile was small and worried. She bobbed a curtsy and disappeared for a good ten minutes before returning. While waiting, I thought of our conversation earlier in the night. Although I had not discovered what I wanted, I felt progress had been made, for Nora had trusted me with details about her life. In the morning I would try again, and this time would ask more directly about how I could protect her from the gardener. Whether because of her plucky nature or because we were both orphans, I felt protective of her. Perhaps I might even ask Elizabeth if I might take Nora with me to train as my full-time lady's maid.

Nestling my head into the pillow, I couldn't help feeling pleased at the thought of how excited my little starling would be at that news.

She opened the door without knocking – 'In case you were asleep, miss' – and entered with a steaming mug of hot milk, but not before glancing over her shoulder.

'Is all well?' I asked. We were both speaking low, so as not to disturb anyone else.

'Of course, miss. Here, sweetened with honey and a sprinkle of cinnamon over the top. That should send you to the land of Nod quick as a flash.' She danced from foot to foot yet showed no sign of leaving.

'If you're afraid of being told off by Mrs Switchley for being here, send her to me. I will happily explain that you are simply carrying out my request. Or is it someone else who concerns you?'

Worthybrook? Bellis? Or was she troubled by the memory of our visitor, Mr Coutts?

She seemed to vibrate with nerves, teetering on the brink of saying something, then stepping back from it.

I was too tired to deal with this. I drained the milk so quickly it almost went down the wrong way, causing me to splutter as I thrust the empty mug towards her.

'There. With thanks,' I said a little gruffly. 'Back to bed for you, so I may catch up on my sleep. Unless I call for you, you may expect a lie-in in the morning.'

She started towards the door but hesitated just before she reached it and seemed about to say something.

'Good night, miss,' she whispered at last.

Disappointed, I turned my back and pretended to busy myself with arranging my pillows.

'Good night, Nora.'

The door gave the quietest of clicks, and I turned to face it again.

'Nora, I'm sorry. If you want to—'

There was a squeak. A gentle thud.

'Nora? Are you quite well?'

The silence seemed a stern reply. With a sigh and a shake of my head, I slid from the warmth of my bed and out into the cold air once more. I opened my door and poked my head into the corridor, looking left and right.

There was no sign of her.

CHAPTER SIXTEEN

Once more I quietly called Nora's name, taking a few tentative steps this way and that. Something warm and wet made me pull back my toes hurriedly. There was a little spillage of milk seeping into the runner carpet. That explained Nora's squeak of dismay, for she must have spilled the dregs of the mug's contents and then hurried off to fetch a cloth to clean up.

Fatigue was winning its battle over me at last. I wandered back to the bed, and climbed into it, listening out for Nora's return to clean up her spillage. Any moment she would be back...

A knock on the door woke me with a start. It was morning already! I must have fallen asleep while waiting for Nora, and now here she was with breakfast. The knock sounded again. Two harsh raps quite unlike Nora's jaunty, light taps. The door was pushed open before I could wonder.

Inside strode Mrs Switchley, carrying a breakfast tray.

'Good morning, Mrs Drummle. We thought you might enjoy breakfast in bed rather than joining the family downstairs. Lady Taykall thought you might prefer it.' She moved with such purpose that it felt as if saying no was not an option – not that I would have, for if this was what Elizabeth wanted for me, then I was happy to comply. It irked me, however.

'Where is Nora?'

'She's indisposed.'

'Oh! I'm sorry to hear that. She has proved to be a quick study and an excellent lady's maid. I suspect she has a bright future ahead of her.'

The purse strings around Mrs Switchley's mouth pulled tighter, but some brave words managed to dart out.

'A hard-working girl, indeed.' She patted the screw of hair on top of her head that passed for a bun. It was so tight it pulled her eyes so that they slanted like a cat's. 'Would you like breakfast in bed or served at the table?'

'Will Nora be up after I have breakfasted, to dress me?'

'I'll be seeing to you today.'

Then she gave a stiff-backed curtsy, and she and her bun left the room.

Worry made the food seem tasteless. I felt responsible for that young girl, and although I didn't wish to pry if she was ill, perhaps I could send her some sustaining food or some such to aid her recovery.

Or was something else going on? I kept thinking about the previous night. Had the gardener, the wretched Bellis, carried out his threat?

When Mrs Switchley returned, accompanied as ever by her bun and pursed lips, I questioned her again.

'I am leaving tomorrow, Mrs Switchley. Will I see Nora before then?'

'I couldn't say. Lady Taykall has suggested a morning walk, so I would suggest this outfit.'

'It was rather surprising that somebody with such a lack of experience had been given the opportunity to serve me,' I pressed. 'Yet she is a most diligent worker. You must be delighted with her.'

'The family have always been firm believers in giving opportunities to those below stairs to appear above stairs.'

She was expert at saying words that told me nothing. I tried again. 'That is surprising to hear, as last night I thought I heard her being berated for being in the wrong part of the house.'

'You must have been mistaken.'

'Must I? How unlike me. So, what ails Nora?' Boredom with the verbal duel made me blunt.

'I came here as a young orphan girl,' said the housekeeper, as if I had not spoken. She shifted, sending the keys swinging and clanking against one another, as if they were other-worldly chains forged in the depths of hell. 'Everything that I know about the world I learned here. I was just a young slip of a thing when I arrived. Wide-eyed and stupid I was, with no idea of how the world worked, but I took the lessons I was given, and I learned quickly. Speed is survival.'

Why had this usually aloof woman changed the subject and started telling me her life story apropos of nothing? I was too fascinated to pass comment and risk breaking the spell, but after several heartbeats it became clear she would say no more.

'You should be proud. It's a great achievement to work your way from the very bottom of the hierarchy to the head of the household,' I said.

Instead of smiling, she pulled herself taller, proud and... something else I could not identify.

'Perhaps you have inspired Nora, for she has ambitions of her own,' I added.

'Well, that's you dressed. If it is all right with you, I shall leave you, Mrs Drummle, and attend to my other duties.'

How abrupt she was. She made me look subtle. She exited the room before I could reply, leaving behind her invisible tendrils of unease. Why was she so slippery about Nora? There was more to her absence than the housekeeper was willing to share with me.

'She took off in the middle of the night, without so much as a by your leave!' Elizabeth rubbed at her temples. 'Mrs Switchley has informed me that the gossip downstairs – and I hate to listen to hearsay, but what else is there? – the gossip, she reports, confirms the girl was unhappy, that she missed her sister and dreamed of joining her in London. Honestly, Estella, what is wrong with girls today, that they do not extend the courtesy of informing anyone of their intentions, let alone giving any kind of notice.'

The tendrils of unease I had felt after my conversation with Switchley were binding tighter around me. 'That is the opposite of everything Nora intimated to me.'

'Another servant down. It really is too much,' my friend muttered to herself, not listening to me. 'Then Mrs Switchley was adamant that you have breakfast in bed instead of joining us.'

To what purpose? She had told me it was Elizabeth's idea! Had she needed me out of the way for some reason? Or... I thought of how she had shared a little of her life story apropos of nothing. Was there a subtext to what she had told me? If there was, it had passed me by.

'Elizabeth, I called Nora to my room last night; it must have been around two o'clock. She brought me milk. Are you saying she did that and then packed and left at that hour?'

At that news she listened to me at last. 'Did you notice anything strange about her? Did she mention anything to you? But no, don't answer – how silly of me to expect you, a stranger in my house, to know my staff better than I.'

'She did seem preoccupied. Perhaps even troubled by something. You need to question Mrs Switchley more closely; and while you're at it, speak with Worthybrook and Bellis.'

As I shared what I had witnessed last night, Elizabeth began rubbing her temples once more. 'No, it is too much. Too dramatic,' she said, dropping her hands at last. 'To imply something sinister is... You're seeing problems where there are none, Estella. I'm surprised at you.'

A little gasp escaped me. 'All I have done is report the truth to you. What you choose to do with that is—'

'I need peace in my delicate condition. We shall speak no more about it.' With a wave of her hands as if swatting away a swarm of flies, she closed the conversation. There was nothing for me to do but accept, for this was not my home.

Perhaps she was correct. My strange upbringing had made me constantly on edge, always ready for battle. Was I starting to see misdeeds where there were none? The way I reacted to situations was... unusual. For all my husband had made me suffer at his hands, my decision to keep him drugged and shackled was not normal. I was unbalanced, and saw the world at a different angle from other people, as if I were sideways and everyone else looked straight on.

And yet, there was no denying certain facts.

Nora had not wished to join her sister in London. She had expressly stated that to me.

Even if she had, why had she chosen to disappear into the night, as if she had something to be ashamed about?

The gardener had told her she was heading for trouble. Perhaps it found her.

CHAPTER SEVENTEEN

lizabeth and I walked the grounds for around two hours, which only seemed to increase her nervous energy, despite my keeping my fears about Nora to myself. Back at the house, I changed from my walking attire – without the aid of anyone – and then rejoined my friend in the Cedar Room, so that we might sit together for a while. Elizabeth had her embroidery out and looked more at ease than earlier. Her smile was open as she welcomed me into the room. The lioness by her side, still attempting to shelter her cubs from harm, appeared less pleased to see me.

'I have been thinking about the girl,' Elizabeth said. 'I will speak to Mrs Switchley about it, for I suspect her strictness is to blame for this Nora leaving, along with all the others.'

'You've mentioned they seem to be leaving in droves. How many have left?'

'We lose about two a month. Local girls seem reluctant to work here, too, so Sir John must rely on outsiders.'

Hence Nora being recruited from her orphanage.

'We pay well, the conditions are good…' Elizabeth continued. 'I can think of no other reason for these problems than Mrs Switchley. She does rather rule the staff with a rod of iron, and although I have asked her to try to be softer and she always agrees, the deed does not follow her word.'

'She's rather terrifying, isn't she?' I observed.

'She gets that look.' My friend pursed her lips together in mimicry, and then giggled and shook her head in that way of hers. 'Oh no, I mustn't. It's so mean of me to mock her, because I do respect her.'

'You are losing staff because of her. Why don't you get rid of her as I have suggested? It would be simpler.'

The lioness seemed to glare at me.

77

'When I spoke with Sir John about it, he shared some of her story with me, and it moved me. She's been here since just before his first wedding, you know.'

'She mentioned that she had been a young girl when she arrived. Although it is hard to imagine her that way.'

'Yes! I cannot imagine her as anything other than the hard woman she is. Yet she came here at Sir John's insistence after both of her parents died. Now, what did he say happened?' She tilted her head. 'Oh, yes, it was a fire. Tragic. They were tenant farmers and when their haystack caught fire they fought to put it out, for of course that was their livelihood and what would get them through winter.'

Elizabeth's eyes welled at the thought of their struggles. Her needle barely paused, however, as she spoke.

'Well, both mother and father perished, leaving little Constance without anyone to take her in. Sir John stepped in, rather than have her sent to an orphanage, even though his mother apparently opposed the move at first.'

'How extraordinary,' I replied. All pretence at embroidery had been abandoned in favour of the fascinating subject, but Elizabeth sewed several French knots before continuing as if the pause had not occurred.

'When I look at her now, I shall try to remember that poor, frightened little girl who had lost her parents. She was such a timid thing that she had a breakdown, you know. Oh yes, it is a shocking thought, is it not? According to Sir John, Mrs Switchley had been living at the house for several years, working as a scullery maid, and then turned quite hysterical for no reason.'

I frowned, trying to imagine the tight-bunned harridan that way.

'Sir John was all for having her put away, for his first wife had died just months earlier, the poor man. He was already dealing with much without… Anyway, it was his mother who prevailed, arguing the girl's case.' Elizabeth gave me a raised-eyebrow look that seemed to say, *What do you think about that, then?*

'That was very kind of her – and quite the turnaround,' I observed.

'She even had it stipulated in her will that Constance Switchley should always have a place at the house. The family showed fierce loyalty to her, and she in turn has done the same. A harder-working woman one simply could not find. It also means that I can never give her notice – she is as much a part of Wynterton as the masonry.'

That explained why the housekeeper felt so secure in her position that she acted as if she were in charge rather than Elizabeth. A housekeeper was a vital role in the household, acting as conduit between the family and the staff. She had to have a steady head for business and be able to manage all the household staff, too, all those personalities and characters with their dramas large and small. And she saw all upstairs, being privy to most happenings within the family that she worked for. Look at Lydia and all she knew of my own household and Mother's. The person holding that position would see everything upstairs and downstairs, know everything going on, and must be a great keeper of secrets.

'What of Mr Switchley?' I asked, blurting the question as soon as it entered my head.

'There has never been one. As is traditional in this household, her title was changed to Mrs when she took on the role of housekeeper.'

'So you will ask her about Nora? I think that is wise. I do not believe she has gone to London—'

'Oh, Estella, not this again. She went to be with her sister, and felt compelled to sneak off because she is too scared of Mrs Switchley. You're being overemotional about it all.'

She exclaimed this while almost throwing down her embroidery in temper onto the side table, then set to rubbing at her temples in vicious circles.

Previously, I would have snapped back a retort. A summer of working hard on keeping my temper meant I managed to hold my tongue.

After a moment, she picked up her work again and we embroidered side by side in quiet for some time.

'You are looking well in your pregnancy. Giving life… It must be a wonderful thing. I cannot imagine it,' I confessed.

'Oh, but it will not be long until you are doing the same, for that is our purpose on this earth, is it not? To bring forth life. What a wonder! Why, Estella, you've gone quite pale.'

Her words had hit home, for the wisdom of the world was that women gave life. Yet I took it.

I was utterly unnatural.

Would I have children? Did I want them? If I did ever have a child… would it inherit my bad blood and humours…?

Elizabeth spoke on. 'Let me confide something in you – I am happy, very happy, to be with child, but… it is a fearful time, too. Childbirth, even in this modern age, is so fraught with danger.'

There it was, the terrible truth. I was not willing to die for someone else. Instead of voicing this, I soothed Elizabeth with words about Sir John being able to afford the best in care for her.

No wonder she was not herself, however; not with such thoughts weighing on her.

Having confided her secret fear to me, a load seemed lifted from her. Her skin pinkened into a glow, and she began talking enthusiastically about her hopes for a strong son, and how she was looking forward to telling her husband about the impending arrival. She shared, too, something of the trials of sickness, which was not only in the morning but could apparently strike at any time.

The stuffed lioness looked on, her dead cubs playing at her feet.

It was a relief to return to my room and have some time alone to think about the mystery of Nora's disappearance. Elizabeth was convinced I was seeing trouble where there was none, and yet unease stalked me like a hunter spotting prey.

My hand lifted to turn the bedroom's brass doorknob, then fell away as I remembered something. There it was, a small creamy-coloured stain of spilled milk on the Turkish carpet runner. There was a strange smell hanging in the air; how curdled milk stinks. Nora had not returned to clean it up. Although I had only known her for a couple of days, I had no doubt that it was out of character not to do so. Instead, she had vanished.

Had she gone willingly, or had that sound I heard been down to more than simply her spilling some milk?

Something untoward surely could not have happened so close to me – mere feet away? If she had been attacked she would have screamed full-lunged, not made a mouse-like squeak. If someone had put a hand over her mouth and dragged her away, she would have kicked and struggled, and again I would have heard. A worse scenario was her being hit over the head. Again, surely I would have overheard such a blow – I had been wide awake and listening actively for a reply from her, so close were we despite the closed door between us.

Someone could have knifed her, I thought. But no, there would have been scarlet evidence on the rug and there was not so much as a droplet.

How had she disappeared from right beneath my nose?

Perhaps if I widened my search, I might find something to help explain.

I made my way along the corridor, knocking on each door, getting no reply, and opening it to search the room. There wasn't so much as a speck of blood to be seen. It was both a relief and troubling.

Returning to the milk stain, I stared down at it, willing it to give me some information. It told me nothing. In desperation, I got down onto my hands and knees. The unpleasant curdling smell hit my nostrils in the way only off milk can.

I was about to stand when I noticed a piece of cloth had fallen down the back of a circular stand, on which stood a glossy-leafed aspidistra. A handkerchief. It was not the fine lace or linen such as would belong to a gentle person; the material was rough, so it was most likely a servant's – possibly Nora's. I popped it in my pocket.

My lips pursed.

Nora had vanished into thin air as efficiently as if she had flown away like the starling she reminded me of. But I kept thinking about the way she had wrapped her arms about her body as if to comfort herself while in my room, how she had glanced over her shoulder as if searching for someone. She had been worried.

And then that little squeak the instant she had left me. A sound of – what? Surprise?

'*Take heed, girl. Or you'll pay a terrible price,*' Brock Bellis had told her that very night.

Something awful had befallen that young girl. Elizabeth might have been happy to live in denial, but I was not. I would solve this mystery, for who else would?

The housekeeper, the butler, and the gardener: they were my suspects, along with Mr Coutts. I had not forgotten the way Nora stared at him in fear, while hiding in the shadows. If no answers could be found at Wynterton, I would turn my attention on him…

Someone was going to pay for what they had done to Nora.

CHAPTER EIGHTEEN

The afternoon had been spent observing everyone who might be involved. Sir John had to be considered, for he was the head of the house, and a man who held firm views that women's sole use was to be bred, like horses. Watching his interactions, however, I was again struck by how he acted as if the servants did not exist — as if, in fact, everything about him simply happened by magic.

Worthybrook was a different matter. He was stern, verging on bullying at times, particularly with the girls. He and the head gardener, Bellis, seemed to spend a lot of time together, considering that one man's job was an outdoor one, while the other's was indoor, and they had little need therefore to ever speak. That underlined my instinctive impression that they were partners somehow in the secrets the house hid.

Mrs Switchley joined their huddle often. What were they constantly whispering about? What was it she and the butler had said during their meeting outside my bedroom in the middle of the night? They had vowed to 'keep an eye on her', that was it.

My investigation was bringing no fresh information. What was required was a new perspective. It would be worth speaking with someone below stairs who traditionally wielded great power there — the cook.

While it would certainly be rather inappropriate of me to visit the kitchen, I considered that a gift might provide the perfect excuse. Casting around my room, I tried to think of what this woman might like, and then saw something that might just suit: a brooch in the shape of a bird.

'I thought of food or drinks but realised you would be surrounded by such things all the time, so instead brought a little luxury that is just for you,' I explained, once I had made my way into the kitchen, much to the amazement of the other servants. 'I wager it is rare that you treat yourself to something less than practical, but everyone deserves something for a special occasion. Perhaps for your coat on Sundays.'

The cook was a battleship of a woman with a bosom so large she appeared almost to have a pillow strapped around her chest. Her complexion was florid, with broken veins on her cheeks that came from constant exposure to steam and high temperatures. She wiped her flour-covered fingers, then reached out and took my gift.

'Why, it's beautiful.' The brooch was of an enamelled starling on a bough, with marcasite scattered along its wings and around its eye to make it sparkle. 'But you surely can't mean to give it to me.'

'I am leaving tomorrow and wish to congratulate you on your stupendous food. My hosts have been wonderful, but what are they without good food, I always say.'

Her red cheeks glowed with pleasure. She nodded her head in appreciation. 'That's very decent of you, Mrs Drummle. The kitchen is the heart of the house, though not everyone acknowledges it. Thoughtful of you. Although...' — She continued with a wistful expression, as if wishing the brooch would metamorphose — 'I do like a whisky with a drop of honey in the evenings for my (parched) throat.' She mouthed 'parched' as if it was a rude word.

I inclined my head towards her. 'After a long day of work, it's the least you deserve. You are short-staffed again currently, I hear?' As I spoke, I gazed around the room, as if merely making conversation, rather than edging towards the true purpose of my visit.

'Always are,' Cook huffed. 'She was a hard worker, was Nora. She'll be missed. Never complained about getting her hands, you know...' Her voice dropped so low for the next word that she virtually mouthed it rather than said it: 'Dirty.' Then she went back to normal. 'Not like some of them others as think they're above such things as peeling and chopping veg, (gutting)' – this last word spoken sotto voce – 'fish, (plucking) birds.'

Her habit of mouthing words was so extraordinary that it made her hard to follow until I knew to concentrate on her lips rather than look her in the eye.

'She would have made an excellent (second kitchen maid), eventually.'

'It must have been a shock when she was given the position of lady's maid, even if it was temporary.'

'That it was.' She chuckled. 'An ambitious one, was our Nora.'

'Yet she has thrown away this opportuhity just to live with her sister.'

Cook's eyes darted around, suddenly trying to find an escape. 'Ah, well. Nowt so (queer) as folk...'

'Did anyone see her leave?' I pressed. 'Bid her farewell?'

'She...' Cook's head whipped about, to see if anyone else was present. She leaned in. 'She didn't even take her (clothes). (Switchley) had to pack 'em this morning.'

Then she began bashing at some dough to show the conversation was over, just as she had finally opened up to me. I stayed her hands with my own.

'Something is happening in this house, isn't it? You want to tell someone, clearly, so... tell me.'

Strong she was, from all the lifting and making, and she easily pulled free of me. 'I have to get on.'

No one had seen Nora after me, apparently. I was more convinced than ever that she had been snatched from virtually under my nose and that the squeak she had made was the only clue that something was happening. But it hadn't been enough to alert me at the time that something was awry.

Again I wondered how on earth it could have happened. No sound of a blow to the head that would incapacitate her, no sign of blood that would show she had been silently knifed. How someone did it, I could not discern, but all the threads of information were coming together to create a picture for me that my young friend had been taken against her will. Possibly even killed.

No, that doesn't bear thinking about.

Yet my animal instinct, honed since childhood, would not be silenced.

The cook would not speak to me for much longer, and so I had to try to make the most of this opportunity. A thought occurred to me...

'Haven't others left suddenly, too? Didn't one of your other maids leave in the night only a few weeks ago? The one who should have been my stand-in lady's maid?'

Tears formed in Cook's eyes. 'That were Lily. I knowed her since the day she was knee-high to a (starling). Come from a good family, she do. The (Batleys) have worked in this house for generations.'

'So where did she go? Did someone threaten her? Hurt her?'

'They said she ran off with some secret lover. Rubbish! Why, she was in—' She opened her mouth to say more, as a shadow fell between us. Head gardener Brock Bellis was standing at the doorway, carrying a tray filled with carrots that had just been harvested, by the look of the soil still attached to them.

He took in the scene. Eyebrows disapproving, jaw clenched, nose flaring. Cook punched the dough hard enough to knock out a man, but her expression was that of a naughty child caught stealing.

'I'm glad you have enjoyed your stay. Fare thee well and safe journey,' she said to the bread she pounded.

'Farewell, and thank you again for the excellent food, Cook. Mr Bellis.' My steps were direct and full of purpose as I left the room. As soon as I was out of sight, I lingered by the door, though, just long enough to hear Bellis' low growl.

'Keep your nose out of things. Otherwise you might be the next to disappear.'

I strained to hear more. The only sound was the heavy thud of Bellis setting his tray down.

Before he interrupted, Cook had been on the verge of saying something important. Something about Lily. She 'was in'… what? Trouble? Love? Some kind of scheme? What did she and Nora have in common, aside from being two young serving girls at Wynterton, who had disappeared into the night? What was their connection with the ever-watchful trio of Bellis, Switchley and Worthybrook?

I should talk to Cook again. I stepped forward—

'Can I help you, Mrs Drummle?'

That haughty voice stopped me in my tracks.

'Ah, Mrs Switchley. I was just leaving. I have given Cook a gift to thank her for her wonderful meals.'

'If you are leaving, you are going in the wrong direction. Let me show you the way.'

Damnable woman. There was no choice but to follow.

The brazen cheek of Bellis, to threaten Cook in broad daylight when I was barely out of the room! In a short space of time I had heard him menace two women: Cook and Nora. Enough of this sneaking about, it was time to confront Bellis.

That a man would threaten women was not surprising. That a man in a position of power – the butler – might also be involved was no great shock. Mrs Switchley's involvement, though, did not make sense to me. She seemed to be covering for whatever those two men were up to, and for the life of me I could not understand it.

Surely she found what they were doing abhorrent? Why would she risk her position to protect them when she could easily tell all to Elizabeth – or even Sir John as she was such a trusted member of staff?

The afternoon was almost gone, and I made the excuse of a headache to get away from Elizabeth. She escorted me to my room and was so concerned for me that guilt nibbled at me, but this was too important to listen to it. Time was running out to find Nora, because in the morning I was leaving.

After giving Elizabeth a five-minute head start, I sneaked from my room and into the grounds. The formal gardens, the orchard, the woods, I checked everywhere and found no sign of Bellis. I even tried by the lake, but its black mirror surface stared back at me unblinking, giving no clue about any secrets it might know.

On an estate so vast, Bellis could be anywhere, but giving up was not an option – not when the image of Nora, young and full of hope, kept filling my mind.

The sun was a fiery eye on the horizon as I walked the edge of the woods that crept towards the back of the house. I came across a clearing where the trees seemed to cup a large shed. With slow, stalking steps, I made my way towards it. Peered in a window. No one was inside. The latch on the door opened at my curious touch. Inside, it smelled of rich, dark soil with an edge of iron. There were seed trays and sacking, and all manner of gardening paraphernalia, while spades, forks, sickles and tools of the trade hung neatly from hooks on the walls. This had to be the head gardener's shed: his office, for want of a better word. I wasn't sure what I was looking for, but it wouldn't be in plain sight, and so I searched…

Hidden beneath some papers in the drawer of a bureau so old that the top was bowed and buckled, was a notebook. A quick flick through revealed a list of names in slow, careful handwriting, each line of every letter laboured over.

Girls' names.

At the bottom, in the darkest, freshest ink…

Nora.

CHAPTER NINETEEN

My fingers traced over each line of Nora's name. Felt the roughness of the paper beneath my skin, the slight raise in the lettering where Bellis had paused in his laborious task and the ink had gathered. Outside, twilight was falling, and I could barely discern the other words written in the notebook.

Dollie. Constance. Jemima. Mary Turpin. Dyllis Evans. Sarah Monkton. Jessica. Jane. Olive. Betsy. Lily Batley. Nora.

It had taken effort to write these names. There was purpose behind them. I shivered at the thought of Brock leaning over the desk, his face as angry as always, as he recorded his latest victim.

But perhaps I was wrong. Despite everything, I still hoped my screaming instincts were incorrect, and the girls had simply flitted away to start new jobs, new lives. Mother had taught me better than that, though; drilled suspicion into me every single day and night for as long as I could remember.

'Men destroy. They dominate, lie, abuse. Lure them close to you, Estella, and then break their hearts and do not give an inch, no matter how they beg,' she had told me.

I always had. For I had witnessed the violence meted out by men. The first time I had been just fourteen years of age. While hidden, frozen to the spot by the speed of the attack, I had seen the blacksmith's wife smashed over the head with a manacle by the journeyman who worked with her husband. Seen her left in a pool of blood... There was also the abuse of my own honeymoon in Paris where I was held prisoner, raped repeatedly, beaten until only the sheerest curtain barred me from death. And just a few months ago, in that dark alley, I had seen a woman attacked by a man who declared his love for her while warning her that if he could not have her then no one else ever could.

No, those names were a record of something dreadful. Hadn't Nora's friend been called Betsy? I tried to think back. She had been rattling

89

off a tale of how her friend had wanted her to leave with her, but then had gone in the night without so much as saying goodbye. I could not be certain of her name, however, for I had only been half listening as we had been searching for the Cedar Room that first evening.

But Lily. That was the name Cook had spoken.

So of the nine names on the list of girls, I knew three, all of whom had disappeared. A shiver scuttled across my flesh.

I tore the page free from the notebook, not caring that Bellis would know someone was on his trail, for perhaps it would put the fear of the devil into him and make him pause before targeting anyone else. Then I slipped from the hut into the gathering dusk outside. As I hurried back to the house, the trees leaning over me seemed to whisper as the wind played through their brittle brown leaves. I broke into a run, checking over my shoulder repeatedly, almost stumbling in my eagerness. For a fear possessed me. Because if I was correct and these girls were all dead, then this gardener was like no other creature I had ever encountered and—

'Estella! Ah, there you are.' Elizabeth stood by the entrance to the southern conservatory, her hand on her stomach. The picture of normality. 'Has the fresh air helped ease your head? Come, it is almost time to change for dinner.'

How could I switch from such terrible thoughts to easy conversation? Yet I found it simple. My smile was a shield, my manners an amulet of protection. But inside, a familiar cold seething was starting to rise that would only be appeased with vengeance...

Sir John joined us for dinner, and unfortunately decided it was time to interrogate me about Bentley.

'I was too caught up in business before, so forgive an old man for his rudeness, eh?' He jabbed his knife at me in a way that did not seem apologetic. 'Now then, tell me all about Bentley.'

'Like you, he is constantly busy,' I said.

'What is he up to? It's keeping him damnably quiet lately.' He stopped chewing long enough to give me a penetrating stare.

It took a moment to dispel the irritation that heated me. I had come to the manor precisely to escape thinking about my husband, not to be badgered by a new source. Fortunately, my childhood had prepared me for an existence filled with tension and threats to my life, and so I did not scare easily.

'Now it is your turn to forgive me. Such dealings are beyond me,' I said. There was one perk to society perceiving women as weak-minded, soft-limbed little beings, and this was it: that I could make full use of it as a mask whenever I needed to. I hesitated, as if thinking. Then shook my head. 'He does tell me but—'

Sir John grunted. 'I'm in town next month. Tell him, eh. He and I can talk then.'

The bumbling buffoon had outflanked me. For a moment I floundered.

'What a remarkable bear that stands behind you!' I said, buying myself some time to think. 'I would wager there is a great story behind bagging it.'

He turned, glared at the rearing beast, then waggled his knife in my direction again. 'You will not forget to tell Bentley, now, will you? I am keen to see him.'

'I will personally make sure you receive a letter from him. You have my word.' A gracious smile, a demure tilt of the head, a lingering look from beneath my eyelashes, all persuaded him to nod and grin approval with those saffron gnashers. He would most definitely receive a letter purportedly from my husband, claiming he was away on business himself. I added Sir John to the mental list of people with whom I was corresponding as my husband. It was fortunate indeed that forgery was another childhood skill, but for how much longer could I keep people at bay? It was only a matter of time before I forgot which lie I had told to whom. Problems were crowding in on me from every direction, with little hope of escape.

With much evasion and leaning into the myth of the empty-headed female, I managed to satisfy Sir John for the time being. Such dodging had been the reason why I had desired to escape into the countryside in the first place. Bentley's friend Startop had visited several times asking about him, and letters from my husband's vile cousin Dupont had started arriving thick and fast from France.

This was a reminder that much as I wanted to stay longer and uncover the black, suppurating canker that lurked in Wynterton, I simply had to return home. Lydia had been left alone with my husband for long enough. He was, after all, my responsibility.

Elizabeth's query about her husband's day brought me back to the present. Sir John reeled off a list of his activities, from dealing with tenant issues to a pleasant hour relaxing in the garden.

'Your gardens are a credit to you,' I said. 'Your gardener is a good man?'

'Eh? Yes, yes, very good is Bellis. Knows his brassicas. A dab hand with roses, too.' Which, judging from the approving grunt from the old man, was the height of praise.

I could think of no way of moving the conversation on to Bellis' background or character, however. And so, frustrated and no further forward, I went to bed. But I had a plan. The next day before setting off for London, I would go to the village, and ask the people there to see if some clue could be shaken free.

CHAPTER TWENTY

Immediately I bid my farewells to my hosts the following morning, I enacted my plan. My carriage came to a halt on a gentle hill in the middle of Wynterton de la Taykall – a large name for a small village. I alighted and looked about me. The cottages all looked well cared for, their roofs and windows in good repair, their tiny gardens well tended. At the top of the hill, half hidden by a curve in the lane, was a church with a fine spire that seemed to point skyward as if wanting to ask a question. Instead, it was I who enquired of an old man more wrinkled than Methuselah, who sat on his step outside a nearby cottage, smoking a pipe, if he knew where the Batleys lived.

'That I do.' He nodded as if he had imparted great knowledge, and puffed on his clay pipe in a thoughtful manner.

'Could you please tell me?'

He worked the pipe to the corner of his mouth and spoke from the other corner. 'Aye. That I could.'

He clamped back down on his pipe, a trail of smoke dribbling from it until he started sucking furiously again. After some further thought, he removed it.

'Live over yonder way, they do.' He nodded with his chin. 'One with the roses about the porch. And the woman beating her rug outside.'

Elizabeth had been kind enough to give me a charming parting gift of a basket of dried lavender, handily tied into bundles ready to put about my home, and so I gave him some as thanks, along with a shiny shilling that was probably enough to pay his rent for the week.

A cloud of dust hung in the air about Mrs Batley as she battered the rug that hung over a line, but she stopped the moment she noticed me approach.

'Would you like some lavender?' I asked. With a smile, I proffered it. She smiled back, tawny eyes warm in a gaunt face worn with care, and reached towards it. 'It's from the manor.' Her hand shot back. 'I was staying there for a few days, and it's so beautiful that I wanted to share some with villagers before I leave.'

'No. Thank you.' The rug got a firm spanking as she spoke.

'Your daughter used to work at the manor, did she not?'

It was as if a spell had been cast over her, freezing her in place. I stepped closer, spoke lower.

'Lily was her name. A pretty girl and a hard worker, I have heard tell. And then one day she disappeared. Do you ever hear from her, Mrs Batley?'

Haunted eyes met mine. 'My girl—'

'Who are you, to be asking about our Lily?' A heavily bearded man had appeared at the open doorway to the cottage. He filled the space, his great arms folded. 'No disrespect meant, but we keep ourselves to ourselves.'

In my experience, there was a time for circumspection and a time for being direct. 'I suspect something has happened to your daughter,' I said, 'and I wish to discover what.'

A great laugh of disbelief rumbled from him. 'Round these parts we know our place and we look after our own. I'm sure it's the same for your class,' he said.

'I only seek the truth. Have you heard from Lily since she left her job at the great house?'

Instead of answering me, he gestured to his wife. 'Rose, I just heard little Thomas calling you. Best get yourself inside. If you'll excuse us.' This last was directed at me. Their front door closed with finality.

My steps were slow as I retraced my way towards the carriage. The encounter had been frustrating but unsurprising given that the family had no earthly reason to trust me.

Still, I had learned something. The Batleys had not confirmed my suspicions, but if their daughter was safe somewhere, why had they not simply told me? Instead, they were wary and reluctant to speak, as if they were frightened. That—

Running footsteps behind me. I whirled.

'Mrs Batley!'

A finger pressed to her lips told me to keep quiet. 'I don't have long. My husband wants me to keep quiet, but I won't have it. The people up at the big house say my girl ran away. That she had a secret sweetheart and ran off with him.' Her words came in a breathless rush. 'Twaddle and balderdash. My Lily would never do such a thing. She was sweet on a lad who lives by the church, William Turpin, and they had plans for the future. He don't believe any of what was being said, neither; says she wouldn't have been untrue to him – and he'd know, wouldn't he?'

Her head whipped over her shoulder, loosening her bun so that strands of brown hair heavily streaked with grey flew free. When she saw no sign of her husband, she continued.

'She ain't the only girl what's gone. Ask the other villagers. Ask William about his sister—'

'Rose.' Deep and sharp, her husband's voice rang out. He strode over to us. 'You got a boy inside what needs looking after.'

'This lady can help us, Sid.' Rose's fingers sank into the front of his shirt – not in violence, but desperation – as she leaned against him. Tears sprang and her voice rose higher.

Her husband shook his head, his own eyes sparkling. 'Don't upset yourself, my love. You know what you get like.'

Her knees sagged. 'She can bring Lily back.'

'I'm sorry,' I said. The words seemed to catch in my throat, blocked by guilt. 'I didn't mean—'

'Didn't mean or did mean, the end is the same,' Mr Batley said. Then he picked up his sobbing wife as if she were a child that needed carrying to bed, and cradled her back to his house.

The last words I heard from Rose were: 'She's gentry, she might be able to help us!'

Other villagers appeared in their doorways, squinting at me as if taking aim with invisible guns. With horror I realised my stupidity at investigating so clumsily, for if Bellis somehow heard what I was doing, I could be placing myself in danger.

The urge to wrap my arms about myself was strong. Instead, I tilted my chin upward and walked regally onward.

CHAPTER TWENTY-ONE

The encounter with the Batleys had shaken me. But Rose Batley's raw anguish at her daughter's mysterious fate also made me more determined, despite my fears. Lily had disappeared in the middle of the night – just like Nora – and never been heard from again. She had left her family heartbroken, along with her sweetheart, William.

Time was getting on and I needed to be on the road soon, but there was one more visit to make first.

By virtue of knocking on the doors of cottages surrounding the church, I found the home of the shiny-faced William Turpin. When I told him I had been sent by Lily's mother his respectfully bowed head bobbed up in surprise. Before he could question me, I explained my suspicions.

'This is none of my business, I know, but if something has happened to Lily then someone needs to find out what,' I finished.

He pressed his lips together and blew an exhalation of relief that had his red cheeks bulging.

'No one is listening to us, miss. Sir John said it was a servant matter, and to speak to his wife – who was kind but...' He shrugged. 'I went to the magistrate even, but he weren't interested in what he called "a skit of a girl doing a flit with a lover, that she will no doubt come to rue". Said the same when my sister went missing, too.'

'Rose mentioned I should ask about your sister.'

'Aye, Mary.'

The name sent a jolt through my body. There was a Mary Turpin on the gardener's list. This was more than my imagination making monsters from shadows. Something horrific was happening to these girls...

'Here, take a seat, miss; where are me manners?'

William used his cap to dust a perfectly clean wooden chair beside the unlit fire, then took the one on the other side for himself. I imagined him setting them out like that, dreaming of the day he and Lily would sit either side of the fire, their children playing in front of it. That day, I feared, would never come.

'What happened to your sister? If you don't mind me asking.'

'She's been gone a long time now – eight years since anyone's heard from her. She had a room at the manor, so we didn't see her much once she got the job, and then one day Mrs Switchley came knocking on the door with a bag of Mary's things. Said my sister had left suddenly. Mam said she'd never do something like that, and losing Mary put her and Pa in an early grave. Do you think that her disappearing and then Lily are somehow connected?'

'Possibly.' A thought tugged my face into a frown. 'How long has the head gardener, Robin "Brock" Bellis, been in the area?'

At the mention of the gardener's name he went so pale that the scar on his top lip stood out, and his red cheeks whitened. I held my breath, waiting for all my suspicions to be confirmed...

'Can't rightly say.' He scratched his head. 'Two years, or thereabout, miss. Why?'

'No reason.' That did not fit with my theory at all; Brock Bellis could not be responsible for whatever had befallen her, for William's sister had vanished six years before the gardener came. So why was her name on his list? Before I found out, I needed to ask one obvious question of William, and get it out of the way. 'William, did Lily have another beau? I must ask.'

'If I may speak plain?'

I nodded.

'If there had been someone else, then I wouldn't have been happy, but would have accepted it. But there were no secrets between Lily and me. We were' – he paused to rub at his eyes with his knuckles – 'we were perfect together. Contented, like. We'd made plans to get engaged after autumn harvesting was done. I'd already got this place for us, and I've a good job as an assistant baker; we'd have had a decent life together.'

Everything Mother had taught me was that men were liars, unfaithful, all that was terrible in the world. But Pip had taught us both that there were exceptions, no matter how rare. I weighed every action William made, every word he spoke and the way he spoke them and... believed him.

'Do you have any idea what has happened to her?'

He shook his head, vehement in his reply.

'You do not like the gardener, though; you paled at the mentioned of his name. Why?'

'The day afore she disappeared, Lily was afraid. She said the butler and the head gardener had spoken to her and said something to her that put the fear of God into her.'

My blood raced through my veins. The butler and the gardener. Working together. At last I was getting somewhere. 'What did they say?'

'She wouldn't tell. Said it was nonsense, that she was fretting over nothing. Next day, she was gone. And here's another thing.' He hitched forward in his own seat, leaning an elbow on his knee. 'Something similar happened with Mary. She told me that the butler, Worthybrook, had cornered her.' At the sight of my questioning frown, he elaborated. 'He said she was being too friendly, and forward-like, and she was going to catch people's eyes. And that if she did, she should be prepared for the consequences.'

Bellis had said virtually the same thing when speaking to Nora. That could not be coincidence.

'Bellis did not work at the manor when your sister disappeared, but Worthybrook did. Could the two men be in partnership—?'

'Miss!' William almost exploded from the seat he stood so quickly. 'If you tell the magistrate this, he'll listen to you.'

I thought about it. Then shook my head. 'Where is the evidence? There is no case here, only supposition.'

My mother's lawyer, Mr Jaggers, had been a frequent visitor to my home when I was growing up, and always he had extolled the imperative of evidence before accusation in all things.

'I am afraid, William, that despite having money and status, the fact remains that as a woman my word will not be enough to initiate an investigation. It would have to come from Sir John himself, as it is happening on his estate.'

He dropped his head into his hand. Then looked up, snapping his fingers, his cheeks red once more, eyes bright with an idea. 'There's a family whose daughter, Sarah, worked up at the manor. She went missing, too. The Monktons, they just left: upped sticks and moved away without telling anyone. I heard a rumour recently that they had moved to a village outside of London – Walworth, it was. Maybe they can help us.'

Sarah. Another name on the list. I asked William about the others but he had no information.

'What about Worthybrook?' I asked. 'Tell me, what is his background?'

'All I know is he was born and raised in Essex, I believe. Joined the household as an under footman when a young man. Don't never come to the village.'

'And Mrs Switchley?' Where did she fit into these evil deeds?

Confusion bloomed across William's features. 'Know nowt about her, really. Po-faced now, thinks she's above us villagers, even though she's one of us, and from what I hear she was no better than she should be when she were young. A wild one, by all accounts. That's all I know.'

Could a wild woman be lurking beneath that stern exterior? Why not? Plenty was concealed beneath my veneer of gentility. Perhaps she was the lover of Worthybrook or Bellis. Or even both. That might explain the strange relationship between the three.

The conversation with William had woven more threads in the tapestry. Yet still I could not see the whole picture. No matter how many answers I got, they always seemed to lead to more questions…

CHAPTER TWENTY-TWO

There was much to think about following my conversation with William – and my return to London gave me an opportunity to set to work in earnest. The first thing I did was send for Joseph, a former servant of Bentley's.

He had proved himself adept at ferreting out people's secrets, and so I had given him some money that he might set up as an independent consulting detective. There had been more than generosity at play, for I wanted to keep a man such as he on my side, while also keeping him too busy to question where Bentley was. He was doing rather well at his new job, by the look of it – and enjoyed it far more than being Bentley's manservant.

He took down the names I had for him, leaning on his John Bull top hat to write.

'My friend has recommended these girls as possible new lady's maids for me, as they were excellent when they worked at Wynterton Manor,' I explained. 'I would like you to find them, so that I can write to invite them for an interview.'

'Would it not be easier to run an advert, Mrs Drummle? You would get plenty of applications—'

'Why, of course I would, but for such a position of trust I prefer recommendations. I am also keen to track down a young woman named Nancy.' I proceeded to tell him what little I knew of Nora's sister.

That had been on the previous day, and while I waited for news I decided to accept an invitation from the Brandleys. I asked the carriage driver to stop a street away from my destination of Mrs Brandley's Richmond house, for I wanted to steep myself in the city and shed the unclean feeling that clung to me from Wynterton's countryside.

The bustle of London life was strangely comforting after the claustrophobia of Wynterton and its eerie peace – as quiet as the inside of a coffin buried six feet under. I stood on the pavement, breathed deep the smell of cigar and chimney smoke, horse manure, and hot-from-the-oven meat pies being sold on the street corner. A milkman tempted passers-by with the contents of his pail. A few steps further on, the aroma of freshly baked bread hit me, as a baker sold his wares.

It was all so familiar to me, for I had lived four years on this street. Mrs Brandley had been Mother's closest friend before she had closed herself off from the world, and it was she who Mother had asked to introduce me to society when I moved to London after leaving the finishing school in Paris.

A little boy dodged around me with a breathless, 'Sorry, miss,' as he chased after a marble that had escaped from the chalked circle he and his chum had drawn on the paving stones. I jumped back, before continuing on my way and knocking on the door.

Soon I was in the welcoming embrace of Mrs Brandley. Her smile was full of a mother's pride, for she was fond of me.

'Be a dear, and fetch Lucy for me,' she asked. 'She is busy with one of her experiments again and quite oblivious to all requests to abandon it.'

I found her in the garden at the back of the house, poring over something. My touch on her shoulder was gentle – but she shrieked in surprise.

'I was conducting an experiment,' she said, hand over her heart.

'Your guests will be arriving any moment.'

'Ah, yes, afternoon tea.' As Lucy considered the prospect of social-ising she pushed her half-moon spectacles up her nose. Seconds later they slid down. It was an endless battle and one she always lost. 'Is everyone here?'

'I am the first to arrive, but the others are surely not far behind.'

She wasn't listening. Instead, she stared at some pieces of paper that seemed to be blackening by the second, as if unseen fire charred them.

'What on earth are they?' I asked.

Lucy Brandley was a fascinating creature, but at least half of what she said was incomprehensible – which, of course, was what kept me fascinated. When first I met her I dismissed her as a shrivelled old maid growing bitter that her bloom had failed to entice a suitor. In fact, she was perfectly happy to be single and allowed to read her books. Her knowledge of the sciences, engines, chemicals and doctoring was incredible – there was nothing about which she had not read a book and become a reasonable expert on. She was a woman content with herself, whose curiosity about the world extended beyond where, when and how she would find a husband. At that moment, she was talking about silver nitrate and gallic acid and salt and...

'Why do you want to salt paper? Do you wish to eat it?'

'It is a test, Estella: an attempt to capture an image on paper. Like a painting, only real. Imagine if a likeness – a true likeness – of someone could be achieved through the correct use of chemicals and light. The problem is, the exposure to light gives me shadows on the paper but then the image continues to darken until there is nothing but blackness.'

That sounded like me. No matter how much light I was exposed to, I grew darker. My visit to Elizabeth had proved that – just look what I had become embroiled in.

Lucy picked up one of the papers and removed the pressed flowers from it.

'See?' She pointed.

The paper was Prussian blue with some pale blobs on it. There was nothing else to see and I said as much. Lucy shook her head, impatient.

'Here, the outline of a fern leaf. And here, the petals of a sweet pea flower, and here, too.'

I stared. 'There's a paler patch, but...' Something seemed to shift in my perception. Faint but definitely there was the scalloped edge of a fern. 'Remarkable!' I breathed. 'But how...?'

How curious that I had been blind to it one moment, and yet upon once discerning the image I could not unsee it. It was obvious.

'If only I could work out how to make the image clearer and then fix it in place.' She sighed.

From inside came the sudden rise of laughter. 'Lucy. Tea.'

She whipped off her glasses and the long cotton coat she always wore to protect her dresses whenever conducting experiments, and together we hurried towards the sound of guests arriving.

Already Mrs Brandley's parlour was filled with chatter, and at the centre was Lucy's mother, her pink cheeks glowing as she bustled about ensuring everyone was seated comfortably. Everything about her, from her energy to her plump skin, made her appear younger than her forty-eight years. Unfortunately, in looks, Lucy had taken after her father, and as a result was rather yellow of skin and sunken of eye.

Over fancy cakes, we women chattered. Eventually we exhausted the subject of our husbands (an even split between those who thought their husband could do no wrong and those whose husband could only do wrong. Everyone assumed I was still in the cow-eyed phase, but that I was also too discreet to speak of relations between my husband and I. Who was I to disabuse them of such a fantasy?).

'What of your friend, Mr Pip, Estella? How fares he? Is he married yet?'

The spoon rattled against the bone china of my teacup momentarily. Mrs Brandley's questions were innocent, for she knew Pip only as someone who was thought of almost as a brother to me, and a most-trusted friend of Mother's. He had been known to me since he and I were eight or nine. She did not know how her queries made me tremble. Had no clue that before my marriage to Bentley, Pip had declared his love to me only for me to foolishly reject him in favour of Bentley. It had led to Pip abandoning me just weeks before Mother died. Did he know she was dead, even? I had not sent word, too distraught at the time, and then weeks had passed and there had been no word from him... and stubbornness was stopping me from sending for him.

'I confess we have had no contact since Mother's passing,' I replied honestly.

'How is your young friend, the new Lady Taykall?' interrupted Mrs Matthew Pocket. I could have hugged her, had not the change of subject been to yet another I wished to avoid. Luckily, she continued the conversation herself – as was her habit. 'Oh, and she has that wonderful house to run now! It really is a glorious place. You have lately returned from there, I believe? Although they do have such terrible trouble holding on to maids, from what I hear – three left in six months. Why anyone would want to leave such acres of gardens and woodlands, such a stupendous house, I do not know. The luck! I went there once, when I was a mere girl, when my fortunes were far better... I do believe at one point Sir John's attentions turned to me. Me! Think of how my life could have been. Of course Elizabeth had the wisdom to marry a man of means, while I married—'

It was always best to divert Mrs Pocket from talking about her former prospects before she married for love. Many believed Matthew, my cousin, was a veritable saint for putting up with such a vacuous, fluttering creature, but I found criticism of her to be hypocrisy in the extreme. She had been raised from birth to be nothing but decorative: discouraged from any useful applications, like most women. She had been encouraged to entertain no thoughts in her head so that a husband might one day fill her up with his own, like an empty ewer. Little wonder she was as much use as a fish in the sky.

'Elizabeth has settled into her new life well,' I said. 'That reminds me, Cecilia, that she was quite fascinated by the talk of you holding a ball at your house in Essex. Have you decided on a theme yet?'

It was a complete lie, but Lady Cecilia Forfar sat up at the query. 'It will be a masked ball – and the invitations are going out this very day.' She clapped her hands as she spoke. 'The last ball is still being spoken of with awe, yet I am convinced that this event shall be even more marvellous…somehow.'

'I thought you said masked balls bored you,' Daphne replied.

'I changed my mind. It is a lady's prerogative. Ah, the trials of being a leading light of society! This will be no ordinary masked ball; Estella, I have you to thank for this, for the theme will be Princes and Paupers. Just like the Parisian gatherings you told us about! Everyone must come in costume, with the rich dressed like either royalty or servants!' There were gasps all round.

Daphne almost tumbled from her seat in shock. 'There are no men dressing as women, are there?' she whispered.

'Who can say? Oh, and I have news.' She leaned forward, eyes bright with gossip. 'Mr Coutts has already confirmed that he shall attend.'

The fans began to flutter.

Mr Coutts would be attending, would he? How I looked forward to meeting him again, and scrutinising him more closely. Perhaps I would discover what connected him to Nora, and what so scared her when she saw him.

CHAPTER TWENTY-THREE

At home – or rather at Bentley's London residence, for home will always be Satis House – I was still pondering, but ridiculously it was not the mystery of Nora but Mrs Brandley's question of Pip that niggled my brain. I had tried not to think of him since my marriage. He had not contacted me about Mother's death, which grieved me almost as much as her loss – for surely he would have heard about it from village talk. For so long he had been my only friend in the world… But all that had changed when he declared his love for me and I rejected him.

But only because you wanted to save him from your love, I reminded myself. Life with me would have been a misery, for real love was not for someone such as I. There was something missing from my heart. Something I saw in others but could not fully comprehend. *No, I did the right thing to push him away,* I told myself for the umpteenth time.

Yet, if it was the right thing, why was there a pain, as if someone was stabbing a knitting needle into my heart?

My heeled boots clicked across the hallway parquet, my own image mirrored in its polished sheen. There, a note waited for me from Joseph. He had found Sarah Monkton. So she was alive. Did that mean others on the list were, too? That would be a relief. Perhaps I had got everything wrong, and there was no crime, only girls escaping service in order to find their freedom. I would only find out once I had spoken with her.

In my dressing room, my housekeeper and keeper of family secrets, Lydia, waited to aid me. Together, we pulled off my satin gloves, unwound from about my waist the broad ribbon of gold and orange velvet, and removed my amber jewels. I changed from the champagne-coloured gown into a less formal dress. Everything was put away in its usual place, for disorder was a loathsome thing to my London persona.

Once more I checked my mirror – I was pristine – and gave a deep sigh at the prospect of spending time with my husband.

A woman's life was one of duty, however, and this could no longer be delayed, no matter how tempting.

I climbed the stairs to his room, braced myself, and opened the door. There he was, Bentley Drummle, the almost but not quite baronet, sitting on a small dining chair, waiting for me.

Toad-like. Powerful muscles. Attitude.

My shoulder blades drew together and the icy urge to run screamed through me. The body doesn't forget the kind of torture I had endured at the hands of that man. Even chained as he was, he scared me, though the admission rankled.

'Husband.' I arranged my face into a smile.

'Bi-bi-bi—' Bentley tried to form words, but it was hard for him lately.

'Bitch? Yes, dear, you've told me that a thousand times before. Apologies for my tardiness, but I was having so much fun I lost track of the hour.' A tinkle of laughter. 'Well, you know time and I are not always friends – that's what happens when one is raised without working clocks in the house. Medicine?'

His whole demeanour changed when I held up the bottle filled with black liquid. He sat up straight, quivering like a plucked violin string. I moved it this way and that, and his head moved with it, as if the two were one. From my pocket was pulled a spoon which I quickly filled with laudanum.

Bentley began drooling.

'Beg.'

He did. He promised me the world, in exchange for a single drop of the opium tincture.

The laudanum had done its work. Bentley could barely lift his head; his eyelids drooped with the effort of keeping them open. I checked the chain that ran from him to the wall beside the bed; it was still intact. In the corner of the room, where the wall met the slope of the roof, a spider had begun to spin a web in the otherwise pristine room. That would not do – Bentley might hurt her. I caught her in my hand, felt her legs tickling my palm as I held her.

Generally, I left the room as swiftly as possible, but that day I lingered. Mother had always known every detail of my life, and had insisted on daily letters to keep her informed. Troubled as I was with thoughts of Wynterton, I needed someone to talk about it with and missed Mother more than ever. I could have trusted Lydia, but felt uncomfortable burdening her further. No, it was far better to keep her innocent of such troubles. My new friends most definitely could not be confided in. If anything, they would provide a useful screen of normality to hide behind should I decide to take action. And so that left my husband: literally a captive audience.

'As you're going nowhere, and can betray me to no one, there is a tale I wish to tell,' I began. Soon everything was spilling forth about my visit, and Nora's disappearance right outside my door, even as we had still spoken. 'The thing I keep thinking about is this: if William Turpin's sister Mary is the Mary on the list – and why would she not be? – then there is more to the gardener's list than simply the names of his own conquests, for she disappeared long before his arrival. But what if two like-minded fellows came together? Discovered their shared love of violence against women, for example.'

Bentley lifted his head with great effort. Bloodshot eyes with pupils like pinheads roamed around as they tried to focus on me.

'Would it embolden them?' I continued. 'I have a theory that two such people together – or even more – would make them less cautious, and push each other to greater, more frequent acts of cruelty.'

Bentley managed to meet my eye and grunt.

'Worthybrook was at the house when Mary Turpin disappeared. Perhaps he and Bellis forged a bond over their mutual fetishes, whatever they might be, and—'

My husband's chin sank to his chest again.

'You do not approve of the theory? Hmm, perhaps you have a point, but you never were a cerebral fellow. No wonder you and Sir John get on so well.'

He rallied again. Wobbled about.

'Are you trying to break free? Dear me, you are so weak you would lose a fight against strong cheese, Bentley, so please stop – you're embarrassing yourself. Where was I? Oh, yes, you remember, of course, your manservant Joseph? He is now – thanks to me – a consulting detective. He already has several clients. What do you think of that? I'm sorry, I don't know what the drooling means… Anyway, he is trying to find out more about the other girls on the list, and already he has found the Monkton family in Walworth. He really is rather impressive. Tomorrow I shall visit them and find out more.'

Bentley seemed to be becoming more alert, stirring restlessly. Perhaps he was becoming used to the opium. That was a worry. I gave him another black drop, and then left him to rattle his chains, ghostlike, alone. My new friend, the spider, came with me. She seemed pleased with her fresh home in my bedroom.

Walworth was a place in south London that I had not before visited. From the vantage of my barouche – for it was another mild October day – I divined that it sat where town and countryside collided, with back lanes lined with cottages crammed in together, each of which had garden enough for a pig or two and the growing of vegetables. The Monktons' cottage was much like the rest, except they had squeezed in some chickens, too, and washing hung everywhere.

A woman of middling years appeared at the door, which had been standing open, and stood with her red, cracked hands on her hips. She had the great forearms and shoulders of a washerwoman, yet for all her physical power, she dropped a curtsy with the elegance of a duchess when she saw my fine dress and furs. Her own clothes were patched and worn, but neatly mended.

'Mrs Monkton?' As I drew closer, the smell of carbolic was almost overwhelming, along with the lanolin that, judging from the shine on her cracked knuckles, she rubbed onto her sore skin to soothe it. 'Forgive the intrusion, but I wish to speak with your daughter.'

'She ain't in.' The reply was too quick, and besides, I had already spotted a girl inside who stood at the sound of my voice.

'Who is it?' There was fear in her voice, but her eyes were dead. No, not dead, but showing a soul so wounded that it had shrunk away to almost nothing. I recognised that expression because I had seen it in the mirror sometimes since Paris.

'Ah, Miss Sarah Monkton, I presume. My name is Mrs Estella Drummle, and there is something I wish to discuss with you. Would you be so kind as to take the air with me? I would love to see the sights of Walworth—'

'That's very kind of you, but she's busy at the moment.' Her mother tried to put herself physically between us. I caught her gaze and held it for three long counts before speaking.

'I mean no harm. I simply wish to talk about Wynterton Manor.'

The girl flinched. Her mother pulled a face. 'Nothing to tell you about. We lived there, we worked there, then we moved away. That's it.'

'I swear to you that my only desire is to help, and to heal past pains.'

A tilt of the head. 'Best way to heal the past is to leave it to scab over, instead of picking at it.'

'Has it helped thus far? Sarah will not have to speak of anything she does not wish to, that I promise.'

A weighing up, and then a nod of understanding. With those few words we two women had exchanged much intelligence. Had she not decided to trust me with her daughter I did not know what my next step would have been, but I thanked her with much gratitude before Sarah and I set off.

Sarah and I made for an odd pairing as we walked in the autumn sunshine: the almost mute serving girl and the gentlewoman. For some time, I asked her only about the sights around us as we found the canal. She pointed out the iron footbridge.

'It moves to allow the passage of barges,' she said. Her voice was soft, as if she did not speak often. 'In the distance, that church spire there, that's St George's.'

We wandered towards it, past ditches and ponds filled with browning reeds, while I tried to decide how best to broach the awful matter.

At last, I was ready to speak. 'Sarah, I am not here as a rich woman trying to force you to do or say anything. You have suffered enough of such behaviour, I suspect.'

We continued walking, pace unchanged apart from the slightest stumble on her part, as if she had encountered an unexpected stone. Her lank hair hung loose about her face, creating a curtain betwixt us through which I could not see her expression.

'Our experiences of life could not be more different, yet there is one place where they intersect, I suspect. I know what it is like to have a man overpower and overwhelm in a way that only a man can to a woman.'

A twitch began in Sarah's thin body, starting from the protruding bones at the back of her bowed neck and running down through her. She said nothing.

'If my suspicions are correct, in this experience we are sisters,' I continued. The only sound was from the distant hullabaloo of everyday life continuing unabated around us, and our gentle footfalls on the dry, dusty path. 'No money, no place in society, nothing differentiates between women who have been through that experience. It is something which binds us together throughout life. Am I right?'

The girl gave a sob. Yet on she walked, not yet ready to speak. We continued southward, several barges puffing by.

Finally, Sarah stopped and sat on a low, crumbling wall, stared at her feet, then shuffled along a little and tapped the space beside her. 'If we are sisters, we can share the same seat.'

I sat so close that I could feel her violent trembling. It broke my heart to see her so shattered at the hands of a man.

'Oh, Sarah, I swear I will make him pay for what he has done. Tell me what happened at Wynterton. Tell me what that fiend Bellis did.'

She looked at me for the first time, her face a wreck of grey features glistening with silent tears. 'Bellis… he…' She wiped a sleeve across her nose. 'He saved me.'

CHAPTER TWENTY-FOUR

Bellis *saved* Sarah? My mind could not comprehend it, and instead of questioning, all I could do was stare at the girl. I weighed the evidence in my mind. His threatening behaviour, which I myself had witnessed twice; his conspiracy with the barking hound Worthybrook, who in turn plotted and planned suspiciously with Mrs Switchley; and, most damning of all, the list. Surely I had misheard, or perhaps she was so traumatised as to be confused.

Sarah did not speak again. We sat side by side on the dilapidated wall and watched a barge pass. A man with a coal-blackened face, sitting on a chair at the back, gave a genial nod of greeting but did not slow the puffing of his pipe. When he was out of sight, she gave a great trembling sigh.

'I was in the gardens, where I should not have been. I was often told off for it, but I love roses and saw no harm in seeking the sight of them. So I sneaked to the walled garden.'

I leaned close to hear her, for her voice was so softened with tears.

'He came upon me and it all happened so quickly. I was pressed up against a wall and his hands were everywhere, and his breath was on me, and there was a smell, the strangest, overpowering smell...

'I-I think I fainted clean away or some such. When I come to, I was on the ground and he was... I wanted to scream, to fight him off, but my body did not seem to respond to my thoughts. I couldn't move! When he saw my eyes upon him, he grew angry and wrapped his hands about my throat.'

My hands were curled so tightly into fists that the leather of my gloves gave a little creak at the strain across my knuckles. But I said not a word, intent on hearing everything Sarah wished to share.

'He had got what he wanted, but it still wasn't enough. He was so angry! He started beating me about the head and then strangling me again, and beating me, and-and-and those were my last moments on this earth, I felt sure. All I could think of was of my parents and how I had let them down, and I prayed to one day see them again, and... then I heard loud whistling. He stopped at that. Stepped away. That's when the gardener walked into the rose garden.'

Sarah's red-rimmed eyes met mine at last.

'He told Brock Bellis he had found me running around inside the walled garden, beating myself and screaming. That I was a lunatic who had harmed my own body. He gave me a shove with the toe of his fine velvet slipper, as if I were no more than dirt, not a poor helpless girl lying there on the cold ground, almost insensible. "Get rid of her. She needs to be in an asylum", those were his words. I still hear them, every time I close my eyes. But Brock didn't do what he was told; he brought me to my parents, and we moved away from the only place any of us had ever known, just so's we could escape the long reach of that awful man.'

There was life in her eyes again. Twin fires of anger and fear burned in the gaze that met mine.

'Who did this to you, Sarah? Can you name him?'

'Why, Sir John, of course.'

Sir John Taykall, that preposterous, addle-pated blunderbuss. But also cunning. And vile. A relentless hunter. And strong for his age.

I had brought Elizabeth and him together. My poor friend! Did he mistreat her, too? Was she in danger? I had watched him with the servants and assumed the way he acted as if they did not exist meant they were safe from his notice. It was the opposite. They did not matter, in his mind. They were there purely to serve him, bring him his meal, or sate another far darker desire – his need to hunt and have, his drive to take lives.

Damn these tight corsets for constricting my breathing so!

''Twas my fault. I had been warned not to linger in the gardens most sternly. Switchley, Worthybrook, and especially Brock Bellis, they'd all expounded on it, but I hadn't listened. It was my fault...!'

I rubbed her back like a mother does a babe. 'Sarah, look at me. I'm going to be quite stern with you. What happened to you was not your fault. You did not want what happened. You had no comprehension of the consequences of a mere evening stroll in a garden; the worst thing that should have happened to you was a scratch from a bush, not' – I faltered, for I was becoming heated and forced myself to take a calming breath – 'not what you had to suffer. If you will not believe it when you tell yourself that, believe it because *I* tell you. There is no reason for me to lie, after all.'

All those girls he had forced his attentions on, and who had no choice but to run in terror in order to stop it from happening again… Because if the truth were to get out, it would not be Sir John who would suffer the consequences, but them. It was always the women who bore responsibility for men not being able to control themselves. My leather gloves creaked again in fury at that thought.

I thought of Nora. Had she run to her sister's side after suffering abuse at the hands of her employer? Awful as that was, it was better than the shallow grave I had feared for her. I would find her and bring her under my wing. She would become a lady's maid, just as she dreamed of.

Another thought followed swiftly: how had Sir John managed to overpower these girls so quickly and quietly? He had taken Nora right outside my bedroom door, as I had listened. Sarah had mentioned not being able to move; was there a clue there?

'May I ask something, Sarah? You mentioned an awful odour. Was that simply Sir John's malodorous breath?'

She closed her eyes and nodded weakly. 'Something more, though. A smell so strong that my head swam and my heart thudded to a slow. Th-there was a handkerchief.' Her eyes flew open again as the memory came to the fore. 'He kept pushing the kerchief over my nose and mouth, and every time that smell appeared and I became so heavy and weak.'

There had been a square of cloth outside my bedroom door, found after Nora's disappearance. The slightest odd odour had been in the air, which I had quickly dismissed as curdling milk from the stain on the carpet; but thinking about it further, it had in fact come from the rough handkerchief.

Still, I could not understand what that had to do with anything. Sarah and I sat side by side, both trembling, she with fear, I with rage.

Think, Estella, think.

A cloth. A pungent aroma. A slowing of the heartbeat.

Memory fluttered its wings. Elizabeth and I running in the sunshine, swooping at butterflies with our nets. My friend opening the kill jar and placing the beautiful insect inside, along with a tiny piece of cloth soaked with a chemical. We two, watching its delicate wingbeats slow to nothing.

Was it possible to do something similar to a person? Perhaps by using a larger cloth steeped in chemicals?

'Do you know anything about other girls being ravaged and brutalised?' I asked.

'There were rumours, but they are not the kind of thing good girls like to talk about.' She bit her lip. 'I am not a good girl any more, though, am I? He took that away from me. So I will say all I know, which is little enough: there's always been talk of Sir John being a cad. Recently, there's worse things being said… Rumours abound that he's started employing orphans because they have no family to protect them or ask questions. Everyone is terrified of him.

'I hate him. He's an animal that can't control his beastly urges for young women. He hunts us the way he used to the poor stuffed creatures that decorate his home. I want to make him pay for what he did. To be judge, jury and executioner to a man whose privilege shelters him from questioning. There, what do you think of that?'

Her look was defiant. I sighed and covered her hand with my own.

'It is perfectly understandable. But do not let him take any more from you than he already has,' I advised. 'I am certain that he will receive his punishment one day, without you having to lose your humanity.'

That would be my job. I had spent all summer and much of autumn trying to fulfil Mother's final wish that I leave behind her lifetime of teachings and instead try to embrace a normal life. But it was *she* who forged me into a weapon against men, she who told me daily to 'never love, never trust, always strike first', to 'break men and make them pay'. Killing that man in the London alley had been a heated moment of spontaneity. Sir John's punishment would have to be cleverer than that, if I were to get away with it.

CHAPTER TWENTY-FIVE

At long last I knew what was happening at Wynterton, and who was responsible. There was a temptation to rush there, blazing like an angel of vengeance, and confront Sir John. Instead, I made myself sit tight and think, no matter how much my soul thrummed at the thought of making him pay for injuring so many young women. He had too much power and influence for that to work, which was no doubt the reason why no one had done so previously. A man with his sort of fortune was always going to be believed and protected against accusation. Besides, there was no proof of what he had done, for the word of one girl of the lower classes would hold no sway.

Justice would have to come not from the courts but from me. Sir John was a master of successfully attacking women, which meant I would be placing myself in great potential danger when I did finally come face to face with him again. Great care was going to have to be taken.

Had Bellis compiled the list of the disappeared, in order to find the girls and persuade them to give evidence? Even though there was power in numbers, I did not think that there was enough power in that instance to have Sir John hanged for his violations. He could buy justice.

Poor Bellis. Knowing he was Sarah's saviour altered all I had witnessed and overheard. Where he had sounded threatening, his words suddenly appeared to be a warning. *'You want to watch yourself, Nora. I mean it. Watch what you're doing, or there'll be trouble.'*

The roughness I had taken for anger could easily be fear and concern.

And what was it he had said to Cook? *'Keep your nose out of things. Otherwise you might be the next to disappear.'*

What I had taken to be Worthybrook and him watching the female charges like wolves over sheep, I realised was more akin to guard dogs over a flock. The same had to be true of Mrs Switchley, too. Perhaps her strictness had been about trying to keep the young serving girls away from Sir John's gaze. Although what her problem with Elizabeth was remained a mystery to me. Unless her implacable nature was a screen for the worry she felt for her mistress.

My friend had married Sir John due to my interference. What if she was in danger?

It was my duty to ensure no harm befell her, and that included creating an unbreakable alibi for her, so no one could accuse her of doing away with her husband.

There were so many strands to consider…

Nora's fearful expression when she had seen Coutts. What did he have to do with any of this? I tried to remember my conversations with him, and my stomach twisted as I examined a growing idea. As I had left Wynterton's dining room I had overheard Sir John asking about 'increasing supply'. What if he had not been talking about fabrics, but girls? Could he be buying them from Coutts?

No, it was too far a leap. There was no evidence to support the theory.

If I was correct, though… he had also mentioned friends who were waiting to be supplied, too.

Stop it, Estella. The world is not as dark as you paint it!

There was enough for me to deal with, without making up new horrors and foes.

Joseph continued to try to track down Nora's sister, Nancy, and Sir John's other victims. Thus far he had only found Sarah. Where were the others? As days passed, my fear grew that Sir John was a killer as well as a beast.

At night, I found it hard to sleep, wondering just how much of a monster this man might be, and my cold imagination provided myriad blood-filled answers. Who might his next victim be? What might my friend, Elizabeth, suffer at the hands of her husband? There was no end to my fears.

If this was what having friends did, perhaps I was better off alone…

There was one person I knew beside Joseph who might be able to provide some answers. My friend Miss Lucy Brandley. We sat in her parlour, discussing the chemicals involved in killing and preserving butterflies and the like.

She thought for a moment only, and pushed her glasses up her nose.

'There's an article I read a few months ago. Now where did I put it? It was regarding the distillation of alcohol and bleaching powder to create a substance that is now being used as a cheap pesticide, and to kill insects for collectors, too.'

She wandered to her shelves and started pulling papers from between books, peering at them, then discarding.

'Could it be used to overpower a person?' I asked.

Her finger hovered on the spine of a book. 'What an interesting question. Ah! Here we are!'

She did not speak again until she had read it, tilted her head, turned the question over in her mind again and finally came to a conclusion.

'There could be a possible application for this new substance – there are several names for it, by the way, but the one that seems most popular is chloroform. Your question has made me think of it in an entirely different way, and I believe it *could* be used to put someone to sleep during surgeries, although no one else seems have thought of it yet. How very perspicacious, Estella,' she said, thoughtfully, 'although there may be a risk of possible fatality. Hmm. Are you going to the masked ball?' With a worried wrinkle of her nose, she switched from astute scientist to socially awkward woman. 'I would rather stay at home.'

'I'm sure Lady Forfar will understand. I will not be attending myself—' I stopped. 'On second thoughts, it could be the perfect distraction for me.'

And it might just help me get away with murder.

CHAPTER TWENTY-SIX

The full extent of Sir John's cunning was slowly becoming clearer to me. Over the coming days I thought often of Sarah's testimony, and how she had been strangled and beaten by him. It sounded as if he had wanted to kill her – and she had perhaps only been saved because Bellis happened upon the attack. Given that Joseph was finding no sign of the other girls on my list, I had to accept that Sir John might have killed them.

Every night I dreamed of Nora. Terrified and unable even to shout out, paralysed by a chemical. I would wake bathed in sweat.

'I will find you,' I vowed. But how could I keep my promise?

I had to think like him. I fought against it, not because it was hard, but because it seemed all too easy for me. The answer was obvious. Sir John was a hunter who loved to display his kills. Even though he was too old to hunt big game, he hunted and kept the carcasses of the insects in his Cabinet of Curiosities. If I was right, he would have killed those girls, using chloroform to overwhelm them, in case he was too infirm to overcome them himself, and he would then keep them close. Even in death.

They were at the house still.

A plan was forming to tackle Sir John, and Lady Cecilia Forfar was the key to it all. A few enquiries to Lucy's mother, and I discovered that Cecilia was in town. I was in luck! There was no time to waste, and so I paid a visit to her London residence in Grosvenor Square.

'What a delightful surprise!' she said. She was in her morning room, and when she realised her visitor was only I, she returned to her chaise and lounged. 'To what do I owe the pleasure?' Her rosebud lips opened to give a barely covered great yawn. 'Do forgive me; organising the ball is leaving me quite exhausted.'

'I have come begging a favour regarding exactly that.'

She did not reply, but instead rang for tea and made a gesture that suggested she wished me to continue.

'I am recently returned from visiting Lady Elizabeth Taykall, and she mentioned that she would not be coming to your ball—'

'Because her husband is too old to bother.' Good old Cecilia, cutting straight to the chase. She always loved a gossip.

'Far be it from me to criticise, but I did think it would make a lovely surprise for her if I were to persuade her to come along with me. It is not entirely altruistic – I long to attend, but Bentley is still away on business—'

'You poor neglected dear!'

'I would never criticise my husband, but...' There was no need to end the sentence. 'I cannot attend your ball alone, but Elizabeth and I could chaperone one another. Herein lies the favour I require from you: would it be a terrible intrusion for us to overnight with you?'

'On the night of the ball? You would both be most welcome!'

'Wonderful! And my thanks. I shall have to get costumes for us both, of course—' I noticed her lips twist one side slightly, as if unhappy. 'My dear Cecilia, what is wrong?'

She huffed and rearranged her skirts before answering. 'It is the most awful thing, Estella. You cannot imagine the trials and tribulations I have suffered. I-I...'

What could it be? Was her husband beating her? Had she discovered he was being unfaithful?

'You must know you can trust me with anything,' I urged.

'I-I-I... Oh, Estella, I hate my costume!' She threw her head back and fat tears rolled down her cheeks as if she were suffering the most appalling apoplexy. 'It is a beautiful gown fit for a princess, the colour of purple periwinkles, and covered in jewels, but I fear I shall simply disappear among the other guests who will also be dressing as royalty, given the theme.'

'Oh!' *How ridiculous*, I thought. Until it occurred to me that it could provide me with an opportunity. 'You rather fancied guests being more daring in their costume... more Parisian... correct?'

She dabbed at her face with a handkerchief of the finest lace, and sniffed her agreement to the question.

'Then why not go as a pauper? It would have everyone talking. Imagine it, you in rags – but rags of the finest cloth, of course. A slashed shirt of the sheerest silk, knee breeches of brocade which has been carefully distressed and frayed to look its best.' My imagination filled in the blanks quickly. 'Your mask would be bejewelled in precious stones all of grey – your breeches could be in grey, too, to imitate the great unwashed.' That awful phrase was inserted for her benefit. 'Think how stunned everyone would be! Think of how you would be tipping your nose at all that is fashionable, while simultaneously being the height of fashion.'

Her eyes shone at the image, but doubt lingered, too. 'It is daring. Perhaps too daring,' she said.

'True… but as the theme of the ball is Princes and Paupers, someone is bound to take up the challenge – and then all eyes will be on them. But perhaps you are right, it is better all talk is about them—'

'Wait! Perhaps you have a point.'

Another idea was forming. One that would aid greatly my murderous plan to rid the world of Sir John Taykall. Would Cecilia agree?

I bit my lip as if thinking, then grabbed Cecilia's hand. 'I might just have the perfect solution. What if you and I dressed in identical costumes? And unveiled them together? That way, you are not alone in your daring dress… yet at the same time, all eyes will be on you in the best possible way, for you are the hostess, and I will be a mere mimic.'

She frowned. Thought. Squeezed my hand in delight. 'And Elizabeth can have my original costume – we are of similar build. Oh, it is the perfect plan, Estella!'

Not quite, for there was still much to consider, yet things were definitely coming together nicely. The ball would provide an alibi for Elizabeth and me. My dressing like the hostess would sow confusion as to whom partygoers were seeing. I could seem to be present even after slipping away.

Hopefully Joseph would, in a few days' time, have more information for me about the other girls who had disappeared. Then it would be time for a swift visit to Satis House, before the ball. Sir John's moment of justice was nearing. He would pay for every scream he had ever elicited.

The fusty, dank air went deep into my lungs and seemed to fill my body. Every dust mote could be felt dancing along my veins, while the utter darkness cloaked me and was absorbed to become a part of my being. I was home. Truly home. At last.

How I had missed Satis House. After Mother's death, and Bentley's subjugation, it had been tempting to repair permanently to the place of my childhood. It had shaped me almost as much as Mother had.

Bentley had been planning to auction it, and had already put arrangements in place before going to the house to see me after Mother's death. Thank goodness I had put a stop to that when tricking him into taking opium for the first time, undoing his arrangements as swiftly as he had made them. Since childhood I had a well-practised skill of mimicking people's handwriting, and put it to use by forging a letter from Bentley explaining that he had decided to indulge his new bride's desire to keep hold of the manor against all manly logic. A couple of servants now stayed at Satis House in order to look after it for me and stop curious people from breaking in.

I needed that house of darkness and secrets. Not only did it connect me with Mother in a way visiting her grave did not, but being at Satis House always gave me a clarity that could not be found elsewhere. Sitting in the darkness, with the faithful spiders for company, was peaceful. With them there was no need for a tiring façade, or vacuous conversations that used so many words but said nothing.

In some rooms, light smashed through widening cracks in the walls, and ivy had started to creep inside to create its own private jungle. The dressing room was intact, however, although the dressing table where Mother had spent so many hours staring morosely at her wizening reflection had been taken to my London residence. Instead, I sat in her high-backed Queen Anne chair and stared at the fire for some time.

I had not wanted another murder on my conscience, had fought my desires, and pushed down my elation at killing. Yet ever since Nora's disappearance I had felt a sense of inevitability. When I killed Sir John it would not only be to quench my desire for revenge, but to stop him from hurting others.

Perhaps it was my destiny to take the lives of men who harmed women. The very structure of the world conspired against my struggles to be a better person. Most men considered women chattels to be used and discarded; they saw no reason why women should have control over their lives, bodies, thoughts. In order to ensure women did have those things, I would willingly fight to the death.

'I wish you were here, Mother. What would you counsel me to do?'

The smoke curled towards me, beckoning, then twisted back on itself up the chimney.

'Well, there was no meaning in that. And so I shall go ahead, regardless.' I sighed and stood, picking up a single candle to take with me.

A fortnight had passed painfully slowly since my visit to Walworth, when I had discovered Sir John's true nature. The wait had been forced upon me, in order that I might have all the information needed, and time for the final pieces of my scheme to come together.

The visit to my childhood home had been both practical (that I might collect the monthly rent from my tenants) and ethereal, because being there fed my strength and stoked my anger.

The wind whistled through the building and howled. *Hurt this man before he hurts you, Estella*, it seemed to say. *Strike hard and true. Make him pay.*

'Yes,' I breathed.

CHAPTER TWENTY-SEVEN

There were many holes in my plan – in fact, it was more of an outline – but in my experience things always went their own way no matter how much one thought every possible permutation had been considered. Better to factor that in and accept that a level of thinking on one's feet would be required.

A few days earlier, Joseph had brought me the information I had been waiting for. There was no trace of the missing girls. All he had found were dead ends.

As I thought through my scheme, I opened a chest of drawers and began sorting through Mother's things. The bureaus filled with paperwork had been the first to be addressed, by necessity, and much had been handed over to Jaggers to sift through, so that all business-related information be held together. There was much that was personal to the Havishams that I was still discovering, however. Paintings of ancestors, family trees, old musical instruments with broken strings, boxes filled with jewellery...

Each item moved broke a little more the spell Mother had cast over Satis House and everything in it, yet I also felt it was worth exploring the family artefacts because it brought me close to her – she who had been behind every action in my life, apart from my one disastrous act of independence in marrying Bentley.

I picked through a trunk filled with old-fashioned underwear – shifts, stays, and the like. A fat-backed spider scuttled out, racing across the material... I held my hand out and smiled at the tickle of her feet across my skin.

'Good to see you, my friend. Here, how about this for your new residence?' I put her in a neighbouring chest of drawers that had already been sorted through. She ran to a corner and slipped from sight beneath the drawer's contents.

For some time I went through Mother's things. There was a certain comfort to the rhythm of taking out each item and putting it in a pile to be discarded. I couldn't help thinking of the young woman she had been when they had last been worn, how in love with Everard Compeyson she had been, and how excited about the future.

What would have become of me had I not been adopted by Miss Havisham, the richest woman in the county? Raised instead by my natural parents, would I have followed after them into some trade or other? But no, of course not, for I had been an orphan child, and would have suffered a life of hardship and deprivation.

Whenever I thought of my true parentage, there was another question that burned always through me: did I inherit my cold, calculating thoughts and hot, violent actions from them? Or was it the strange way I had been raised that had twisted me into the weird monster I was? If only I knew, I might understand myself better—

My fingers butted against something hard among the fabrics. Once pulled free, I saw it was a book, a journal of some kind. It fell open to a much revisited page, judging from the softness of the paper, and the fading to the ink. Mother's distinctive writing dashed across the page with impatience, and lingered for sweeping flourishes of indulgence.

> My heart is his and only his, and when I die, if they were to cut me open and look at it, they would find the name Everard engraved across it.

Oh, Mother, what a melodramatic fool you were for that man.

If only I could have stepped back in time and warned her of the future unfolding, but by the time she wrote those words the once silken threads of her life were already being woven into a horsehair shroud. It hurt me too much to read more hopeful, lovesick entries, and so I set the journal aside.

Further searching inside the drawer revealed letters tied in royal-blue velvet ribbon. The writing on the outside was a perfect copperplate, as if the author were taking care to appear flawless and not give away anything about their true nature. The bow undid at my barest touch, the ribbon slithering to the floor.

My darling Pandora,

I will never deserve you. That you bestow your love on me is my constant wonder. To be in your company is to find a happy home, to have you in my arms is to...

Sentimental claptrap peddled by a sharp, subtle whipster. No doubt gilded words such as these had ensnared more hapless women than just Pandora Havisham for Everard Compeyson. I could read no more. Mother's inexperienced heart, still grieving from the death of her father not twelve months before she was targeted by Compeyson, had been tenderised by each honeyed manipulation.

The wind wailed around the house in agreement as I emptied the trunk. Right at the bottom lay a wooden box. A pretty thing, but built for solidity, with decorative brass corners that matched the sturdy little brass legs, and an ornate plate that housed a lock. It would not open. I searched around for a key, but found none; I tried to unpick it with two hatpins, but had no luck. When shaken, something could be heard slipping around inside it. More papers perhaps, but also something else that was heavier. A secret that called to me.

A tingle of curiosity. Mother did not have any secrets from me, nor I from her – not after those weeks spent together after the terrible accident that ultimately led to her death. We had cast into the light all shadows that had grown between us through the years. Yet here was something locked away. Curious, I decided to take it with me, for it was almost time to leave for the next part of my journey.

There was one more important thing to do. I visited a certain spot between the malthouse wall and an oak tree, where the earth had been disturbed a little over a score of years ago. The conditions perfectly suited a certain plant that now grew there: one with berries that were almost black. Once picked, down to the kitchen with them I went, and crushed them up, along with some herbs and spices, and added them to several bottles of alcohol that I planned to gift at Wynterton.

Sir John stood in his Cabinet of Curiosities, his hands on his hips, a deep 'v' upon his forehead as my words sank in.

'What did you say, my dear? It's nonsense, not possible. You're getting that pretty little head of yours in a muddle.'

A huge butterfly with wings with long streamers on them that brought to mind a swallow's tail scintillated between brilliant blue and blinding white as candlelight flickered over it. Sir John had been in the middle of pinning it to the black velvet when I entered the room.

Seeing it made me think of the pretty young girls, their fluttering innocence stolen from them. They were as delicate as butterflies and had been destroyed just as easily. I wanted to smash the glass and release them, but they would never fly again, no matter how much I wished it otherwise. Men like Sir John knew only how to destroy the things they most coveted.

Instead of saying any of that, I pressed the back of my hand to my temples as if trying to calm myself.

'The truth, Sir John, is that Bentley has gone away for a few weeks and I have got myself into a terrible bind with the servants. I could use Elizabeth's advice on organising them. If you would be generous enough to allow her to stay with me for a few days, I would be so grateful.' I looked up at him from under my eyelashes. 'If it weren't too great an inconvenience I would ask for your aid, but servant matters are so far below a man of your importance. I do not want to let Bentley down, but cannot deal with it alone. The fact that I have arrived here unannounced to beg this favour surely shows my desperation. I fling myself on your mercy, sir.'

'Humph... Well, even so—'

A belch of his halitosis washed over me. I whipped out my fan and fluttered it in a manner I hoped looked demure, wondering if the poison of his vile lies were what had made his mouth rot.

'What's Bentley thinking, leaving you behind? Pretty little thing like you should be with your husband, how else will he sire a son? Some women get ideas once they are married; I hope you are not one of them. They think they are safe, protected, that nothing untoward can happen to them. They learn.' He shook his head as if saddened. 'They are made to learn. Ah, but it is a wicked world we live in.'

'It is indeed. Why, some of the wickedness of which I hear tell I would scarcely believe, without the proof of my own two eyes.'

Our looks were swords crossing. Cursing myself, I gave in first: the weaker sex caving as he expected, glancing away and around the room.

'Speaking of such things is most upsetting,' I added. 'It makes me fear for my travels home, alone... I hope you can forgive my weakness in this, and the inconvenience it causes you to be without your dear Elizabeth.'

The honey satisfied him and he at last gave his agreement.

Elizabeth shifted beside me, her hands cradling her stomach. 'But Estella, I need to take care now that I am expecting. I must not be selfishly gadding about.'

Was her desire to stay really from concern for her unborn child, or fear of her husband? I could not tell.

Sir John threw his hands in the air. 'Enough of this womanish back and forth. It has been decided.'

He took my hand and kissed it, his wet mouth lingering on my knuckles so that he almost seemed to suckle it for a moment.

'Skin as soft as a rose petal,' he murmured, rubbing an avaricious thumb over the damp spot he had left on my skin.

My laugh was coquettish. 'Oh, Sir John, take care that this rose doesn't have thorns that will make you bleed.'

CHAPTER TWENTY-EIGHT

After dinner, Elizabeth oversaw the packing of her clothes, while I went down the servants' back stairs to the kitchen. Cook was there, surrounded by various footmen and serving girls.

'Forgive me,' I said, announcing myself. 'My visit is brief, but I wanted to bring you a gift for accommodating my unexpected visit. Your food was as divine as ever. This is for you.'

I pulled back the covering over the basket I carried, revealing several bottles of whisky. I passed them around to Cook and anyone else who was nearby.

'It is a whisky with my own special blend of spices, sugar and bitters, to warm you on these damp nights. Raise a glass to me tonight, I beg you, and drink my health as well your own.'

'We will.' Cook gave an appreciative nod. Everyone else echoed it. '(Most) kind of you.'

'Be sure to give all the men get a draught as well, for you all labour so hard.'

'I'll make sure of it. I'll get everyone to (raise a glass) to you.'

Hopefully, most of them would be fast asleep thanks to the berries picked at Satis House. The more the better, if my plan were to work. For although I and Elizabeth would be leaving this house and attending the ball, where we would be seen by hundreds of guests, I would be returning that very night, and death would ride with me – and perhaps take my life instead of Sir John's.

Of course I was scared, but I tried my hardest to hide it even from myself. There was no certainty anyone would drink my sleeping draught that night. It was a gamble.

But what a dull life it would be if all was certain.

Elizabeth sat opposite me in my carriage as we raced away from that monstrosity of a house, her feet on a foot stove, blankets over her knees, and furs about her shoulders.

'Warm enough?' I quipped.

'I'm still not sure why you need me.'

'How about because I like your company?'

She returned my smile, at last, and shook her head. 'You're very good at getting your own way, Estella.'

'If only that were true…' *…then by the time the sun rose again, Sir John would no longer be breathing.* 'Elizabeth, I have a surprise.'

Her head turned so quickly she must almost have cricked it.

'Lady Cecilia Forfar is hosting a masked ball tonight – and we shall attend! Our outfits are waiting there for us, and we will overnight before continuing our journey.'

'Oh no, Estella, I'm really not feeling up to such *vigorous* socialising. This journey to your London home is really as much as I could manage.' She put her hand protectively over her stomach, as was her new habit, and I could not help wondering how she would feel about the child growing inside her if she knew the truth about its sire. Would she love it regardless, or always wonder if his evil had been replicated within it?

Was that where I got my instincts for violence – from the father and mother I had never met, whose blood ran in my veins? Or was it from my adoptive mother's daily indoctrination of me, that I should always hate men and try to destroy them?

'A long journey will be too much, surely,' I said. 'Better to have an enjoyable break than an uncomfortable ride through the night, for no reason.'

'You make a good point. Wait – does that mean that the problems with your servants were a ruse?'

I held my hands up in mock surrender. 'You may be married to an old man, but you are young, my friend. Besides, I could not face the ball without a companion, and Bentley is away, and I saw no harm in this little subterfuge. Forgive me?'

For this… and for what I am about to do.

The Forfars' Essex country seat was a well-choreographed dance of servants moving from room to room putting finishing touches here and there. An extra blanket for one guest's bed, an extra pillow for another. Ensuring everywhere was spotless. When Elizabeth and I walked in, Lady Cecilia Forfar was inspecting the flower arrangements, real and artificial blooms together, that adorned every table, and swagged across wall and windows, and down the sweeping banisters.

'…remind Cook that the Duchess of Marlborough likes her steak so rare it may still moo.' Then she saw us. 'Estella! You persuaded her! I'm so pleased you came, Lady Taykall, it's simply wonderful to see you.'

Cecilia's own husband of a year or so, Lord Thomas Forfar, was older than she, but at five-and-forty was still in fine fettle. He also indulged her every whim, hence no expense being spared on the balls and routs that she loved to stage.

'You need not have feared attendance to your ball,' I commented. 'There is a queue of coaches stretching all the way down the drive and along the road, filled with people eager to arrive.'

Cecilia clapped her hands together and gave a delicate jump of delight. 'I am most grateful to you for your part in this,' she added. 'Everyone is talking about my Princes and Paupers theme.'

I demurred, the picture of modesty. 'Nonsense. I may have made the suggestion, but it is you who has brought it to life.'

It was the right thing to say, for she glowed with pale pink pleasure the colour of the inside of a conch shell.

She raised a questioning eyebrow and whispered. 'Is Elizabeth quite well? She is so pale.'

I made the well-known gesture for being pregnant, my hand sweeping out then in again to denote a bump. Cecilia's grin was one of sincere delight.

'And you?' she asked.

I considered. Pregnancy was a great excuse for all kinds of behaviour, and may explain away any absences of mine, but as tempting as it was to fake a soupçon of suspicion of being with child, it may also have brought with it unwanted scrutiny. I tried to recreate the look of sadness seen on other ladies who had not fallen quickly.

'Oh, dear Estella, do not fear. It will happen for you soon enough – you have not been yet married a twelvemonth.'

Apparently there was a clock ticking, waiting for me to get with child. For the time being there were more pressing matters to worry about.

'And no Bentley with you?' Cecilia asked.

'No, as I mentioned, he is away.'

She pressed no further. It was a testament to how vile my husband was, and his unique ability to bully people or create an uncomfortable atmosphere merely with his glowering presence, that more people did not miss or seek his company.

'Have our costumes arrived?' I checked.

'They have. And ours are identical – as planned.'

'Perfect!'

Absolutely perfect for getting away with murder…

CHAPTER TWENTY-NINE

A roar of laughter and applause rose through the throng of revellers, as Cecilia and I made our entrance together, down the sweeping mahogany staircase. We paused, laughing, around twelve steps from the bottom, so that we could be seen above the sea of faces that stared up at us.

The rich were enjoying 'slumming it' Parisian style at the masked Princes to Paupers themed event. Some were dressed in the most ostentatious finery, precious gems reflecting the light so that people seemed to shiver with their treasures. Rubies, emeralds, diamonds of every cut, carat and colour encrusted women's bodices and skirts, and men's waistcoats. At the opposite extreme were those who had embraced the amusement of dressing as a pauper for the night, even if their clothes were made from cloth that cost enough to feed a family for a year. No matter how people were dressed, they hid their faces behind masks, adoring the freedom it gave them, because for one night only no one was who or what they seemed; all were opposites and revelling in it.

None more so than Cecelia and me. From the first time I had mentioned how sometimes at Parisian balls women dressed as men and men as women, Cecilia had been fascinated. Desperate to do it, but aware of how scandalously it could be received, she had not had the courage to act alone. When I had spilled beer on the two men who had taunted the runaway boy all those weeks ago, it had been in order to create confusion, so that they would not notice me pickpocketing them. Misdirection would also be key at the ball, if my absence were not to be noticed. My offer to dress as a boy had won Cecilia's gratitude as an act of support, and would also help me enormously as the rest of the night played out, as no one would be certain if it was Cecilia or me that they saw.

Cecilia and I stood side by side in front of all the guests, who continued to roar approval, clap hands and stamp at the shocking spectacle of we two ladies dressed as serving boys. They took in our artfully torn white silk shirts, pale blue cummerbunds wrapped about our waists to cinch them in, and loose, voluminous pantaloon-style yellow and dark blue striped trousers (Cecilia had not wanted to wear dull grey), and our matching, glittering masks over our eyes.

Around 700 people had been invited to the ball, for this was one of the biggest events of the ton's social calendar, just as Cecilia had hoped. The hall, staircase, and all five drawing rooms were lighted with chandeliers, lamps and even illuminated vases and beautiful hanging crystal lustres.

Cecilia broke first, making her way down to her waiting husband, Lord Thomas, while I joined Elizabeth in her shimmering gown and matching tiara, both the exact shade of purple periwinkles.

Soon we were all – yes, all 700, for Cecilia was determined to make this event the one people would be talking about all season – enjoying a raucous, deafening standing supper, spread across the dining room and one reception room. The banquet was delicious, and of course pineapples were displayed on each table, grown in the estate's hothouse at great expense. All was served on a mix of French and English plate which showcased the wealth of Cecilia and Lord Thomas, and even the wines were of the finest vintage available, so that no one could be left in doubt at the hosts' fortune. If they could serve such quality produce to such a huge number of people, it could only be imagined how much finer the fare was when it was only they two.

By the time the food was done, it was nine o'clock, and everyone was in high spirits. Even Elizabeth. The orchestra struck up, and as I handed my friend a glass of champagne, her toes tapped in time with the reel and her eyes sparkled like the contents of her glass. We circulated, smiling and nodding to some we passed, stopping to converse with others. Across one of the ballrooms (for the event was so large that two of the rooms had been given over entirely to dancing) I spied a crowd of fluttering fans. At its centre must surely be an eligible bachelor, marooned in a sea of mothers pointing out their unmarried daughters' best assets. I glimpsed the object of their attention. Something about the way he moved, coupled with the deep green, high-waisted jacket that showed off his fashionably tight black trousers, made me recognise Mr Coutts, despite his mask.

Of a sudden, our eyes met. He raised an eyebrow so high it arched over the top of the golden mask that banded across his eyes, and gave a *Mona Lisa* smile before returning to the conversation swirling about him. Was this charming peacock a link between the evil Sir John and the orphans that he was rumoured to be procuring, according to Sarah, for his nefarious deeds?

'Estella, is that Colonel Magrew and his daughters? It's so hard to tell who is who with their masks, but I believe it is!' Elizabeth's voice cut through my thoughts, and soon we were swept along once more, past bright chandeliers and dark corners.

Everyone seemed more comfortable, more themselves, behind their masks, or secreted in dim corners of the room. That came as no surprise to me, daughter of darkness that I am. In the brightness of day there is nowhere to hide. No room for intrigue, scandal, or gossip; such things wither beneath the sun. It is at night they blossom. In the shadows people feel safer, more hidden, and thus more able to drop their daytime performance of what other people think they should be... and become their true selves. The masks of polite society are easier to cast off when faces are hidden by physical masks.

The floor shook with dancing, the music flew through the room, everywhere people were talking and laughing and fanning themselves, red skin showing around their masks. Hours flew by as we explored. There was so much to see and do and discover. Outside, the air nipped deliciously after the oven heat produced by hundreds of bodies, but still there were crowds watching the entertainments on the lawns. A contortionist had us all scratching our heads in amazement. A gasp of oohs and ahhs went up as a man juggled fire. A great plume of it appeared as he blew like a dragon – and then he swallowed it! Further away from the house stood bronzed people, standing like statues, and moving stance only occasionally – just in time to make those walking by shriek in surprise.

Elizabeth was growing tired. I escorted her back inside the house and found her a seat with some acquaintances, before leaving her for another walk through the shifting multitude.

Eventually I discovered the library, which was set up with card tables, for those who wished for a break from the exertions of dancing through the night. It was there that I espied Mr Coutts again. He smiled across the several people between us.

'Would you like a drink?' he mouthed, and did a little mime, perhaps supposing that I was Cecilia.

I shook my head and tried to move on, but he was strolling towards me.

A woman with shining red cheeks and a glazed smile waved her almost but not quite empty punch glass in the air, in time to the music, and some of the contents sloshed onto Coutts' jacket. He arrived by my side dabbing at himself with his kerchief.

'You do love to gain notice for your attire wherever you go, don't you?' I said. My gaze slid from him to the rest of the room.

'Ah, Mrs Drummle. I thought it was you, but could not be certain whether it was your twin, our lovely hostess. As for your question, I must answer: I do,' he admitted.

I did not reply.

'I am rather partial to standing out from the crowd, sartorially.'

I pretended to start in surprise. 'Hmm? Oh, I didn't see you there! I thought you had gone.'

His chuckle was warm, despite my ribbing.

'You have managed to escape the marriage-makers,' I added.

'Heaven save me from them. I have no desire to marry again.'

'Again?'

He studied the contents of his glass and drained it before replying. 'My wife. She died birthing our daughter.'

So that was who he had lost. I had thought he talked too eloquently of grief to not have suffered it himself.

'I am sorry. You did not mention her before—'

'No,' he cut in, voice sharp. He looked around, swallowed. 'No, because... Because I...'

Mr Blincoe appeared, hurrying to his master's side like an obedient hound. He seemed a little flustered, but said nothing.

Still trying to gauge Coutts, I attempted to find out more about his business. Was it really fabrics? It seemed so, for the man knew as much about materials as I – more, in fact.

'Mrs Drummle, you do not wish to get into this business, surely,' he said at last, in a most decided manner. 'I assure you it is not for you. I could never allow it.' He seemed to freeze for a beat, before adding in far more reasonable tone: 'Although I would never say never.'

'Your moods are so changeable you put Mercury to shame. How goes things with Sir John? He has a reputation for being a sharp man of business; does he live up to it?'

Coutts' head tilted. His fingers went to his right sideburn and stroked the hairs. The pause stretched on.

'He is a determined man,' he replied at last. 'He is more of a businessman than I ever could be.'

'Even with your successes?'

Was it my imagination, or did he tug the hairs of his sideburn in discomfort?

'I—'

Blincoe spoke for the first time. 'Mr Coutts is being modest. Both he and Sir John are towers of industrial greatness.'

'Towers? My word, that is terribly impressive.' I tried my best not to smirk.

Bells rang, just as the orchestras stopped playing. A master of ceremonies announced it was time for refreshments to be served. That meant it was already two in the morning. I must away.

The crowd swayed and swelled like a sea, and I allowed the waves to carry me from Mr Coutts and his clerk of business. As everyone queued to help themselves to tables groaning with soups and savoury dishes, ices and confectionery, and grapes, peaches and nectarines grown in the hothouses, I made my way to the stables, pulled on a large travel cloak hidden there earlier, and saddled up the finest horse I could find.

Time for Sir John to get his comeuppance.

As fireworks exploded in the sky, I rode like the storms that hit the Kent coast of my childhood, fierce and fast and unforgiving.

CHAPTER THIRTY

My nerves jangled like the keys on a chatelaine as I rode through the familiar grounds leading to Wynterton Manor. It was about fifteen miles from the ball in Essex to Wynterton, just over the Suffolk border. There was no real plan in place. I carried a bottle of poison, hoping I could find Sir John asleep and put it into his bedside water carafe. If people assumed he had died from old age it might be easier for Elizabeth to accept. Even so, a knife nestled in my pocket, in case a more physical solution was required.

Could I really kill in a cold and calculated manner, though? Even if it was someone who was so perverse and evil? I had to. If I told the authorities about him, left him to face more usual means of justice, I could not guarantee that someone of his wealth and power would not simply pay off investigators, and buy his freedom. If I did not act, nothing would change. He would go on attacking girls. Elizabeth would remain in mortal danger.

However the night played out, Sir John must meet justice – and if that meant I died in the attempt, or was caught and hanged, so be it; I would pay the price willingly.

In order to slay a monster it is sometimes necessary to become one oneself.

Yet my hands trembled while tethering my horse in the wooded glade near the house. As I walked to the monstrous, hotchpotch house which crouched low, waiting to pounce on me, I noticed a light blazing. All else was in darkness, and no one seemed to stir. Through the window, I saw Sir John in his study, his feet upon his desk while he read a book. There was a large golden rose embossed on the cover, and I imagined it might be about growing roses, as he adored gardening. Suddenly, he jumped up and walked past a stuffed tiger that seemed surprised to have found himself beside a roaring fire in merry England,

and climbed a ladder, presumably searching for another book on his shelves.

I hurried to the neighbouring room's window. Where the two wooden frames of the sash window slid over each other, was a crack that was wide enough for me to force my knife into. I jiggled the blade, felt it click against the latch, and forced it across until the latch clicked open. A firm push and the sash dropped into the open position. Giving thanks for the ease of movement afforded by my servant-boy costume, I climbed inside.

I pressed my ear against the study door. Grunting and shuffling noises. It sounded as if Sir John was still up the ladder, but what if I was wrong? Biting my lip, I eased the door open…

There he was, back to me, atop the ladder, flipping through a book. A dissatisfied tut, and the book was slotted back into place. I slipped into the room and crept closer as he continued his search.

'Found you!'

I jumped at his exclamation. He had seen me! But no, he was reaching for another book, balancing on one foot, his body at a dangerous angle.

He teetered. Arms windmilled.

That was my chance. I ran full pelt, Mother seeming to ride on my shoulder, urging me forward with a battle cry. Straight into the ladder I went, pushing it with all my might. It slipped from beneath him and the old man tumbled through the air. His foot connected with my ribcage, sending me careening back, falling on my rump with a thud that jolted up my spine, making me cry out.

At the same time, there was a crack. Sir John's head connected with the large marble mantel. The twin dogs carved either side of the fireplace glared down at him, hellhounds disappointed not to have a new playmate – for Sir John was not killed, only stunned.

He sat up, rubbing the back of his head.

I pulled my cloak closer about me so that he could not see my boy's garb, and hurried forward.

'Are you quite all right? That was a nasty slip!'

'What—?' He winced. Tried to push himself up.

'Just a moment, let me get you something to drink. Here, this brandy will help.' It was a generous double, with a large helping of poison.

'Estella, what-what are you doing here? Are you and Elizabeth returned?' He gave a little yelp. 'Damnation, that hurts!'

'Drink up, it will help your head.' It would permanently relieve it.

He took another gulp while I picked up his book. Why did he adore his rose garden so? Of course, even the worst people needed a hobby; I myself found great comfort in knitting. I thought of the rose bushes, lovingly tended, protected by a high wall all around the garden. It was the place where Sarah had been attacked.

'Better? Now, I think we need to get help, for look, there is quite a bump forming. Come.'

He got to his feet, unsteady from the blow, and took the opportunity to put his arm about my waist.

'Bentley... Bentley is a lucky fellow, eh?'

'And I can hardly believe Elizabeth's luck.'

Between the concussion, the alcohol and the poison, he was surprisingly pliant as I opened up the French doors and we stepped into the cold night air.

'Why are we in the garden?' His voice was slower than usual.

'Just a little further. We don't want the servants to see their master so weakened, do we now?'

He nodded, but it was slow and a little line appeared between his eyes, questioning. But a man such as Sir John would never truly believe that I, a mere woman, would act against him. Still, he looked around the garden where we stopped and his hands fluttered up to his neck and pulled at his necktie.

'Why are we here?' He swayed to one side. I needed to act fast. Still, I could not help toying.

'Your rose garden is a pretty spot, is it not? So quiet and secluded from the main house. No one can see us here, no matter which window they look from, and not even if they were taking the air in the garden.'

A high red-brick wall ran around all four sides of it, and the only access was through a neat green-painted wooden door, recessed into the wall. Apple trees grew beside the wall, adding further height, and in front of them were the rose bushes and flower beds in pretty patterns. In the centre was a fountain within a stone bowl that was edged with carved roses and leaves. There were so many rose bushes, and although most no longer bloomed, some still had flowers despite the lateness of the season. It made my stomach clench and my skin tingle. Over to the left was one that was freshly planted, with soil only recently turned. That was where we would start.

I turned to him. 'Roses are the flowers of love, friendship, even mourning, are they not? Now, dig!'

'Madame, what are—'

'You have dug here before. Dug deep. Numerous times now, I believe, and you've even planted a rose bush over each spot, if my guess is correct. Tell me, were they randomly chosen, or do the different colours have meaning?'

He huffed and turned to walk away but it was easy to catch his shoulder and spin him back. His feet seemed to tangle and he folded to the floor, eyes wide. Tried to stand. Tried to push himself up using his hands. No use. He flapped them in the air, a toddler about to have a tantrum.

'Help me up, woman. Don't just stand there.'

He saw the knife in my hand then, pulled from my pocket, and screamed. Although he was so weakened by the blow to his head and the poison leeching through his blood, it still echoed into the air and made me hiss in frustration. Pressing the blade against his neck, we waited, both panting, but tense, breathing in unison as we waited for discovery.

There came no sound of running feet.

Putting my mouth so close to his ear that the long hairs sprouting from it tickled my lips disgustingly, I whispered. 'There is no one to hear you, Sir John. Your staff all lie in a deep slumber – thanks to a little help from me.'

This time when I told him to dig, he crawled forward and obeyed. Cadaver fingers sinking into thick, fleshy earth.

'My hands,' he cried. 'It hurts. Have pity on me.'

'Your death will be quick if you comply. If not, I will bleed you slowly.' I flourished the knife. 'Continue.'

All the time he whimpered. He had not the strength to shout again. At last he formed quiet words as the hole he created widened and deepened.

'Is this to be my grave?'

'Perhaps. It is beautiful here… but no beauty can make up for a life cut short, can it?'

'Have mercy, I pray you. Why are you doing this? What have I ever done to you?'

'To me? Why nothing, sir. But you know what you have done to others.'

'I-I… It is a man's duty to keep women in line. To—'

I pressed the blade against his lizard-fleshed neck just hard enough to illicit a gasp. He renewed his digging. But his movements were increasingly sluggish. It was almost time and I grew worried that I was wrong about this garden…

Another prod of the knife made him scrabble deeper, faster, and finally something was revealed in the mud. Something white.

The bloodless face of Nora.

CHAPTER THIRTY-ONE

There she lay, my little starling. There was no mistaking those fine, sharp features.

Rain began to patter down on all three of us in that dark rose garden: fat drops, that seemed to detonate on the ground. Nora's face was soon washed clean, her once shrewd, now cloudy eyes stared up at the stars, sightless. I reached down and gently closed the lids. My fury was the white heat at the centre of a furnace, capable of melting metal to liquid. I feared it would be my undoing. It took several breaths before I regained control enough to speak.

Sir John shrank back at the sight of the lifeless serving girl and gave a mewling cry.

'Are you afraid?' I asked. 'Are you as afraid as she was?'

No answer.

'Girls go missing in the middle of the night, and it's covered up because, as awful as it is, it's not unusual for a master to take advantage that way. But that's only because the remaining servants imagine the girls run away after what you have done.' I shook my head. 'The truth is far worse, though, isn't it? As if rape were not bad enough... you also murder.'

When Joseph had been unable to track down any of the other girls on the list, I had hoped I was wrong. Hoped my own monstrous imagination was creating fears that were not real. Perhaps the drilling from Mother to never trust anyone, to despise men and always think the worst of them had given me an intuition for such things, or perhaps it was the treatment I had received at the hands of my own husband – those terrible, endless nights as he had forced himself on me and almost killed me with his brutality.

My animal instinct had brought me to the rose garden. Discovering that the gardener had been a saviour rather than sinner had made me think over all our encounters – including our first, when he had barred Elizabeth and me from entering the rose garden. Fear had made him sound aggressive as he spoke to us. As I had realised that, I had come to a second conclusion: if I were to bury a body at Wynterton, I would have chosen the seclusion of the rose garden.

Being proved correct in all surmises was the worst feeling in the world. Nora's face was devoid of all her nervous giggles and determined concentration, slack after being robbed of her soul. Tears gathered but I swallowed them down, though they stuck in my throat. There would be time for crying later.

The garden was wall-to-wall filled with rose bushes. There were so many more than there were names on Bellis' list. Surely they could not all mark the graves of girls? If they did, then he had been doing this for far longer than anyone had known.

'When did you begin? Was it frustration at being too old to journey to Africa and bag more big cats? Was it your butterfly hunting that gave you the idea of how to net a larger prey?'

'I'm as shocked as you at this discovery,' he slurred. All I saw in his expression was self-pity.

'I've been wondering how Nora could be snatched so easily, so silently. Then I realised: the chloroform. You put it on a handkerchief, did you not, and then covered her nose and mouth with it so that she was incapacitated in seconds. You've still strength for your age, thanks not only to all the gardening but this other hobby of yours, and so were able to carry her into the neighbouring room, close the door before I was even out of bed to check on her. But how did you move her body about the house without being seen?'

With a snarl, he lunged at me. Punching the back of my knees to try to make my legs give way. How easily I shook off this killer of women.

'Think of how scared those poor maids were,' I continued. 'I tracked down one who escaped you, but here lie the ones who died at your hands. What was her name?' I nodded to a bone-white dome of a skull that had been uncovered alongside Nora's remains.

'I... It was an accident!'

'Her name.' The bite in my voice made him jump, but the pressure of the knife against his skin produced a reply.

'I don't know! Please!'

143

'Did she beg, too? Did you listen? Show her mercy?' A cloud of confusion passed over his white, pock-marked, moon-like face. I kicked him. He huffed and fell face down. 'Of course you didn't. What were their names?'

'I'm... I can't... Mary! I think one of them was Mary.'

'Mary Turpin. Dollie. Constance. Jemima—'

'Don't you dare mention her!' He slipped around in the sucking mire until he could sit upright again, the rain pattering down on him.

'Why does she—?' It took a heartbeat for me to realise. 'Your second wife. You...? Is hers the one life you regret taking? What happened – did she find out what you were and confront you? Is that why you drowned her?'

'Lies! She was threatening to speak to her brother about me. He was a duke, he could have had me hanged, the stupid woman. She forced me to kill her!'

His own wife! Thank goodness he had not raised a hand to my friend, although surely it would only have been a matter of time.

'Dyllis Evans. Jessica. Jane. Olive. Say their names.'

He tried. Got muddled. I put my foot on his chest and with a shove he fell backwards into the mud with a soft splat.

'Betsy. Lily Batley. Nora. I want you to say them all.'

I repeated the names. He got two right, no more. Cried, rubbing his knuckles into his eyes so that his tears made tracks in the muck he had smeared all over himself.

'Nora. Say Nora's name. Tell me what you did to her.'

'The girls, they are nothing. Their lives would be wasted anyway, so why should they not be made useful?' he whined. 'Don't tell anyone. I can make it worth your while.'

'Sir John, I solemnly promise I won't tell a soul.'

Hope blossomed in his eyes, features relaxing as he lay on his back in the filth, his head between Nora and the skull of one of his victims.

'I will be generous, good lady.' Sir John's voice was soft with relief and something more. He clutched at his stomach and gave a soft gasp of discomfort.

'No payment necessary,' I replied. 'We will both take this secret to the grave. Here.'

Lifting the skull free from its resting place I handed it to him. He took it and stared stupidly at it. Cradled it to him.

'I-I-I'm dying, aren't I?' he gasped.

'Realisation comes at last.'

'Come-come closer. There is something you need to know.' His voice was barely a whisper. I knelt down...

A hawking sound. A gob of spit landed on my cheek. Sir John laughed, his whole body shaking with mirth. 'Think you can outwit us, little star?' he hissed.

I flinched at the endearment Bentley used for me when he was at his most violent. Had he told Sir John what he had done to me? I found myself tugging my cloak closer about me, to shield myself from this vile man. Still he laughed, weak but hysterical, tears running down his cheeks. My stomach warped and roiled. The urge to stamp my heel down on him and crush him was overwhelming, my foot raised—

Wait. What had he said? *Us.*

'There's more of you.'

His laughter turned into a cough that had him curling in on himself. Bloody spittle spattered his lips.

'We make quite the little club, I and my friends of similar... appetites. Get rid of one of us and two more spring up. Like pulling weeds,' he wheezed. 'You think you can change the world by taking my life, Estella? Females exist to be used by us – it is our God-given right.'

My worst fears were realised. Sir John was not acting alone; he was part of some horrifying club of like-minded men.

'Who is in your club? Who supplies you with the girls?'

He lay back in the soil, a beatific smile on his face, giving in to the encroaching embrace of never-ending sleep. I slapped him.

'Who supplies you? Is it Coutts?'

He muttered something that sounded like 'Fool'.

'If I'm such a fool why am I still standing, while you die?'

He was right, though: I was a fool. Too much time had been spent gloating instead of questioning him.

'Sir John! Tell me!'

A heavy nod. He curled on his side, still holding the skull to his chest. His eyelids fluttered. Closed. His breathing growing deeper.

'You will never get away with this.'

It was a clarion call of discovery. I spun around as Mrs Switchley stepped from the shadows.

CHAPTER THIRTY-TWO

Mrs Switchley's expression was not shocked or angry, it was appraising as she stood on the puddled path. Her gaze travelled slowly, taking in the full scene before her.

My coming days flashed through my mind's eye: arrest, baying crowds, disgusted looks as I glared from the dock, the judge sentencing me to death speedily so he could get back to dozing, the sound of the trapdoor opening, the drop as the floor disappeared beneath my feet, then the dance of the hanged... I saw all as I pulled myself straight, for I would not cower like someone who felt guilt at their actions.

More movement from the shadows. A slight rustle. Out stepped Worthybrook and Bellis.

I was caught red-handed. Cornered. Outnumbered. There were too many to fight, but I crouched anyway, my knife balanced in my hand, ready for battle.

'You will never get away with this,' Mrs Switchley repeated. Her face twitched into a momentary sneer of disgust. 'Alone.'

A surprised breath escaped me and hung in the cold air.

I thought of Mrs Switchley, telling me about how young she was when she arrived at the house.

'Wide-eyed and stupid I was, with no idea of how the world worked, but I took the lessons I was given, and I learned quickly.'

At the time I had missed the significance of her words. Standing in that garden of death, it seemed all too obvious. She was a victim. She had learned to survive the awful lessons doled out in Wynterton.

Elizabeth had mentioned that the young Mrs Switchley had suffered some sort of breakdown – Sir John must have been the reason why.

In fact, Elizabeth had told me her housekeeper's given name.

'Constance,' I breathed. How foolish of me not to have remembered it earlier, for it featured on the gardener's list. I had not associated the names of Constance or Jemima from the list with two adults, for I had been so fixated on *young girls* vanishing. 'What happened?'

'Exactly what you think,' she said. 'I was lucky; at least I survived. He was still honing his craft back then, and had not yet become a killer.' Her back remained ramrod straight, her voice stern. How I admired her control, because I knew myself how much it took to maintain that façade.

'Why did you stay here?'

'To stop what happened to me happening to others. Sir John's mother showed me such kindness after the death of my parents, and when she realised what her son was doing to me every night she stepped in to protect me, so it would never happen again.'

Sir John had told a different tale to Elizabeth, one that made him sound like a hero stepping in to stop young Constance being sent to an orphanage, while his mother opposed the idea. How typical of an abuser to paint themselves in a flattering light, when the truth was all ugly shadows. While his mother had wanted only to protect, he had seen a chance to take advantage.

'I loved Sir John's mother as if she were my own. She promised me a home, even wrote it into her will, but in exchange I must keep an eye on Sir John and protect the family name. I would have stayed anyway. I have done my best over the years to limit his access to the young girls but—'

'There is only so much you can do.'

'He is the devil incarnate.'

'And he never hurt you again?'

'Even after her death, he was too afraid of his mother to act against her wishes. Eventually, I became too old for his tastes. Rather than get rid of me, he found it safer to keep me close and promote me as a reward for what he saw as loyalty to the family.' Her upper lip pulled into a sneer of disgust that he could think her a colluder. 'I do my best to keep the girls away from him as much as possible, watch over them as they work upstairs, and ensure they get safely below stairs as quickly as possible. So many times I have wanted to go to the magistrates, but Sir John is friends with them all. You know, he was in the court of George the Third briefly? With those connections, if someone speaks out against him it will be they who are punished, not he.'

'I most assuredly would not attempt it.'

'And yet look what you have done. Eliminated the problem. Perhaps I should have simply done this instead... I do not think I could have.'

For a moment I could not meet her eye.

'To work,' she said in that decided fashion she used for her underlings.

Throughout our exchange, Bellis and Worthybrook had neither spoken nor stirred. At Switchley's word, they moved forward, holding garden spades.

'Bury Sir John—'

'No,' I urged. 'I want him and all of his victims to be discovered, so that people know his true nature. The families of the missing will at last discover the fate of their loved ones.'

'Then should we uncover more?' asked Bellis.

'Perhaps just one more, further away, so that it is obvious what feeds these roses,' I said. 'But what of the rest of the staff? I've drugged some with laced whisky, but might we be discovered by any who haven't partaken?'

Worthybrook spoke. 'Those of the household servants you did not drug with your generous gifts have orders from me that will keep them out of the way.'

'I've taken care of the groundsmen who usually check the grounds through the night,' said Bellis, as he dug. 'I got them riled up about not receiving a gift, and so we all had a protest drink or two, while complaining loudly about favouritism. They all got drunk.' He leaned on his spade and pointed at the ground. 'Here's another. May she rest in peace now, at last.'

We hung our heads in silence for a moment before the housekeeper spoke. 'I am here to ensure you tidy up after yourself, so no one will know what you have done.'

'Then come closer.' I beckoned. 'Take a moment longer and watch a sort of justice be served.'

We stood over Sir John, who was curled up, cuddling the skull like a child does a favourite toy. Mrs Switchley pulled a small looking glass from her skirt pocket and held it to his face. It did not cloud.

'When he is found in the morning, everyone will know his secrets,' I said. 'If they investigate this garden further, I believe they will find the remains of all the missing girls apart from Sarah Monkton – who escaped thanks to you, Bellis.'

He growled quietly. 'And his poor wife, Jemima. She lies at the bottom of the lake because of him. I saw Sir John push her from the boat and watch her drown, weighted down by her sodden, heavy skirts. I jumped in and tried to save her, but it was too late. When I came out of the lake, Sir John was crawling along the ground having some kind of attack. Wish I'd let him die, but I didn't even think of it.' He shook his head, appalled by his instinctive act of charity. 'That's how I got embroiled in all of this.'

So that explained why the gardener had become involved, and why he had compiled the list of Sir John's known victims.

Switchley took up the story. 'We suspect that Jemima had discovered his secret and confronted him. Knowing her nature, I believe she would have given him the opportunity to do the honourable thing and confess to the authorities. It was the last thing she did.'

'Can I trust you all to keep my secret?' I asked.

The housekeeper inclined her head in that regal way of hers, answering for them all. All she said was, 'We must get rid of our footprints.'

Bellis tore some branches from a nearby bush and we set to, using them as brushes to sweep away all signs of our presence.

'The dumb waiters,' the housekeeper said suddenly, as she swept. 'You asked him how he moved the girls, and it was via the dumb waiters, once they were insensible. He would transport them down to the abandoned part of the manor on the ground floor.' *That dark corridor with its animal-like aroma and dread atmosphere.* 'No one goes there but him. It affords him the privacy he desires – desired.'

Another thread woven into the picture.

We straightened up and surveyed our work. Only Sir John's footprints could now be seen. My accomplice consulted her pocket watch.

'The scullery maids will be laying fires soon. You need to leave.'

'Can you keep everyone away from his office for a little while longer? Since childhood I have been a skilled mimic of people's handwriting. I need to forge a suicide note in Sir John's hand so that people believe he destroyed himself because he was filled with remorse.'

A snort of derision. 'That man?'

But she set off at a rapid pace towards the house, all business, and I followed.

In Sir John's office, while I forged a confessional letter from Sir John, I told Mrs Switchley to search the room.

'I need to try to find paperwork – Sir John said there were others like him. I believe there is a sort of club of them who share his tastes. Do you know about this?'

She swayed in shock at my words, but stayed upright. Finally, she shook her head. 'He always left the hiring of the female staff to me. I have done my best to take on older women who were less to his tastes, and was strict about always working in pairs, and not loitering above stairs…' As she spoke, she moved around the room, opening drawers and searching meticulously.

'None of this is your fault,' I said gently.

'In the last couple of years he began hiring many of the staff himself. They seemed to be orphans.' She looked at me and for a moment in her wide eyes I saw through the cracks to the real Mrs Switchley. Horrified, traumatised, helpless. Fighting to keep Sir John's evil at bay must have felt like King Canute trying to hold back the tide. 'For the most part they seemed to be from Kent and Essex.'

'We need to find anything that might tell us where these orphans are from exactly, or who might be in this group of like-minded men to which Sir John referred. Anything that can help us stop this from happening elsewhere.'

With a final flourish for his signature, I finished Sir John's letter explaining how old age and a lifetime of evil had finally caught up with him and made him destroy himself. Then I joined the housekeeper in her search, and asked again if I could trust her and the men. Switchley had experienced abuse at Sir John's hand, but not they. Why should they stay silent?

'Don't forget Brock Bellis witnessed Sir John's murderous evil not once but twice. As for Worthybrook' – her face softened in a most uncharacteristic way – 'we have been friends for many years. Soon after joining the staff he began to suspect my history… When I shared the truth, he tried to become my protector. He would marry me, if it were possible, but I could never do such a thing. If it were with anyone, it would be him, though. Instead, he has helped me look after all the girls as much as we can. But it is harder than ever now. We hoped Sir John would slow with age, but he seemed even more crazed these last few years. Ah, here!' She held aloft a handful of papers. 'They are receipts for fabrics from Mr Coutts, but see how the amounts don't tally with the goods.'

I looked at where she pointed on the bill. 'That's extortionate. It simply cannot be for the fabrics listed, even if they were cloth of gold.'

It was not proof positive, but it was enough to make me beyond suspicious that Coutts was involved. The question was how? From these invoices it seemed that he might be supplying the girls, but I could not be certain. What was the link between Coutts' factory, orphans, and this terrible crime?

CHAPTER THIRTY-THREE

I t was easy to insinuate myself back into the crowded ball without gaining anyone's notice. Everyone's cheeks were red, eyes bright, the chatter loud, and music filled the air. The chalked dance floors teemed with revellers as the orchestra played that old favourite, 'The Regent's Medley'. Every dropped pendant on the chandeliers, every gem adorning hair, throats, bodices, every raised glass sparkled in the candlelight. Cheers and laughter came from the card room. Outside, a group of people were singing.

I was a different creature than the one who had left, however. No matter how dark my imaginings had been regarding Sir John, it was different to see it with my own eyes.

So many lives never lived. So much potential snuffed out.

Bellis and Worthybrook had agreed to 'discover' the body of Sir John at the start of the working day. Mrs Switchley would accompany a scullery maid into Sir John's office and find the suicide note. Then at last, the true story of what had happened to those girls would come out. They would be given a decent burial and laid to rest as they deserved.

I picked up a delicious elderberry-flower flavoured ice to cool me, for even though it was a chilly night I was hot after that ride, and so exhausted that I felt I could happily curl up where I stood, and sleep for a week. The ride had given me time to berate myself: if only I had not got so emotional in the rose garden I could have got so much more information from Sir John. Anger had made me stupid.

'Mrs Drummle!' Mr Coutts appeared by my side, his eyes merry behind his emerald-green mask.

My stomach turned at the sight of him. If only Mrs Switchley and I had found solid evidence against him, but he and Sir John were too clever for that. While the impossibly expensive bills for fabrics were highly suspicious, they were not proof enough to either stand up in court, or persuade me – yet – to dispatch him.

Beside Coutts was Mr Blincoe, who looked about himself as if overwhelmed. Why on earth had Coutts dragged the poor man with him to this?

'How are you faring?' he asked. 'I kept thinking I saw you, but it was always our gracious hostess, Lady Forfar. Oh, you have some mud on your face. May I?'

He wiped my cheek with his handkerchief.

'Sir, you overstep the mark.' My heartbeat was loud in my ears. His touch disgusted me, but if I was going to get to the bottom of the mystery, I was going to have to work harder at my acting skills. I cursed myself for not checking my appearance properly. My travel cloak had protected me from the rain and mud, so my serving-boy costume did not appear suspiciously grubby, but how foolish of me to forget my face.

'My apologies—'

'Nonsense, it gives me the perfect opportunity to overstep with you. Would you allow me to visit your manufactory? Where is it located, I forget.'

He threw a look Blincoe's way, then back at me. 'A woman as *decorative* as yourself should be satisfied to fulfil that purpose alone. A lady's role is to be beautiful not practical.'

'Like a vase? Or a brooch?' I suggested.

'I rather think I may retire soon.' His voice was curiously small as he made the desperate attempt to change the subject.

'And admit defeat, sir? I may be as much use as a vase, yet my staying power is stronger than yours.' It had to be. I needed people to see me, as the ball was my alibi if the finger of blame were ever pointed at me.

Killing Sir John had been neither easy nor hard, it had simply been necessary, for had I not acted, he would have gone on murdering innocents. Nevertheless, it had wrought a permanent change in me. The first time I had killed could almost be excused as being in the heat of the moment. This time had been executed with cold-blooded aforethought. It was as if I had stepped through a door and was now in a different room from most other people, and my life would always be split into before and after. This is how villains are made, one wrong-doing after another, each slightly worse than the last. What I would be by the time I came to the end of my life was something I dared not consider.

Had it been worth it? Yes. I would never forget all those young women, targeted by Sir John, a devious man who hunted them the way he had hunted big game on the continents. Nora would stay with me for the rest of my life, I knew. She should have been training to be my lady's maid, making silly mistakes and laughing at them. Not lying in a shallow grave.

But even as one mystery had been solved another far more complex had opened up before me.

For all the heat of the ball, I felt a chill through my body because it was not normal to be so calm and rational in the face of taking a life. My existence was spent in darkness, no matter how much I tried to live in the light. Perhaps I brought the shadows with me. Beside me was a knot of young women in bright-hued tones as pretty as a posy of flowers, talking quietly and sharing confidential smiles. Was it better to be innocent like them? And therefore be possible victims? Or to be like me and find darkness even where no one else suspected it existed?

I would rather be a devil, I decided, if it meant being able to vanquish far worse ones.

My feet began to tap to the music. 'Would you think it rather forward of an old married lady to ask for a dance?'

Mr Coutts looked astonished, then recovered. 'It would be an honour.'

'Actually, I have just espied Elizabeth. Would you ask her, instead?'

Coutts was the perfect gentleman, dancing not one but two strathspeys with my friend. She deserved some happiness before her world was shattered. Besides, it gave me an opportunity to study Mr Coutts, much like those in the marriage mart – but my reasons could not have been more different. I was in horrified awe at how well he hid his cunning behind a vacuous charm.

By half past six, many of the attendees were retiring. For those who remained, an elegant *dejeune* was served of tea and coffee and drinking chocolate, along with some light morsels. Elizabeth and I took our refreshments with Cecilia, who was radiant with success. Her husband, Lord Thomas Forfar, looked delighted for her, but suggested gently that it might be time to end the party soon. Heads were drooping heavily, all were ready for slumber. I was weak with exhaustion, for it had been a long, hard day, and I sipped my breakfast tea, closing my eyes for a moment when…

A horseman was riding hard up the driveway. All stopped and looked, for he was whipping the horse into giving everything it had and he lay flat along its back. Its eyes rolled, its flanks were covered in foam. The ground trembled through my thin-soled shoes as the hooves pounded.

The messenger boy hauled on the reins, expertly managing the sudden sliding stop of the horse.

'Where is the master of the house?' he asked, leaping down. The butler hurried forward, still adjusting his wig, for he had not been expecting to have to work just yet.

'You have a message for Lord Forfar?' he intoned. To his credit he managed to sound more awake than he looked.

'For him and for all, but most especially for Lady Taykall. Is she here?'

'I am she.' Elizabeth looked at the boy and then at me as if for reassurance. We held hands and together stepped closer, as the murmuring crowd drew into a knot of curiosity.

The boy fell to one knee and bowed his head. 'Grave news. Sir John Taykall is dead.' Elizabeth gasped; her hand tightened on mine. 'And that is not all.'

CHAPTER THIRTY-FOUR

It was almost a pleasure to be back at my London residence. Elizabeth had returned to Wynterton, and both Sir John's son, Winston, and Elizabeth's blood family had gathered around her to protect her from the ensuing scandal. I was no longer needed by her, and so returned to my house to be looked after by the ever-faithful Lydia, my housekeeper, lady's maid and chief secret keeper in one.

I sat on the velvet chair and looked into the mirror of Mother's dressing table, which had been transported from Satis House months earlier, as soon as ever I could arrange it. All my life I had watched Mother peering at her reflection, picking up jewels and trying against her hair or mine, and then setting them down in the exact same place with a sigh so deep it shook her entire body.

With almost as deep an exhalation, I set down the two hatpins in my hands. I had been using them to assault the lock of the box found hidden in Mother's chest of drawers on my last visit to Satis. It simply would not unlock, despite my best efforts. I chose a nail file, and tried again. If I could just...

No, I could not feel the tumblers. I tried again, sticking my tongue out in concentration, as thoughts rose, unbidden.

For some reason I was having trouble sleeping, and could not understand why. It definitely was not remorse for killing Sir John. Why on earth would I feel terrible about taking a life after all he had done? And yet, since taking his life, sleep was hard to find and when it did, my dreams were troubled. Despite Sir John being a monstrous man, killing him had been, for me, another step down a dark path.

Where did my ability to think in such a cold, calculating way come from? I had *known* Sir John had buried those girls in his rose garden because it seemed logical to me. I would never meet my true parents, but perhaps I could get answers about them from someone who had known them: Mr Jaggers. It was not the time for such a personal quest, however.

Above me came a creak and heavy thud, as Bentley moved about the attic which was also his prison cell. Ignoring him, I went at the lock with hearty enthusiasm.

Killing Sir John should have been the end. Instead, I had discovered something far bigger and more terrible was at play, and would not be able to rest until every man involved had paid for their misdeeds against innocents.

The nail file snagged on something inside the lock. My tongue protruded further between my teeth as I carefully twisted it and…

It slipped. Bloody thing. I abandoned the nail file and tried the hatpins again.

Did the other men in Sir John's depraved club employ the girls the way Sir John had? Possibly. More likely was that employing his prey as maids in his own household was a pattern in Sir John's behaviour, and other deviants would be more straightforward. I imagined they had their victims delivered somewhere secure, where they could be safely held, used, and disposed of. Anything else was too risky. Sir John was set in his strange desires, though. He enjoyed watching the girls in his home, like a hunter seeing a doe wandering in a forest glade, thinking itself safe until the crack of the gun fired. Sir John wanted those girls to feel comfortable so that they dropped their guard – putting off his own moment of domination over them, that he might savour it more when it came.

How did I know that? I did not. I felt it. The stalk, the thrill of the chase, the capture and kill. The thoughts came as naturally to me as did other women's thoughts on recipes.

The pins were not strong enough to turn the lock. I tossed them across the dressing table in frustration. Then picked them up and put them back in their usual place, lined up exactly parallel with the other hatpins. The box would remain firmly closed for now.

Leaving it on the dressing table, I stood, swept non-existent dust from my skirts and headed towards the creator of the creaks upstairs. Whether I liked it or not, questions must be asked – and I had never been one to run away from a problem when it could be met head-on.

The attic door swung open to reveal my husband sitting on the edge of the bed. Bentley jumped to his feet; the chain that ran between the wall and the manacle on his ankle clanked at the movement. His whole body quaked as he pulled the lace of his shirt cuff over his hand and wiped from elbow to fingers across his sweating forehead.

Usually he was a sleepy, drooling wreck when I came to give him his next dose, as I liked to keep him always under control. That day he was clammy and agitated, unsurprisingly, because he had been due his laudanum several hours past. I wanted him good and desperate when I spoke to him…

I went to the corner of the room beside the door and settled in the comfortable armchair there. I stared at my husband.

He stared back with red-rimmed, bloodshot eyes. Threw his hands in the air suddenly.

'Lord! Where is it, Estella? Where's my medicine? I need my medicine!'

'Shouting won't get you anywhere, Bentley. You will receive your heart's desire, but first some answers… Tell me about Sir John and those missing girls I was talking to you about the other day.'

The sweat on his face went from a sheen to dripping.

'What girls?'

'Very well.' I stood, started to the door—

'Wait, wait, wait. I do remember you talking about some missing girls. What does Sir John have to do with anything?'

'I never noticed before what a bad actor you are, Bentley. I know all about your relative and the special prizes he keeps buried in his rose garden—'

Bentley's head jerked as if a slap had landed on him.

'There we go. Those girls. Tell me, husband.'

That tall, broad barn of a man gave a curiously high-pitched and girlish laugh, and he licked his lips. 'Sir John will kill me.'

'He will never kill anyone again, now I have dealt with him.'

'Lord! You surprise me, little star.'

'Constantly.' Although Mother had spent my every waking day indoctrinating me to hate men, and although I had violence already growing in my heart, I did not snap and act out until Bentley had done what he did to me in Paris. He wrote the final sentence that changed the story of my life.

I held up the bottle of tincture, so deep brown it appeared almost black. Bentley's eyes snapped on to it.

'I-I don't know anything, really. Never asked – knew just enough to know I did not want to have more knowledge.' He spoke to the laudanum rather than me. 'Sir John's always had very specific taste in that department… Helped himself to the staff. What was the harm?'

In my fury, I slammed the bottle onto the arm of the chair. My husband flinched as if it had been he who was in danger of being crushed beneath my blow rather than the vial, then snarled like a dog. Lunged at me, arms outstretched, fingers clawed, rabid with threats.

'Give it to me, damn it!'

The chain that ran from wall to leg manacle was not long enough for him to reach me. But he could reach his washstand, and his own wooden chair. Snatching up the latter, he held it high above his head then flung it at me, causing me to duck.

Slowly and with great ostentation, I produced a delicate lace handkerchief and wiped his spittle from below my eye. 'You seem to be getting a little overwrought, dear. Perhaps it is best if I leave—'

'No! I beg you! Just give me my medicine—'

'If I poured the precious contents of this bottle onto the floor, could you lick it up fast enough, do you think, before it disappeared between the cracks?' The cork made a little squeal as it came free. I tilted the bottle ever so slightly…

Bentley dropped to his knees, clammy hands slapped together in supplication. 'I'm sorry. I didn't mean it. I'll do anything—'

'Tell. Me. About. The. Girls. Did you force yourself on them, too?'

His nostrils flared at the insult. 'Why would I lower myself? A serving wench? Lord!'

A single dark drop fell onto a floorboard. Bentley whimpered.

'I don't give two hoots of an owl about servants,' he said. 'I took you because you are my wife, and it's my right. It is totally different from what Sir John did. He was in the wrong, of course, and ungentlemanly, even, but it was not my business.'

'Where did he get them from?'

'How should I know?' Another drop fell. 'Estella! Why would I know? I swear on everything I hold dear—'

'You hold nothing dear.'

'My life, then! I swear on my life, may the Lord strike me dead if it's a word of a lie.'

'It is, in my opinion, more than coincidence that the majority of Sir John's victims were orphans,' I said. 'He chose them because they had no one to turn to, and it would be easier to pretend to befriend or terrorise or isolate or whatever he did to get them alone so that he could strike. This makes me wonder... did he get them all from one orphanage? Did the parish beadle or other such person not wonder why he continued to need so many replacements?'

Bentley looked at me, slack-jawed, while I told him this. 'He... I...' He shook his head, as if trying to shake free a memory. 'He did say he had found a man. Someone with connections who could provide him a steady supply. He'd never have to worry again.'

A supply of girls. So it was confirmed. I almost smashed the bottle in fury.

'But he did not reveal who they were. Someone from the criminal underworld, that's all I know.'

'Do you know of others who share Sir John's tastes?'

'It is none of my business.' He sounded exasperated. 'You are missing the point. I do not get involved.'

His pallor was the grey of filthy shirts in want of a laundress. The sweat dripped into his eyes and made them water with the sting. His teeth were chattering as he spoke. He was going from useful desperation to becoming so distressed he was barely coherent.

'Good boy. You've done well.' I poured laudanum into a heavy-bottomed glass. His body sagged in relief. 'Oh! One more thing,' I said.

'Please.' His beg was a whisper of desperation.

'Have you heard of a man named Coutts?'

'The viscount? Isn't he something to do with fabrics? Sells to Sir John, I believe. What about him?'

When asked if that was all he sold, my husband looked confused. He knew nothing of Coutts selling anything else to Sir John. Putting the glass on the floor, I pushed it towards him with a broom kept for exactly this purpose, so that neither Lydia or I were ever within reach. Bentley snatched it up and drank it in one gulp.

'Please, Estella, I want some more.'

He held the glass out to me, eyes as wide as an orphan begging for an extra helping of gruel.

'I have remembered a name,' he said. 'Koblin. When Sir John was boasting about the man who could get him anything or anyone, that's the name he mentioned. I only remember because it sounds foreign, and I said he shouldn't trust foreign types.' He wore an eager smile. 'Did I do well, Estella? Did I earn more medicine?'

'When did he mention this Koblin?'

His eyes darted left, right, up, down. 'I-I don't know! Two years? Eighteen months? A while ago.'

I gave him what he wanted, and left the room as he sank onto the ground, a lazy beam on his face.

There was no such smile on my own.

Two years. That same time frame repeated again and again. That was when Coutts' fortunes had changed dramatically, and when Sir John started procuring orphans from this Mr Koblin. Those two things had to be connected. But how?

There were more girls out there who needed saving from savage men, and if I was going to succeed then I needed to find this Koblin.

If only I had remembered what Nora said about her orphanage, but I recalled nothing about its name or where it was; and perhaps she had never told me. It was more important than ever that Joseph tracked down her sister, Nancy, but it was no easy task. I would also instruct him to start searching for information on Koblin.

As I swept across the hall, I called out to my housekeeper. 'Lydia, I shall be out for several hours.'

'Yes, Miss Estella. A letter arrived for you, while you were with Mr Bentley.' She brought it to me, and as I took it from the silver tray she held, I was struck once more at how she seemed to shrink almost daily with age. What would I do without her?

I turned my attention to the large scrawl on the paper.

Keep your nose to yourself or it might get cut off and buried beneath the roses.

CHAPTER THIRTY-FIVE

My fist clutched the threatening note, crumpling it into a ball. Someone connected to Sir John's club knew of my existence and was determined that my involvement stop there. Unease flickered through me. How did they know about me? Did that mean they knew what I had done to their partner in crime? They must.

Come on, Estella. Chin up.

A whole group of men – killers – knew about me. Had that shadowy figure of the underworld, Mr Koblin, himself written the note? To be able to boast that he could get anything anyone desired, he must have had many connections.

I quaked at the thought. I had done enough already. Some would say more than enough. Perhaps it was time to step away and leave it up to others to finish the job. Whom, though? The authorities? No. Whoever was involved had to have power like Sir John – they were the authorities. Besides, it was unlikely anyone would believe me if I did inform, for I was a mere dunderheaded woman. Prone to hysterics and easily confused.

'Have you seen this?' I showed Lydia and forced a laugh. 'If the senders knew anything about me, they would realise this is going to have the opposite effect.'

My housekeeper looked quite pale. 'Oh, Miss Estella, do take care.'

'Never fear, sweet Lydia. It is time for me to consult one of the most, if not *the* most, famous lawyers in the whole of London.'

The mention of Merryweather Jaggers' name struck fear into the hearts of criminals and judges alike; he made the guilty want to confess to all misdeeds, and the innocent wonder if they were actually guilty after all.

Not I, however.

Mr Jaggers had been Mother's man of business. It had been he who brought me as an orphan of barely three to Mother so that she might adopt me. Growing up with him as a frequent presence in my life had meant he and I had a unique relationship. Instead of feeling interrogated by him, I had by his example learned how to question and intimidate others. He also felt a certain softness of heart, for want of a better phrase, towards me that was not displayed to anyone else in the world, and sometimes when he looked at me I wondered if he was the only person in the world who saw me in all my horrifying reality – and whether he felt some responsibility for the monster Mother had helped forge me into.

Despite a lifetime of shared history, that early morning visit was my first to his office, as I usually summoned him.

At the heart of the office stood a small, skinny man of sprightly demeanour and eyes that twinkled with raven-sharp intelligence.

'Mr Wemmick, chief clerk, at your service.' He gave a brief bow. 'Would I be right in guessing you are Mrs Drummle?'

'Is Mr Jaggers available?' I asked.

'In court, but due to return soon.'

He had the most extraordinarily wooden countenance I have ever seen in my life. There is a saying that came to mind that if someone were to smile, their face would crack. Wemmick was the only person whose countenance I feared might be irreparably damaged if he were ever to try looking genial.

Yet in many ways, that clerk reminded me of another: Mr Blincoe. There were certain mannerisms – a gesticulation of the hand, or turn of phrase – that were similar to Mr Coutts' employee. They even shared a love of jewellery. Wemmick was covered in an eclectic mix of colours and styles of adornments. I recalled Jaggers had once told me that Wemmick collected the jewels from unfortunate clients who were at the gallows, waiting to die.

'They give them to him in gratitude to us,' Jaggers had said as we sat in Satis House, either end of the dining table. Just we two (for Mother refused to eat or drink in front of anyone), the darkness pressing down on us, and only the light of two candles valiantly keeping it at bay.

'Do you take similar payment?' I had asked.

He had wagged his great forefinger at me. 'I do not. Clients pay me to represent them to the best of my ability. That is what I do. No more and no less. And I take not one penny more, for if I did it would open the door to other people begging me to take less.'

Wemmick saw me looking at his array of jewellery. 'My portable property,' he said. No smile threatened to damage him, but his dark eyes twinkled. 'Always keep your investments portable, I say. That way they are always with you to keep an eye on. Although my esteemed employer prefers more traditional business investments.'

Blincoe's own love of jewellery was more curated than Wemmick's, for the cameo, oval mourning ring, and even the adornment that hung from his watch chain were all silver and black, as if he were captured in dark shadow and the light of a full moon, all matched.

Another thing I was certain the two clerks had in common was knowing all about their master's business. So I broached a subject about which I both desired to ask Jaggers and also would rather have scooped my own eyeballs out with a spoon rather than put into words...

'Where is Mr Pip these days?' I enquired.

'I could not say.'

My laugh was light. 'Mr Wemmick, I have known your employer long enough to know that "I could not say" is really "I know but will not tell you". Pray do tell, for I will confess something to you: we are friends from childhood, but the last I heard was that he had lost his fortune and prospects. Surely that cannot be true. If it is, however, I would like to help him.'

The clerk shook his head until his mouth went from straight line to as downturned as a humpback bridge. 'These are not sentiments for the office.'

'Please. At the time of this news I was nursing my mother, and have been in mourning for her since. This is the first opportunity I have had to discover Pip's fate. You see, my mother died feeling that she had done him a terrible wrong, and so now that she has passed, it is up to me to put it right.'

When Pip and I were children, Mother had asked him to visit her every week, ostensibly that she might watch us play together, but in reality it was so I could practise cruelty on his soft, innocent heart. Only when she realised he truly loved me, not long before her death, did she finally comprehend that he had deserved none of the pain inflicted by us both.

Wemmick glanced at the clock, throwing his sharp features into profile. 'I am going on an errand. You are welcome to accompany me.'

He did not wait, but pulled his cloak about his shoulders and set out from the office, dodging through the busy street. When we were a few yards from his place of work he began to talk, without appearing to check whether I was with him – in fact, I was, my feet going nineteen to the dozen beneath my skirts, in order to keep pace.

'It was a bad business all round,' he said, eyes straight ahead. 'I'm telling you this only because Mr Pip himself said you were childhood friends – and strangely all this links back to something that happened to him as a lad of nine. Yes, yes, I'll speak to him, asking him to represent your husband...' This last was directed at a woman who clutched at him, pressing a filthy coin into his hand, her face tracked with tears. 'But it don't mean he'll listen. He's a law unto himself, is Jaggers. And deep as Australia.'

Wemmick did not slow, leaving the woman in the wake of his flapping cloak. Everyone appeared to make way for him, despite the seeming mass of people. He continued to speak as if not interrupted.

'As a young 'un, Pip aided an escaped convict he came across on the marshes. He did it because he was afraid, but the point is the convict – a man called Abel Magwitch – never forgot this act of kindness, for it was the only one he had experienced in a hard life.'

Before I could tell him that I already knew those facts, and had myself briefly encountered Magwitch along with Compeyson that same night, during a truncated attempt to run away from home, Wemmick rapped on the window of a building. It flew open and a head poked out: a boy wearing a mildewed and battered top hat so large that it fell over his eyes. Wemmick pushed a note into the boy's hand, then turned on his heel and set off once more.

'Even when he was transported to Australia, this convict, Magwitch, remembered the boy Pip. And when he made a fortune as a sheep farmer, he sent all his money, anonymously, to Pip that he might become a gentleman. But when Magwitch was caught back in England, all his fortune was forfeited and Pip lost everything.'

His feet moved as fast as his words. A man with a face so crossed in scars that he looked like the back of some messy embroidery threw himself at Wemmick, begging him to speak to Jaggers. 'Justice will be done if he represents me!'

'Caught forging again, eh, Colonel? Well, justice and the law are two separate things, don't confuse 'em. We'll see what the law can do for you once you cough up the fee. It'd be best for you if justice is not brought into proceedings.'

As we moved on, I asked: 'Why on earth had the convict returned to England?' That was a piece of the puzzle that did not make sense to me.

'It was not enough to know that he had raised Pip up, he wanted to see it for himself. He loved the boy, despite their brief encounter. It seemed that he had, you know, taken to him as a father to a child.'

'And so now Pip no longer has a fortune he is back at the forge where he was raised? A blacksmith once more?' Finally I asked what I truly needed to know.

Wemmick spun round. 'Why, no, he's in Cairo. His friend, Mr Herbert Pocket, has taken him on as a clerk in the insurance business. Both moved to Egypt several months ago.'

My steps faltered. Stopped. Pip had left the country, without even saying goodbye?

Wemmick stopped, too. We had come full circle, I realised, and stood once more outside the office. I tried to formulate a reply, but instead stood, wordless, blinking, as the hopes I had hidden in my heart for Pip and me shattered to pieces that seemed to cut with every breath I took. I had thought my dream was to help him, perhaps by offering a role within the Havisham estate as manager or some such. Truly I had not thought it through properly, because – standing on the street outside Mr Jaggers' place of work, I finally realised it – aiding Pip had not been the real motive. No, instead, there had been part of me hoping he would help lead me back from the monster I was becoming. He had always seen the good in me, despite all evidence to the contrary.

The last time he had spoken to me had been to beg me not to marry Bentley, but instead to take his hand in marriage.

'May God forgive you for making this mistake, Estella,' he had cried.

Yet it was Pip's forgiveness I craved. And with him I had hoped to grow the tiny seed of decency within me that only ever flourished when in his company.

There was no one left to save me. Apart from myself – and I did not hold out much hope of that working.

A strong smell of perfumed soap made me turn, and see Mr Jaggers approaching us with long, heavy strides. His appearance was a large black full stop to our conversation, and together we entered the office in silence.

Mr Jaggers was a fury of cleanliness as he stood with his broad back to me, water slopping from a bowl as he scrubbed his hands and nails. The perfume of the soap cleansed the air.

'You have come to my office.' His voice made it sound like an accusation rather than a question.

'Obviously.'

'To what purpose? A lady should not be here, surrounded by criminals – especially not alone.'

'Information. About my heritage. And a game.'

After drying his hands on an unusually large jack towel on a roller inside the door, Jaggers went to washing again. At last he was washed and dried to satisfaction and took a seat behind his paper-strewn desk. His high-backed black chair with its rows of brass nails around it made his expression more severe, if that were possible.

'You seem annoyed,' I observed.

'"Seem" is not a fact.' Jaggers sat back and bit his forefinger. Grey sunlight from the smeared skylight above his head made me squint. I moved my chair. 'What brings you to this place of all places, Estella?'

I slid over a payment, to guarantee my confidentiality. 'It has been some time since we saw one another; the reading of Mother's will was the last time.'

'True. Go on.'

Neither of us liked to give away more than was necessary, which sometimes meant our conversations were more like monosyllabic tennis.

'I have a game for you, or rather, an interesting legal hypothetical. I know you enjoy such discourse.'

It was not a smile, but his eyes definitely warmed, his great bushy eyebrows ceased their beetling and he stopped chewing his finger.

'Let me put a case before you,' said I. 'One of abuse of power and murder most terrible.' I then set out a hypothetical case of a baronet who had been procuring young girls and dispatching them after they had served their horrendous purpose for him.

He grunted. Stood and put one foot on the seat of his chair. 'Your story is inspired by Sir John Taykall, who recently destroyed himself among the bodies of his victims. Deny it.'

'Why would I? The best tall tales are inspired by true life.' I bestowed a smile. Above me, from a top shelf, two death masks appeared most interested in my discourse. 'I put the case that this fabricated baronet, hypothetically speaking only, would be procuring these young girls from somewhere. Most likely one source only.'

'A trusted ally would make sense.'

'And if the ally or allies felt threatened, and knew that someone was in danger of discovering their secret, they might lash out. I ask only for the entertainment, you understand.'

There came a rasping sound as he scratched the strong black stubble of his dark cheek.

'Now I come to the fun part of the game. Where would one seek such a person? Someone who could provide young girls as if they had no value but monetary? Who would sell them into sexual slavery and death, without a thought? Your arms are long and reach far into the underworld.'

'Estella—'

'It is merely a game. That person would need punishing, in the game. Justice would be served – and not necessarily via the law, for we know never the twain shall meet.'

The death mask with an inkblot on his eyebrow was particularly fascinated. I kept catching his eye and wondering what he swung for. And if a similar fate would be mine.

'Estella, I would advise this particular game end.'

'On a completely different subject, I received this. I believe I need to seek out the sender before they come at me.'

I pulled the anonymous note from my pocket and smoothed out the creases as well as possible on Jaggers' desk. He stayed standing as he read it.

Those great eyebrows of his sought each other out. Was it my imagination or did he tremble slightly as his finger returned to his mouth?

And from nowhere, I remembered something...

Mr Jaggers' name had been spoken by someone at Wynterton. Had it been Sir John? Was my trusted lawyer involved?

I looked at him again. And noticed a bead of sweat trickling down the forehead of the usually unflappable Jaggers...

CHAPTER THIRTY-SIX

Mr Jaggers pulled a huge black handkerchief from his pocket and wiped his face as he read the note again. This time he spoke the words aloud. '*Keep your nose to yourself or it might get cut off and buried beneath the roses.*'

'It is such a neat little nose, see?' I tapped a finger on the end of it. 'It would be a shame to lose it. A threatening, anonymous note proves I am on the right track – and also that the person responsible knows somehow that I was the one who dispatched their comrade, Sir John. Hypothetically speaking, of course. How on earth is that possible, though?'

Unless, I added silently, *Mrs Switchley, Worthybrook or Bellis had loose lips, but it seems highly unlikely given that they helped cover up my crime.*

Out loud, I continued. 'And so, I ask you to try to find this theoretical individual or group who deal in the sale of young girls to despicable men, and who have absolutely nothing to do with sending this note – for why would they have reason to send me such a thing?'

My tone was light. My expression as full of steel as the blade I kept with me always.

Mother's words swirled about my mind, the ones she had made me repeat every day from the age of three. 'Never love. Never trust. Always strike first.'

While I did not love Merryweather Jaggers, he was someone to whom I turned automatically. While Mother had been ruled utterly by her heart, the head was sovereign for Mr Jaggers. In many ways he was as close to a father figure as I had ever had, and he had taught me much about evaluating people and situations. Even so, his evident discomfiture on this subject planted some doubt that perhaps I should trust him a little less, and instead, when dealing with him, should use the lessons he himself had taught me.

'I will not help you in this, Estella,' he said. 'My expert advice would be to do as the note suggests. There is nothing to gain in pursuing this game.' His emphasis on the word 'game' was heavy as a crypt door closing.

I pulled my fan out and snapped it open, fluttering it before my face to obscure my expression. 'No? Not even if I gave you a name to investigate? That of Koblin?'

He did not flinch or blink. Although that meant little when dealing with Jaggers.

'Very well. You know best.' I would have to rely on Joseph's investigations instead. 'There was another matter, however – you recall I wanted information as well as a game?'

'Be swift. I am due back in court soon.'

'Straight to it, then: tell me about my parentage.'

'They are dead to everyone who walks this earth.'

'That does not prevent you from telling me anything you know. Their names. Their professions. Any perceptions you formed of their character. Where they are buried, even.'

'It was a long time ago.'

'Your memory is long.'

'Why do you wish to know after all these years? There is no benefit to knowing.'

'Yet still I want the information. Give me a name, at least. Did you meet my mother?'

He flung his finger at me in that way of his. That single bead of sweat on his forehead was joined by another. 'She handed you over to me herself. She did not want you, Estella; that is my eyewitness account. She was a rough woman of violent temper. When I met her, she was accused of murder. There, does that comfort you? I thought not.'

Murder. Body and mind seemed to be pulled in two directions at once. That single word was a blow that left me blinking rapidly, fighting tears of shock. How I wished it was not true!

Yet... there was a guilty relief to knowing where my urges came from.

It is not my fault.

'Do you know where she is now?' My words scratched my throat.

'Perhaps she is in the same place as your father. I was recently informed of his burial within the grounds of Newgate Prison. He died in the infirmary, I was told, and so did not get to travel down the Birdcage Walk there – that long, infamous passage that gives prisoners a final, iron-lattice-obscured glimpse of the sky as they walk from their cell to the place of their hanging, watched by baying crowds. But he is buried beneath the flagstones of that selfsame Dead Man's Walk.'

Words refused to form at first. At last, I managed a single sentence. 'My father was a criminal also?'

'I did not wish to tell you, remember that.' His finger wagged. 'I have tried to shelter you from the truth, but as you demand to know I shall furnish you with some information. Even though it hurts you.'

The death masks above were twisted not in fear but mirth at my folly.

Mr Jaggers sat at last, leaned his elbows on his desk and his chin on steepled fingers. 'Estella, I present to you a case of a young lawyer whose world was filled with despair and grime and all the worst of humanity. Even the young mother he came across had not a care for the child she had birthed. A pretty little thing, the babe was. And the mother made it clear that she would destroy the infant rather than allow her to be with her father, not because he was a particularly bad man but because of the woman's own desire to hurt him through the child.'

My natural mother had wanted to kill me?

Hurting a child was something I would *never* do. How could she even contemplate it?

'I put the case that the young lawyer wanted to do one decent thing before the mire of the law closed over him forever, and shut him away from all soft feelings. By chance, he knew of a rich, broken-hearted woman who desired a child above all else.'

My hand crept to Mother's ring on a chain. Notwithstanding her many faults, she had never tried to harm me.

'He believed her when she swore she would protect the child – and I put the case that, in her own way, she did just that. As for the child, that lawyer saw her raised up beyond anything she ever could have achieved had he left her where she was. What a case, eh? Now, what good could come from that child learning her lineage? Precedent shows that if it were to be discovered by others, her position might be imperilled, and so I say: leave the past in the past.'

'Mr Jaggers.' I leaned on his desk, too, so that I might speak softly. 'I appreciate all your care and kindness—'

'I admit nothing.'

'Of course. Let me argue the defence that the past is never truly in the past. There are always threads connecting us to it, and they cannot be severed. They create the tapestry of our lives. Has my whole life not been woven from Mother's past as much as my own?'

His gaze dropped from mine.

'Now, you said that someone told you about my father's death. Was it a reliable source?'

'It was Pip.'

I could not have heard correctly. Yet when I asked him to repeat it, still he said the name of my childhood friend.

'Why would he know such a thing?'

'Because your father was the convict that Pip aided. It was Abel Magwitch.'

So many emotions were inside me, trying to prise me apart, and all I could do was wrap my arms about myself, throw my head back and laugh. Laugh until tears ran down my face.

No matter how hard I tried to run towards the future, those threads of the past always pulled me back and wove my present.

At last I stopped the strange laughter and dabbed at my eyes with a fine lace handkerchief embroidered with my initials – EH, not ED.

'I am rather confused,' I said. 'Let me clarify things, to ensure there is no misunderstanding. My father and Pip had a chance encounter on the marshes when Pip was a child?'

'That is the matter as it has been put before me.'

'But… that means I met him – my father. Do you remember the night that you caught me sneaking back into Satis House, covered in mud, after trying to run away to find my parents?'

Mr Jaggers leaned back in his chair and seemed to deflate as my words sank in. His voice lacked a certain force that was usually present when he next spoke. 'You told me you had encountered two convicts: one of honeyed words and evil intent, and another who was rough but saved you. You left the two of them fighting.'

'Correct. I discovered just last year, if you remember, that the man of honeyed words was that cad, Everard Compeyson. It appears that the rough convict was no other than my father? I am stunned.' The puzzle pieces seemed to fall together to create a never-before-seen picture of my life. 'So he – if I understand correctly – was aided by Pip that night—'

'By his own account, Pip gave him food, and a file from the blacksmith's where he lived. That is why Abel Magwitch, the convict, your father, always remembered the boy he encountered, and decided that if he were ever to earn any money, it would be for Pip. He wished, he claimed, to raise the boy up so that he would have opportunities that Magwitch himself had never had.' Mr Jaggers normally spoke in a bombastic, almost bullying tone, but his voice was quieter as he, too, saw the newly realised picture of my life.

'He thought of Pip almost as his own child, by the sound of it. Did-did he ever know that his daughter lived?'

'Never, to my knowledge.'

I blinked rapidly, trying to understand why my heart clenched so.

So my mother and father were both dead. Both convicts. At last I had the answers I had sought about my lineage.

My leaden feet carried me from the office and onto the street. Through the thronging, shouting, stinking, kaleidoscopic crowd.

Father some kind of career criminal. Mother a murderess.

I had hoped that I would find something good and kind in them that I could cling to, and claw my way out of the darkness that Miss Havisham had thrust me into. Instead I knew now that it was a part of me inside and out. Hurting people was what I had been raised to do, and it sang in my blood. There would be no escaping my fate.

Mr Jaggers had handed me over when I was three, a mere babe, in the somewhat surprising and uncharacteristic hope that I would be given a good life, and a fresh start. Perhaps he even dared hope that letting a child into Miss Havisham's life would help allow her shattered heart to become once again whole. All his hopes were in vain. Perhaps seeing his most charitable plan fail had been the final step in Jaggers' journey towards complete cynicism.

If people knew, they would shun me.

If people knew how alike I was to my blood kin, they would hang me.

On I moved, trying to work out how I felt. Yet there was nothing there. An echoing chamber of emptiness where my emotions should be.

Carriages rolled past, but I took no notice. Barely even registered the horn being sounded to warn people the Post Office mail coach was coming at full pelt. The pounding hooves grew closer, the horn's call louder, the guard's encouraging urges to the horse team, but I did not look up at the everyday sounds. From the corner of my eye, I saw a blur of familiar black and maroon livery of the coach... and something else moving swiftly towards me from behind and one side.

Hands on my waist. A strong, firm shove that sent me flying into the road.

Face biting the ground, skin scraping on gravel. Screaming, whinnying. Horses hooves flashing above me. Sound and vision overwhelming until... nothing.

CHAPTER THIRTY-SEVEN

Pain. Throbbing, dizzying pain. A groan escaped. When I opened my eyes, a great crowd of eyes stared down at me. And far above me, it seemed from my place on the ground, were the great flared nostrils of a chestnut horse, bending its head to check on me and giving a snort of annoyance at finding I still lived. Steam rose from the flanks of its companions.

'Gor, you frit the life outta me then. You all right? How many fingers m'I holding up?'

Three digits with enough dirt beneath the nails to grow potatoes were waggled in front of my face, close enough for me to smell the hay and horse sweat on them. The owner of the digits sported a scarlet coat with blue lapels and gold braid, and a black hat. In his belt were two pistols, and in the hand not being waved before me he held a blunderbuss. He sported the distinctive Post Office uniform of the mail coach guard.

'I am quite well,' I gasped. 'Thank you, guard.'

'Mrs Drummle! Estella!' A voice filled with concern came from the crowd. 'Excuse me; make way there; pardon.' And the owner pushed his way through and appeared at last.

'Why, Mr Coutts, what a pleasant surprise.'

It is a curious thing that manners are so ingrained into the British that even in a state of great disarray, they will converse politely. It is a place of comfort in which to retreat when life is at its most discombobulating. I almost found myself commenting on the weather, but before I could, Coutts had knelt by my side in the mud, his face a frown of handsome concern.

'I was across the way when I saw what happened,' he said. 'You are lucky to be alive. If you had fallen in front of the coach…'

Apparently, thanks to the luck of where I had tumbled, and the skill of the coach driver, disaster had been averted by a horse whip's breadth.

He and the Post Office guard helped me up – the guard first having to lay down his blunderbuss so that he could aid me. I swayed. Mr Coutts supported me.

'Sir, I have hailed a cab.' The soothing tones of Mr Blincoe sounded out. Coutts started.

'What were you doing here?' he asked in a low voice that seemed only for his clerk. But Blincoe's answer was at a normal volume.

'I was running an errand, delivering the price list for the latest line of linens to Moriart and Son. As we discussed, sir.' His voice went up a little, as if in question.

A flush crept over Coutts' neck and cheek.

Meanwhile, my wits were returning and I wondered what either of them were doing here. It seemed a mighty coincidence. Were they present because they were doing Koblin's bidding in trying to kill me?

The guard consulted a great watch, then returned it to his coat pocket with a tut. 'If you are sure you are well, I had best get on.' He swung up to his seat on the mail coach, sounded his horn again, and was on his way almost before I could blink.

Coutts and Blincoe helped me to the cab the clerk had hailed, supporting me as if I were an invalid. I could hardly wait to get inside, away from them.

'Let me accompany you,' said Coutts.

'No, I am quite well now.'

The driver was informed by a member of the crowd what had happened to me.

'You don't wanner be travelling alone,' he said.

'I really would prefer—'

'A lady such as yourself should not—'

'Truly, I am fine.'

The entire crowd appeared to know my well-being better than I, and would not allow the all-too-keen Coutts and Blincoe to leave me.

Coutts seemed stiff and awkward, running a finger around his collar when he thought no one was looking. His eyes darted everywhere but at me. Meanwhile, Blincoe asked questions about what had happened.

'My head is rather throbbing. All I remember is walking along the street and then suddenly...'

The joy of being a woman was that men accepted such empty-headed answers without question. The truth was, despite the grazes and bruising to my head and the right side of my body on which I had fallen, I remembered those hands on my waist. Felt again the force of the deliberate push into the path of the coach.

Someone had wanted me dead.

I was trapped with the very men who I suspected had harmed me.

I had been delivered unharmed to my home. There had not been so much as a threatening word uttered. It was all rather strange.

The morning had been rather eventful, what with hearing about my heritage, and then an attempt being made on my life. Therefore, the remainder of the day was spent at home recovering. Lydia checked me over and shook her head, but pronounced that physically I was intact.

Despite my having little idea what was happening, someone appeared anxious to stop me looking into things. I could only assume that I had been followed to Mr Jaggers' offices and that had placed a terrible fear on them, causing them to act rashly and push me under the wheels of the coach.

I spent most of the afternoon and evening staring at the fire. Pondering. Why had the unflappable Mr Jaggers been so worried? He was well placed to be a criminal mastermind, with his connections, and knowledge. And who better to dodge the law than a lawyer with a fearsome reputation? I imagined him watching me leave his office, then sending word to a minion to end me...

Surely not.

Perhaps he was not the man who ran things, but instead a member of Sir John's club? I did not like the thought, but studied it anyway.

There was far more reason to suspect Mr Coutts.

He had been at Sir John's. Nora had seemed afraid at the sight of him. He had been present when I was pushed. And according to tea talkers and gossips his cloth manufactory business had become highly profitable just two years earlier, seemingly from out of the blue. The same time that Drummle said this Koblin man was supplying Sir John with orphan girls. There were the invoices, too – something underhand was afoot. Could it be that Coutts' real business was far darker than manufacturing cloth – could it be selling girls into sexual slavery?

Most men, let alone women, of my station would be unaware such things happened in the world, but although my life at Satis House had been very sheltered, I had become friends with revolutionaries during my time in Paris as a young lady. They had opened my eyes to many injustices against the poor and vulnerable of society, and shown me how easy it was for such people to be taken advantage of.

A coal shifted, sending orange sparks flying up the chimney, just as Lydia entered the room to inform me I had a visitor.

'Joseph! How is business?'

'It is going well, thankee. Here is your blunt.' He proffered some cash, and a handwritten note. 'And that is where the girl Nancy lives.'

A wave of relief washed over me. The little starling Nora still haunted me: those huge eyes staring from her thin face, taking everything in, and her babbling mix of nonsense and sharp observation. I needed to tell her sister what had happened to her.

'It might be best if I dealt with her,' he offered. 'She… keeps dubious company… in Ratcliffe.'

'You say it as if I should know the place.'

'Rather, I would be surprised if you did. It used to be a hamlet filled with shipbuilders, merchants and crew, but now that it is being swallowed by London it has a reputation for being filled with all the worst this great city has to offer. Criminals. Murderers…'

I should feel right at home.

'…and, I hesitate to say it, but she is light-skirted, Mrs Drummle. A doxy. Lady of the night. Prostitute.'

'Thank you, Joseph, I understand. I am shocked, and will leave the matter,' I lied. Better he thought that than wonder why I was seeking out such company. 'On a more appropriate note, Mr Drummle wants you to acquire the location of Mr Coutts' manufactory? I believe he wishes to speak about a possible investment in the business. Oh, and also get whatever information you can on a Mr Koblin. He is, I warn you, a shadowy, dangerous man, by all accounts, so keep your wits about you. Mr Drummle urges you to use all caution and discretion.'

'Really?' Joseph ran a hand over his moustache, smoothing it. 'Might I speak with him, to get more information?'

'Mr Drummle is currently out.' I lingered on the word, the significant look between us implying that my husband was busy drinking, gambling and possibly whoring. I shifted in my seat and twinged from my earlier fall.

'I should be able to get that to you this afternoon,' he said. There was soft pity in his voice as if he thought my husband had beat me yet again.

If pity gave me a cloak of invisibility under which to hide my true avenging nature, I would put up with it. There were debts to justice that someone owed, and I was going to collect.

My carriage came to a stop down a street so narrow and tall, and so strewn with washing lines, that barely any light reached the bottom. James, the footman, opened the door for me with an expression of one who was seriously considering looking for a new employer after being brought to such a place. On every front step, children squatted, with dirty noses and ragged clothes, and that air of being far older than their years because they had seen so much of the dark side of life. Faces appeared at windows to see who was visiting, as James rapped on a door that looked as if it might come off its hinges if he hammered too hard. While we waited, a couple tottered down the street, arm in arm, holding one another up as they sang. The gin fumes from them were almost enough to make me drunk. James knocked again.

'All right, all right! Keep yer 'air on!' The door flew open. An older, stouter, more gaudy version of Nora stood framed there, in a red gown and green boots, hair piled up untidily, as if it had been arranged the night before and then slept in.

Hands on hips, Nancy looked me up and down. 'Blimey, should I curtsy?'

CHAPTER THIRTY-EIGHT

Emotions ran through me that I was not used to, as I stood on Nancy's doorstep. I cleared my throat to try to stop my voice from wobbling. 'I'm here about your sister. Nora told me about you when she looked after me at Wynterton Manor. Might I come in and speak with you?'

A group of young men, who had already passed by once, ambled back the other way along the tumbledown street, their necks so craned in my direction that one almost stumbled down a hole.

'Got a good enough look, 'ave yer?' Nancy called to them, her curls jiggling as she shook her fist. Then to me: 'Come in, come in.'

Her room was blackened with age and mould. A three-legged table, propped up on one side with half-bricks, stood in front of an unlit fire. Atop it was a ginger-beer bottle, with a candle stuck into it. In the far corner was a narrow bed piled with a nest of blankets.

The only seats were two stools, and while Nancy invited me to sit, she remained standing, hands still on hips. She was fifteen if she was a day, and all bravado.

'How's Nora, then?'

'I am afraid the news is not good,' I began. And so I laid out the sorry tale of her sister's demise, watching her face crumple then harden. 'She has been laid to rest at the church in the village,' I finished. 'Along with the other remains that were discovered. I'm so sorry.'

Nancy wiped at her face. 'She weren't never getting a happy ever after. People like us don't.'

'You were raised in an orphanage, is that right? Where was it?'

'I ran from that place when I was four.' She was proud of it, defiant. 'Knew even at that tender age that I was worth more than three meals of thin gruel a day, even with an onion chucked in twice a week and half a bread roll on Sundays. I was that thin I disappeared if I turned sideways.'

She laughed, but it was hard and angry. 'Leastways, I was small enough to slip through the bars and escape.'

On the streets from such a young age; it seemed unthinkable. Just a year older than I had been when I was adopted. Yet I knew her story was not uncommon.

'How did you survive?'

'Lady like you don't need to know any more than that I used the only thing what I was given so as to stay alive.' Her bravado fell away, and suddenly I could see Nora in her vulnerability. 'Got lucky, I did; got taken in by someone who put me to work and looked out for me.

'Nora, she being that bit younger, she stayed on. We'd send each other little messages. Different flowers with meanings to convey that all was well – or not. Yellow flowers for happiness, that kind of thing. Not that either of us ever admitted to anything other than a yellow mood, for it made us happy just to know we were there for each other. But I thank heaven, dear lady, that at the last she had found friendship and hope in you.'

'Nancy, I have so many questions, but one in particular that I hope might help me find the people behind your sister's death. Do you know the name Koblin?'

She hesitated before shaking her head. 'Perhaps? I'm not sure.'

'How about Coutts?

'I-I think I've heard that somewhere...'

'Your sister seemed to recognise him from somewhere, on the night she died. Might he be someone either of you have worked with before?'

'Not wishing you to shrink from me in disgust, but... I don't always know the names of people I come across, if you get my meaning.' She pulled her shawl closer about her.

'Nancy, stop. You have no reason for shame. Those who use and condemn you do. So, it's possible you have encountered Mr Coutts and not realised—'

'Me, maybe – but not Nora. Not that way. There's not much you can trust me on, but you can on this.' She was shrinking before me. My questioning was doing that, and I hated it... but had to press on.

'Would you tell me the name of the place you were raised?'

'Why yes, it was—'

The door opened with such force that it hit the wall. 'I hear we got a special visitor, Nancy. Introduce us, then.' The words were growled, as if they came from the white shaggy dog in the doorway, rather than the muscular, stout man it cowered behind. As for the man, he was about five-and-thirty, with at least three days' of beard on him, and scowling eyes. His black velveteen coat and breeches were covered with beer and other indecipherable stains, and the handkerchief about his neck may once have been striped but it was hard to tell beneath the sweaty grime. He snatched his brown hat from his head and growled again. 'Remember your manners, or do I have to remind you of 'em?'

Nancy looked between us. Love verging on adoration shone in her eyes, but also fear. Somehow I knew without words that she would forgive him anything. She probably believed that any attention was better than none, that his violence was an indicator of passion and therefore love – of the depth of his feelings. I would not let her take a beating because he was annoyed at some perceived slight on *my* part.

'Forgive my intrusion, I was just bringing sad tidings about Nora—'

'Oh, Bill, my poor sister is dead!' Nancy flung herself at him.

'And are you here offering compensation?' Bill asked, his voice a rumble.

'I am. Here.' His eyes lit up at the money I offered. Nancy would almost certainly see none of it, but at least I had tried. Bill had an expression on his face that was not only calculating, it was positively totting up the possibility of more pounds, and I knew just what he was thinking: why be content with what was given, when he could take more from me through force? 'Did I mention that I am an acquaintance of Mr Jaggers, the lawyer? I say that, but he thinks of me more as a daughter. If you need me for any reason, contact me through him.'

Bill's fists clenched, but he forced a smile tight enough to crack walnuts. Nancy put herself between us.

'On your way. You've brought only grief here,' she said, her voice angry. But she gave me a wink. 'I don't need a stuck-up mare like you coming here, looking down your nose at the likes of us, salving your conscience by telling me about Nora. What did you ever do to help my sister?'

I beat a hasty retreat to my carriage and the driver raised his whip, ready to snap it over the horses, when there came a sudden banging on the door.

'The orphanage was over in Cobham, Kent. Look there and you'll find some answers. And I've just remembered something else,' she whispered. Bill stomped towards her. She raised her voice to a shout. 'You don't want to be going that way – dodgy area, that. You want to go left, down that road instead; that will lead you out.'

'Thank you. But what—?'

She gave an almost imperceptible shake of her head. The look she gave me was bold, just like her sister's. For a moment my hand covered hers and then she slipped away and the coach set off. The last thing I heard from Nancy was a nasty laugh after Bill asked: 'What did you send her that way for? It's the worst part of London, and that's saying something.'

'Snooty cow needs eddy-catin' about the lawless places of the city. Never know, if she keeps her eye out she might just learn a thing or two in that hellhole.'

CHAPTER THIRTY-NINE

The coach rattled over the rough, muddy road, lurching me from side to side as we made our way slowly through the street in the direction Nancy had pointed. The further we went, the narrower the way became, and the more pitted. Her neighbourhood had been dilapidated, but this was so much worse, for it was a rookery, a slum where people lived all on top of one another, with sickness running rife, and children rarely made it to adulthood. A place where gangs of the lawless gathered together. Where the detritus of society existed, because nowhere else would suffer them.

And the stench! It seemed to reach inside and strangle me, it was so overwhelming. My fingers scrabbled at the lavender sprigs tucked into the band at my waist, pulling them free so they could be pressed to my nose. It made no difference.

London was the capital of the richest nation in the world – and had the worst slums in the world. It was a place where hope no longer screamed for attention, but sat in the broken doorways of roofless buildings, watching passers-by with vacant eyes, knowing they, too, were forsaken.

Why had Nancy wanted me to come to this place of the damned?

'Where are we?' I asked one of the footmen.

'Mill Lane, Mrs Drummle. That ditch' – he nodded to a filthy waterway around twenty feet wide, the green-brown slime in it thick and with a slight sheen. I pressed the lavender against my nose even harder, trying to breathe through my slightly open mouth, in order to limit the stench assaulting me – 'that's known as Mill Pond, although it's a tidal stream. Then across the way is Jacob's Island, the worst rookery in the whole city.'

There had to be a reason why Nora's sister had wanted me to see this godforsaken place, but it seemed unfathomable. 'We should turn around wherever we can and return home,' I said. 'Has it always been like this?'

The footman scratched his head, leaving his powdered wig crooked. 'Thirty or forty years ago it was thriving, people say, but no longer. Morality and laws abandoned this place years ago, and now only the dregs of society live here.'

We passed yet another large red-brick building that was falling apart. Rusty iron bars guarded the broken glass windows. Half the chimneys tottered on the roof, as if tempted to slide to the ground and join the crumbled bricks that had once made up the other half. But it was not abandoned, for smoke poured from those broken chimneys. In a courtyard stood donkeys, heads bowed with fatigue, backs sinking in the middle from the weight of their burden, ready to pull carts piled high with goods. Above them, squeaking as it swung in the breeze, was a filthy sign declaring the name of the business: Coutts' Finest Cloth Manufactory.

Could this near-derelict building really be owned by the dapper Mr Coutts I knew? It seemed almost impossible to comprehend. Yet it must be, for why else would Nancy direct me here?

My curiosity not only called me, it wailed. I had to go inside. The footmen looked momentarily aghast when they realised I planned to enter – but they knew better than to offer comment unless asked. Their presence made me bolder, too, for although I did not know what I might find inside, I knew I was safer having them with me.

From within emanated clanks and rumbles from machinery.

I slipped inside by simply opening up a normal-sized door within huge double doors that would have been large enough to admit a coach and six.

I had opened a portal into a sort of hell; the rumbling and clanking of beasts was so great, the ground shook with it. Clapping my hands over my ears, I tried to look beyond the rectangle of daylight cast by the still-open door behind me, for I had been too stunned to close it, but my eyes needed time to adjust to this unaccustomed gloom. Barely any daylight fought through the filthy windows. Instead, lanterns flickered everywhere, hung high above the great beasts that roared: beasts that I could now see were machinery with jaws and ever-moving parts that were carding, spinning, and weaving cloth. All around were tiny shapes.

Scurrying mice, I thought stupidly, like my friends of childhood.

Of course, it was not. It was children, some almost adults, but others, those who crawled like spiders beneath the great looms to pick up fallen lint and cottons to stop them clogging the machinery, were aged around four or five, I'd hazard.

Many of the children stood, like herons, on one leg, balancing the ends of spindles on their lifted knee.

In shock, I stepped further into hell, my feet moving seemingly of their own volition. Eyes were moving in my direction, alerted, no doubt, by the still-open door and the fetid breeze that still managed to bring freshness into the damp heat of the manufactory.

A little shape darted forward, as tall as me, but so slightly built as to be frail as shadow.

'Help us, miss. Save us,' she whispered, or perhaps she shouted, for either way, I saw her lips move, but heard no sound over the machinery.

I found myself nodding without thinking, befuddled by the noise so great it seemed to reverberate through my body and take up occupation in my mind, shaking up my thoughts.

I had admired how Coutts, struggling to maintain his 'old money' status after his father had gambled away the family's fortune and holdings, had launched himself into the new industrialised world. But this was horrifying.

The children were filthy, heads bowed with fatigue, coughs racking their bodies, backs sinking with the weight of work, no hope sparking in their eyes. They were sunken with despair. No laughter rang above the clunk and thunk of machinery.

In the corners of the room were piles of rags, which at first I assumed were oily offcuts kept to clean the machinery – until something stirred within. A child popped her head out, lifting it free, with rags still sitting atop her head.

That feral nest was her bed. Others slumbered on it, too, I saw.

I realised the children slept there in the factory. They must work and sleep in shifts so that the machinery was never still.

This was all highly illegal. I remembered Bentley and his vile cousin Dupont discussing some act or other that had reduced the hours children could work in factories – from memory, those aged nine to thirteen were limited to eight hours, while those aged thirteen to eighteen couldn't be worked for more than twelve hours a day. Bentley had been convinced it would lead to factories having to close due to their profits being cut into, as they would need to employ more children than before to do the same amount of work.

'It will lead to increased crime, too; mark my words. Lord! Naturally vicious they are, and need to have it exhausted from them. With all that spare time the little devils will be free to run riot, pickpocket, do all manner of nefarious activity. Low-life, common-born oiks like that don't care about the law, they break it at every opportunity – that's why this country is going to the dogs unless we watch it. Too soft!'

He had finished his rant by outlining how he and others planned on getting around the new law by bribing one of the four inspectors who had been hired to check on working practices across the country. 'Is that not illegal?' I had asked, and rapidly been told that was 'not at all the point'.

Those with money were always above the law, in my experience.

So this horror was the reason why Nancy had sent me this way. But what was the link between Coutts' fabric business, those suspicious invoices, Koblin's child prostitution ring, and Nancy and Nora? Nancy did not know him as a client of hers, and Nora had never had to sell herself, yet my little starling had stared at Coutts, as if she knew him from somewhere. Perhaps the children supplied to Sir John and his ilk came direct from the factory, but if that was the case, where did Koblin come in? Nothing seemed to fit together neatly—

A hand on my shoulder startled me.

CHAPTER FORTY

ey up, what's your business here?' A wiry little man, shorter than I, with a flat nose and cauliflower ears, leered at me. In his belt was a gun, the handle of which he stroked like some might a cat.

He was joined by a larger man who, judging from the crumbs down his leather waistcoat, had been busy eating immediately before he hurried over. Even so, he had a long, rusty knife drawn.

Just then a great shout was heard over the machinery's clanging.

'Mrs Drummle!' Mr Blincoe bustled towards me, surprise writ large across his features. His eyes, though, were hidden by the reflection in his glasses of the candles high in the sconces and the lanterns.

With a gesture, he got rid of the guards.

'You have guards?' I asked in surprise. 'That seems unusual for a cloth mill.'

'The cloth trade can be rather cut-throat. You would be amazed.'

He beckoned me to follow him, his hand on my elbow as he gently guided me up some stairs. On this floor was a large double door in the wall, which presumably opened up to allow bulky or heavy items to be dropped down into a wagon. Beside it was an office, and it was into this that Blincoe led me. He shut its door, and the sound of the factory was only marginally muffled, but still it was a relief.

'Mrs Drummle, are you lost? How are you after your fall? What brings you here?'

'Why, business.' Of course, the lie came swiftly to me. 'I wish to speak with Mr Coutts about a possible investment on behalf of myself and my husband.'

'I'm afraid he isn't here at present, but perhaps I can be of—'

The door flew open. Framed inside the rectangle of light was Mr Coutts, panting as if he had run from somewhere. Behind him hurried the huge footman I recognised from his visit to Wynterton; he carried Coutts' bag for him. His clerk gave him a look of astonishment and explained the reason for my presence.

'Mrs Drummle is interested in investing,' said Blincoe. His voice was warm, educated, soft as honey on a summer's day. I must try to match his charm if I was to find out how this place was connected with Nora.

'The workforce is younger than I envisaged,' I said. 'Are they able to work effectively? Would adults not be better?'

'They are fast and nimble. Their little hands make light work of things bigger digits might fumble, and if they were not here, they would be in the workhouses alongside their parents,' said Mr Coutts.

He and Blincoe exchanged a look. From it I inferred their belief that a woman was too soft of heart and head to understand such necessary business decisions.

'I once saw a man drawn up by the strap.' Coutts' words came out as rapid as a cough. He nodded towards one of the looping straps that dangled down from the top of the machinery. 'Drawn right up, then smashed in the machinery. It took him five hours to die.'

The usually taciturn Blincoe gave a nod, and then cleared his throat. 'That man might be alive today had children been employed instead of he. They really are better at this work; far more dexterous, and therefore so much safer.'

Rumble and clunk, rattle and clang went the heavy weaving machinery.

'Are they all from the same workhouse?' I asked. 'Or perhaps orphanage?'

Again I tried to find a link to the two orphaned girls.

'Little ones do maximise profit, though it can be upsetting to see for those of a more delicate nature,' Blincoe answered on behalf of his cowardly master. He at least had the courtesy to look ashamed; his head bowed slightly.

'How much do you want to invest?' Coutts interrupted.

'How much did you require?' I replied with a light laugh.

'Shall I draw up a contract? One to satisfy all parties?' asked Blincoe.

'Make it so.' Coutts' nod was curt.

This was all moving rather fast, and I still had found out nothing. 'I would have to check with my husband first,' I said, thinking of a way that I could stall, 'and where did you say the children were from?'

'I'll leave you together. You have much to discuss, I'm sure,' said Blincoe. He finished with a look to his master to confirm he was doing the right thing. Coutts gave a nod of approval before all but slamming the door shut on his clerk.

'My husband and I—' I began.

'How many times must I tell you? I shall be blunt,' interrupted Coutts, straightening his cravat and smoothing his high, stiff collar. 'I do not want your money. A woman involved in my business... It will never happen.'

'Is that because I'm a woman, or because you're ashamed of the hideous conditions, so barbaric, that you keep your workers in?' I asked.

He stared at me, then out through the windows that allowed him to look across the factory floor at his workforce crawling around, scurrying like spiders, helpless, as if he might want to reach out and crush them. The machinery roared for several beats and when he spoke again, the wild anger in his eyes had been replaced by something else.

'I will not have you here. I will not take your money. Now go.'

'I do not think my husband will be as scrupulous as I about this investment,' I insisted. I wanted to delay. I did not want to end the conversation completely. 'Did you ever know a girl named Nora?' I blurted out.

'You should leave.'

He had me by the elbow and walked me, almost carried me, out. His footman, caught unawares, hurried after us.

'I would unhand me if I were you,' I said. Quite chirpily. Conversational. He was going to regret this.

'Mrs Drummle, listen, I pray you.' His voice was urgent. 'My daughter—'

I was looking forward to making that strutting peacock Mr Coutts unhand me. While he muttered something I did not catch about his daughter – no doubt that he wanted to raise her to be far more genteel than I – my hand went to my hair, feeling for my hatpin to jab him with. Mr Blincoe appeared at the same moment as the huffing footman. I always tried to behave in front of witnesses. Apparently, Mr Coutts had the same policy, for his hand dropped to his side.

'Are you leaving, Mrs Drummle? I thought that I was drawing up a contract for us all?'

'Mrs Drummle changed her mind.'

'Mr Coutts changed *his* mind,' I corrected.

'Shall I see her out? Sir?'

'I can do it.' And he did. In fact, both men saw me right out of the door, and then shut it on me.

I stood looking at the wood. Quite stunned. With a sigh of frustration, I turned around and turned back again at the sound of the door opening. There was Mr Blincoe.

He neatened his cravat.

'I am sorry if you felt too upset by what you saw to invest. We don't normally have people over to the factory itself. We have an office in a more central part of the city, where we usually conduct business with our investors. Would you prefer – or perhaps your husband – to meet us there and speak instead?'

'Your master seems to have concluded business for me,' I said.

He blinked rapidly at that. Perhaps I could appeal to him. Coutts had been surprised to see Blincoe when I was pushed under the carriage. Perhaps the servant had been following his master to see what he was up to? It was a gossamer-thin theory, but there was nothing to lose in pursuing it.

'Mr Blincoe, may I speak bluntly?'

He adjusted his eyeglasses in discomfort, and for the first time, I saw his eyes properly. Usually, they were hidden in the reflection. They were intelligent and intense, the pale blue of a freezing cold day on the marshes, with unusual silver flecks. His gaze dipped down briefly then raised again to meet my look, as if giving a silent agreement.

'I'm appalled by the conditions. It's so at odds with everything that your factory seems to stand for, when Mr Coutts puts forth such an air of neatness and professionalism, of quality. I do not think that he is a man who is all that he seems.'

The clerk blinked rapidly. 'You see much, don't you, that others don't,' he said quietly.

'Certainly I question how you can work with such a man as Mr Coutts.'

'When one has a family to support, one will do whatever is necessary to keep a roof over their heads and food in their bellies.'

In some ways, he was almost as trapped as those children. But not quite. There were other options open to him, rather than blindly giving in to Coutts.

I tried a different tack. 'Have you been doing business with Sir John for many years?' I asked.

He shook his head. 'It's a fairly recent occurrence. And, of course, all of that is over since Sir John's sad demise.'

'What was he buying from you?'

'He was an investor, not a buyer. Although he had been in receipt of some wonderful fabrics for his wife, that I believe were made into several gowns. They were more perks of the investment than purchases, though.'

'What is your most opulent fabric?'

He told me, along with the price. It was nothing like the figures in Sir John's invoice.

'Do you know a servant named Nora?'

A light shrug. 'I am quite bad with names. Is it somebody who worked here?'

'Oh, no, it was a servant girl at Sir John's.'

'Oh, in that case,' he said, 'I certainly wouldn't know her. We're barely ever there. I've only been… twice? Yes, twice. The second time was when we made your acquaintance.'

'Well, thank you for your help, and thank you for being more polite than your master.'

He watched as I stepped into my carriage. As I did so, I saw two young girls go up to him, holding a little stack of fabric squares, and apparently asking him something. One of them looked like the girl who had mouthed 'help us'. He nodded as if in reply to a question, and they both ran over to me.

They pressed cloth into my hands.

'Samples,' said one. The bolder. The one who had mouthed to me. I took the little fabrics, and as we drove off, I flicked through them.

And saw, roughly stitched across one swatch, in large, hasty stitches, some words.

HELLP. RETERN AT MIDNITE.

CHAPTER FORTY-ONE

I sat at home, clutching the cloth just as I had the entire journey from the manufactory. The soft silk fabric in my hand was at odds with the thick thread that slashed the large stitches across it.

Those poor children. No one was looking after them. At best, like countless children across the country, they were trapped in the inescapable mire of poverty. At worst, they were somehow a part of this child-slavery ring.

Once again, I felt that sense of connection with them. That desire to do something to help, the way that Mr Jaggers had stepped in to keep me from a life on the streets, prostitution, slaving in a filthy, dangerous factory and most likely becoming maimed, or whatever other horror life might have inflicted upon me.

It was clear to me that Coutts' factory was using child slavery. Where did he get his supply of children from? From the same place that Sir John Taykall had sourced his serving girls? Only by taking those poor girls up on their invitation to return at midnight would I find out more.

Decision made, I dashed off a letter to Joseph with information from Nancy about her orphanage. Hopefully, he would be able to find it.

'Begging your pardon, Miss Estella.' Lydia had entered the room without my noticing, and stood before me with a smile on her face – the kind I had noticed often played on the faces of mothers when looking at their children. 'Miss Lucy Brandley is here to see you.'

Stuffing the cloth into my pocket, I rose to meet my friend, who was busy pushing her glasses up to the bridge of her nose when she entered the room. Sometimes in public she took them off, ashamed of the way both men and women shot her judging glances for marring her looks with them. With me, she did not care, though, safe in the knowledge that such things did not matter to me. Why should a woman stumble around blindly when she could rectify her sight so easily?

After greeting one another warmly, she sat in her favourite armchair by the fire. It was a testament to how often she and her mother would come to visit me that they had favourite chairs, although I was never very comfortable even with them visiting. It was hard to relax knowing that one's husband was chained up in the attic and that people might be a little… judgemental should they discover that fact.

Lucy could not sit still. Her eyes were as wide as the pink spots of excitement glowing on her cheeks.

'Estella, I am to fly like a bird!' she announced.

Lydia almost dropped the tray of tea and muffins she was setting down between us, as Lucy expanded on her bizarre claim.

'It is common knowledge that there is a hot-air balloon in Vauxhall Gardens,' she said, in the tone of someone who had only recently learned this, for Lucy was someone who spent most of her time reading rather than looking about her. 'Well, Mother's friend, the Colonel, has said they are now offering flights for people. He wishes to go up – and has invited me along!'

I stared at her completely nonplussed.

'There is a group of us going, all Mother's friends, of course, and she said I could invite you and Mr Drummle.'

The mention of my husband made me swallow my muffin the wrong way, and Lucy had to pause to pat my back.

'Can you imagine being up in the air like a bird? Fifty years ago it would have been unthinkable, now it is so commonplace that a woman can go up. This truly is an age of glorious innovations by mankind.'

'Humankind.'

Lucy nodded vigorously in agreement, but continued talking. 'Do say you will accompany me, Estella! Think of the sights we will see below us.'

I would rather have stabbed myself to death with my sugar tongs. 'If God had wanted me to fly, he would have given me wings.'

Lucy laughed, then caught my expression. Much as I hated to give in to weakness, I had never quite got over falling through rotten floorboards and plummeting far down to the ground below when I was a child. I had been led there by Camilla Pocket, my dreadful so-called cousin, a middle-aged woman who had been determined to kill me one way or another in order to stop me from inheriting the Havisham fortune, and get it for herself. She and her co-conspirator, Sarah Pocket, had failed on numerous occasions throughout my life, and I had them to thank for engendering in me a tiger-like survival instinct from my formative years. But because of that particular encounter, which had almost killed me, I was afraid of heights.

I was ashamed of this weakness as I did not like to be controlled by anything – I was the one who controlled, usually. However, when up high I found myself shivering and remembering the sensation of the ground giving way beneath me, the rush of air over my skin as I plummeted, my stomach seeming to lift high into my mouth and fall through to my feet, the sensation of weighing nothing more than a feather, and then the shattering pain as I hit the ground. A wide white scar like a rope against my inner thigh was a permanent souvenir.

After hearing an expedited version, Lucy was full of understanding. Yet her eyeglasses drooped to the end of her nose and did not get pushed back into place.

'The thought of being in a hot-air balloon may make my knees quake, Lucy, but I will watch your flight from the safety of the ground.' My offer made her smile once more, and her eyeglasses were returned to their usual perch.

It would be a pleasant late afternoon outing the following day, and would give me the chance to get to better know Colonel Palladon. He had apparently been a family friend for many years, but he and Mrs Brandley had grown closer of late. The invitation would give me an excuse to take a keener look at him, to ensure my friend and her mother were safe. I rather felt that, as Mrs Brandley had looked after me for four years, it was my turn to look after her a little and confirm that she was safe with the Colonel.

Lucy was now content, and tucked into another muffin while talking of the latest article she had read about fulcrums. Hardly my area of expertise, but as she spoke a thought popped into my head.

'I wonder if you might help me with something…' I stood and fetched the wooden box I had brought from Satis House. 'It's locked. I could use brute force and smash it to pieces to discover the contents, but I'd rather not as it belonged to Mother.'

Lucy turned the box this way and that. 'A simple task. You have tried to tackle this face on, by picking the lock, haven't you? But sometimes it is better to check the back – hinges are often a weak point.'

She tapped them, but I was none the wiser. The screws were recessed and covered, so what was she going to do?

'All I will need is a pair of tweezers.'

I fetched mine. Lucy was soon squinting intently at the hinges again.

'See these pins? All I must do is pull them out...' With a steady hand Lucy used the tweezers to grip the metal pin that ran through the centre of the hinge and ease it out. It was fiddly, but slowly it slid out, and she repeated the process on the other hinge. Then I opened the box from the back, the lock giving a crack as it was forced to give way.

Inside was a stack of letters. The top one in particular looked soft and fragile from frequent handling. Resting on it was a pouch with something inside.

Lucy was often distracted from her surroundings because she had her mind on other things – this separation from others could, perhaps, be the reason why she and I got on so well – but it would be to underestimate her badly to think she was not sensitive to people's emotions, and she understood without my having to explain that I wanted – needed – to go through the box's contents in private in order to feel closer to Mother.

'We shall collect you at four p.m. tomorrow,' she said, as she left.

Once alone, I set aside the pouch that rested on top of the pile of correspondence, and started reading the top letter. It was the cruel break-up note that Everard Compeyson had sent Mother on the morning of what should have been their wedding day. It was not the first time I had seen it, but once again the deliberate cruelty of his language struck me. He had attacked her heart, integrity and even her looks, degrading her and blaming her utterly for what he had done.

Never could I have loved such as you, Pandora Havisham. I was sent by your brother to steal your heart and humiliate you as punishment for stealing his inheritance from him.

Liar! Arthur, Mother's half-brother, had been cut from the business by their father because he was a wastrel. He must truly have been a useless article for Mr Havisham to have chosen to leave the brewery and the rest of their great fortune to a woman rather than Arthur.

How pathetically easy it was; how you grovelled at my feet and clutched to your breast every crumb of faked affection I cast down. Weak woman!

The paper was particularly yellowed at that last paragraph, where my mother must have run her finger beneath it while reading in the dim candlelight again and again over the years. That day had broken her. She had started the day glittering with golden hope, been cast into a crucible of despair, and come out as something different, something hard and heartless. Even adopting me, a longed-for child, had not brought her joy. Instead, she had forged me in her furnace of bitterness, telling me daily to trust no one, to hate all men and wreak revenge on them for all the ills they unleash on women. 'Break their hearts,' she would hiss as she tucked me into bed at night. 'Promise!' Poor, unwitting child I was, I had done whatever it took to please her, and thus become something monstrous and unfeeling, different from the rest of the population.

Yet still I wished she were with me.

I expected more letters from Compeyson, but instead they were from Mother to him. Unsent. Full of begging and tears and pain and weakness, from those early days of heartbreak before she hardened. This was the woman, full of softness and emotion, who had never shown herself to me until she was on her deathbed. Then, at last, we had talked about the suffering in both of our lives and, in sharing, had bonded in a way we never had before. How glad I was that she'd had the sense not to send these letters to the master of her destruction.

My cold heart cracked for her.

Setting the letters aside, I picked up the pouch. It clinked lightly as I opened it, looked inside – and recoiled in shock.

CHAPTER FORTY-TWO

An eye was staring back at me!

That could not be possible. Cautious fingers pulled the drawstring pouch's mouth more widely open, and this time I steeled myself before looking inside.

That could not be possible. Cautious fingers pulled the drawstring pouch's mouth more widely open, and this time I steeled myself before looking inside.

A single eye met my gaze.

It was staring at me from a shield-shaped, gold-edged pendant barely bigger than my thumbnail, and surrounded by alternating pearls and rubies. I pulled it out and looked more closely at it. The eye looked back at me as though it saw all.

Of course, it was a lover's eye pendant. They had been terribly fashionable when Mother was a young woman, after Prince George of Wales sent to Maria Anne Fitzherbert a picture of a close-up of one of his eyes, soft with love – the idea being that no matter where she was, she would always be under her lover's amorous gaze. After that they had become highly fashionable. A way of carrying a secret piece of your lover with you, while no one else would be able to recognise them.

I found them simultaneously intimate and disturbing. There was something about this partial portrait that was curiously animated beneath its slightly arched eyebrow. As though there was a living spirit behind it, and it was peering through a keyhole to look at me.

Perhaps it was the flecks of silver that made it seem to glint as if alive. I could imagine Mother, sitting beside the fire, one hand clasped over her walking stick as usual, the other holding the pendant. Rubbing her thumb over the eye, stoking her malice, wearing away the enamel paint of the tiny portrait until the silver backing showed through. Trying to decipher from that single blue eye the expression of the whole face, while wondering whether, if she had only seen the signs of his evil intent earlier, she could have saved herself a lifetime of heartbreak and loss. Had she felt watched over by him? On first receiving the pendant, had it been a comfort to her, which she showered with kisses when they were apart? Was that what had worn the paint away? In the end, had she felt that he could *see* her torment and was enjoying it?

Putting the pendant down, I paced to the window and stared out, unseeing.

Ah, Mother, how I long to speak with you! And not only to ask you about the pendant, but to share with you all my troubles.

She had always been a part of me. From childhood, we had spent every moment together. When I at last left home, she had demanded a letter from me every day we were apart. What would her advice be now? To walk away from danger and protect myself? Or to walk through fire in order to avenge the young girls?

My skin prickled, warning me I was being watched. When I turned, the pendant was looking at me, eyebrow arched in arrogance.

I marched across the room, and tossed the eye into the box, slamming it shut. At the earliest opportunity it would be returned to Satis House.

For the time being, I had more important things to do. A change of attire, for one. For a disguise was called for, and I found the clothes of a man offered me both anonymity and freedom of movement, and both would be useful if I was to return to the factory. There were things I needed to find out. Things that I could only discover by speaking directly to the children.

The clocks were striking twelve when I arrived back at the manufactory. Despite the hour, it still belched out smoke, and the clatter of machinery was as deafening as before, but at least it disguised any sound my arrival might make. I needed to talk with the children without Coutts and Blincoe noticing. There were five guards, but they were huddled around a brazier of glowing coals, flapping their arms and stamping their feet. What looked like a hip flask was passed around between them. There could well be more who were better at their job, so I kept alert and patted myself on the back for deciding to wear my black boy's clothing.

Inside, it looked as if a fresh circle had been added to hell: one of machinery that flailed away the human spirit with unflinching efficiency. Despite the hour, children scurried here and there, darting beneath the clacking looms to fix problems, or hunched over them, their fingers ever moving. But it was not those who were working that I needed; instead it was those who were curled up together like puppies in a pile, rags pulled over them for extra warmth, snatching what little sleep they could before having to work once more. It seemed cruel to wake them, but if I was to find out what was happening at this place then I stood less chance of being noticed speaking with them than stopping a worker at the machines.

The two girls who had given me the stitched note appeared.

'You came!' The boldest of the girls was stick thin and sharp-faced, with blonde hair hanging in tangles. She had a way of pushing herself forward while simultaneously holding herself back; it brought to mind terrified dogs, who want to take a morsel from a proffering hand, but fear it is a trap.

'I may not have much time.' I glanced around, checking that Coutts, Blincoe or some other crony was not marching over to order me from the premises.

'Don't worry, I told you to come at this time 'cause the guards get bored and sloppy. Start boozing around now. Drink 'emselves to sleep most times – cor, if the boss knew he'd do his nut in. He's gorn home for the night.'

'You gave me this cloth. So, tell me, what do you mean by it?'

The bold girl looked fierce and proud, despite the dark shadows under her eyes. 'I did that. Taught meself letters from labels on boxes, posters that blew in from the street, orders, and the like. I'm Sarah-Jayne, by the way. This 'ere is Hilda.'

Some of the others around us began to stir. Frowns, looks of fear, glances of suspicion, all were thrown my way. Some curled up as hard as they could, like clenched fists, turning their backs to me. The ones that really broke my heart, however, were those who lit up as hope fired in their hearts.

You cannot save them all, Estella. What are you going to do, take them all into your home?

I rejected the doubting voice.

'We're worked 'til we drop,' Sarah-Jayne said. As soon as the words were out, she skittered back, as if expecting a beating. 'You ain't one of 'em, I can tell. Don't 'ave the look,' she said. 'But can we really trust you?'

She looked at Hilda, who shrank back into the rags, while pressing her hands together as if silently begging me.

'Trusting me is a brave thing indeed,' I said. 'Without it, I cannot help you – and I promise you, I will do everything in my power to aid you if something illegal is happening here.'

Shocking as the conditions were, thus far nothing I had seen broke laws except perhaps the hours the children worked.

Hilda tugged at Sarah-Jayne's sleeve and nodded.

'I dunno...'

'You asked me to come and I did. Doesn't that show I can be trusted? And here.' I gave her my card. 'Can you read that? That has my name and address on it. You know who I am now.'

She turned the card over and over in her hand, then it disappeared into the folds of her clothing. A barking cough shook her tiny body, for the air was always warm and damp to keep the cotton thread strong and supple.

'When we beg for a break or for more 'an a chunk of bread and bowl of gruel 'at's all water, we're punished,' she said. 'Beaten and told to work with weights attached to our backs.'

These were horrifying tales, but sadly typical of the sort of stories that were starting to appear in newspapers and be discussed in parliament.

'Could you run away?' I asked.

'The guards watch our every move, they do. If we tried and failed, the punishment'd be terrible. Besides, where'd we go? We got us a roof over our heads an' food – though barely enough to survive on, at least we do survive. We're treated as no more than moving parts in machinery – as if we're cogs, and when one of us breaks we're as easily replaced,' said Sarah-Jayne.

Hilda nodded so hard her whole body was involved, and smacked her fist into her open palm.

'Don't mind 'er, she's deaf – so she can't talk, neither,' Sarah-Jayne added, voice sharp in order to get my attention again.

But still I looked past her, at a knot of older children shuffling towards us. Their legs were painfully bent inwards at the knees, and their faces pinched with pain as they walked. Sarah-Jayne noticed them.

'That's what 'appens when you stand on one leg for hours on end every day of your life.'

The clothes I wore, so fine, had been made with cloth produced in factories just like this one.

'That Coutts is a liar, keeps promising 'e'll fix things 'ere, make it a better, safer place to work, but it never 'appens,' said one of the older boys who sat down beside us.

Sarah-Jayne and Hilda looked at each other and rolled their eyes. 'Like 'e ever could,' the girl said. Her voice dripped with contempt. 'But ain't just conditions.' A sea of emphatic nods, hisses of soft 'yes' all around me. 'It's...'

'Shut up! All of you!' A larger lad pushed himself to the front of the crowd. Scared and angry, both fists clenched, chin jutting forward, ready for a fight. 'You'll get us all into trouble!'

'We're already in trouble, Billy, in case you dint notice.' Sarah-Jayne's whisper was fierce.

'Well, I'm a-going to tell on you all.'

'Wait!' I begged. 'I can pay you for the information. Would that make it better?'

He sneered. His back was badly twisted, his knees knocked. 'What good'll money do us? We'll never be able to leave this place to spend it.'

'Then say nothing, at least, to your masters, for speaking to them doesn't seem to have improved your lot.'

The boy picked at his arm, thinking. 'Yeah, maybe.' Pick, pick, pick; he started to bleed. 'If we're found to have kept secrets from 'em it will surely be worse for us than ever it is now.'

'It can't get no worse, Billy,' said Sarah-Jayne.

'What? What's happening?' I demanded.

'Workers go missing. In the night. By morning it's as if they never existed.'

CHAPTER FORTY-THREE

A chill stole over me. It was just like at Wynterton. But I had to be sure.

'Who goes missing? Surely, explanations are given?'

'Who goes missing? Surely, explanations are given?'

'Girls, boys, always the younger ones—'

'No one older 'n thirteen, usually,' interjected one of the other children. Her voice was wheezy, as if the humid conditions had stolen her breath.

'Aye. There's no warning. It started 'bout two years since, not long after the factory moved 'ere and everything changed—'

'Back when was paid wages,' said a boy with his forefinger missing and a huge scar running across his hand and down his wrist.

'Are you not paid any kind of wage?' I asked.

Myriad deadened stares met me.

Sarah-Jayne continued. 'If we ask about the missing children, Coutts 'n Blincoe tell stories 'bout 'em falling ill, being sent to an infirmary, or reunited with parents and the like, even though we're all from orphanages. We want to believe it, but...'

Hope wiped the lines from her face, and she looked so young. She blinked and the fear was back.

'Sometimes they say they've gone to another factory,' whispered the boy. 'Wherever they go, we don't hear from 'em again.'

Could Coutts have got the children from Koblin, the same person that provided Sir John with Nora and the like? Or was he the one running this whole thing? Supplying innocents to men such as Sir John? With such a large number of children disappearing, the excuses did not ring true.

'Have you heard of Sir John Taykall?' I asked.

A gasp. Hilda grabbed Sarah-Jayne's arm and nodded furiously.

''e comes sometimes. Picks out girls. Says they'll be doing special things at his house.'

'Shut up!' Billy shouted. I looked around, scared. The last thing I needed was the guards being alerted.

'I won't! Others come, too. Posh blokes in fancy clothes 'n plummy voices.'

They will pay. Every one of them will pay.

The children, it seemed, came from several orphanages, but there was one in particular that kept cropping up – the same place where Nora and Nancy came from.

'Can you 'elp us?' begged Sarah-Jayne.

'I...' I hesitated. 'I can, but it will take time.'

Hope hardened instantly into bitterness. 'You're just like them. Nothing is going to change 'ere. We're starving, we're dying! 'n no one cares.'

'No! I do! But if I am to be an avenging angel of justice, acting as judge, jury and executioner, then a case must be built that is irrefutable. And it must leave no one out who is involved. I must make sure everyone who has done this to you all is punished—'

'Look at us! We can't wait. We need to be saved now, for who knows if we 'ave a tomorrow?'

They were right. But so was I. What was I to do?

Some started to cry. Others clung to me. Several looked furious. Billy lurched forward on his unsteady legs, red dots of anger on his grey cheeks.

'I knew we shouldn't trust you.' His voice was as tight as his fists. He lifted his head and shouted: 'Help! Guards!'

The children broke, scattering in this direction and that, scared mice. And I ran with them. But not to the front door, but upward, towards the office and the large goods door I had spotted beside it on my first visit. Below me a hullabaloo was breaking out. Deep voices shouting, children's voices crying.

Hopefully I would be out by the time the guards got some sense from the chaos. Any moment I might feel heavy hands grappling me, dragging me down. My legs pumped as I ran, my lungs on fire. Closer, closer... I slipped through the door, to the outside and onto a rickety staircase and a gantry across to another building. Which way?

The guards all seemed to have run inside. I raced down the stairs, and on to freedom.

As I slipped away, I looked over my shoulder, checking that no one saw me leave. If I had looked but a moment later perhaps I might have noticed a shadow detach itself from the darkness and come after me. Oh, the times since that I have revisited that moment, and wished I had! But instead, I continued on, oblivious of the tragedy about to unfold...

After returning home from the factory, sleep refused to come. Anger and the urge to act had fizzled through my body, despite my exhaustion from the long day. I paced up and down in my bedroom, pausing only to feed a titbit to my spider.

I had to act against Coutts. Yet Bentley had given me another name: Koblin.

Every piece of evidence slotted around the peacock perfectly, though. The overheard conversation where Sir John had requested his supply to his friends be increased. The look on Nora's face when she saw him. The suspiciously high bills for materials that simply had to be for more than fabric. The children at his factory literally telling me their friends were disappearing in the night, after people with 'plummy voices' visited.

So who was this Koblin? By the sound of it, he was the one truly in charge. Coutts was a minion, doing his bidding. It made sense to me, as there was nothing about Coutts that screamed he was a good businessman. My guess was that he was being paid handsomely for his part in the disgusting scheme.

Despite gaining a slightly clearer picture of what was happening, in many respects my visit to the factory had been a disaster. Coutts would now know that someone had broken in and spoken to the children. My actions had probably put them in even more danger. And possibly put me in more danger, too, as they would tell him that the intruder was a woman. Plus, Sarah-Jayne had my card, and I would not blame her if she gave me up under pressure.

I deserved to be in danger for messing up so badly. What a buffoon I had been, blundering in and assuming everyone would immediately trust me.

Danger was closing in on me. Despite wearing a nightdress, I suddenly felt as if I wore a corset laced too tight. Heart pounding, breath gasping. Dizzy, I slumped onto the edge of my bed, trying to calm myself.

I reasoned through the scale of my peril. The note threatening to cut my nose off and bury it beneath the roses. The hard push that almost sent me under the wheels of the mail coach. The guards discovering I had broken into the factory. Coutts would surely know immediately who the strange female intruder was, for who else could it be?

I lay down, and pulled the sheets over my shivering body. The warmth did not banish my trembling, nor did my wrapping my arms about myself.

Stopping was not an option. I had to help those children. If my life had been different, my fate might have been similar to theirs. The only way to save them and myself was to push onward.

If only I could find Koblin. Joseph had found nothing so far on him, apart from a few scared whispers that he was a dangerous fellow, to be avoided at all cost. When pushed further, people clammed up. I looked forward to making his acquaintance and introducing him to my knife. Then there were Coutts' other clients. Who were they? They needed to be hunted down.

Returning to the factory to look through the office's paperwork was not possible until things had died down. Which left me with the orphanage where Nancy and Nora had grown up. There I might find nothing – or discover everything I needed.

First thing in the morning, I would summon Joseph, discover the address of Nancy's orphanage, and go there. The decision felt right, but still I lay awake, wishing for sleep, starting at every sound. What else did these abusers of children know about me? How many of my secrets were they aware of? Were they watching me at that very moment?

Time was running out – for us all.

CHAPTER FORTY-FOUR

The plan had been to go to the orphanage immediately after breakfast. Instead, Bentley had proven annoyingly restless. He had shown a shocking amount of ingenuity by pulling up some floorboards in an explosion of rage and kicking his way through the plaster ceiling, before leaping through the hole.

Luckily, the chain still attached to his leg had not broken as he had hoped. Instead, we had discovered him in one of the unused bedrooms, swinging as if from a gibbet, though upside down and from one leg rather than his neck. He was rather red of face and bellowing enough to bring every concerned citizen from miles around to his rescue. I'd had to resort to hitting him about the head until he was senseless, sending him into a dizzying spin, before Lydia and I were able to get him down and drag the heavy oaf back to his prison.

I had still been buttoning my sleeves after changing into more suitable attire when Lucy, her mother and the Colonel arrived to take me to Vauxhall Gardens.

The day had been a fruitless waste, I thought, as I walked alongside Miss Lucy. As she chattered happily, I tried to hide my brooding heart behind noises of agreement at set intervals. Yet brood I did over the day's antics. Everything made me think of the previous night.

The open space and clean air.

The fetid stench of the factory.

Members of society, perambulating, showing their fine figures.

The children with misshapen bodies and missing limbs.

Men and women wearing the latest fashions.

The rumble and clank of machinery making the cloth for these fine clothes.

Lucy, her mother and the Colonel continued into the heart of the gardens. It was a wonderful place still, although slightly more tired around the edges than it had once been, and one did not wish to be seen there after dark, when its nature changed to become more tawdry.

Beside me, Lucy started to bounce up and down with excitement before she was subdued by a reminder from her mother to act with more decorum.

'But look, Estella! Look!'

Before us was a huge hot-air balloon, moored firmly to the ground by strong ropes which creaked as the balloon swayed in the slight breeze.

'Oh, Lucy, now that I see it, I am really not sure you should go up in that...' Mrs Brandley's voice was quite weak at the thought.

'Mother, please—'

'She shall be quite safe with me.' The Colonel had a rich voice full of smiles – although the emptiness of his promise irritated me. How on earth could he keep her safe if the balloon plummeted from the sky?

He doffed his tall top hat at Mrs Brandley, as if in further reassurance. The movement revealed a surprising bald patch, as he had thick white hair around the sides and back, and his snowy beard was also luxuriant, along with his thick eyebrows. All that white made his apple cheeks look all the redder.

For a mere moment he took both Mrs Brandley's hands and gave them a comforting squeeze.

'I trust you, dear Colonel,' she said.

Just minutes later, he and Lucy were floating impossibly into the sky. Below, Mrs Brandley and I fanned ourselves with almost enough vigour to take off ourselves, and only stopped once our friends returned to terra firma. Not that Lucy really did, for though her feet were on the ground her heart still soared above as she described in detail how it felt to look down from such a height.

'The land looked like a patchwork blanket laid down before me. It felt almost as if I could reach out and pluck something from miles away – pick up a huge castle that would be as small as a pillbox in my hand. It's as close to being a god as it's possible for a person to be.'

The only thing to ever make me feel like a god was when I held the power of life or death...

Shadows were deepening, the sky turning lilac. Beautiful lanterns lit up everywhere.

'Shall we stay for the fireworks? And then home?' suggested the Colonel, and we all agreed, just as a familiar face appeared in the crowd.

Mr Coutts. Looking every inch the dandy in his royal-blue dress coat that sloped his shoulders to perfection, and nipped in at the waist to accentuate the breadth of those shoulders. His silk shirt so pale it almost outshone the gold necktie.

Was it a coincidence that he had appeared here? Or was he toying with me?

He tipped his hat to us all as he approached, greeting everyone.

'No Mr Drummle?' he enquired.

'Bentley unfortunately had to stay at home and take care of some business. He was... complaining about being left hanging by something or other... No Mr Blincoe?'

'He is here. He is never far away, we are always in sight of one another.' He looked about him and waved at his clerk, who was speaking with someone a small distance away.

The conversation quickly turned to Lucy's flight. All the time he made polite conversation, white-hot anger roiled through my veins. What a vile man! Hiding behind that geniality, impeccable manners, and peacock clothing was an abhorrent creature.

Yet he hid it so well.

He asked questions of Lucy and listened with interest to the answers. The look in his eye was gentle and sincere.

I will cut out his lying tongue.

A whizz. A bang high above us. An explosion of colour in the rapidly falling darkness. The crowd 'ooh'ed as one. Everyone's eyes were skyward, smiles on their faces. Apart from Mr Coutts. From the corner of my eye I watched him. Saw his smile fall to the ground, his posture slump, and—

He twitched suddenly, like a runner about to start a race. Alert. Without saying farewell, he walked from our little gang, slipping through the crowd.

A glance at my friends showed their eyes still skyward, fascinated by the display. It was easy for me to take a few steps back into the crowd, let people slot into the space where I had been, and then slip away.

Craning my head this way and that, I spotted Coutts – the only rapidly moving person in an otherwise still tableau.

As he reached the edge of the crowd he glanced around. I froze. Had he noticed me? It appeared not, for he stepped from the wide clearing and melted into a wooded area.

Perhaps he was keen to get some company. Vauxhall Gardens was reputable by day, but after darkness its nature changed, and its reputation tarnished. Many men met courtesans there.

It was hard to keep track of him among the trees, away from the lanterns. There were only the regular fireworks to illuminate the surroundings. My skin prickled, eyes widening, head turned this way and that, trying to sense...

An explosion. There! Quite a distance in front of me was his distinctive shape in his dress coat. He seemed to be talking with someone far smaller and slighter. Before I could see properly, the firework above glittered and faded to nothing, leaving me more blind than before.

I crept forward. Could hear quiet voices. Coutts and a woman. No, girl, from the cadence. I could not hear what was being said. I held my hands before me and felt my way forward.

Bang! Light flashed.

Coutts and his companion had moved forward, too. Whispering urgently. I squinted. Sarah-Jayne. That was the girl. Coutts had hold of her, trying to drag her away. She was tugging back, heels dug into the ground. She lashed out...

We plunged into darkness again. Fear doused me – not for myself but the girl. My heart beat so loudly it must surely be heard. What was Sarah-Jayne doing there? Had she been following me? Run away from the manufactory? Was she trailing Coutts to find out more about him? But what would the point of that be when she already knew everything she needed – that he was the evil master of all her suffering?

Another flash. Sarah-Jayne and Coutts were further away. She was being held still by someone else who had joined them. It was the beefy footman who, along with Blincoe, went everywhere with Coutts.

I had to reach her! Pulling out my knife, I stalked forward blindly.

In the spaces between darkness and light I was somehow falling away from them. Another flash – and they were gone. But where? I spun around, listening. Nothing.

Nothing but a sense someone was watching me. Making the hairs on my body stand to attention.

A brilliant multi-coloured flash overhead. I twirled. There was no sign of anyone. My blade glittered… fell into darkness again.

'Sarah-Jayne!' I called in desperation. 'Mr Coutts!'

No reply.

More fireworks exploded, but they showed me nothing but trees, trees, more trees.

I was all alone in the woods.

There was no choice but to make my way home, with a terrible fear in my heart.

The following morning, I pondered what to do about Sarah-Jayne as I breakfasted. While removing the embroidered cosy from my boiled egg, I decided that she must surely have got away and it would be impossible for me to find her now. She would be on the streets some-where. I prayed she would use the card I had given her, and somehow find me.

As I cut the top off my boiled egg, I decided it would be best for me to visit the orphanage, and try to find the other perpetrators involved. What I needed was solid information, not more clues as flimsy as muslin.

While shaking open the huge Sunday newspaper to read as I ate, I changed my mind again. Perhaps Sarah-Jayne had been dragged back to the factory, and I should go there.

My circular thoughts were annoying. With a sigh, I read to distract myself – and dropped my spoon in horror at the story at the bottom of page five.

A young girl had been found floating dead in the River Thames. Her arm torn from her body. The grim dawn discovery, just downriver from Borough Fish Market, was barely more than a caption to accompany the drawing of the girl.

The sharp nose, the high forehead, the deep lines either side of her mouth that seemed to prematurely age her… The artist impression looked exactly like Sarah-Jayne.

My eyes blurred with tears. With shaking hands I rang for Lydia, and barked an order as soon as she appeared.

'Send for the police. Immediately.'

It was time for the truth to be told.

CHAPTER FORTY-FIVE

The bobby sat in the same armchair Lucy had occupied the previous day. He put down the newspaper and shook his head, drumming his fingers on his blue top hat, which was tucked under his arm since removing it after entering the house. That was the first and only sign of respect I had seen since.

After a moment of thought, when he considered all I had told him, he spoke. 'Let me get this right.' His voice was high and nasal. 'You saw this drawing of a girl in the paper, and you think you know her because you saw her briefly while visiting a factory?'

'Correct.' I tried to keep my answers short and factual. If I said more, my irritation might spill out.

'And now you're accusing a viscount of killing her?'

'Yes.'

'Because you think you saw them arguing in Vauxhall Garden.' He checked his notes and scratched his head. 'But you've no idea what was said and can't even be certain it was her because it were pitch-black.'

'It was definitely her. Fireworks were going off.'

'Yes, I forgot about them.' His fingers drummed on his hat again. 'And, er, it's all part of a conspiracy to sell little 'uns to the peerage, but you don't know who.'

I licked my lips. 'The way you say it makes it sound ridiculous, but I can assure—'

'Where is your husband, Mrs Drummle?'

My voice was icy, my back ramrod straight. 'What does that have to do with it? He did not witness the argument between this young girl and Mr Coutts. I did, which is why I summoned the police.'

'Now, now, you shouldn't get yourself so worked up. You'll make yourself ill,' he advised. His blue-and-white striped duty armband on his left arm denoted him as a constable. The patronising, jolter-headed lobcock was unlikely to rise any higher in the ranks, in my opinion. 'Have you been reading penny dreadfuls? They can get the imaginations all riled up. Or perhaps you had a bad dream.'

I stood and looked down on him. 'This is a serious matter—'

'You're forcing me to speak plain. You're making a fool of yourself with this fantasy, Mrs Drummle, and if you continue to pursue it I shall have to speak with your husband myself. He might be best off fetching the doctor to you; he can give you something to calm your nerves.'

My fingers ached, they were clenched so tightly into fists. The haughty put-downs were on the tip of my tongue, waiting to launch…

But I could not free them. Instead I had to bite my lip – literally – to contain them, because the last thing I needed was the police asking questions about Bentley and realising he hadn't been seen for months. Instead, I uttered possibly the biggest lie of my life.

'You're right, officer. I apologise.'

He left the room so swiftly that his smart blue tailcoat streamed behind him. Still, it was not fast enough for my taste.

I had tried to do the right thing and tell the police so that justice could be served. What a waste of time that had proved. Another girl dead and only me to hunt down her killer. This was insane! I wanted vengeance, I wanted blood, but it was starting to feel too big, too wide-ranging for me alone. I needed help, but with the authorities dismissing me as a little woman with a big imagination, to whom could I turn?

There was one other option left to me.

Gerrard Street, in Soho, was not one I was familiar with, and the grand four-storey houses that lined it made me pause in astonishment, not because I was unfamiliar with such sights but because I had never imagined Mr Merryweather Jaggers to reside in such surroundings. He was a successful lawyer, and his clothes were of good quality, and certainly everyone knew that his gold watch on its great chain was valuable, yet it was impossible for me to imagine him living somewhere palatial. This was a man who had nothing outside his life but work, as far as I knew.

Perhaps there was more to him than I had assumed.

After all, despite knowing him my entire life (at least the part I could remember, for there were only snatches of remembrance from life before my adoption, and one of my earliest recollections was of my little fingers fisting in his velvet lapels as he carried me away to Mother) never had I been invited to his house. Instead he had always come to us when we summoned him. It struck me as slightly odd, now that I thought of it, for I had lived in London for five years.

Not that it was a secret where he lived, for he liked to make sure everyone, including thieves and worse, knew his address and the treasures he kept within, as a sort of test for them. Not one of them dared to rob him, for they knew his reputation as the best, most ruthless lawyer in London, unbeatable in court. What fool would risk the long drop by stealing from him?

There was one house which stood out from all the others. And that was how I knew I had reached Mr Jaggers' home. A grand place, yes, but with paint peeling off the door and window frames. I took my gloves off and rapped on the door with bare knuckles. Several flakes of black paint fluttered to the ground – and at the same time, someone hailed me. Upon turning, the smell of soap enveloped me, and Mr Jaggers huffed to a stop, lips parted.

How extraordinary! Mr Jaggers hurrying for someone.

'I hope you don't mind my calling on you—' I began, just as the front door opened. There stood a middle-aged woman, presumably the housekeeper from her garb and the pale complexion of one who spent all of her time indoors. Her large eyes widened at the sight of me – confirming my suspicions that Mr Jaggers did not have many callers, and likely none of them were female. Her lips were parted as if to speak, but her employer was faster.

A look passed between them. Interesting. Perhaps they were more than master and servant? For although she looked worn out and faded, it was clear that she had once been beautiful.

There was something else, though. Mr Jaggers looked positively agitated, slipping between me and the front door as if to block my way. Was he trying to prevent me from entering the house?

CHAPTER FORTY-SIX

Molly, do not worry about my lunch, my caller and I are going for a walk. If that's agreeable with you, Mrs Drummle?'

The housekeeper closed the door as I narrowed my eyes and replied. 'Please, Jaggers; you know how I despise that name. Why have you suddenly stopped calling me Estella?'

He offered his arm and set off at racing speed in the general direction of St James's Park.

'Nothing like a walk to blow away the cobwebs,' he panted, as if he had never been for a walk in his life. This was not his routine; it was a subterfuge to keep me from entering his home. Why?

The last time we had spoken, at his office, I had remembered hearing his name at Sir John's house and momentarily suspected him of involvement in this hellish mess. Then he had told me of my father's fate, and the thought had been temporarily pushed aside. After being pushed in front of the coach, I had examined it again and rejected it, for it was unimaginable that he would want me dead.

There it was again, though: that sense that he was nervous. He was not acting like himself. He was acting like a man with something to hide.

The idea refused to be tidied away. What if Jaggers was somehow involved? My body instinctively jerked away from possible danger.

'Did you stumble, Estella?' he asked. Of course. Jaggers missed nothing.

He knew so many criminals. It would be easy for him to have the contacts to create a gang of low-class wrongdoers who would do his bidding. He also had dealings with those of the upper classes who could afford to buy themselves young girls. So easy for this man who was a bridge between the worlds of darkness and light.

And so I began to walk a mental tightrope, confiding to Jaggers all that had befallen, and my suspicions that Coutts had murdered

Sarah-Jayne, in the hope that he might be able to help me if he was not involved, while carefully watching his reaction to see if he gave anything away to indicate he was. Jaggers was a master dissembler; it was the key to his success as a lawyer. Yet he was always different with me, and I knew him like no one else.

He harrumphed once I had finished talking. 'There are few secrets in the city that I cannot discover the truth of, if I put my mind to it. Note that I make no promises, though. Note that, and that I will only tell you what the evidence reveals.'

'I understand.'

He gnawed his finger for a moment, then wagged it at me. 'Wemmick has found out something of Coutts' background, following our last conversation—'

'The one during which you said you would not get involved.'

His index finger got another gnawing for that. 'His father, the viscount, lost every penny to his gambling debts. Francis Coutts started a small business that had modest success. Then his wife died in the childbed.

'All witnesses agree, although it is only hearsay, that he loved her dearly and was distraught at her death. Despite hiring a wet nurse and nanny to care for the child, he was so overwhelmed with grief that his business suffered greatly. He almost lost everything, but by some alleged miracle managed to turn things around and become a success again. This time a considerable one.

'The change in his financial fortunes has been incredible. If one were not of a factual state of mind, it might be tempting to suggest it was *suspiciously* so. That would be pure conjecture. There is no evidence whatsoever of any criminal activities or connections.'

'I see.' I stopped walking and stared my companion right in the eye. 'No *evidence* of any criminal activities. Would suspiciously high invoices count?'

I told him of the paperwork I had come across. He dismissed it as proving only that Coutts' charges were high. I gave a tut of discontent.

'Can you tell me anything else about Coutts?'

Jaggers dusted off an imaginary speck of dust from his cuff. 'His daughter passed away just as his fortune altered.' There was no telltale sweat bead, no reluctance to meet my eye, no twitch... Either he was telling the truth or he had regained total control over himself.

'Have you ever come across a Mr Koblin?'

Jaggers stopped walking. 'There are rumours in certain circles. I do not hold with idle chit-chat.'

'Indulge me.'

'His name has been mentioned once or twice in connection with some dark crimes. No one seems to know anything about him. Wemmick and I both look forward to the day we meet him – for it is only a matter of time, mark my words. He is a specimen to be studied with great interest.' Mr Jaggers began walking again, with a new spring in his step at this prospect, as he continued. 'I will remind you of my original thoughts on all of this: leave well enough alone. You would do well to listen to me.'

'I always listen to you, for I greatly respect your opinion. However, respecting it does not always mean doing as you advise, for I have my own thoughts and views. A young woman has died – a girl, really. Doesn't that matter? Does that not stir you to action?'

'As tragic as that is, girls die every day in this city—'

'That doesn't make it acceptable. Is it the fact that it is a girl that leaves you so unfeeling? Or that she is from the lowest of classes?' Heat was rising inside me. I poured ice on it, for losing my temper would not win over Mr Jaggers.

'Every day of my life is filled with stories of death and the worst deprivations. Do not think me naive of what goes on in the world.'

'It isn't naivety that bothers me, it's your lack of caring about what you see.'

'Estella, I would remind you of the evidence. You have seen that my working life is entirely given to the law. I put the case to you that I work tirelessly for those who fall foul of the law.'

'You do. But you do not care for the outcome apart from for your own professional pride.'

'Someone sent you a note warning you to keep out of this matter. Whoever is behind it all knows who you are, Estella. The danger to you is all too real.'

He raised a hand as he spoke. A cab pulled up beside us, and he gave my address.

'You are ending our conversation rather abruptly,' I observed.

'Forgive me. I must get home for lunch.' For a moment his thick black eyebrows drew together, as if in worry, before returning to bullying the rest of his face.

As the cabbie set off, the heat of the conversation dispersed and I began to feel the chill of the day. I pulled on my gloves – how annoying, there was only one, I must have dropped the other. I rather suspected it had happened on Mr Jaggers' doorstep, and so asked the driver to stop there before taking me home.

There was no sign of Mr Jaggers as I stepped down from the cab, but there was my glove, resting against the door. Swiftly, I picked it up – just as the door opened.

'Oh! I thought I heard a visitor arrive,' said the housekeeper.

Behind her in the dark hallway was a large mirror. The light from outside reflected in it, making it so eye-catching that I stared at my reflection caught within it. My face right beside the housekeeper's, as if we stood side by side rather than opposite one another.

Molly's eyes stared back at me, twofold. Two pairs of identical lips. Her expression mirrored. I could see exactly what she looked like as a young woman, for the image was right beside her, captured in the looking glass; she had been exactly like me.

And when life had worn me down and lined a map of woe on my face, I would become her double.

What did it mean?

My blood seemed to pound in my ears.

It could not be… It was not possible…

Yet the evidence of my eyes was irrefutable.

'Estella!' Mr Jaggers called me, hurrying over just as he had before. Eyes wide in consternation.

Only this time I understood why.

'Mr Jaggers, deny it if you will, but you implied that both my mother and father were dead. I put it to you, sir, that my mother is alive. I put it to you that she is standing before me.'

CHAPTER FORTY-SEVEN

The three of us stared at one another in a triangle of shock. I was stunned. I had always trusted Mr Jaggers, and yet he had spent virtually my entire life lying to me by omission – not to mention his barefaced lie to my face when I asked about my mother recently. He was the first to unfreeze, hurrying us all inside. Too stunned to argue, I let myself be swept along, into the gloomy hall, up the dingy stairs, and into a room painted dark brown, in which little light leaked through the filthy windows. Mr Jaggers' obsession with cleanliness clearly did not extend to his home.

But then, there was nothing homely about this room. It was dominated by a dining table, there were no armchairs in which to sit comfortably, and tucked in one corner was a desk covered in papers, on which stood a shaded lamp. Beside it was a bookcase, filled with books about evidence, criminal law, criminal biography, and trials, acts of parliament…

Could this man really understand my sense of betrayal when he had nothing in his life? Nobody that he really, truly cared about? I had thought that he cared about me like a daughter, but clearly not if he could lie so easily to me about something he knew meant a great deal.

'Molly, leave us,' he ordered.

'Molly…' My voice was a dangerous warning – to him. 'Stay right where you are.'

She said nothing, but kept her eyes attentively on Jaggers, waiting to be told what to do. I had two diametrically opposed intuitions at the same time: that his word was law and must be obeyed, and that despite her looking subdued, she was like the wild animals caged up in London Zoological Gardens – not tamed, just contained.

'The jig is up, Jaggers. Stop trying to control this situation,' I said. 'This woman is clearly my birth mother, for we look identical aside from the years between us.'

He pulled one of his dining chairs towards him, and put one foot on it, leaning his elbow on his knee. A finger wagged in my direction.

'This woman birthed you, but she is not a maternal woman. Need I put forth again the facts? This is a woman who threatened to destroy her daughter. Indeed, she hid her daughter away and pretended to that child's father that she was murdered. She herself has confessed to me that she told the father: "Yes, I strangled our daughter to death."'

My mouth twitched, repelled. She actually went as far as to say those words? What a despicable liar she was.

'Think on that, Estella. Think of the power of that statement. Think of what kind of woman would make that statement and what kind of mother might just have carried it out.'

Molly made no noise of denial. She hung her head, as if in shame. Her eyes were narrowed, though. I recognised my own acting in her. Had it actually entered her head to kill me, I wondered... it sounded as if it had.

'You look like your mother – an awful lot like her, but you are more like your father in character,' continued the lawyer. 'You do what you need to do to survive, but you would never go out of your way to hurt someone for no reason.' If even *I* did not know if that statement was true, how could Jaggers be so certain? 'Molly would. Take care, Estella, lest you are putting your head inside a lion's mouth, like a circus master. How long before it will close its jaws on you?' His boots gave a creak of emphasis.

'What you say may be true or may not be, but it is up to me to hear all information and make up my own mind.' No tremor of indecision was in my voice.

'See the evidence.' His boot slapped onto the floor. 'Show her your wrists, Molly.'

'Master,' she pleaded, but when he gestured impatiently she did as she was told. Her body was as tense as a piano string.

'See the power.' He traced a possessive forefinger over the sinews. One wrist had deep scars across it.

She must have tried to harm herself, poor woman – but no, I realised: the marks were from continued wearing of a manacle. I looked closer. A sudden image sprang to mind of her pulling at the iron clamped about her wrist, throwing herself back and forth in a frenzy, trying to break free, the way a wild animal willingly gnaws off its own leg in order to escape the snare.

'Few men have the power of wrist that this woman has,' Jaggers said. 'What sheer force of grip there is in these hands! Never have I seen stronger in a man's or a woman's than these. Make no mistake, they are powerful enough to squeeze and squeeze a throat until life is extinguished.'

I thought of my first victim. Of wrapping the scarf about his neck and pulling with all my might...

'Be under no illusion, Estella: your mother is a murderess.'

Her hands were so like mine. My cousins had shamed me for them, calling them 'coarse and common'. Her wrists were identical to the ones I always disguised carefully with delicate sleeves and lace gloves.

In trying to turn me from Molly, Jaggers had pointed out what we had in common. It was nothing to be proud of, but it was a fact, nevertheless.

She was my mother. I was her daughter. The same blood ran in our veins. The same hot urges.

'Molly, let us go down to the kitchen, which I assume is your domain. There' – I looked at Mr Jaggers pointedly – 'we may speak without interruption.'

As we descended the stairs down to the kitchen, there came the aroma of mutton cooking. So that was what Mr Jaggers was having for his lunch. The room was cosy as well as functional, and beside the fire there was a rocking chair, over the back of which was folded a brightly coloured crocheted blanket. Just like upstairs, a table dominated the centre of the room, but this one was cluttered with bowls, utensils, and a dusting of flour. Off-centre in the wall, opposite a series of small windows that let in the daylight (and which were considerably cleaner than those upstairs), was the gaping black hole of a dumb waiter, just like Sir John's. Despite it containing nothing more sinister than a variety of bottles and decanters, goosebumps bloomed across my skin.

Most of me no longer suspected Jaggers of being involved with Sir John, Coutts and their evil cronies. His reasons for being nervous around me were obvious now, and yet... A splinter of misgiving remained. He had kept this from me. What else had he lied about?

One thing at a time, though.

'Molly, do you believe that I am your daughter?'

A single nod.

'Did you pretend to your husband, my father, that you had murdered me?'

Another nod.

My stomach contracted. She was so different from me! Yet the parallels between us could not be denied, either. At last, I had found someone like me, and having found her, I did not want to let her go ever again.

'Does Jaggers keep you here against your will?'

Her eyes tightened. 'He never beat me. Instead, he controlled me with his words and looks, with threats of what would happen to me if he decided to withdraw his protection and send me back to the streets. No food. No shelter. It's always been my choice to stay, but it never felt as though I did have a choice.'

I opened my mouth—

A clattering from above made us both look up. The vigorous splashing of water.

'He'll be quiet in a minute, once he's washed up,' said Molly.

More splashing.

'Sounds as if he might have to get his penknife out and clean under his nails to calm himself fully,' I observed. 'Scrape out the lies he has told.'

Gargling floated down to us.

'Oh, he's very upset. He only does that when he's in a state.' Molly met my eye and we both smiled. Even laughed a little.

'Would... There is so much I need to know. Will you tell me all?'

'I will. But first a cup of tea.'

At last, holding a steaming mug between her hands, and with her feet resting on the fender so that they warmed beside the fire, she began to tell her story...

CHAPTER FORTY-EIGHT

I was a snip of a girl when I met your father. I was working at a pub, sweeping and washing up, mostly, but some serving, too. Hated it, I did.' Her lips curled. 'Hated sleeping above the inn's stables, and always stinking of horse sweat, horse piss, and spilled beer. Hated the sweaty, drunken men who grabbed at me, offering to pay for a refill by "showing me what a real man could do". Hated every single day being the same.'

Her scowl grew. It made me smile because my reaction would have been the same.

'Then in walks Abel Magwitch. Handsome, rough-and-ready fella: dark hair, dark eyes, and a dangerous air. We clicked together like two halves of a locket. When other men hounded me, he went toe to toe with 'em. Defended my honour, he did.'

My heart swelled. My father sounded like he had been a decent man, even if he was a thief. He had done right by Molly, and by Pip. He would have tried to be a good father for me, too, perhaps, if given the chance.

'He'd lived on the road, scraping a living, for as long as he could remember. His first arrest was for stealing turnips, you know; he was only four. After that, he was regularly took up, and with his record growing ever longer it weren't long before he was considered a regular rough.'

My father's life of crime had been about survival, not enjoyment. I thought of the boy I had met on the way to Wynterton. My father had been even younger than he, and forced to survive alone.

'We took off together. We didn't have no plan, we stole everything we needed to stay alive,' continued Molly. 'It was a life of adventure on the road, with no one telling us what to do. Endless laughter, blazing rows and making up under the stars. There was never an in-between for us, it was all or nothing; he breathed life into my days and warmed my bed at night.'

Her words spoke of passion, but she was so guarded it was impossible to imagine. She gave only the smallest glimpses into her emotions, for she mostly kept her face a careful blank. I found her near impossible to read – yet it was the very thing that drew me to her, for in that I recognised myself. Cold, careful, cunning.

'The fun stopped when I was seventeen and pushed you out into the world one mild, sunny winter's day, as we sheltered in a ditch. An extra mouth to feed. A responsibility. I wasn't the centre of Abel's world any more, you were. He'd keep you warm by putting you inside his shirt, your head resting on his chest where I once had. Sang you to sleep at night.'

I was no expert in emotions, but she sounded jealous. Of me. Her tiny, helpless newborn.

'Do you remember the doll he made you out of a peg? No? Put horsehair on it, even made a dress out of a bit of rag; pretty it was. Surprised you've no memory of it when it was always either tucked under your arm, or you were sucking on it.' She looked me directly in the eye for the first time. Skewered me. Then flashed a smile. 'The daffs were just poking through the hard ground when you was born. Lovely day, it was. Shame you ruined my figure.' It was almost identical to mine, despite the passage of years. 'I had to watch Abel after that. He wasn't the flirty type, but he was kind; couldn't see when women were flinging themselves at him, so I had to make sure to see 'em off meself.

'Your pa started dreaming about a house, stability, a steady income. Silly dreams – and boring ones at that. He'd just come out of Kingston jail on vagrancy committal, and was trying to get some work at Epsom Downs Races, when he caught the eye of a ne'er-do-well with tickets on himself as some kind of gent. Everard Compeyson was his name, and I curse the day that first I heard it.'

My body stiffened. I was aware he had known my father, but hearing it first-hand felt more shocking.

Molly spat on the fire. She spoke over the sizzle. 'Compeyson thought 'imself the gent, wearing his fancy black clothes to show off his perfect pale complexion – not a pockmark or scar on him. Got lah-di-dah manners, and used big words when he talked. He offered

Abel work, said they'd be partners. Well, Abel was all excited, saying his prospects were on the up.' A certain set to her lips indicated she had agreed with him at last about this. She looked at me again, and this time her smile seemed fonder. 'You was toddling about, getting into all sorts.'

We had been a family. I tried to imagine it and failed. But I yearned for it. If only things had worked out, could we have been a normal, happy family?

'Anyway, Compeyson would come up with all sorts of clever ways of parting fools from their cash. Swindling, handwriting forging, and even banknote forging, there was nothing his quick mind couldn't turn to a con. If Compeyson wanted a big 'ouse breakin' into, it'd be him who'd detail how and your pa who'd be slipping inside, and getting chased by the owner with a gun. If he created a forgery, it was your pa as had to pass it to people. He fronted everything, which meant he was the one always in danger of being caught, while there was nothing to link Compeyson to a single thing.'

She picked up the poker and jabbed at the fire as if wishing it were Everard.

'And it wasn't because he couldn't have done it. No, he had the silver tongue to sell tea in China. He could have been on stage, that one, with his ability to mimic people he'd only met once, from gestures to voices right down to their walk. Only thing was, sometimes he liked the game more than the end result, you know?'

I shook my head, puzzled. Fascinated, too, to hear more about the man who had shattered my adoptive mother's heart with his lies. I realised my fingers were fisted in my skirts.

'He enjoyed toying with people – destroying people for the fun of it, even though it might have been more profitable to carry out the plan properly.'

I had often wondered why he had not married Mother (even though it would have been bigamously, the chances of anyone discovering his first wife would have been slim) and thus gained control of the entire Havisham fortune. Instead, he had ended things on their would-be wedding morning. At last I understood why: because he had enjoyed crushing her, and had not been able to hold back, even if it meant losing a fortune.

'And now we are reaching the end of the sorry tale, for Compeyson played on my jealousies until I killed a woman, simply because it amused him.'

Interesting wording. She did not take any responsibility for her part in the woman's death. Was I like that? I did not believe so. I was culpable for the lives I had taken, that much I knew for certain. But it was from her that I had inherited my murderous streak, my violence, my rage. I studied Molly's face, a mirror of mine, and felt both repelled and connected. Her flesh and blood and character was the mould from which I was pressed. We were simultaneously opposite and alike; two sides of the same coin.

I'm no longer an orphan.

Molly's words interrupted my thoughts.

'See, after six months or so, your pa kept arguing for more money – for he was paid pennies, while Compeyson kept the silver. So he wound Abel up, saying I was being light-skirted. Abel dint believe a word. Next, that fork-tongued ruination of Eden started on me, telling me that Abel was a bit too friendly with a woman of middling years who he'd bumped into; a woman who had shown him kindness as a child.

'"He's not so much helping Maggie as helping himself," Compeyson told me. He was hissing lies day and night until my head buzzed.

'So I watch 'em, and she's crying and he's holding her. I marched right up to 'em in the tavern, you in my arms, and told him straight, "It's her or us." He told me I was being stupid. But he didn't deny it, see?

'I've always been fiery.' She squinted straight into the flames, which carved harsh shadows that moved as if demons writhed inside her. 'The inferno inside me burned away all love, all reason. I looked him square in the eye and told him: "You leave her alone. Otherwise, I swear to you, I will take everything from you that you have ever loved. I'll make you wish you had died by my hand, you'll suffer that much."'

No! I would never act that way. She had caved to petty jealousy and obvious manipulation – and used her own daughter as a weapon.

Her eyes saw only the past, and her lips twitched. 'I said to him: "I swear to you on all that's holy and unholy, you will never see your daughter again." You were screaming in my arms as if you understood my threat.'

The tension disappeared as if something had snapped. She flopped back in her seat, which rocked with the force. I recognised her expression as she spoke: it was as deadly as my own.

'What was I to do after that?' she said. 'I had to go through with it once I'd said it. So I took you to a pal, got her to look after you and tell no one of your whereabouts. I'd never actually have hurt you, I just wanted your pa to believe I had.'

How heartbroken he must have been, thinking that I, his daughter, had been murdered at the hands of his wife. It was a strange sensation, sympathising with a man over a woman. I shifted in my seat, trying to make myself more comfortable with the feeling and failing.

There was a long silence. 'Why did you kill Maggie?'

A shrug. 'Back at home there's no Abel, but Everard is there, whispering and buzzing at me. "Maggie's been laughing at you. They both were. Take control, Molly. Show 'em you mean your threats." I was angry enough to burn down the world. I don't remember walking to the barn where Maggie was kipping, I only remember her telling me not to be stupid – just exactly like Abel had. My hands wrapped about her thick neck.' Her voice dropped, as if talking only to herself. 'And her eyes bulged, the whites gone all red. Her tongue lolling out like a dog panting.'

The coal shifted. The clock ticked. I did not speak. Did not know what to say. This was where I got my murderous streak from, but finally knowing gave me no comfort. She had killed an innocent woman.

'Jaggers got me off. He made me dress in finery a bit like yours, that made much of my slender delicacy and hid my strength. He convinced the jury that little ol' me was too weak to have done the deed, for Maggie was a much taller, bigger-built woman.

'That case made him the big shot he is today. No one had heard of him before that. Do you know how I paid him for my defence? He demanded you. Promised he could ensure a better life for you than my wildest dreams, and it looks like he delivered. So not hanging for murder cost me my child.'

Again her tone was not penitent, it was self-pitying.

'And here I am, trapped.'

'Trapped how?'

'At first Jaggers said he would show people the truth of me if I left. That I'd hang for what I'd done. Eventually, I trapped myself, though.

I grew too comfortable with regular meals, a comfortable bed, warmth in winter. And when I fancy some male company, he's not averse.'

I was captured by a certain movement of her hands: a tilt of the wrist and a flutter of the fingers. A gesture exactly like mine when I was nervous and trying to hide it.

'Jaggers told me how Compeyson is dead now, thanks to Abel. I'm proud of him for never resting until that fiend was delivered to the reaper, for leaping at him and holding him under water until he couldn't trouble no one else ever again – even though it meant Abel sentencing himself to death, too. Bet the devil didn't see that coming. That's the thing about the likes of Everard Compeyson: they underestimate people because they think no one can be as clever, or brave, or cunning or whatever you like as they are. And why? Because even though those types is so clever, and more often than not plans several steps ahead, and has the cunning to get others to do his bidding so his hands are never dirty, why, they are so used to taking the *credit* for everything that they actually believe they *do* everything! Well, Compeyson learned that lesson the hard way.

'No, I can rest easy now, knowing everything is settled at last. And look how I even have my girl back. Got everything I could wish for.'

She said all of this while talking to the fire once more. Yet the side-eyed glance I caught had a glitter to it like sunlight on a knife blade.

CHAPTER FORTY-NINE

My feet were heavy as I trudged up the stairs after my conversation with Molly, and followed the sound of sloshing water until I found Jaggers. He was busy scrubbing his dark skin almost to bleeding.

'Did you wash away your guilt yet?' I asked.

He did not pause his ablutions, but his coal-black eyes looked at me squarely.

'There is none. My actions in this instance were always for your best interests. I would do the same again to save you from the life you would have had with Molly.'

When we had spoken in his office, he had confessed that he had saved me in an unprecedented urge to do some good, in order to cancel out the cynicism that was overtaking him – cynicism born from the terrible deeds he witnessed daily in his working life.

'I understand that you saved me. What angers me is that you kept the truth from me.'

Despite everything, this man had been a constant in my life from childhood, and never had I known him to act in any way that might damage me.

He started washing his hands again. 'I kept Molly with me to stop her from trying to find you, and bringing ruin on you. If I were a fortune teller, I would tell you that Molly will offend again if not controlled constantly by a jailer.' As he rubbed dry his skin, a spot of blood smeared on the towel. 'But I am not a fortune teller, Estella. You know what I am, don't you?'

A dealer of facts who says nothing lightly, and without evidence, I thought, but did not say.

He held up two gnawed fingers and a thumb. 'There are three things you should know, which I'm sure Molly missed out. One—'

231

'I am capable of counting, thank you—'

'The woman Molly murdered did not attack her; she was completely innocent. Two: despite believing that your mother had destroyed the child he adored – you – your father hid away so that he would not be compelled to give evidence against the wife he loved. Three: now this is hearsay, but you might find it of interest, as it comes from Pip, who heard it direct from Abel Magwitch himself, on his deathbed...'

Pip was there with my father when he died? Once again, my childhood friend seemed to know more about my life than I did myself. No doubt he also chose to keep it all from me 'for my own good' rather than trust my good sense. How infuriating.

'Abel Magwitch was a broken man after losing you and Molly. Compeyson took advantage of that grief to work him harder and give him less, and when they were both finally caught, all evidence led to Magwitch. That was why he was given a worse sentence than Compeyson: that and his lack of education and fine manners.

'The grief of losing you is, I believe – though do not know, mind – the reason why your father formed such a strong and immediate bond with Pip. Coming across an orphaned child of the same age his daughter would have been cast a metal-hard bond in the man's heart, and from that moment he worked only to be able to one day give that boy a chance in life – one he had never had; one he wished he had been able to give to you.' Jaggers' face was soft with a longing I could not decipher. Then he flung his foot onto the seat of a chair, and his usual air of bullying confidence returned. 'He strived for you even when he believed you were in the ground, Estella. Whereas that woman, Molly Magwitch, has given you life, but naught else.'

He was right. Yet I could not abandon the hope I felt at meeting Molly. With her in my life, I felt less lonely. Less like a freak. Instead of explaining that, I watched him plunge his hands into the water bowl once more, and left with a soft goodbye.

As I rode home in a cab, I picked at the memories of the day. My birth mother was alive. A murderess without remorse. I looked exactly like her, and clearly that was not where the resemblance ended... I wanted to trust her. I missed Mother desperately, and as if by the magic of my constant longing, suddenly I had a new mother figure. Could I trust my birth mother? My head told me a firm 'no'. My heart felt lighter at the thought of having her in my life, however. The link between us felt forged from iron.

I was no longer alone. I could perhaps tell her about Bentley, and she could share the load. Then there were the orphans to save, and the threat to my life; it would be wonderful to have someone as steely as me on my side. In Molly I saw someone who could know all of me, even the parts in shadow, and love it all. Was that not what a mother was supposed to do?

Then there was Jaggers. My feelings towards him were somehow even more complex, for he was one of the few people – men – I trusted. Yet he had been keeping a huge secret from me for all the years he had known me.

I would think much on that once home – and truly it was a relief to see the cab had turned into my street. The day had been long. Something light to eat, and then perhaps a bath to soak—

Wait, what was that?

A movement caught my eye. A slight figure tottering. Falling to the ground. Fighting to stand up.

'Stop!' I rapped on the roof of the cab, and leapt from it as it slowed, running to the slumped form.

The cabbie picked the girl up and carried her to my home, as instructed. As the front door swung open, something fluttered from her hand.

My calling card.

I looked closer at the girl's features and horror dashed over me. It was Hilda!

CHAPTER FIFTY

ilda's face was as red, white and blue as the British flag. Blood smeared across her features, and soaked into her clothes so much it was hard to see the actual injuries. Patches of flesh not obscured by blood were either blue with bruising or a deathly white. Her knuckles were split, nails torn, and there were scratches all over her forearms. She must have fought like a wildcat to get away.

The cabbie set her down on the couch, and backed away, rubbing his hands on his trousers anxiously, face grave. I sent him on his way with a large tip and sincere thanks, while in the same breath calling for Lydia to fetch an errand boy to send for the doctor.

Kneeling beside Hilda, I felt at her neck. There it was: a soft fluttering. She was alive. I poured a couple of drops of brandy into her mouth to help with the shock.

Coutts. He had killed Sarah-Jayne, and was now acting against the other children who had spoken to me; picking off agitators. There was no way to discern how he knew, but the truth of my supposition was there before my eyes. Not that Hilda was any more able to tell me what had happened than Sarah-Jayne, for even if this girl lived, she was deaf, unable to speak, and could almost certainly neither read nor write.

My quiet ruminations were interrupted by Lydia's voice from the hallway. 'Now is not a good time. You shall have to come back.'

'This cannot wait. I must—'

'Joseph?' I called. 'Is that you?'

He strode into the room, Lydia close behind him. 'Apologies for bursting in, but I know you would want to hear the results of my investigations immediately— Oh!'

'I told you it weren't a good time!'

'Peace, Lydia. Joseph, could you run and fetch the doctor?'

'I've already sent a boy, miss, but then this arrived, and I'm all at sixes and sevens, so much is happening at once. What a to-do!' Lydia held out a piece of paper. 'I read it because he said it was urgent, and what with everything going on I wanted to be sure before bothering you.'

Whatever the note contained had got my usually steady housekeeper and confidante in a spin. I did not mind her reading it, for she knew everything about my life and my secrets, and helped me look after Bentley, but her reaction had me concerned.

'Come here, you,' she added as I took the proffered note. A boy peered around her, his mouth a round 'o' of shock.

'Who is this?' I asked.

'Errand boy that delivered that. You'll see why I've kept him here…'

She did not need to finish. I scanned the note – and crumpled it in my fist in anger.

'Aye, I thought that'd be your reaction.' Lydia sounded grimly satisfied.

Everything was coming at me from all directions. I closed my eyes. *Think, Estella. Think.*

But all I saw were those words. Writ large and confident with swirling loops.

I know your secrets. Keep away from my business or you will pay dearly FINAL WARNING.

Bentley in the attic. The man I had murdered in the alley. Sir John, dispatched with an unflinching heart. So many secrets that could lead to my being hanged for my crimes…

I opened my eyes again. Panic would lead to my downfall; forging on was my only option.

'The doctor is on his way? Very well, fetch a bowl of warm water to bathe her wounds, and that is all I can do for Hilda for now. Next is you, boy.'

The errand lad shuffled back. I dropped down to my knee so that we were the same height.

'It is quite scary in here, isn't it? It is normally calm, but today…' I kept my voice warm. 'Who sent you with this note?'

His skinny shoulders lifted and dropped. 'Dunno, Miss.'

'You do not know his name? Have you seen him before? Would you recognise him again?' Each question was answered in the negative.

My stomach churned as if it contained a weir. I fought against my rising fear.

'Could you describe him?' asked Joseph.

The boy shook his head, like a dog shaking off water. Wrung his cap between his hands. All the scrutiny was probably making him too anxious to think.

'If I were to give you this shiny shilling, could you describe who gave you that letter?' I asked.

The boy gazed with longing at the coin glinting in my palm, before dragging his eyes from it with reluctance. 'It wouldn't feel right taking your money, miss.'

'You must have seen something.'

'Yes – but he was wearing a big hat pulled down, and a kerchief pulled up like, like a highway robber, out of a story, and he kept his face turned away from me most of the time, and he, and he was hidden in shadows.' The words tumbled out.

'Hmm. Can you tell me anything about his voice?'

His head tipped to one side for a moment. 'It was deep, but he sounded like he was putting it on.' Sharp lad!

'Here's the shilling. And if you remember anything else about the man, or can find out anything about him, there will be more money waiting for you.'

Lydia led him out. As I watched, I felt the chill of fear creep further inside me. This anonymous writer stated that he knew all my secrets. Could it be true? How could Coutts – or Koblin, or anyone else for that matter – have discovered them?

My eyes travelled upwards as if seeing through the ceilings to the attic where one of my secrets resided. Bentley was the only one of them that could speak my name and thus provide proof positive; perhaps it was time to act— The realisation came with a jolt: there was someone else who knew I was a murderess. Mrs Switchley, and her helpers, Bellis and Worthybrook. There was no reason to believe they would betray me, but…

Never trust. That had been the mantra Mother had made me repeat daily from the age of three. Assuming the Wynterton trio would keep my secret because otherwise it would reveal their own part in Sir John's tawdry life and death had perhaps been a mistake.

The doctor arriving interrupted my musings. Hilda lay pale and unmoving as he began his examination. Perhaps it was my fears at play, but she seemed greyer than when first she arrived. Was another girl going to die at the hands of Coutts?

'Joseph, let us go to the library and we can talk there while the doctor is at work,' I said. Hopefully, he would provide another link to Coutts – and another nail in the factory owner's coffin.

We began walking across the large Turkish rug—

A weak cough. A rasp of someone taking a huge breath.

I turned. Hilda was awake, her eyes fixed on me.

'Save them. You must… save… them…'

CHAPTER FIFTY-ONE

The shock that Hilda could speak was almost as great as her words.

'Save them.'

I would do everything in my power.

After uttering her plea Hilda had passed out again, and the doctor had not been able to bring her round. If I had been impatient before to see her open her eyes, it was twice as bad now that I knew she could speak! If she woke up again her words could finally tell me all I needed to know. If...

Waiting has never been my forte, however. And so, desperate to act, I ordered the phaeton be prepared for me – faster than the carriage, more manoeuvrable for dodging swiftly through the streets of London.

'I'm coming with you,' Joseph insisted. He would not take no for an answer. 'Shall I drive?'

'Certainly not.' It was perfectly acceptable for a lady to drive her own phaeton, and particularly under the circumstances I would not allow any discussion. For the sake of decorum I allowed him to help me up. He had to push my skirts out of the way so he could sit in the snug driving seat, too. Picking up the lead straps, I urged the pair of horses forward across the cobbles.

'Use the whip,' said Joseph.

'The horses need no beating to do their mistress' bidding.' We overtook three carriages, and picked up more speed.

'Where are we going?' Joseph shouted over the sound of the wind whipping past us.

'I know that girl. She is from a factory Bentley and I were interested in investing in – and so to the factory I go. I...' I hid my hesitation by concentrating on cornering through a sharp left turn. 'I fear that my talking to the workers may have put them in danger. Therefore it is my responsibility to put things right.'

If Coutts was trying to kill the children who had spoken with me, what of the others who whispered to me on my night visit? I had to get to them.

'Is this anything to do with the orphanages, Mrs Drummle? Watch out for those—!'

The pedestrians jumped back onto the pavement before I could react.

'You were desperate to speak with me. Tell me your news,' I said, ignoring the question. I leaned forward over the reins, concentrating hard.

'I've uncovered a link between Mr Coutts and an orphanage in Kent. It's the one you mentioned in your last note to me.'

Nancy and Nora's orphanage.

'There are rumours that— Oh!' He paused to grasp onto the side as I turned into another street at breakneck speed, the phaeton tilting slightly then thumping back down onto the road. 'The-the, er, where was I? He was seen visiting it – my witness is a reliable man – and it's said he is in the process of buying it, and another orphanage, too, this one in Essex.'

The more orphanages he owned, the more children he would be able to supply. He was expanding his business.

'I say orphanages, but they appear to actually be baby farms.'

'Baby what?' I must have misheard him over the city sounds, the horse's pounding hooves, the wind flying past me.

'Baby farms. A disgusting practice that started innocently enough many years ago. They were originally set up by women wanting to help families struggling with their infants for one reason or another. Perhaps a husband left with a newborn when his wife died in childbirth…'

The way Coutts himself had been. Was that what had initially drawn him to the business?

'Families who needed someone to look after a child for a short time, because they were dealing with sickness or some such complication. The reasons were endless why people might need a helping hand in raising a child, and baby farms were the perfect solution. They were paid to look after the children until their own families were able to again.'

I slowed the phaeton. Was it left or right here? No, straight on, and then that right turning a little distance away. 'Go on,' I urged. 'It all sounds unremarkable currently.'

'It was. Until, inevitably, criminal types spotted a way of making easy money. The baby farms were paid well to feed the children and look after them – but families were not always able to travel to check that was what was happening.'

'And so sometimes the "farmers" would take that money for themselves, and barely feed the children.' My guess was met with a nod I caught from the corner of my eye.

'Other times they killed the children and kept all the money.'

'Why pay even for gruel and the cost of a blanket, when you can keep all the money?' I was a cold-hearted murderess, and yet that was something too wretched, too hideous for me to comprehend. Tears formed. I shook them away – I needed to see where I was going, not give in to emotion.

Joseph, not hearing my muttered words, continued. 'When relatives were finally ready to collect the children, they would be shown a grave and told the child had just died of a short illness. Sadly, all too common an occurrence even in these modern times.'

Joseph's words were whipped away by the wind as soon as they were spoken, yet how they raked my soul.

'You have proof Coutts is doing this at his orphanages? We can go to the authorities?' Even if I could not prove my worst suspicions, the baby farming was enough to have him arrested. The relief was palpable, because the truth was that I was so far out of my depth that there was a real danger of my being overwhelmed. There were too many people involved in this terrible scheme for me to act; too many people to save; too much responsibility. I was but one woman...

'No, all I have is rumour. I wanted to speak with you first, and see what you wanted me to do next. I could—'

He did not finish. We had arrived. There was only me to stop all of the horror. I leapt from the phaeton and ran full pelt towards the factory doors, fired up and ready to do whatever it took to save those children.

I hauled at the huge double doors. They did not give. I yanked furiously at the handle of the small door cut within them. All to no avail.

There was no smoke belching from the chimneys, I realised. No sound of machinery rattling.

I hammered on the door, demanding someone open up.

No one came. The only footsteps were Joseph's coming up behind me. He tried everything I had, of course, and was no more successful.

'Do you know how to pick a lock?' I asked.

'That would be breaking the law.' His puckered brow showed shock. 'Children's lives could be at stake.'

We both studied the lock. Joseph kicked it. Once. Twice. Despite its rot, the door held. In desperation, I stood on tiptoes and peered through the barred windows – but they were all covered up on the inside, so that I could not see a thing.

What had happened to the children? What would Coutts' next move be? If this was a game of chess, then it felt very much as if we were reaching the end of the game. Was it already checkmate? No, there had to be something more I could do.

'Come!' I climbed back into the phaeton, and held my hand out to help Joseph up. 'I'm going to go to that baby farm. I'm going to get the proof that I need, and I'm going to get that place shut down by the authorities.' *Or by my own justice.* 'I'm going to find the children from this factory, and make sure they never have to suffer again. It is time for action. Are you with me, Joseph?'

He held out his hand for me to shake. 'You are a truly good person, Mrs Drummle. I am with you. All the way.'

CHAPTER FIFTY-TWO

Barely into the county of Kent, in some no-name place, huddled a dismal row of squat, grey buildings, lassoed together by a low wall that was more fallen down than standing. A small stream ran beside it, the banks trampled to mud, indicating that the cattle I could see in the distance used it for a watering hole.

Joseph and I crept up to it on foot. The phaeton was hidden behind a knot of trees almost a mile away, so that no one would spot our approach. Having him with me was both a good and bad idea. His presence would cause complications if things became threatening – certainly, I would not be able to use my knife to do any threatening of my own. In spite of the constraints, however, it was a comfort having someone by my side.

'You stay here as a lookout,' I suggested.

'I could not possibly allow that. I am here by your side as your protector and mouthpiece.'

Mouthpiece? Oh, of course, he expected to do all the talking for me. How foolish of me not to have realised that would be the case.

'As a man, you know best, of course. But might I suggest a woman's softer touch might be better here? You mentioned on the way over that the place is run by a woman who started as a wet nurse. Perhaps she might respond better to an appeal from another of her gentle sex?'

He opened his mouth to object, but I pretended not to notice.

'Also, if I go in and get caught having a look around... well, I am a lady, a gentlewoman, so no one will imagine I am up to no good,' I continued, and walked into the largest of the buildings before he could argue.

Inside, I did not call out to announce myself. Instead, I took the opportunity to look about me. Even though this was the largest of the buildings huddling together to escape the biting wind and miserable surroundings, it only contained three rooms. The first was where someone clearly lived and slept, for a fire crackled in the hearth, and a low cot piled high with blankets sat in the corner, as well. Pots and pans hung over the mantel, but the tankard sitting on the table obviously got more use than they. In the second room there was nothing but a tin bath and an empty pail. The third room was the one I wanted: the office.

The owner of the office appeared to be trying to build their own private mountain range from paperwork. Teetering towers surrounded the desk in the centre of the room, so that they must have felt as if they were in the Swiss Alps. A sigh escaped my lips. Where to start? There was nothing to do but dive in – almost literally. The first paper I read had a name across it that made my heart stutter. Mr Koblin. The man who could get anyone anything. So he owned the orphanage. And Coutts had visited it with a view to buying it. At last, the link between Coutts, Nora, the orphanage and Koblin had been made.

Keen to discover more, I pulled some papers towards me from a random section, causing a small avalanche, and studied the writing.

It didn't make sense. Columns marched across the page. In one, with 'children' at the top, were various names and their ages. Another column was entitled 'dead', and according to it, many of the children were. But another column seemed to be recording fees given for those dead children, and beside that were names – one of them was Sir John Taykall. I recognised other names, too. Wealthy men of high rank in society, with unimpeachable characters.

Why would someone pay the baby farm for dead bodies, as seemed to be the case according to the paperwork? The sums were high, too.

My frown deepened. I studied other papers, and found similar. Digging futher, older papers, more yellowed, with ink that was fading, gave a different story. Soon I was able to piece together the history of the business – and understand.

It had indeed started as a baby farm, with the owner being paid seven pence halfpenny per child per week, which was enough for each child to eat well, plus a small profit for the owner's time. Greed had not taken long to flourish, however. Children began to die with alarming regularity, according to the death certificates I uncovered, along with reports from the beadle who had only done the most cursory checks, presumably. Yet families were still being charged fees for those poor little souls who had passed on.

The owner, Koblin, then made it into an orphanage as well as a baby farm – and thus he was paid by the authorities to care for the unwanted youngsters of the world.

In the last two years, things had taken an even more sinister turn. From what I could gather, there seemed to be some kind of double accounting occurring. Paper after paper showed the same thing, until I worked out what was happening…

Koblin had realised there was something even more profitable than killing the children and charging for their keep anyway. He was now selling children to the highest bidder – to gentry, no less. So he was making huge amounts of money from those sales, and still being paid by authorities, parents, and the like to look after them. And if anyone did check up on them, they would be informed that the children had recently died – thus no one would investigate where they had disappeared to, for they were assumed to be six feet under.

But why would rich men pay high prices for children they would most likely describe as guttersnipes? Lacking in education or training, and considered by most of society to be the dregs; who on earth would pay over the odds for them?

Part of me knew the answer already. Knew the depraved depths men could sink to. Yet I kept digging through the papers, denying the evidence before me, biting my lip to stop the threatening tears from falling.

The evidence was irrefutable.

These young girls and boys were being sold to men with the worst desires and deviancies. Men like Sir John. There were a dozen names that came up with alarming regularity, most of which I recognised. And then one name made me double over, my stomach heaving at the sight of it.

It could not be!

He seemed so… normal. Kind, courteous, reliable. But his name was there again and again.

Lord Thomas Forfar. My poor friend Cecila. We had stood side by side at the ball, dressed identically, laughing, while her husband looked on seemingly with pride. All the time he hid this abominable secret.

At least there was no mention of Jaggers. Any vestiges of suspicion about him disappeared. His sole reason for acting suspiciously had been because of my mother. Not that it meant he was forgiven just yet.

Straightening up again, I tried to think clearly about all that had been learned. I still did not understand the link with Coutts and the factory, even though it was now irrefutable, not least because Joseph had an eyewitness who had seen Coutts visit.

There was the timing, too. Two years ago Coutts' business had enjoyed a dramatic change of fortune – at the exact time Koblin made his dastardly business change. And Sir John had boasted to Bentley about finding a supplier of girls two years ago. It all fit together.

Presumably Coutts found factory workers from the orphanage. From what the children had told me, he also sent children from the factory to Sir John's club members. Was he now buying into the orphanage business, in order to become Koblin's business partner rather than a client?

And what of Nora? She must have been sold to Sir John from this place, for it matched her description. She must have seen Coutts visiting the orphanage, and recognised him when he came to Wynterton.

No wonder she had looked so afraid. If only she had confided in me.

Finally I understood almost everything. All that was left was to find where this Koblin lived. I would enjoy making him beg for death. And then it would be Coutts' turn.

The urge to find Koblin had me plunging into the papers again. Did he live here? Or was he lording it up in some manor funded by the screams of children? I searched for any piece of paper with his name on, muttering it under my breath over and over in fury.

'Koblin, Koblin, Koblin,' I said it so many times it seemed to run into one long word, 'KoblinKoblinKoblinKoblinKo—'

Wait. I said it again, more carefully.

'KoblinKo. BlinKo. Blincoe?'

Could it be…?

CHAPTER FIFTY-THREE

Could it be that the clerk was in charge of the master? Was the silent, obedient Blincoe the mastermind behind it all? The heel of my palm ground into my temple, trying to knead in some sense as I thought of my encounters with the two men.

All those times Blincoe had stood slightly behind and to one side of Coutts as if in subservience, barely saying a word.

But it was always him whispering in Coutts' ear. And always Coutts responding. From the beginning I had been confused that the great businessman appeared so vague on business matters. It was because he was a mere puppet, whose strings were being pulled by the real brains of the operation: his clerk.

He had been hiding in plain sight, watching everyone while being almost invisible himself, whispering orders and…

My hand flew to my mouth, but not fast enough to hold in my gasp.

Nora. All this time I had thought she was staring at Coutts.

She had been looking past him, to the man in the shadows. She had been trying to get a better look at Blincoe.

The sound of approaching footsteps.

Joseph? No, these were heavy, plodding, with one foot dragging slightly. There was just enough time for me to stuff a couple of pieces of paper into my pockets, and turn to face the opening door.

'Ooo the 'ell are you?' shrieked a voice.

I had been discovered.

The woman standing before me was plump as half a dozen pillows squeezed into a corset, with her capacious bosoms threatening to spill over. Pewter-grey curls peeped out from beneath a filthy mob cap, and her cheeks and nose were red as a robin's breast – presumably from gin, as she reeked of it.

'Wotcherdoin'?' she shrieked.

I have found over the years that it is possible to get away with most things one should not be doing if one is confident about it. It is the privilege of being monied and well spoken. I pulled myself up to my full height (several inches taller than she) and spoke in the most haughty and icy of tones.

'My good woman, I would think it is obvious to all but imbeciles what I am doing here. Do you dare to question your betters?'

Her eyes, which were an unusual combination of hazel and blood-shot red, squinted. It was almost possible to see cogs turning as she tried to understand what the well-heeled lady before her could be doing.

'When is Mr Koblin arriving? I was told he would be here on the hour. It is outrageous I be kept waiting.'

Her look turned sharp – as sharp as the blade that appeared in her hand. 'He never meets anyone 'ere for business. Now, ooo are ya? An' ooo knows you're 'ere?'

I held my hands up, fingers spread wide. 'Please,' I stepped towards her, 'do I look like a danger to you?' Another step...

I pushed at the closest paper mountain, sending it tumbling onto her. With it, I launched myself. Landing on her was like landing on a soft mattress. Her breath was knocked from her in one huge huff, and her knife skittered across the floor. I grabbed it up, triumphant.

She gave a great heave, her mighty bulk shifting me as if I were a feather. I was flung clear, landing at the bottom of yet more paperwork, which whumped down on me faster than a wet slag heap. Blinded, I kicked out and flailed until I was free once more. The manageress was still pulling herself up, as my hand closed on something cold and heavy buried alongside me, and I lunged forward, flinging myself through the distance between us, aiming for her head.

There was a crack. A cry. I had only caught her shoulder, but that would do. Her arm hung as if broken or dislocated, the knife once again on the floor. Panting, I kept hold of the – what, had I picked up, anyway? A statue? No, an iron doorstop in the shape of a terrier dog sitting up, begging – doorstop, and gathered up the knife with my free hand.

'Shall we start again?' I said. 'Sit there, and let us talk amiably.' I held the knife against her neck just long enough to produce a trickle of blood to show exactly how friendly things could be if she did not supply answers.

'Estella!' Joseph's voice hitched with anxiety. 'Estella, I'm coming!'

Ah, wonderful. What I did not need was the aid of a good man whilst interrogating...

He burst through the door. 'I'm here!' he announced, unnecessarily.

'Oh! Thank goodness. What would I do without you? I was attacked by this creature—'

'I knew I should have come with you. I heard the rumpus and came as swiftly as possible. Although, by all that is holy, you have managed to overpower this creature.'

'I am sure it was only momentarily.' I did not need anyone suspecting my true nature, least of all Joseph, a man of keen instincts.

More men were on their way. With shouts and cries, their boots thundered on the floorboards. Joseph stood his ground, while I did as instructed and hid behind the door like a helpless maid.

Joseph was quite the pugilist. A left hook, a right jab, and one man was knocked out. The second through the door was more wary. The two men went at it, one, two, one, two, punching with all their might. The other man kicked and bit, too, and his reach was stronger; he was starting to dominate. Around the room they battled.

Come on. Come closer!

Finally, they were right beside me, and—

I swung the begging dog and cracked the strange man over the head. He slumped to his knees then his face crashed into the floor.

Joseph's look was one of thanks and confusion. Time to act the little woman again. I dropped the doorstop as if horrified.

'Oh! What have I done? How awful! But we do not have time for me to pity myself – we must get information from this woman before her fallen comrades regain consciousness.'

We tied the men up using the tie-backs for the curtains, then looked once more at the woman, who had shrieked through the entire encounter.

'Are there any more likely to be on their way?' Joseph asked. She gibbered and shook her head.

'She seems terribly afraid,' I said. 'Perhaps it would be better if it were only me questioning her. The danger is over now, everyone subdued. You could fetch the phaeton, while I get the information.'

He frowned. His mouth puckered to one side. He nodded, reluctantly. 'Only if you feel safe.'

With a moment's more assurances, he left me. The woman blasted me with her gin breath as she laughed. 'Played 'im like a fiddle, din'cher?'

'And for my next trick I will make you sing.' I pulled her knife from my pocket.

CHAPTER FIFTY-FOUR

The woman stared at my knife and swallowed hard. Her pewter curls trembled, and her double chins wobbled in fear.

'What kind of hellish business do you run here?' I asked.

'Have mercy! I'm just earning a crust like everyone else, mistress.'

'You sell children to deviants.'

' 'T'ain't against the law to ask for money to raise a little 'un, nor to sell 'em into apprenticeship.'

'To learn the craft of being used and abused? To be raped? And murdered? Because that is the bright future you are selling them into.' My voice cracked. I gripped the knife harder.

Her mouth set, a line as flat as the land outside. 'Saves 'em from sickening from want or cold. No one wants these orphans, so what are we meant to do with 'em? I'm just trying to give 'em a future – I don't know what happens to 'em once they leave here with their new masters.'

'And if they stayed here they would die for sure,' I hissed. 'Maybe trip into the fire, or be smothered while changing the bed sheets. According to your paperwork that has happened more than a few times. Or perhaps fall out of bed and break their necks? And let's not forget the uncommon amount of children who seem to tumble into the tub and drown on washing day. How do you get away with it? Tell me – or would you like another cut in your neck to match the one I made earlier? This one might go deeper.'

'The beadle!' she shrieked. 'The beadle turns an eye blinded by coin, o'course. The surgeon, too – might open up a body, but he finds nothing because he don't want to. T'would make more work for 'im.'

'Who are you selling the children to? I've found some names, but want them all.'

'I don't know!' She looked affronted. 'What do I care? I'm paid to feed an' care for 'em while they're under this roof. So that's what I do.'

'I've seen how much is spent on food here. Where are the children kept?'

'Yonder buildings. Got their own toys, cosy as yer like.'

'Tell me the name of your employer.'

She shrank back as if the blade sliced her skin. 'Can't.' Her voice was but a whisper.

'I already know it.' My smile was colder than a mountaintop. 'Mr Koblin. Describe him for me, at least.'

She shook her head, until I threatened her again. Tears leaked down her vein-mottled cheeks.

' 'E's tall, 'bout yay high.' She indicated with her hand. 'Dark hair, wot's greying. Woulda bin 'andsome in his time. Always wears lovely clothes in all black.'

Too vague. It sounded like Blincoe but could be anyone.

'Oh, and o'course there's his scar. Runs from eye to beard.'

I have you, you hound!

'What of another fellow? A peacock, with plummy voice.'

Her eyebrows drew together. 'Don't know 'im. Unless you mean Coutts. Came looking for a wet nurse for his babe two years ago or so, I believe. Mr Koblin said 'e was going to do something special for 'im. Dunno what 'e did to deserve that.'

Another mystery, another child imperilled, another string to the rope I was hanging myself by. It was too much, too big for me alone to tackle. But if not me, who else? No one.

When asked where 'Koblin' might be found, the woman was equally unknowing. ' 'E don't let me in on 'is movements, an' I'm glad on it,' was all she would admit.

Once she was trussed up, I went to the other buildings, opening the rooms using the set of keys that hung up just inside the front door. Inside were grubby children crammed into rooms barely bigger than two beds pushed together, a dozen in each. Poor, malnourished creatures. All angles they were: knees, elbows, lines of ribs showing through torn clothing, the knobs of their backbones clear to see on those curled up. Many had sores and wounds that would not heal.

'You're free. Run,' I told them. But run where? The memory came to me of an inn Joseph and I had passed on the way here... 'Head east, over that rise, until you reach The Leaping Stag. I will tell the innkeeper to feed you all and board you.'

It would do until I could think of a longer-term solution for them.

'Go, quickly,' I urged. They shambled away as fast as they could, holding one another up. Some had burn marks on their skin where they had been tortured, or long, thin scabs across their backs from whippings.

As I watched them, I tossed the unfamiliar knife in my hand, catching it easily, testing its weight and balance. Only once all the children had disappeared did I turn and make my way back to the trussed-up prisoners. Joseph would be returning in the phaeton soon, so I would have to dispatch them swiftly... luckily for them.

As soon as I arrived back home, I enquired about Hilda, and was overjoyed to discover she was improving. It put a much-needed smile on the face of Joseph, too.

The journey back had been full of emotional turmoil for poor Joseph. I felt rather awful for him, truly, because he was wracked with guilt for having left me 'helpless and alone' with those ruffians. For, as far as he was concerned, one of the men had come to after I had freed the children. The man had knocked me out, I claimed, and must have stabbed his colleagues and then destroyed himself in a fit of madness. Joseph had discovered me lying seemingly senseless among the carnage. The local constabulary had been called, and had also accepted that version of events.

It was not a story that held together particularly well if scrutinised, but what was the alternative? That a fine member of the gentle sex unleashed fury in cold blood? It did not even enter anyone's head.

The baby farm was closed forever. And it was to be hoped that the police would go through the paperwork and put together the rest of the evidence as I had.

'This was an adventure of the greatest magnitude, Mrs Drummle,' said Joseph. 'Let us be grateful it is now ended.'

I made an agreeable face, but knew this was far from finished. The children at the baby farm were safe, yes; what of those from the factory, who had now disappeared? And what of the threatening note I had received claiming to know all my secrets? It was only a matter of time before Blincoe made good on his threat. He had men with great power in his thrall, and if he told them of my interference it would not matter where I ran to in the world, I would never be safe.

No, no one would be truly safe until Blincoe had been dealt with. Perhaps Hilda could shed some light on where he might be holed up.

While Lydia gave Joseph a stiff brandy for his nerves, I went up to the guest room where Hilda had been put. She lay in plumped-up pillows, her body clean of blood and grime, and looking much the better for it, although it also meant her injuries could be more clearly seen. There was bruising on her broken nose and two black eyes had puffed up so that she could only see through slits, and the doctor also suspected several of her ribs were broken. I knew exactly how painful all those injuries were, for they were almost identical to those I had suffered – and worse – at the hands of Bentley within days of our wedding.

Still, she somehow managed a smile. My cold heart warmed. I had been right to like her; she was plucky. Just like Nora. Just like Sarah-Jayne.

'How are you feeling?' I asked.

She looked confused, beckoned me closer. I repeated the question, and this time she looked directly at my lips.

'Everything hurts. But I'm alive,' she said.

'And can talk.'

She laughed, then winced. 'I couldn't speak for many years, until Sarah-Jayne befriended me and taught me – just like she taught herself reading and writing. People always thought me being deaf meant I was stupid or lazy, but not Sarah-Jayne. She called me her secret weapon.

'I don't hear well, but I lip-read – so I can tell what people are saying from across the room, even when there's loud machinery going. It means I know what is being said between the boss men. Know their secrets…' Her head slumped to her chest. 'Maybe if I hadn't told my friend, she'd still be alive.'

'What happened to her?' I had settled into a low chair beside her bed, and shifted slightly so that my face was full on to her. That way she could see my lips. 'Did Coutts kill her?'

I still did not trust that he was innocent in all of this. Blincoe might be the mastermind, and he the puppet, but it was his factory, his workers, and he must have been aware what was going on. That made him as responsible as Blincoe in my book.

'Him? Nah! He's too cowardly for that. No, Sarah-Jayne made the most of the chaos you created to get out, and was following you, to see if we could trust you.'

My fault! If only I had seen her, I could have protected her.

'The plan was to sneak out and back before anyone noticed. I-I don't know what went wrong. Blincoe and some cronies that come to the factory regular, they dragged her back there and made her dance the line, for punishment.' Her eyes closed and she shuddered as she spoke. I gently tapped her hand so that she looked at me.

'I don't understand what that means.'

'There is a cross-beam above the machinery, and sometimes to punish us we are hung from it by our hands, without our shirts on, and beaten with straps or sticks. We call it "dancing the line" 'cause of the way our legs jiggle about as we're struck. They tied a twenty-eight-pound weight to Sarah-Jayne before making her dance the line.'

'Why?' I did not want to hear. Wanted to close my ears and not know the answer. Sarah-Jayne deserved better, though; she needed me to hear the truth.

'They done it to make the torture worse for her arms to bear, o'course. To make her *suffer*.'

Those monsters.

'She was in agony before they even started beating her, and they beat her long after she had stopped a-begging for mercy. The quiet is always the scariest... They dint stop until they was too exhausted to lift the straps.'

That poor child. I shook with anger.

'And then they threw her in the river.'

'Hoping she would sink without trace,' I said.

She nodded. 'When we started at the factory twas just Mr Coutts running it and the work was good. Hard an' long hours, but we was paid fairly an' fed well. Then his wife up and died, an' the factory started struggling to get orders... This Blincoe comes in from nowhere. Suddenly everything changes.' She seemed bewildered. 'We moved premises. Had to sleep in the factory, we did, instead of in separate living chambers. Our shifts was twice as long, for half the wage, then no wage at all. The food was less and less, too. Some of us talked of running away, but where to? No one cares about the likes o' us.'

A cough wracked her body and she cried out in pain, holding her ribs.

'You need to rest, Hilda.'

'Let me talk a little longer, miss. Someone needs to hear our story in case I meet my maker, and there's no one left to speak out.'

CHAPTER FIFTY-FIVE

We put up with all the awful changes at the manufactory, too broken to care.' Hilda's voice was ragged, each word dragged from her exhausted body. She was determined to tell me everything, though. 'Then children started to disappear. Coutts got angry then. He an' Blincoe, they had a big row, right on the shop floor. He'd complained to Blincoe before 'bout the way we was treated, but his so-called clerk has a heart of flint, if he's got heart at all.

'When they argued about some of us disappearing, though, Blincoe, feeling safe 'cause no one can hear him over the thunderous machinery, said to Coutts: "Have a care for Flora. I'd hate an accident to befall her what left her with a slit throat." He had no idea I could lip-read everything. Well, Coutts went paler than raw cotton. After that, I paid more attention to what they was a-saying. And it seems like Blincoe has a hold over Coutts, 'cause he's threatening the life of his child.'

'Why doesn't Coutts report Blincoe?'

Hilda shrugged. Gave a gasp of pain. 'Far as I can tell, there's someone has hold of the babe, and is ready to slit her throat if there's so much as a hint that the authorities have been alerted. Coutts durst not take that gamble with his own child's life, not even to save the lives of other children. One wrong move or word and...'

She dragged her finger across her throat.

She added that she had not seen Coutts since Sarah-Jayne was murdered, and she and the other children had been herded to another location nearby where they had been promised better accommodation. Clean cots, good food. Instead they were locked into a dank and dismal place, where they slept on the floor; although at least they had been given gruel, bread and an onion each, along with water.

'It wasn't enough to stop our bellies grumbling and growling, like, but it's enough to keep most of us quiet. I had been keeping my head down, but that Blincoe! He come in absolutely raging about you. Had me grabbed by one of the big men who do his bidding, an' that man beat me for being Sarah-Jayne's friend.' Her voice thickened with tears. 'But he dint tie me like he had Sarah-Jayne, so I managed to tear free somehow – Lord knows how – then I ran and I ran and I ran, and still had your card what you give us, and a good thing, too.'

'So the children are still being held in the property?'

'Far as I know.'

'Would you recognise it? Could you take me there?'

She thought. Then clenched her fist and beat the mattress. 'It's all a blur, miss. I might remember if you took me there, but... I don't remember rightly.'

'Peace, Hilda, peace. You have been through enough; little wonder you cannot remember all. But I promise you, I will do everything in my power to find the other children, and set them free. And make certain Mr Blincoe receives a punishment even worse than dancing the line.'

What should I do next? There was only one person with whom I could discuss things without fear of it going further, and so I trudged upstairs, unlocked the attic door, and sidestepped around the man-sized hole in the floor. Bentley grunted at me in greeting, eager for more laudanum. After he had been dosed, I showed him a letter addressed to him, which had arrived that morning and been forgotten about in the rush of the day.

'Looks as though it's from your vile Parisian cousin,' I said. 'But first, let me bring you up to date on a few things...'

That huge brute of a man listened, meek as a lamb, and slurped some drool back into his mouth as I told all. It felt good to lay it all out.

'I am unsure of my next step. I could scour the buildings near the factory, in a bid to find the children, but it would take a long time. Time those children do not have. Time that Blincoe might use to reveal my secrets to the world at large.'

Bentley's head lolled down, chin resting on chest.

'My other option is to see Coutts. He might know where his "clerk" is; they might even be together at Coutts' house. Or he may have an idea of what building Blincoe is using to keep the children in.'

A gentle snore was my husband's reply.

'Hmm. Perhaps sleep would be a good idea.' Exhaustion weighted my limbs and made my head feel filled with London fog so that solutions were always just out of sight.

Had Coutts willingly been part of Sarah-Jayne's capture? It was him I had seen her with in the woods. Perhaps he had handed her over to Blincoe in order to keep on his good side. Certainly, whether he was a good or evil person, it sounded as if he was too afraid of Blincoe to ever act against him.

Unless perhaps his daughter were made safe.

Until I found out where exactly the children were being held, I could do little more for them. Even though my bed was calling, I could not rest. The next step must be taken – I had to see Coutts and find out exactly how much control he had over everything that had occurred.

Shaking away the sleep that was dragging my eyelids downward, I remembered the letter and opened it. It was indeed from Dupont. I scanned it, growing more widely awake by the word.

> *Bentley,*
> *I am most concerned following the letter from your wife, telling me you are gravely ill. Please reply by return to ease my fears, otherwise I shall travel to be with you as I do not trust that woman to look after you.*
> *Sincerely*
> *Jean-Françoise.*

No such letter had been sent by me. If not by me, then by whom?

Someone had played me at my own game and forged my handwriting – which meant they almost certainly knew about Bentley being held captive, and that he and Dupont were the closest of allies. It had to be the person behind the threatening letters, who pushed me under the coach, who said in their last note that they knew my secrets. I had thought it was Coutts, but knew at last he was the servant to the master, Blincoe – and so that was who must be toying with me. He was showing that he did indeed know everything…

How was it possible he had uncovered all in such a short time?

I had to go to Coutts and see what he could tell me. Then I would hopefully have a way of moving against Blincoe.

Strike first, Mother had taught me. Always strike first. But Blincoe always seemed to be one step ahead. I had no idea what to expect once there. How heavily was Coutts' daughter guarded? The reason for the constant presence of Blincoe and the large footman was obvious: they were his guards, always watching and listening. There must be more guarding his daughter.

I felt outwitted.

I felt afraid.

CHAPTER FIFTY-SIX

There was nothing for it but to visit Coutts and beg him to tell me all he knew. For even if he had no power, he had to have information. In exchange for that, I would try to aid him and his daughter, if I could.

On the way to Coutts' house I went into a general store nearby and bought a bottle of laudanum. Thank goodness it was so easily bought from shops and markets, without even a register to keep track of the purchaser or date. If Coutts' child was under guard then cunning might be the best solution, though in what form I could not be certain.

Outside his house, I decided to keep watch, rather than march up to the front door. The bush in which I was hiding was thornier than it had looked in the darkness. Thankfully, my cloak was thick, as were the men's breeches I wore, but the back of my hand bled from a deep scratch. I did not dare move, though, as a heavyset man with a neck wider than his head appeared at the window, his silhouette black against the yellow gaslight inside. He glared into the darkness, as if suspicious that someone was out there, waiting...

No one joined him, however. Perhaps that meant he alone stood guard. I could only hope. I started to stand – and froze. A woman had appeared beside him. She held a chubby toddler on her hip. There was something about the way the two adults spoke to each other, and her hand strayed to her gown where a pocket might be, that alerted my senses. Finally, the curtain dropped back into place.

Carefully, oh-so, carefully, I prowled the perimeter of the house, trying windows and doors, all of which were locked. Hands on hips, I cast about, wondering what on earth to do. Looked down in despair.

Ah… now there is an idea.

I was standing right beside the coal chute. The coalmen used it to make their weekly delivery without having to disturb the household, opening up the small metal door and pouring the huge coal lumps down the angled channel into the basement. It looked just big enough for a slender woman to slide down.

With a thump, I landed on top of the coal pile. Slid down quickly, carefully. Then stopped. Let my eyes adjust to the darkness, lit only by the orange glow leaking from around the furnace door. Listened for sounds above me. All seemed quiet.

Up the stairs I crept, all the time waiting for discovery. At the top of the stairs was a door which I eased open, finding myself in a dark, cool storeroom filled with various root vegetables. I moved on, each step expecting to be discovered.

There was no one in the kitchen, or along the corridor. Where were all the servants? Up more stairs I went, my heart pummelling my chest. At the top was a passageway and several doors. Choosing the nearest, I eased it open a crack, and put my eye to it. The main hall was on the other side. On the floor were hand-painted tiles of blue and gold, and the walls were lined with mahogany panels.

A door across from me opened. Mr Coutts strode out, looking every inch the lord of the manor—

'Where are you going?' From the shadows emerged the man mountain I had seen at the window.

The luck of the devil was with me! If Coutts had not appeared at that moment, I would have stepped from my hiding place, straight into that guard.

'I am retiring for the night.' Coutts might have been dressed as if he was lord of the manor, but he sounded nervous. His eyes were red-rimmed and dark-circled, face drawn. His waistcoat was buttoned up incorrectly.

The man mountain looked him up and down. 'Get going, then, and don't dawdle. Don't want me getting the wrong idea and hurting Flora, eh?' His smug laugh was a volcanic rumble. He watched Coutts hurry up the stairs and listened for the door to open and close, as did I, still safely ensconced in my dark alcove. Then he went into the room Coutts had just vacated, and I heard a tinkle of crystal along with something being poured. It sounded as if he was helping himself to the owner's drinks cabinet.

Quiet as a cat, I crept up the stairs. It had sounded as if Coutts went into a door on the right side of the corridor, and close to the stairs.

Sending a silent prayer up that I was not about to walk in on Mr Coutts in a state of undress, I opened the door of the closest room.

He was in bed, pulling the covers up under his chin in shock. 'What—?' He stopped his question when my finger flew to my lips.

'I am here to help,' I whispered.

'Wait... Mrs Drummle... Estella? Is that you beneath the grime?' Like me, he spoke quietly.

I gave a low chuckle. 'Well recognised. Now, are we likely to be disturbed?'

'I – what – I'm – this is most inappropriate.'

'Never fear, I am not here to molest you.' I laughed again. 'But I do want answers. I know your daughter's life is in danger. I know that you are Blincoe's marionette, and he is the puppeteer behind everything. Now tell me, where might I find him?'

Coutts' face, already pale, blanched further. 'Do not tangle with this man. He is already obsessed with you!'

I flinched. Then laughed. 'Not dismissive of a mere woman? Or afraid of what I am capable of?'

'You have no idea what *he* is capable of.'

'I have heard first-hand about some of his deadly work. Is it your daughter I saw a few moments ago, on the hip of a woman?'

He pulled the sheets higher up under his chin. 'Peggy never lets Flora out of her sight. She has a knife in her pocket always, and likes to show off her knife-throwing skills at apples she lines up.'

'How many guard you both here?'

'Five men, strong and savage; Blincoe is away at present.'

My guess was that Peggy and the other guards had become a little too comfortable in this luxurious garret, particularly as Coutts and his daughter posed no threat to them.

'Why have you never fought them?' I asked. I got my own knife out and started to toss it in the air and catch it. Coutts' mouth was a circle of astonishment. Finally he found his voice.

'Have you seen the size of the men? They are too many! Unfortunately, I am built for conversation rather than combat. No, unless I can guarantee my triumph, it is too dangerous.'

Almost certainly. Yet, if I had a child, and someone threatened her, I did not believe my reaction would be ruled by logic.

'You could buy laudanum – or poison – and put them to sleep easily.'

He gulped at the word poison. 'Blincoe is always with me, or that so-called footman who follows me like a guard dog. Even when it seems I am alone, they are watching. I dare not try anything because one wrong move and my daughter's throat will be slit.'

I returned my knife to its sheath, finally understanding. The world was filled with fighters and those who accepted their fates with stoic resolve. Most people imagined themselves fighters, but when tested were not. Perhaps I fought so hard against the world because there was nothing for me to lose.

'Tell me, do the guards indulge in the finest of your food and drink?'

When Coutts confirmed as much, I handed him the laudanum bottle I had brought with me.

'Blincoe is away, and you have the means to escape. This is the time! Lace their favourite tipple with this. Be generous, though not so generous that they might be able to taste it. If you're unsure what to put it in, I suggest their pot of tea or coffee first thing in the morning. As soon as they are asleep, take Flora, and run.'

He looked too afraid to even touch the bottle, the sheets still held beneath his chin.

'It's your only chance to save yourself and your daughter. Do you really think they will ever set you free? Not now there is easy money and a good life at their disposal – they will kill to protect that, even if you will not.'

The nod he gave was reluctant but he let the sheets loose, and his grip on the bottle was strong.

'Good. Now, tell me all you can about this Blincoe – and did you know he also has a pseudonym of Koblin?'

'That and others, I believe. I wish I had never set eyes on him. After the death of my wife, while bringing our beautiful child into the world, I fell apart, I am ashamed to admit. I searched for someone to take Flora for a time, for looking at her was too painful – she looks so much like my Anne. There was an advert in the newspaper, and so I wrote and Mr Blincoe got in touch, writing that he ran a reputable establishment, complete with wet nurses for my newborn.

'When I met him he was so neat and business-like, and so charming, it seemed impossible that he could be anything but a gentleman of his word.' He drew a great, shuddering breath. 'We quickly became friends – or that is what I thought, fool that I am. I shared my business troubles.

I am not a natural-born businessman, and lack of capital was a constant issue, but I had been determined to be a success for the sake of my wife and child. Anne's loss, though... it hit me hard and the business was falling apart because of it. I even shared with him the terrible troubles my father had suffered. His compulsion to gamble consumed him. Even when all our money had gone, he offered up the family land, until bit by bit that, too, was gone... and then he lost the house. The ton turned their back on him, on us.'

'Let me guess. He offered to help you. As a friend,' I said.

'Why, yes.'

What a nincompoop. He looked amazed that I had guessed Blincoe's ruse.

'Blincoe offered to step in and help me, unofficially, just until I got on my feet again. How grateful I was! I did not always approve of what he did, but he explained that moving premises and cutting wages and expenses was the only way in the long-term to save the business and therefore the jobs of the workers. It was for their own good, he said, and they would be grateful eventually for the tough decisions we were making for the short-term.'

Coutts pulled his knees up in bed and leaned his arms on them, then shook his head at a memory.

'At first grief had me blind. Unquestioning, I accepted all he said, and was grateful for it. He started asking for introductions to various people in society, which was easy for me given my privileged background. I opened doors to lords, barons, viscounts...

'Blincoe suggested that, for my own sake, we pretend that I was the driving force behind the business, while he was merely my clerk of business. I am ashamed to admit it appealed to my vanity. He was always there, whispering in my ear, telling me what to say or do. "Now tell them you will accept no less than ten pounds for this order, and then tell them that I have reminded you of an appointment you have, which is more important than this one, but you will leave it with your underling to deal with." It was always something like that.

'He brought in servants who would "help" me. He didn't ask, it just happened and' – he hung his head – 'I let it happen because my grief incapacitated me.'

My fingers traced over the hilt of my knife, listening. How cunningly Blincoe had manipulated Coutts. He had identified how useful he would be, and moved swiftly but subtly to gain power. I almost admired him.

Almost. Not quite.

'Grateful as I was, eventually even my haze of grief was not thick enough to blind me to the fact he was hiding things from me. When I finally did check up on him, it took only moments to discover he was skimming most of the profits for himself. I confronted him, as a gentleman should always be above reproach. He... he told me he was selling children to-to...' He could not speak.

'Why did you not take action? Inform the authorities?'

'You do not understand. I had signed every piece of paper he put in front of me, and it looked as if I was the one...' He could not bring himself to say the words, instead waved his hands wildly. 'He showed me signed witness statements swearing I was the one who did-did *that*. Bought the children myself and partook of them. It's a lie!'

I tilted my head, scrutinising Coutts as he cowered in his bed. The wild expression, the horror screaming through his whole body, the sheer outrage...

Yet he had not acted to protect either his own child or the children at the factory and orphanage. It took great effort to keep my sneer hidden.

'All evidence led to me,' he said, 'for I had ostensibly initiated the meetings and led them. I had thought we were talking about cottons and silks and all the time... Still, I threatened to expose him anyway, for my word as a gentleman of rank is surely unimpeachable. That was when he told me that Flora would pay for my actions with her life.'

His eyes were twin saucers of fear. He was being honest. What a coward he was. But...

My summer of trying to be like other people made me try to see the situation from his point of view.

Blincoe might kill little Flora. Even if he did not, Coutts might be imprisoned, and then his daughter would go to an orphanage or workhouse – or even worse. Blincoe would sell her to the highest bidder.

I understood why Coutts had done what little he could to protect her, but still anger needled me.

'So you let him carry on selling those poor youngsters to a horrifying fate. Is that also why you gave Sarah-Jayne to him when she ran away? I saw you grappling with her at Vauxhall Gardens.'

'No, I was trying to get her away! I saw her in the gardens, being followed by Blincoe. He did not see me at first, but I saw him – and the murderous expression on his face. So I tried to get her to come with me to safety before he reached her. She would not trust me. Especially after she saw my dastardly footman coming towards us. Sh-she fought like a wildcat, even as I begged her to listen to me, and ran from me—'

'Can you blame her? Even though she knew Blincoe had a hold over you – yes, she knew that – she also knew you were too weak to stand up for her and the other children. Why should she believe anything you say? They have no one to advocate for them. You failed them.'

He had the courtesy to hang his head. As did I. It did not lessen my desire to slap him; I held back because there was more I needed to learn.

'Where might I find Blincoe now? He isn't at the factory; it's all locked up.'

'Do not look for him. If he has taken his eye off you, give thanks.' Coutts scooted forward. 'Estella, you hold a dark fascination for him. He is a man obsessed.'

CHAPTER FIFTY-SEVEN

'Since the moment he met you at Sir John Taykall's home Blincoe has been trying to find out all he can about you,' said Coutts. 'You are all he speaks of. All he can think of.'

A muscle twitched in my cheek; the rest of me was frozen in place. Why was a man with such dark power fascinated with me? Coutts gazed up from the bed to me standing over him.

'Do not blame the candle for the moths it attracts,' I said. 'Men falling in love with me is not something new.'

Mother had sent me to the best school in Paris to learn everything required to break men's hearts. It was something I excelled at, even with men old enough to know better – in fact, often they were the fools who fell hardest, desperate to recapture their youth. If Blincoe was in love with me, perhaps I could use that to my advantage, I thought, and persuade him to hand over to me whatever proof he had of my secret life. Certainly, it would be easier to draw him to me if he thought he was getting a kiss rather than a knife in the heart.

'I beg you, heed my warning. He wanted me to get close to you so that I could find out more for him,' said Coutts. 'I-I did my best to do his bidding in front of him, but to push you away whenever he was not close.'

That explained why I had always found Coutts so changeable.

'Once Flora is safe, you can help me stop Blincoe once and for all—' I began.

He was shaking his head before I was halfway through the sentence. 'If he can do this to me so easily, what else is he capable of? How many other people does he have in his pocket, either because they enjoy his "produce", or through fear of blackmail or other reprisals? He has friends in high places – he told me as much. And unfortunately, I was the one who introduced him to all of them, not realising that he was not only promoting my business but through cunning means finding buyers for his other business. They are men with great power and specific tastes.' He shivered.

Once a coward, always a coward.

'Very well. But use the laudanum! It's your only chance to get your child away. Once done, travel to this inn.'

I bid him write down the details of a remote inn on the Thames estuary.

'From there, row out to the middle of the river. There is a buoy there, where you can flag down passing steamships. They will let you buy passage onboard, so you and Flora can start a new life somewhere.'

He grasped my hand and sobbed over it in a way that made me feel most uncomfortable. Would he do as instructed? Or – my stomach curdled in fear – would he be too scared?

His and Flora's fates were in his hands now. At least I had given them a fighting chance.

There was much to think about following my conversation with Coutts. I had escaped his room by climbing from the window and using the ivy-covered trellis that sat conveniently below it. Although I had learned plenty, still I did not know where Blincoe was, or where he was holding the children. It was the small hours of the night, the clock on my mantel striking twice to denote the hour. Exhausted and frustrated, I peeked in on Hilda, who was sleeping peacefully, then allowed Lydia to send me to bed with a cup of hot milk. It did not still my mind. How could I possibly be abed when lives hung in the balance?

All of this had started because I had striven to be a normal woman, and visited my friend, Elizabeth. My arrival at Wynterton had, without my even realising it, been the first domino that fell, causing them all to tumble down and sweep me along with the momentum, and even the discovery of all the young girls and women murdered by Sir John – including one of his wives – had only been the beginning. If he had not killed Nora virtually in front of me, none of it might ever have been revealed. That had led to my realisation that other men with similar tastes to Sir John had been provided with youngsters by the same people who had supplied him. The hunt had led to the factory, then the orphanage and baby farm, and Koblin, and the mastermind behind it all: John Blincoe. I had to find those hidden factory children, dispatch Blincoe, and then do something about the men who had been placing orders from him.

And all of this because I had tried to be like other women. No matter how much I raced towards light, the darkness always chased me. Perhaps that was a good thing, though, because the obsidian blackness was urging me to keep my fear in check and hunt out Blincoe. It would stretch forth and blot all those men out.

I closed my eyes, and heard Mother whispering to me. *Destroy them, Estella. Break them.*

It felt so real I could almost feel her breath tickling my ear.

Mother had honed me into a weapon of destruction, to avenge all women mistreated at the hands of men. She would approve of what I was doing now.

What I wanted more than anything was to return to Satis House. There I could feel her spirit more strongly.

'I wish I could talk to you, Mother. I need your guidance, your poisonous words, your venom and bitter cunning. I miss you so much.'

The desire was strong. To walk the overgrown gardens. To wander the dark paths and breathe in the still, dusty air, frozen in time. To feel the cold seep into my bones. To hold in my hands familiar items and return them to the exact same spot...

My gritty eyes opened. I turned to my side and punched the pillow into shape in frustration. *So tired...*

I realised I was staring at my dressing table. Mother's dressing table, to be precise. There was no time to go to Satis House, but I could sit there and perhaps find some connection with Mother that way.

No sooner the thought than the deed. I sat before it, on the velvet chair that, though faded and threadbare, was comfortingly familiar. In the light of a single candle, with eyes half closed, I could almost believe the reflection in the mirror was Mother's. That my nightgown was not crisp white but the yellowed pigment of a wedding dress worn for more than two decades.

Idly, I picked up and put down items on the dressing table. My hairbrush, combs, cosmetics... There was the box of Mother's; the one

Lucy had broken into for me. I pulled out one of the letters, and with it fell the drawstring pouch, the contents spilling from it. Compeyson's eye stared at me.

I had met him once, when I was eight – though at the time I had not realised who he was, nor that the man he had fought with then had been my father. Since the revelations by Wemmick and Jaggers I had been afforded no opportunity to think about it, but I did now. I had run away from home and found myself wandering on the marshes, when the cannons blasted, announcing that convicts had escaped from the prison ships, the Hulks, anchored just off the Kent shore. What could I remember of my father, Abel Magwitch? A filthy creature, who had appeared from nowhere, roaring across the mire to save me from the clutches of the other convict who had lifted me from the ground and threatened me. A rough voice and features obscured by mud. That was all.

I remembered Compeyson more clearly, although not much considering he was the man responsible for shaping my entire life by shattering those of my father, my birth mother, Molly, and my adoptive mother, Miss Havisham. All I remembered about him was his voice, as charming and persuasive as the Pied Piper's music. There was a vague impression of him being handsome, but cruel – he had slapped me. I sat at Mother's dressing table, remembering Compeyson's proud bearing, as if he had been wearing the finest clothes rather than rags. The way he had dropped me the second he heard that other convict shout. The sight of him turning at the sound, eyes widening, his wide-brimmed hat allowing only a sliver of moonlight to fall across his eyes and highlight his fear.

A single eye glared eerily back at me from the lover's eye portrait.

'Where are you now, Mother?' I spoke aloud. 'Are you torturing him in hell, as you hoped?'

No reply came, of course.

That eye bored into me. As if, even in death, Compeyson held secrets. Like Mother before me, I ran my thumb over the painting, expecting to feel the tiny ridges where she had worn the enamel away to the silvered backing that showed through here and there. I did not. It was perfectly smooth. Holding the image to the candle, I studied it and saw that the eye had flecks like silver ice chips, painstakingly painted in.

My hand jerked, throwing the pendant across the room as if I had been bitten by a rat, as I realised...

Someone else had those unusual eyes.

CHAPTER FIFTY-EIGHT

The realisation was akin to watching one of Lucy's cyanotypes appear: at first I had not been able to see anything and then the blobs had changed into flowers – even though the process of them developing was a gradual one, the moment of changing from me not seeing to seeing was quite sudden. At that moment, staring at the lover's eye pendant, what had been in front of me for so long was all too clear to see.

Those unusual eyes were ones I had seen recently.

They were Blincoe's…

But this was Compeyson's eye.

It was impossible. It simply could not be. Yet there it was: the impossible answer was the only possible solution – Compeyson lived, and he was the mastermind behind all the evildoings I had encountered.

What a fool I was! Compeyson had taken me in completely. I stared at the eye again, and there was no shadow of doubt in my heart.

He lived! The greatest liar to walk the earth had fooled us all!

'How can this be?' I cried aloud.

Jaggers himself had come to Satis House to tell Mother and me of Everard Compeyson's death. He told us how Abel Magwitch, my father, dragged that fiend into the Thames. Both were sucked under a steamer's great paddle wheel, fatally injured and died. What were Jaggers' words?

'I have been informed there is no doubt.'

A groan escaped my lips as realisation hit. Jaggers had told us the body of Mother's former fiancé was found four days later. He himself had not seen it. Our lawyer had been informed by the authorities that Compeyson's body was decomposed and could only be identified by his clothing and the papers in his pockets.

Mother! Poor Mother, who had looked forward to meeting him again in hell, and becoming his torturer. If she were still alive she would be beating her chest with clenched fists and shrieking like a banshee at the news. I could almost hear her.

Lure him! Shatter him into so many pieces he can never be put back together.
'I promise, Mother. Even if it costs my life, I will end his days.'
My legs buckled, the room tilted, and the floor rose up to meet me.

I came to on the floor. Had it all been a dream induced by extreme fatigue? The pendant was staring at me from the other side of the rug. I crawled towards it, hoping, praying, that I was wrong.

Compeyson's eye stared out at me, his eyebrow arched in derision.

Yet it was also Blincoe's eye.

Twisting into a sitting position, I tried to think rationally. Was it possible? Molly had mentioned what a great mimic Compeyson was. The reason why he, as Blincoe, reminded me of Wemmick was probably because he had been deliberately hiding behind some of those gestures in order to disguise his own.

But he had taken on the persona of Blincoe long before pretending he was dead. Why? It was yet another question without answer.

Blincoe's 'obsession' with me did make sense, however. He must have recognised me the moment we first met – perhaps because I looked so like Molly. From that moment I was a fox that thought it had evaded the hounds, when all along it was being herded into a corner, and so to its death.

How he must have laughed. How very clever he must have thought himself as he watched me running around, clueless and unwitting. Compeyson knew all my secrets. There was nothing I could use to take him unawares.

My hands fisted. I wasn't cornered yet. This fox still had cunning left. Perhaps Compeyson did not know about Molly. He might be prepared for me, but not for me *doubled*.

It was typical November weather. A London particular, brown as the Madeira wine it was named after, had descended. The thick fog trapped smoke, and made breathing deeply impossible. Soot flakes fell like snowflakes. Even though it was morning somewhere up above the fog, every window was filled with the glow of gaslight or candles as if it were the middle of the night, and no one could read by the daylight even by a window, as it was too dark. The fog even crept inside, making it hard to see across large rooms. It was as though the sun had died.

Through this I attempted to hurry to Mr Jaggers' home. A vain attempt, as the fog was so sturdy that one of my footmen had to walk in front of the carriage holding a lantern, thus enabling the driver to see where he was going. Trusting Molly was a gamble, but I was desperate enough to try it. Even the smallest advantage might be enough to tip the scales in my favour.

Finally we arrived, and Molly answered my impatient jangling of the doorbell.

'Mr Jaggers isn't in,' she said. She seemed shocked when I told her it was she with whom I needed to speak. We perched on opposite sides of his dining table. There was little to gain from meandering around the point.

'I have news,' I said. 'Compeyson is not dead. He is alive.'

She blinked, recoiled, as if a shot had been fired aside her. So quickly she recovered her composure, though. It was disconcerting. Was that how I appeared to people, I wondered. No wonder I struggled to fit in with such a lack of emotion on show. Yet it also felt good to see someone else like me.

'That is not all: he has me in his sights, and is determined to act against me. There are certain things he knows about me, which he is threatening to make public unless I leave him alone.'

'How bad can your secrets be, a lady like you?' Her look was appraising. 'Taken a lover, have you?'

I smoothed my hair at the back. 'Suffice to say that I am my mother's daughter.'

Her mouth opened. Closed. 'You mean?'

I inclined my head regally, never once losing eye contact.

'Then leave him be. That's my advice. He's slippery, cunning, and dangerous. Appease him if you can, because if you cannot... it will be ill for you.'

'Mother Molly.'

She blinked again, my words another crack of a bullet. I ploughed on.

'Leaving him alone is not an option. Lives hang in the balance – mine and others. If we act now, we can save me and them, and stop this evil man forever.'

There to be punished by my waiting mother in the afterworld.

'I don't know. Mr Jaggers would not approve—'

'Hang Jaggers. He will understand once I explain all to him. Just think of it, Molly – you can get your revenge on the man who manipulated you into killing a woman.'

Him and her out-of-control jealousy...

'Think of the look on his face.'

She smiled at last. It turned into a frown. 'Don't underestimate him. He likes to toy with people, make 'em think they have the upper hand. Then he pulls the rug from under 'em, and cor, do they regret it.'

'I can tell from my limited dealings with him.' It was not easy to confess my own shortcomings. I had underestimated Compeyson in all his many guises and names, and that had allowed him always to be one step, or even two, ahead of me. 'Together, I think we can bring him down, though. You know him of old, and we are both wily. What say you?'

A moment's thought. A great sigh. A nod.

'He will not know what has hit him when mother and daughter strike together. Lord knows we both have enough reason to hate him. Apart, we might not be able to destroy him, but together—'

'He has no chance.'

First, though, I needed to find out where he was. For now all I could do was go home and hope that Joseph, Jaggers or Hilda came up trumps for me. Molly and I headed to my home together.

'I will not leave your side now you need me,' she vowed.

After eight long months of grieving Mother, it felt wonderful to have someone on my side again.

On the carriage journey home, my head lolled in exhaustion.

'You're fit to drop, girl,' said Molly. 'Here, rest your head.'

She offered her shoulder. A moment's hesitation... then I gave in.

How strange and wonderful it was to lean on someone and feel their steady warmth, and feel contentment. As a child I had often wanted to climb on Mother's lap, but she had not liked it. On the rare occasions she held me, it had not lasted long. I did not know if I could trust the feeling inside me that reminded me of sitting in a comfortable chair in front of a warm fire on a cold day. At that moment, however, I needed it more than I cared to acknowledge. My eyes grew heavy and I let sleep carry me away.

CHAPTER FIFTY-NINE

The house seemed odd when I walked in. My steps echoed more than usual. I called for Lydia and received no answer. No one came to my ring of the bell in the parlour, either. A horror took hold of me, chilling me to the bone, as I hurried up the stairs.

'P'raps they didn't expect you home, and they've just taken a half-day. While the cat's away the mice will play,' Molly suggested, trailing after me. I did not reply, just lifted my skirts higher and sped faster along the corridor and then up the attic stairs...

The door at the top was open.

The room was empty.

Bentley was gone! I spun around, bracing for attack. A body slamming into me. The roar of anger.

There was nothing. No sign of Bentley anywhere. Where the hell had he gone? How had he broken free?

And what would he do next? Oh dear Lord, if he told people the truth about me I was done for. If he waited so he could get his own personal retribution, it might be even worse.

Something was on the pillow. A note.

I warned you that I knew your secrets. Come to the address below if you dare. If not, the children die.

So Compeyson had liberated my husband. Together, who knew what they were capable of? Molly and I sat in the kitchen of my home, staring at the note as we had for the last ten minutes, while I explained there was no choice but for me to follow the instructions written on it.

'You're walking into a trap,' said Molly.

I shook the paper at her. 'What choice do I have?'

She chewed her lip. Stayed silent.

'Exactly! No choice at all! He thinks I'm alone, though, but I'll have you with me. It gives us the upper hand, even if only for a few moments.' Fear rolled through me at her doubtful expression. 'Think how marvellous it will be for us to finish that plague of a man.'

Still Molly said nothing.

'Here, take this.'

'It's madness.' Her voice was flat as she spoke, but she took the huge carving knife I handed her, and felt its weight with an expertise I respected. 'But I will come with you if you insist on this folly.'

I did. Even with Molly on my side, the chances were this confrontation would end badly for me. All I hoped was that somehow, together, we could get the children away before I met my reckoning.

So this is how it will end, I thought.

I was not ready to die. I would not accept my fate and walk stoically into it; no, I would fight tooth and nail. But if I were to die in this encounter then it was a good way to go, I decided, and for a just cause. Besides, Compeyson was a worthy adversary.

'Give me a moment to change, and then we shall be on our way. One should always be well dressed when facing death.'

Through a labyrinth of dark, narrow alleys and courtyards we made our way together, through fog that created night of the day. People stood in doorways, and slid inside to watch our progress. This was not the sort of area where it paid to get involved in the business of others – in fact, the price for doing so might be one's life.

Finally, we were at the address we had been given. It looked empty.

'Hide here, count slowly to one thousand, and then come after me waving that massive knife,' I instructed.

She grabbed my arm before I could walk away. 'I've been thinking. It's too easy.' Molly stared up at the building we had been instructed to come to, just a couple of streets away from Coutts' factory. 'It's all in darkness for starters.'

'Well, that does not mean—'

'It's a red herring. He's never straight, that man, not when he can send someone on a detour. What if he's toying with you? What if he's got the little ones at the factory, and just wants you to watch, helpless, as he kills them, and you too late to save 'em because you've wasted time here?'

Interesting. If I were in Compeyson's shoes, and were completely without a moral compass of any kind, that was the sort of idea that would occur to me. Good on Molly for spotting it.

And so Molly and I crept over to the building and peered in the windows, looking not only for children but any other signs…

'Do you smell—?'

'Paraffin.' Molly nodded.

No time for prevarication, I smashed a window and climbed inside, my fine dress catching on the glass but my many underskirts protecting me from being cut.

The smell of paraffin was even stronger inside; strong enough that I was not tempted to light one of the many lanterns around the place. As a child of Satis House, raised in darkness, lack of light held no fear for me. It took a mere few beats of my heart for my eyes to adjust, and then I walked about, searching, listening…

There was no sign anywhere of the children.

What was Compeyson playing at?

I reached for the door – and just happened to glance down. I froze.

There were a series of matches winkled in between the planks of the door, their heads facing downwards. If the door were opened, they would scrape along the floor and ignite – as would the paraffin. The place would go up like a candle, and most likely set alight the poor person who had opened the door, too.

How ingenious.

Despite myself, I was impressed by Compeyson. Molly had saved me. But I did not want my murderous nemesis to know that, so after climbing out through the window, Molly and I found a long plank and set off the fiery trap by pushing at the door.

Then we set off towards the factory. It was time to end things, once and for all.

The deafening machinery was mute. It stood still, looking like the skeletal remains of long-dead monsters; like those discovered by a woman named Mary Anning, in the red sandstone and white chalk cliffs of Dorset. Most of the lamps inside the factory were unlit, but a few cast a glow that softened the darkness enough for me to see where I trod, and make my fine dress glitter with each step.

The place seemed deserted. My skin prickled, my animal senses telling me differently.

I climbed the stairs to the office. Each creak loud as a gun being fired. The rickety wooden building reminded me of the barn at Satis House: the one I fell through the floorboards of as a child, and which had left me with my fear of heights. I clung a little tighter to the banister, but continued on my way.

At the top of the stairs I turned left on instinct, opened the office door…

The children were all huddled inside, tied up. Skinny as skinned rabbits, eyes large, grubby faces pale, waiting for the butcher's cleaver to fall and end their lives. All fight drained away. And in front of them was the butcher himself.

Everard Compeyson.

CHAPTER SIXTY

rifter. Abuser. Heartbreaker.

The man who broke apart my family with lies and manipulation, and drove Molly to murder.

The man who broke my adoptive mother's heart so profoundly he sent her to the edge of madness.

The man responsible for Pip losing his fortune, and having to move to Cairo.

The man responsible for my father's death.

The man who altered the course of my entire life countless times.

My nemesis.

Fury surged through me. Sudden. Hot.

Compeyson's eyes sparkled in the lantern light, plain to see now that he no longer wore glasses. He untied one of the terrified children and shoved him toward me, all the time pointing the gun at me.

'Check her for weapons.'

The poor thing looked terrified as he emptied my pockets, but my demeanour was serene.

'You will find nothing,' I said.

'Then you are rather more stupid than I gave you credit for,' Compeyson replied.

Or perhaps cleverer. There was a reason beyond vanity that made me choose that particular gown. The front boning of the bodice held a dagger; the ornate handle appeared to be part of the neckline's decoration, and the blade slid down a hidden sleeve that pointed down towards my waist. Utterly deadly and hiding in plain sight, rather like myself. I thought, too, of Molly waiting outside, counting down to the moment she would enter with her large knife and impressive temper.

How hard it was to stay still and allow myself to be tied up by the boy. The whole time Compeyson kept the gun trained on me. Every now and again he closed one eye as if about to fire, then gave a chuckle rich and dark as fruit cake.

My bonds were tight, the long strips of discarded material used to tie me as effective as ropes. I had been placed so that I sat on the floor, hands behind my back, ankles tied together. Compeyson tugged on each bond to check they were secure, and grunted with satisfaction. Then he stood over me, and as he looked down the moonlight caught him at just the right angle and – there he was, the convict from the marshes of my youth.

The material bit into my skin. Despite myself, I struggled, hating the feeling of being trapped.

Compeyson's lips twitched in amusement.

'You recognise me at last, Estella Havisham?' He seemed to savour that last word in his mouth, as if it were a tasty morsel. 'Tell me, how did you manage to escape your murderess mother's clutches?'

I shook my head. 'I have no idea what you're talking about.'

'How came you to return to the land of the living when Molly maintained she'd strangled you to death? And...' He paused to pull up a chair and sat on it, tucking his gun back into his waistband.

'Make yourself comfortable,' I said.

'Oh, I always do.' He smiled. 'And how came you to be adopted by my former fiancée, no less? It seems we are inextricably connected, you and I.'

He almost purred as he spoke. He clearly liked the sound of his own voice. My heart was racing. I had deliberately made myself vulnerable so that Molly could strike at Compeyson with his guard down. She had to rescue the children. Me? I would take care of myself, somehow. Perhaps the key lay in keeping him talking.

'My name is Mrs Estella Drummle; how do you know my maiden name?' I asked, playing stupid to buy time. My fingers tingled from lack of blood. I flexed them.

'It took very little digging to discover your maiden name, and the fact you're adopted. And one need only look at you to know who your mother is – looking at you is like travelling back in time and seeing Molly once more. Fitting the pieces together is child's play.' He tilted his head to one side and considered. 'I sense the hand of Jaggers.'

How sharp he was, to have seen so much and put it all together while I ran around in a fog of confusion.

He reached forward – I flinched back, and then cursed myself for showing weakness when a smile bloomed over his face. One of his fingers trailed from my collarbone downward. Was he going to rape me? Shivering in fear despite myself, I made myself stare into his eyes, those distinctive silver flecks exactly as they had been depicted in the lover's eye portrait. His finger paused at the top of my dress' neckline. He bit his lip. Then pulled at the fine chain about my neck, bringing up the ring that was hidden in my clothing.

'I remember this ring. You were wearing it the first time I met you, with that fool Coutts, and I thought it odd that you should wear paste jewellery. But it tugged at a memory, and… it is the engagement ring I gave Pandora Havisham.' Compeyson threw his head back and laughed. 'I admit, it shook me a little, to see this past memento, and so I left the room – but not without first instructing Coutts to find out what he could about it and you. Your replies to him confirmed my suspicions, and from that moment I made it my business to find out everything I could about you and Pandora. May she rest in peace.'

The playful smile returned to his lips. Anger shot through me.

'Did you ever care for her?'

'Who?' He frowned. Already he had forgotten about Mother, despite talking about her mere seconds ago. 'Oh! Pandora? Hmmm… No, no, I don't believe so. Although she was rather generous, which made her company less trying that most. Anyway, where was I?

'Yes, it has been great fun toying with you. Sending you silly little notes and seeing you running about town like a bored dog chasing his own tail. Although you did become far more of a thorn in my side than I anticipated.' He cocked his head, birdlike. 'Stubborn, too – just like your father, Abel. You were not scared off even when I pushed you in front of the mail coach.'

Beneath Compeyson's gaze I felt like one of Sir John's butterflies about to be skewered to a cloth and displayed for all eternity.

'When did you realise that you could make money from selling the children to deviants?' I asked.

'There has always been a market for such things. But Coutts' contacts in high places meant they would pay well. Oh, don't look at me as if I am doing anything wrong, I am merely the supplier. It is like blaming the person who sold the gun for its owner pulling the trigger and killing a man. I am simply earning a living—'

'From other people's misery. You are as responsible for the deaths of those children as the ones who did the deed,' I hissed. 'I am not the only one who knows who your clients are. They will dangle from a gibbet, just as you will.'

A breeze seemed to stir beside me, brushing past my ear. *Tear out his heart!* Mother's voice whispered.

How I wanted to! But it was better to keep him talking. I changed tack.

'You say I came back from the dead, but I am not the only one who has achieved that. You have, too, Everard Compeyson. It would seem the celebrations over your death were premature.'

'You want to know how I did it, don't you? I can see the question burning away behind your eyes. Come, admit it, Estella!'

I blinked slowly. He showed his teeth again, he laughed so hard.

Laugh away, Compeyson. You will not be coming back from the dead again – not once I have finished with you. Savour this moment, for I will make you scream for mercy soon…

CHAPTER SIXTY-ONE

I will tell you, for you strike me as someone who will appreciate the tale – you and I are similar in that regard, Estella.'

Everard Compeyson's smile fell away as he thought about the moment of his near death.

'Your father came within a whisker of making his dream come true and sending me to the underworld. When I heard that he was back in the country, I could get no rest knowing he was free as a bird. He was the reason I had been captured after escaping from the prison Hulks all those years before.'

That had been the night he and I had first encountered one another.

'Abel could not bear the thought of me being free as well as him, so the fool fought me, pinned me down and yelled for the guards as hard as he could until they found us grappling in the mud. It was so petty of him! If he had only let me be, we both would have been free to carry on our lives in the world, but instead he willingly gave himself up so that I might be captured, too.

'When I heard whispers last year that a certain prisoner who had been transported to Australia had risked his life to return to London, I made it my business to hunt him down. He was on a rowboat when I and some officials I had tipped off finally caught up with him. If we had arrived but a minute or two later we would have been too late, and he would've managed to flag down the steamer and get aboard, thus escaping England.'

Fierce pride infused every word he spoke. His chin was lifted high as his eyes gazed into the past.

'Even then, he refused to be beaten by me. He launched himself from his boat into mine. Madness! Twining his hands in my clothing, he dragged us both overboard. I fought back, the steamer bearing down on us... It was a confusion of sound and sensation as we were suddenly caught up in the great paddle of the steamer, the current it created whipping us up, dragging us down, tossing us about like a child's rag doll. It is how I received this great scar on my face.'

He traced the ugly line that ran from his eye down into his beard.

I gave him my most dazzling smile and laughed. 'How proud I feel of my father.'

Compeyson's cold look was calculated to strike fear into my heart. It did. I kept on smiling, though.

'When I came to, I had been washed ashore. Soaking wet, freezing cold, but somehow, by the luck of the devil, I had survived your father's murderous plot.'

I raised an eyebrow. 'In fairness, he was only responding to your own dastardly plot.'

He continued as if I had not spoken. 'I stumbled about for who knows how long, knowing I should leave the riverbank because I was likely to be spotted by someone, but… I hate to admit a failing, Estella, but I was too weakened and foggy-brained to be able to navigate my way across the marshes without getting hopelessly lost. But, by God!'

He slapped his thigh, making me jump.

'It was all for the good. Do you know why? Because fortune was with me. I stumbled across a body in a most indecorous state. It had clearly been there for a couple of days, and by the look of him he was a sailor, washed overboard somewhere out at sea. The fellow was about the same size and build as I, and so… I stripped the body and swapped clothes. A little disgusting, but rather ingenious, I am sure you will agree.'

He actually stopped and looked at me as if waiting my approval.

'Very clever,' I said.

'I knew you would understand! You would do the same, would you not?'

Quite possibly, in all honesty. Agreeing with my arch-enemy was disconcerting.

'I had hoped it might buy me a few extra hours before they realised it was not me. Now there I was lucky again, because my plan worked even better than I had hoped. Far from only buying me a day or so of extra escape time, by the time the body was discovered it had been rotting for so long it was no longer identifiable at all, apart from the papers in the pockets – which were, of course, all in the name of Compeyson. Imagine that!'

Another thigh slap of self-congratulation. Compeyson was far larger than life and more charming than Blincoe, the self-effacing clerk.

'For several months I had been working on Mr Coutts, using an alias of John Blincoe – I do love a good alias, don't you?'

'I cannot say that I have ever needed one.'

'Really? You do surprise me, given the interesting life you lead. The husband in the attic, the forgery skills, your adeptness at detection, to name but a few.' He picked a stray cotton thread from his black velvet lapel before continuing. 'To cut a long story short, I made my way to Coutts' house – a long, tedious journey that holds no fond memories. I knew he would look after me, for he is weak and so very *nice.*' That last word sounded like an insult.

Where was Molly? Surely she had counted to one thousand by now?

I wriggled in my bonds, but they did not give. Fear was rising inside me, but I slapped it down. Molly would come. She had to.

Think, Estella. Buy more time!

'What is your plan now? I understand why you want to kill me, but why the children? They're your workforce, your means of making money,' I said.

'Them?' He looked about him as if seeing the children as actual living things for the first time. They huddled in the shadows, too cowed to move or even cry. They were frozen in place, just like the machinery they worked on. 'They are easily replaced. The children are nothing, mere commodities to be used then discarded when of no more use – like a worn-out cog, the teeth of which no longer bite.'

A muscle in his jaw ticked.

'No, they have been problematic, not least because of your interfering. Little devils have been complaining about conditions. The ringleaders have been eliminated, but I've decided it's not worth the risk of keeping them. But here's the clever thing...'

Compeyson leaned forward again, full of enthusiasm once more as he thought of something he felt might impress me.

'I will profit from their deaths. Impressive, eh?'

'You'll make money?' I cursed my incredulous question.

'The insurance will pay out for the loss of the building and machinery, and everyone will assume the children kicked over a lamp accidentally and caused a tragic accident.'

Any second now Molly will appear... Any moment...

Compeyson stood and dusted himself off.

'It has been a genuine pleasure talking with you properly, at last.' He gave a bow. 'Unfortunately, it is almost time for me to take my leave.'

With that, he picked up a canister of oil, and began dousing everything in sight.

There was no telltale movement in the shadows. Where was Molly? Had she been caught? Killed?

Slowly it dawned on me, like iced water dripping down my back.

Molly had abandoned me.

No one was coming to help me.

CHAPTER SIXTY-TWO

ompeyson threw oil over everything. It dripped from the walls, and puddled on the floor. Even the nests of rags the children slept on were drenched. The smell filled the air so that a sneeze could almost ignite it.

Some of the children sobbed, but a dark look from their master was enough to muzzle them with fear.

He turned to me with the flourish of an actor, coat-tails flying out behind him.

'Farewell, Estella! You know, for years I dreamed of teaching Abel Magwitch a lesson for never simply buckling under and doing as he was told. He was always questioning, always thought he knew best. He did improve after Molly disappeared – his family had been a stabilising factor in the years I knew him, and so it was obvious to me that the best way to hurt him was to rob him of you both.' His smile sparkled with triumph. 'It was so easy! But the bitterness of the man after we were arrested; he simply could not understand why he should be treated differently from me. I am a gentleman! And he… eurgh, he was a wretched creature – you really should give thanks that you take after your mother in looks. He spoiled everything when he stopped me from escaping the Hulks. Damnation, I had to serve time in prison. Me! And then he dies thinking he has triumphed over me.

'Meeting you has been such a wonderful, unexpected bonus. At first I thought it odd that my past had returned to haunt me: Magwitch, Molly, Pandora… But in taking your life, I beat them again, unequivocally.'

He took one of my hands and lifted it in order to kiss it. As they were tied together, both came up – and I launched forward to scratch his face. He dodged back; I missed, and fell flat on my face.

'It's been a pleasure. And now, adieu.' Compeyson tipped his hat, opened the door, and kicked over a lit lamp all in one movement. In seconds all was aflame. Above the screams of the children, I heard the click of the door being locked.

The flames and heat grew with every second, as did the children's helpless cries. I pulled the blade free from my bodice, and flipped it in my hands until I could awkwardly saw through my fabric ties. Thin ribbons of blood snaked down my skin, but it was done. Another snick and my ankles were free.

'Take this, cut one another's bonds,' I ordered, pressing the handle into a child's hand.

I ran at the door and kicked it. It did not open.

'Children, try to find something we can use as a battering ram,' I shouted over the roar and crackle of flames.

Those children who were free began to rush around in the ever-diminishing circle that was not burning, trying to find something we could use to batter the door down. They pulled at machinery, trying to free things that were screwed into place. Time was running out.

I must get them free!

Dropping to my knees, I studied the lock. Pulled pins from my hair and set to work. My hands were shaking too much.

Calm down, Estella.

I closed my eyes, tried to shut out the children begging to be saved, the fire that would consume us, the smoke reaching down into my lungs to choke me. There was only me and the lock, the pins sliding over the barrels. If I could just... One of the pins snapped. I cursed and threw the other one to the ground.

A cough convulsed my body. My eyes streamed from the smoke. One of the children slid to the ground, her little body overcome.

No! These children would not die here! Everard Compeyson would not get away with this!

I will hunt him down! I will—

Another cough doubled me over. I clung on to one of the door's hinges for support.

A memory stirred. Had me straightening suddenly. Lucy opening Mother's box via the hinges...

'Who has my knife?' I snapped my fingers. 'Quickly!'

A little boy darted forward, his jaw naturally jutting forward so that his bottom teeth showed permanently. He had the saddest, biggest eyes I had ever seen aside from on a seal pup.

'Don't worry. You will be safe,' I heard myself saying.

Please let me keep that promise.

The huge metal hinges were as long as my hand, and the pins as thick as my fingers. I worked the knife into the crack between pin and hinge. Bore down on the blade. My hand, slick with sweat, slid off. I wasn't strong enough to do this alone.

But the children were watching. The little boy with the seal eyes saw what I was trying to do. With swift words, he explained to the others. Something big enough to use as a battering ram had been hard to find, but there were lots of little bits and bobs scattered about the place. Soon, several of them were working on the other three hinges.

'Ready? One, two, heave!' We all bore down. The pins lifted up enough for us to pull them free. With a swift kick from me, the door sagged open, and we broke through, gasping, stumbling, coughing onto a gantry outside.

We were free!

The fire was spreading quickly. Flames licked along windows, making any glass that had not smashed over the years shatter in the heat. Smoke spewed into the sky. One tendril seemed to twist and beckon for my attention, a crackling cry of my name. A movement catching my eye...

A figure disappearing across the rooftops.

Compeyson. That jackal.

The children were not safe yet, though. The stairs from gantry to ground were being caressed with orange fingers.

'Quickly, down those stairs, children.' They did as they were told, as a crowd gathered below, drawn by the fire.

I looked at the children running to safety. And across towards Compeyson. I took a step in his direction, looked down at the tiles... at the ground so far away... My legs turned to water beneath me and I sank to my knees.

Damn my fear of heights!

The heat was building, the fire intensifying. A decision must be made: would I go down to safety or pursue my enemy across the rooftops?

I could not move. I kept telling myself to. My head was screaming at me, yet my legs did nothing. I was trapped by my own terror.

A great cracking and rumbling, a shaking and breaking had me clinging to the gantry. The stairs had given way and fallen to the ground, the crowd below shrieking and hurrying back to avoid the debris.

Was I to die there on that narrow walkway between two buildings, hunkered down like a frightened rabbit?

Move!

On trembling legs, I pushed myself up. My stomach churned, my vision swam, but I stepped onto the slope of the next building's roof.

Do not look down!

I set my eyes on Compeyson's disappearing back, and gave chase.

CHAPTER SIXTY-THREE

atred pushed me on. My shoes made clattering sounds on the tiles. Every couple of steps, a tile would slide away beneath my feet, almost making me fall. But I kept my eyes on Compeyson, his black cloak flying out behind him.

Below, the mob screamed and yelled, and generally enjoyed themselves as they watched the horror unfold. I slid, grabbed a chimney to steady myself, felt it swaying precariously.

Compeyson glanced over his shoulder, presumably alerted by my loud progress as the chimney stack I clung to came loose. I flung myself free just in time. It tumbled down the sloping roof and smashed below. His eyes widened, and he leapt the small gap from one building to the next.

Swallowing down the fear-filled bile that swam in my mouth, I again let sheer hatred push me on.

Every time I fell to my knees, I thought of Nora, and stood up for her. Every time Compeyson disappeared from view, I saw streaming behind him all the deviant men he had supplied with innocent children, and I found a fresh spurt of speed. When my legs turned to jelly, I thought of how hard Sarah-Jayne had fought for her life, and she lent me strength.

The thick fog enveloped us, above, below, all around, blotting out the buildings, muffling the baying mob's shouts, so that it seemed only Compeyson and I existed. Chasing through the clouds, through the heavens, for all eternity.

Where had he gone? I slipped and slid around another chimney – to discover him standing waiting for me, holding a gun.

'We meet again, Estella.' He drew that dazzling smile of his across his face, but his eyes were as cold as a December morning on the marshes of my home town. How I wished I were there at that moment. Anywhere but up high above the city of London, with a brilliant madman training a gun on me.

The fog seemed to huddle around us. Thickening until we appeared almost to be floating.

'Here we really must say our last goodbyes. A shame, as you have been the most interesting adversary I have ever come across.' He gave a sigh. 'You have Molly's murderous streak, Abel's stubbornness and overdeveloped sense of right and wrong, and I recognise Pandora in you, also. Her cunning—'

'Oh, do shut up. Like so many men, you are overfond of the sound of your own voice, and feel a bizarre need to explain everything, just in case I don't understand. I do. You have won, and now you shall kill me – but please do not *talk* me to death.'

He blinked rapidly. Then gave the kind of hearty laugh only possible from people who know they are the victor and can afford to be magnanimous.

'Turn around, Estella. I do not want to look you in the eye when I shoot you.'

I felt up my sleeve for the knife that hid there… It had gone. It must have fallen during the chase.

Perhaps I could throw myself at him. The distance was too great, I would be dead before I reached him. To the left of him was a skylight. Could I jump through it? No. Again, it was too far.

The options had run out. I turned my back to him and closed my eyes. My heart did not thump. It was a slow, steady beat of calm acceptance. It reminded me of when I had tried to give up all control over my life and relinquish myself wholly to Mother's plans. It would not last long, I knew, and so I had but one hope – that he kill me quickly, before—

A shot rang out.

I... I was alive? I patted myself as if checking for holes. There were none. I spun around.

Compeyson lay crumpled in a heap, eyes open and unblinking. Still clutched in his hand was the gun.

He had killed himself.

Compeyson's eyes, wide open and staring straight at me, made me shake. They seemed to follow my every move, just like the lover's eye painting. Desperate to get away from that gaze and the smothering brown blanket of fog, I slithered on shaking legs to the skylight, and managed to open it and lower myself to the room below.

I had only made it down the first set of stairs when I was met by some constables and the mob, running up them.

'We heard a gun! Are you all right, miss?' asked an officer.

'I am. But there is a body on the roof...'

Two shimmied straight up through the open skylight, while a third took off his jacket and put it over my shoulders.

'Thank you,' I said through chattering teeth. For now it was all over, a great shaking seemed to have taken hold of me. 'The children, are they—?'

'All safe and well. Thanks to you – they have told us what you did. You're quite the hero.'

A face appeared at the window in the ceiling, peering down at us.

' 'Ere, miss, you sure there's someone up here?'

'He's right by the skylight, you can't miss him,' I replied. But even as I was saying the words, I was reliving what I had seen. Compeyson's eyes, wide and staring, the gun in his hand...

And no blood.

What an idiot! How could I not have noticed the lack of blood? But between physical exhaustion from lack of sleep, my terror of heights, the sheer relief of being alive when I had thought I would be murdered... Somehow, in all the rush, I had seen only what Compeyson wanted me to see.

He had faked the whole thing – and proved that once again he could fool me. Of course he had. I now owed him the most precious thing I possessed: my life. What's more, he had sharply shown that, whenever the fancy took him, he had the power to take it.

EPILOGUE

ydia brought me a cup of tea in bed and fussed over me as only she was allowed. It had been a fortnight since my chase across the London rooftops, and she had not quite recovered from the fright of it all, for she loved me as if I were one of her grandchildren.

From above came a heavy tread, and the sound of scraping that one might suspect was the sound of a chain dragging over bare floorboards, reinforced with metal plates – but only if one had a fanciful imagination.

'How is Bentley?' I asked.

'All better now he's back to his routine,' she said. 'I think he quite likes it, really. He misses his laudanum otherwise.'

It would seem that Compeyson had sent a note to Lydia, forged in my hand, ordering her to empty the house of all but Bentley due to a 'grave danger'. He then freed Bentley himself, in order to scare me into our showdown. Lydia and I had created a code word to use going forward, so that she would know when it was me writing to her.

Bentley had been found just an hour after his liberation, wandering near the house by some neighbours, who had assumed he was either so sick he was delirious, or so drunk he was addled. They had, thank goodness (or badness?), taken no notice of his claims of being kept prisoner in his own home and drugged, for what was more ridiculous-sounding than a delicate gentlewoman such as me overcoming a powerful specimen such as him?

A house spider the size of Mr Jaggers' fob watch ran across my bed, those long legs moving like pistons, her bulbous black body crouched low. I held out my hand, and she clambered onto my palm. Her presence made my homesickness for Satis House more manageable. I had been too busy to visit, thus far.

'How is Hilda's training progressing?' I asked.

'She's a quick learner, and a hard worker. And I think she will be loyal to the family after everything you've done for her.'

I let the spider run from hand to hand, my eyes on her rather than Lydia as I replied. 'I think so, too. She's the perfect choice to become my new lady's maid. And she can't hear Bentley moving around upstairs, which is a boon.'

Although we would have to be careful never to discuss him within her sight.

'Shall I fetch her up now and help you dress for your meeting with Mr Coutts?' asked Lydia.

'Please. And has Mrs Switchley arrived yet?'

'She's down in the kitchen, having a cuppa. She wouldn't sit in the parlour, like I asked – said it wouldn't be proper.'

'Well, she's going to have to get used to her change in station eventually,' I said, putting the spider down on the bed again, and standing, ready to face the day.

It had occurred to me that the formidable Mrs Switchley was capable of so much more than her position as housekeeper at Wynterton. The place held too many bad memories for her, perhaps, and so I had written offering her an alternative, should she choose: to help Mr Coutts start up his new fabric factory, and then ensure that it was run fairly.

Coutts was weak rather than evil and had been in fear for the life of his daughter, so his punishment from me was that he must put up with Switchley's terrifyingly efficient ways… and also that some of his profits go towards the education of his young employees.

The meeting taking place that day would put some of the finer details down into a contract which Mr Jaggers would draw up.

Lydia helped me into a dressing gown, and then left me to my toilette – but not before pausing by the door.

'Have you worked out yet why Compeyson let you live, miss? If you don't mind my enquiring? Oh, and would you like me to bring a little titbit for her ladyship?' She gestured to the spider.

'I'm sure she would appreciate that. As for Compeyson… He certainly wanted me dead when he tied me up and set fire to the factory.' For a moment I was back there. The searing heat. The roar of the flames. The choking smoke. 'It is inconceivable that he accidentally missed me when he fired the gun, because we were too close. Yet, no matter which way I look at it, letting me live was a senseless thing for him to do. Perhaps it was because he knew his clients' names had been discovered, and so he would have to face justice eventually? At that point his business would be ended anyway. Most likely, however, I think it was simply because he was acting on the whim of the moment.'

Molly and I had discussed it several times, and that was her opinion, too. She had slunk from the crowd when I had emerged, soot-blackened and exhausted, and nodded her head at me. It had hardly been an emotional reunion. When pressed on why she had not come into the factory as per the plan she had looked taken aback.

'Cor, I got muddled with my numbers! I don't know how to count to one thousand, do I?' she claimed, her voice just a little too high. *At some point*, I thought, *I shall check that assertion with Mr Jaggers.*

It should not have shocked me that the woman who had pretended to kill me as a babe, and willingly given me up in order to keep me from my father, was not capable of loyalty. Yet somehow, it had. Perhaps because I had thought we were more alike than we in fact were. Jaggers had warned me she could not be trusted.

'*You are putting your head inside a lion's mouth,*' he had said.

My pride and my pathetic desire to bond with my replacement mother had made me deaf to him. It was a harsh lesson, but had been learned. Anyone who said I had cried myself to sleep at her betrayal was a filthy liar. I would not turn my back on her, though. She was my only blood relative, and that made me curiously reticent to eject her from my life.

At some point I would study that weakness, but for the time being I was too busy. The authorities claimed they could find no paperwork at the orphanage linking anyone in the peerage or otherwise to any nefarious deeds, because the place had burned to the ground by the time they arrived. Compeyson, it would seem, was nothing if not thorough at covering his tracks.

But I knew the names of the men. I remembered every single one. I was going to kill them all. Which reminded me...

'Lydia, are my bags packed for my trip?'

'All done, miss. You still wish to leave this afternoon?'

'Most assuredly. Lady Cecilia Forfar will need my support in the coming days, once she is widowed. Her husband's death will come as a great shock to her, poor dear, and I will not abandon my friends in their hour of need.'

Lord Forfar, who had appeared prominently on Compeyson's list of child buyers, was going to take a tumble from his horse and break his neck. By coincidence, just the day before, Molly had shown me how easy it was to snap someone's neck, with the right technique – so she did have her uses.

After leaving Cecilia, I would continue on to Wynterton to call on Elizabeth, before returning to London to continue my work. I needed to take care of those men quickly, before they realised that everyone in their little club was dying.

It would be nice to think that once my work was done I would be able to rest for a time. But somewhere out there was Compeyson. Watching. Waiting. He knew all my secrets. And I knew his. Perhaps that would be enough to create balance and keep us at stalemate.

That is what I hoped he believed. That way he would not see me coming.

A Letter from Barbara

Without the amazing writing of Charles Dickens there would be no Estella. What he created in *Great Expectations* was the ultimate enigma, however, as she burned with disdain and even flashes of violence during her childhood encounters with Pip, but then turned into the perfect image of Victorian female behaviour – beautiful, poised, well-mannered – while having no emotional heart with which to feel. Dickens never explained how she made that transition however, as it happened during her time in Paris, and so I told it in *Estella's Revenge*. In those pages I explained how Estella was warped into a woman with deep psychological issues thanks to her childhood in Satis House where she was raised in darkness by a bitter mother who indoctrinated her daily to 'never love, never trust'; the deadly machinations of her jealous cousins, the Pockets; and society itself.

What was so interesting was that the breadcrumbs of Estella's personality that I created were already present in *Great Expectations*; I was strict that everything I wrote must be possible within the world Dickens himself had imagined, and the character he had honed. In this novel I have taken Estella a step further away from that, while still holding true to the original text in all the 'facts'. Jaggers, Wemmick, Molly, and so on, always act in a way that is true to their characters, even as I add to their back story. And as for the biggest surprise that *Estella's Fury* holds… it is absolutely feasible within the world that Dickens created – and I can't tell you how delighted I was when I realised that my mad idea was possible!

In *Estella's Fury* you might notice some little nods to some other novels of his: the fog of *Bleak House* for example; but more than anything the horror of childhood in this era echoes part of *Oliver Twist*. When I had the idea of exploring baby farming, a real practice, it didn't occur to me that *Oliver Twist* would be a useful text. Only as I started to write *Estella's Fury* did I realise that this tale of orphans, sex trafficking, and the use of child labour to fuel the industry, was exploring (in a very different way) similar themes.

If you want to know more about the terrible existence child workers suffered in the cotton mills, then I recommend you read about Robert Blincoe – for it was his life that inspired Dickens. The injuries I mention in *Estella's Fury* (the bent legs, the terrible chest infections, the lost limbs) along with the punishment of 'dancing the line' are, tragically, all real. I hope that it doesn't seem too incongruous that I used Robert's last name in the book, but his life affected me deeply when I researched it, and I wanted him to be woven into my work of fiction as a thank you.

There is just one place where I've knowingly strayed from historical accuracy. The balloon flights in Vauxhall Gardens didn't start until 1836, but I've pushed it forward a little so that Lucy can enjoy a flight, as it's something she would enjoy so much.

I do hope you enjoyed reading *Estella's Fury* as much as I adored writing it. You can find out more about me and my books, and the next instalment in Estella's journey, by visiting my website or following me on social media.

www.barbaracopperthwaite.net
x: www.twitter.com/BCopperthwait
Instagram: www.instagram.com/barbaracopperthwaite
Facebook: www.facebook.com/AuthorBarbaraCopperthwaite
Bluesky: www.bsky.app/profile/authorbarbara.bsky.social

Acknowledgements

This book was meant to be dedicated to my nan, Hilda Price, just like *Estella's Revenge* was. She inspired the character of Hilda: hearing impaired, brave, tough, clever. Nan lost her hearing when she was three, in 1910, after almost dying from scarlet fever; as I'm sure you can imagine, she often met with prejudice and abuse because of her disability, but she never let it stop her from doing anything that she wanted, including dancing.

So this book was always going to be for her. But I don't think she would mind at all that instead it is for my brother, Rory, who died far too young, aged just 61. At the time of writing this, he has been gone for just one month, and we are all of us in the family trying to navigate our way forward in a world that feels emptier without him. Among his many passions were books, words, and the English language. I hope this book is good enough to deserve his name in it.

Acknowledgements are always a list of thanks, but can sometimes feel perfunctory. The teams that stand behind me really have held me up and supported me through this difficult time, and I can't thank them enough. Everyone at Hera has been incredible, but particularly my editor, Jennie Ayres. She is as passionate about the character of Estella as I am, and has been there for me every step of the way, pushing me to make this book the best it can be – always with such kindness and understanding. Thanks also to Keshini Naidoo for everything, along with Dan and Kate.

Copyeditor Ross Dickinson deserves a special mention for his forensic knowledge, keen eye, and endless enthusiasm. His little comments of encouragement always make me smile! And proof-reader Abigail Fenton, thanks for your eagle eyes.

Thanks to Sophie Hannah, and her Dream Authors. And the Savvy Writers Snug.

The book community, from bloggers to bookstagrammers, has been incredible at embracing Estella Havisham, and there isn't enough room to thank individually everyone, but you know who you are and I'm so, so grateful to you. I'm also incredibly grateful for *Estella's Revenge* being nominated for the Theakston Old Peculier Crime Novel of the Year 2025 – what an incredible achievement, and totally unexpected!

A massive thank you to Catherine and Claire, who run the Heath Bookshop, in Kings Heath, who have backed *Estella's Revenge* and now *Estella's Fury* with such enthusiasm. Both books have been partially written in their fantastic shop. I'm lucky to count these two amazing women as my friends.

While I'm on the subject of friends, big thanks to Julieanne Caie, as ever. You're one in a million.

Rona, Ellen, Mum, I love you so much. Paul, I couldn't keep going without you by my side – and without you keeping the house running when I'm lost in the 1800s! I don't need to write here how much you mean to me.

Last but by no means least, thank you, lovely readers for embracing Estella in all her angry, stubborn, violent, vulnerable, weirdly moral beauty.

Barbara Havelocke